WHAT C**...**

about *A Morning Moon*

". . . . recreated the immigrant odyssey to America with deft sensitivity."

—Gloria Goldreich, HADASSAH Magazine

". . . . warm hearted, neatly turned, with humor and appealing people . . . ."

—KIRKUS REVIEWS

". . . . interweaves letters and dramatic episodes to produce an engrossing novel."

—Kaye Stoppel, LIBRARY JOURNAL

". . . . intriguing information about the times and much humor . . . ."

—Elsa Solender, BALTIMORE JEWISH TIMES

about *A Splendid Indiscretion*

". . . . considerable humor and color . . . marvelous ensemble scenes that vividly portray the exquisitely developed humor of this superb comedy of manners."

—Melinda Helfer, ROMANTIC TIMES

about *Her Man Of Affairs*

". . . . reminds me more . . . of Austen than Heyer . . . ."

—Phyllis Ann Karr, HAUTE TON

about *A Regency Match*

". . . . well-written, with real people thinking real thoughts . . . ."

—Elaine F. Peltz, HAUTE TON

about *The Reluctant Flirt*

". . . . a triumph in the genre . . . ."

—Phyllis Ann Karr, HAUTE TON

PAULA JONAS

TO SPITE THE DEVIL

PINNACLE BOOKS
WINDSOR PUBLISHING CORP.

PINNACLE BOOKS are published by

Windsor Publishing Corp.
850 Third Avenue
New York, NY 10022

First Printing: July, 1994

Printed in the United States of America

Acknowledgements

For much-needed handholding, for encouraging support and for expert advice on an astounding diversity of subjects like the topography of Spuyten Dyvil or the best way to maneuver a flat-bottomed cargo boat in the wind, I offer my sincerest gratitude to Helene and Leo Benardo, Ruin Checknoff, Paula Klein, John Morrow, Terry Paiste, Minerva Reid, Lyda Rochmis, my daughter Wendy Sheridan, and the more-than-helpful, knowledgeable librarians of Fairax County, Virginia. Of the dozens of historians whose writings were an inspiration, I must name at least three: Bruce Bliven, Michael Kammen and A.J. Langguth. More than gratitude goes to my husband, whose unfailing, deeply instinctive kindness has been my security.

And a very special thanks to Tory Pryor and Mercer Warriner, without whom this book could not have come to be.

The regal and the parental tyrant differ
only in the extent of their domains
and the number of their slaves.
                              —Samuel Johnson

Book One
Taking Liberties

Winter, Early 1774

Dear Hannah,

What a delight that you come for a Visit next week! I have seen you but twice since your Wedding, and I am eager to bursting for this Chance for us to have a good coze. Since you come Alone, we shall be able to put our heads together and talk privately and frankly about the Joys and Tribulations of Wedded life, the Former of which you are the Expert and the Latter of which I am.

What we shall not *talk about is Politics. I am sick to Death of hearing Papa pontificate about Tea and Taxes, about the Devilish doings of Sam Adams in Boston, and about Who in this County are the True Loyalists and Who are Not. We shall speak of nothing but Female subjects, we shall nibble on Sugarplums and Dragees, and we shall giggle to our hearts' content.*

Before you put one foot in the Door, however, I must prepare you for the new addition to our Household so that your first sight of it will not be overly Shocking. We have acquired a new Painting! It hangs over the mantel in the Drawing Room. Benjy, Babs and I have taken to calling it The Monstrosity (when Papa is out of hearing, of course). I warn you, it is an object so truly Dreadful that I despair of ever enjoying the Room again.

It is the Painting that my father commissioned from that itinerant Limner I told you of. The man came by to ask if Papa would like him to do portraits of his Daughters, but instead of us, Papa chose to have a Painting of the Hudson River! He and the artist discussed the project at great length, but the result is as ugly and Vulgar a piece of art as ever I have seen.

I know you think I exaggerate, Hannah, but when you come you will see for yourself. The Work is painted on wood and fully six feet wide. It depicts a stretch of the Hudson from New York City north to where the River widens and becomes the Tappan Sea. The focus of interest is on the eastern Shore of the river, where the area from Brooklyn to Westchester County is depicted in painstaking detail. New York City is shown at the right corner of the Canvas, but one's eye comes to rest at the left, on our own Spuyten Duyvil. There, Papa's property is reproduced in a golden yellow so Bright that it appears to be the only spot in the Painting on which the sun shines! Quite the Heavenly kingdom!

Papa is convinced that the work is a Magnificent landscape, but in truth it is merely a glorified Map, with Papa's modest property standing out in its ludicrous yellow "sunlight" as if it were the Promised Land.

I suppose I shall grow accustomed to it in Time, but meanwhile I tend to avert my eyes from it when I pass it by. I promise that, when you come, we shall find Another Room in which to sit.

With fondest affection, I remain your loving Friend,
Patience.

Letter from Patience Hendley
to her friend Hannah LeGrange
Spuyten Duyvil, New York,
11 January, 1774

One

They'd hanged her father in effigy right outside her front door.

Patience saw it first from a distance. She'd climbed the snow-covered hill, turned into the drive and, eyes still dazzled by the bright sunshine on the snow, looked toward the house. The sight of it usually pleased her, not because it was one of the finest of the domiciles that overlooked the Hudson from the heights of Spuyten Duyvil (though it was), but because the three steps of the light sandstone veranda led the eye up, first to the wide, welcoming front door, then to the white trim of the gambrel roof, and from there to the distant, purple-misted palisades on the other side of the river, and the sky.

But today her eye did not get past the door. She noticed through her snow-blindness that something strange was dangling in front of that door, dancing wildly in the brisk February wind. She broke into a run, her skirts whipping about her ankles, her heart beating with a frightened premonition. But she couldn't make out what the thing was until she reached the steps.

There was no mistaking that it was meant to be Peter Hendley, her father. She stared up at the dancing puppet, aghast. It was so grotesque it froze her blood. Hanging by its neck from the pediment over the door, the doll-figure was three feet tall, crudely stitched of dowlas cloth and stuffed with straw. The head dangled pathetically from its noose, half covered with gray yarn tied back with a black bow in an exact copy of her father's way of wearing his hair. And in a particularly cruel touch, the figure's left foot was twisted round to the back to represent Papa's crippled leg.

Fearfully, she looked over her shoulder. There was no sign of the carriage yet, but the family would be coming home from church at any moment. She had to get the dreadful effigy down before Papa could see it, for if he got a glimpse of it, he'd fly off the handle for certain. A loss of temper was ever Papa's way of covering over his disturbed feelings. Such malice directed against him would surely cause him to suffer. He'd rant and rave at everyone in the house, too shamed to express the underlying cause, but Patience would know what hurt he was hiding beneath the angry display.

Under the circumstances, it was fortunate that she hadn't stayed with the family for the social exchanges that always followed the Sunday church service. She'd slipped out of the family pew before the last hymn, as she usually did, to avoid being greeted by the gossips. She hated to hear them wish her "Good Day, Your Ladyship," and follow up with the inevitable question, "Have you had news from England?" They knew perfectly well that she'd not had a word from Lord Orgill since the day he'd left her. The question was always asked with pitying condescension, and Patience despised it. So she'd left early and walked home. And thank goodness she had, for she now could protect Papa from this hideous insult.

She reached up to pull the figure down, but it hung just out of her reach. She jumped up, caught at one of the legs and yanked. The leg ripped off in her hand. She tottered back a step, dropped the dismembered thing and shuddered.

Taking a deep breath to overcome her revulsion, she jumped up again, but the wind blew the figure out of her reach. The effort dislodged her bonnet and the lace-trimmed cap beneath it. The wind lifted the cap and whirled it away before she could catch it, but the bonnet dangled by its ribbons from her neck. With her next jump, equally ineffective, the braid she'd wound up and pinned at the back of her head came loose and flipped like a thick rope against her back. In this state of breathless disarray she heard a voice behind her. "Seems like you're in need of some help, ma'am."

She whirled about. It was Tom, their indentured man. He was standing on the lowest step of the veranda, looking up at her with an amused gleam in his dark eyes. She was struck at once with a confusion of feelings—an inexplicable gladness at seeing him, a flush of embarrassment at her bareheadedness, and a sting of annoyance at his poorly hidden amusement. "Can it be that you find this . . . this *thing* comical?" she demanded, masking her feelings with a veneer of stern coldness, just as her father would do in like circumstances.

"No, ma'am. Only offering my assistance."

"How did you know I needed any?" She eyed him suspiciously. Tom, she knew, was a rebel sympathizer; he and his riffraff cronies had probably done this ugly deed.

"I was just passing by, on my way down to Peach's, when the wind blew this pretty trifle into my face." He grinned up at her, holding out the lace cap. "Yours, ma'am?"

Instinctively, her hand flew to her head, but she realized that the gesture revealed her embarrassment. "Yes," she muttered, forcibly lowering her hand to a position of greater dignity, "thank you."

She took the cap from him and stuffed it into the pocket of her overskirt. He, meanwhile, came up the steps and peered up at the effigy with knit brows. "What *is* that thing?"

"Don't pretend you don't know, Tom Morrison! Who else would have done this but you and your tavern friends?"

His expression immediately hardened. "I had naught to do with it, nor have I heard aught about it," he said stiffly.

She didn't know whether or not to believe him. He had rebel leanings, she was sure of that, but he was not the sort to lie. He had a way of looking at one with a gaze so direct it had a piercing honesty. And his way of standing—broad shoulders pulled straight back, large hands hanging down in easeful confidence at his sides—was not that of an equivocator. There was something stalwart and straightforward about him that demanded respect, despite his being a bondsman.

Ignoring her scrutiny, Tom studied the effigy. "It's supposed to be Mr. Hendley, I reckon, but 'tis a sorry likeness." He made a disdainful gesture, as if dismissing the figure's importance. "But what else can your father expect, calling for a Loyalist meeting as he's done? He must have known he'd rile the towns-folk.

"If your 'townsfolk' think that this vulgar, childish attempt at intimidation will work, they are sadly mistaken," Patience said proudly. "Papa will not be frightened by a mere straw man, no matter how monstrous."

"No, I don't suppose he will," Tom agreed with a shrug. "But I didn't stop to argue with you. Only to offer my help."

"How kind."

"It *was* kind. After all, this is my one day of the week free of servitude. 'Tis freedom dearly earned, and very precious to me. I prize it above all."

She put up her chin. "Then take it, by all means. Don't let me keep you. Take your precious day of freedom, and waste it as you usually do, at Peach's tavern with the rest of the rabble, drinking and wenching and plotting sedition. I can do this with-out your help." She turned her back on him and, determined to show him she had no need of him, made another leap at the effigy. But in spite of her determination, the effort was again unsuccessful.

She glanced over her shoulder to see if he still watched, and she discovered, to her surprise, that he'd come up right behind her. And that wickedly amused glint was back in his eyes. "What—?" she gasped.

"Well, ma'am, if you want to do it yourself," he taunted, plac-ing his large hands on her waist, "then go ahead and do it." Before she could catch her breath, he'd turned her round to face him and lifted her up in the air as high as the full stretch of his arms permitted.

Now she was able to reach above the effigy. Shaken as she was by his hold on her, she nevertheless managed to grasp the rope and pull at it. The whole contraption fell to the ground. Then she looked down at him. "Thank you, Tom," she said, trying to sound stern. "You may set me down now."

He lowered her with insolent, lingering deliberation, holding her so closely that every part of her body, from her thighs to her breasts, pressed against his chest in passing. Sharp words of rebuke formed themselves in her mind, but before she could bring them to her tongue, she became aware of the rapid hammering of his heart, a thrum of excitement that matched the pounding of her own. At the same time, she was utterly astounded by a sudden clenching of the muscles in that private part of her that no virtuous woman would name. It was a spasm of pure physical desire, stronger than any she'd ever before experienced. She didn't know what to make of it, except that it filled her with shame. By the time her feet touched the ground, a wave of heat had spread through her whole body. Such feelings were shockingly unseemly for a woman in her position . . . perhaps for any decent woman at all! And on the Lord's day, too!

Cheeks flaming, she pushed away from him and took a backward step, her eyes meeting his for the briefest of glances before dropping away from the burning glitter in his. "You are t-taking *liberties,* Tom Morrison," she stammered, flustered.

"Yes, ma'am," he said, his voice hoarse and a little breathless. "Every chance I get."

Two

Tom left the Hendley grounds and started down the hill toward Fordham, his head lowered against the wind. He kicked at clumps of trampled snow along the road, disgusted with himself. Bondsman though he was, he liked to believe he could behave like a gentleman. Yet just now, with Mistress Patience—of all the people in the world the one whose approval he most desired—he'd acted like a boor, a lout, a damned roughneck . . .

Before he could finish the thought, he heard a commotion in the bushes at the side of the road, and three men jumped out, laughing, shouting greetings and pounding him on the back. "Did you see it?" chortled the largest of the men, locking his arm about Tom's neck in a gesture of good-natured affection. "Weren't it grand?"

"Jotham, you clumsy lout, did you devise that piece of stupidity?" Tom growled, pushing him off.

"Are ye sayin' ye didn't *like* it?" Daniel Styles's high voice, always startling in a man with so barrel-chested a frame, rose even higher. "I can't b'lieve my ears."

"I told you he wouldn't approve," said Nate Cluett, the youngest of the group, and Tom's best friend.

"What's wrong with it?" Jotham Dillard demanded, his face clouding with disappointment. "Ol' Hendley'll have a fit of apoplexy when he sees it."

"But he won't see it," Tom informed him with unkind satisfaction. "I helped Mistress Patience pull it down. She's probably thrown it into the fire by this time."

"Blast you, Tom!" Jotham cursed. "Y' should've left it hang."

"What for? It was just a bit of nasty mischief, with no real purpose to excuse it."

"I told you he'd say that," Nate remarked again.

"Damn it, there *was* a purpose!" Jotham swore. "Hendley's calling the Tories together, ain't he?"

"Did you think a stuffed sack would fright a man like Peter Hendley? Scare him enough to cancel his meeting?"

"It might've," the big man insisted, "if you hadn't interfered."

"If that's what you think, you're a damned puddinghead." Tom stuffed his hands in his pockets and strode off.

The other three followed glumly, not speaking. But by the time they'd crossed the green and reached the tavern, their spirits rose. Hard cider and rum awaited them. After they'd drunk a couple of double stonewalls, they knew, good fellowship would be restored.

Nate suggested that they sit outside the tavern, for the wind had died and a warm sun had made the air unusually mild for February. They took seats on the benches and kegs that lined the west-facing wall and shouted for Samuel Peach to send out their drinks, but Samuel, the innkeeper (and one of their circle), shouted back that they'd have to wait. He was too busy with transients to serve them immediately.

Peach's tavern attracted many travelers, for it was well situated. It was located at the north end of the King's Bridge, which connected the mainland with Manhattan Island. The bridge crossed the Spuyten Duyvil Creek, a narrow body of water that joined the Haerlem river with the Hudson. Anyone traveling from the north to New York City had to pass through Fordham Village, nestled in a valley where two main roads—the Albany Post and the Boston—converged at the King's Bridge. And Peach's Tavern was the only hostelry nearby.

Tom went inside to help Samuel serve the customers; it was

the one way he had of paying his shot, for bondsmen earned no wages and thus had no money to spend on drink—or on anything else. To hear the rattle of coins in his pocket was one of Tom's unfulfilled dreams. His friends, knowing his predicament, would have been glad to provide him with drinks, but he was too proud to accept. Acting as part-time serving man for Samuel Peach was Tom's way of providing himself with the wherewithall.

Freda, the shapely tavern wench whom Peach employed and who lived in an attic room above the tavern, smiled at Tom from her place behind the bar. "Want t' come upstairs?" she whispered when he came over with his tray. "I can slip off for a quarter hour or so."

"Later, Freda," he said absently. When he'd first set out for town he'd hungered to hear those words, but now, for some reason that he did not understand, he'd lost his appetite for her.

When the crowd in the taproom thinned, Tom took a mug of cider for himself and went outside to sit with his cronies. They welcomed him with eager friendliness. They'd all mellowed, even Jotham. The incident of the effigy seemed to be already forgotten.

Tom sat down on an empty keg and leaned back against the tavern wall, turning his face up to the sun. It was pleasant to sit in the sun with a mug of hard cider in hand, free to relax and think his own thoughts. He shut his eyes and let himself recreate in imagination how Patience had looked today. He'd never before seen her so, with her hair uncovered and hanging down her back in a thick braid. He loved the dull-gold color of it and longed to feel it in his fingers. Without the cap she always wore, he could finally see how the color of her hair made her dark eyes seem even darker. He let himself dwell on those eyes, eyes he thought seemed to hold oceans of secret thoughts. The shape of her face captured him, too. It was an almost perfect oval, but the roundness of her chin softened it. It also softened her expression when she frowned, something she did much too often. She had lovely, full lips that didn't seem suitable for frowning. The woman tried so hard to keep her expression forbidding, as if she were afraid to show the world how sweet she really was.

The one thing he tried to keep himself from remembering was how she'd felt in his arms. But his mind kept coming back to it, will-he, nill-he. The contours of her body seemed to have imprinted themselves upon his chest. The memory could still bring a shudder through his frame. But it was foolish to dwell on it. She could never be his. Never in this world. She was rich, she was wed (legally if not in reality), and he was her father's bondsman. The impossibility of it, if he dwelt on it, could drive him mad.

Samuel Peach, at last finding time to spare, came out and took a place on a bench near his friends. *"A February sun is dearly won,"* he intoned, a broad smile puffing out his already chubby cheeks. He was known for spouting adages, for he'd memorized hundreds of them and could find an appropriate one for any occasion.

Freda followed him out and stood leaning against the doorway, one hand provocatively resting on her hip. "So you went an' hanged the puppet, eh?" she asked the men. "Do you think old Hendley has been frighted out of his wits by now?"

Jotham sat up in alarm. "Hush, ye damn wench! Do ye want someone to overhear?"

Samuel shook his head at her. "Fool girl! *Better to let the foot slip than the tongue.*"

"It doesn't matter now," Daniel Styles reminded them. "The effigy was burned before Hendley ever seen it."

"Aye, that's right, dammit," Jotham growled, his mellow mood dissipating. "Tom helped Mistress Patience take it down before Hendley even got home from church."

"Why'd ye do that, Tom?" Samuel asked.

"Never mind," Nate said. "It's not worth hassling over. The whole episode wasn't meant to be anything but a little prank."

"A pointless little prank," Tom muttered.

"So Mistress Priss-faced Patience cajoled you into taking it down, did she?" Freda taunted jealously.

Tom sat up and frowned at her. "Stay out of this, Freda."

"She's right," Jotham said. "Patience Hendley's too blasted high-and-mighty fer her own good."

Tom glared at Jotham in disgust. He usually felt a bond of affection for the huge fellow, for Jotham Dillard, a blacksmith who owned the town's forge and livery stable, had made something of himself by the skill of his hands and the sweat of his brow. But on the subject of Mistress Patience, Jotham could be infuriating. He never had a kind word for her. Tom hadn't taken offense before, because rumor had it that Jotham had once offered for her and been rejected. One couldn't blame a man for resenting a woman who'd rejected him. But somehow, today, Tom felt that enough was enough. How many years should a sensible man carry a grudge?

Meanwhile, Daniel Styles joined in the deriding of Peter Hendley's eldest daughter. "You always call her Patience Hendley," he was saying to Jotham. "Y'mean Lady Orgill, don't you?" He snickered nastily. "It's Her Ladyship, don't forget. Not Patience Hendley."

"Her La-di-da Ladyship," sneered Freda. "She ought t' be taken down a peg, just like her father."

"Aye, the Tory bitch," Jotham cursed.

The words put Tom into a rage—a rage as sudden and unexpected as it was violent. He flung himself at the larger man in an explosion of temper. "You goddam horse's ass," he swore as they both fell to the ground, Tom pummeling the bigger man unmercifully about the head and shoulders, "if you ever call her names again, I'll break your bloody neck!"

"Hey!" cried the startled Jotham, holding up his arms to protect his face from Tom's furious fists. "Come on, Tom, leave off! I didn't say nothin' so terrible."

"He didn't mean no harm," Daniel said as he and Nate tried to pull Tom off.

"Women's jars bring men's wars," Samuel quoted piously, while carefully remaining aloof from the fray.

Tom let himself be dragged to his feet. Then, thrusting their hands from him, he glared at them all. "I don't want to hear you saying anything against her any more. Any of you. Do you understand me?"

"What's gotten into you, Tom?" Daniel asked, utterly perplexed. "Since when did you decide you had to be her defender?"

"Aye, I'm wonderin' the same thing," Jotham grunted, getting clumsily to his feet. He thrust his face within inches of Tom's and demanded accusingly, "Have ye suddenly turned Loyalist?"

"Politics has nothing to do with this," Tom said, shoving him aside. "I just don't like it, that's all. I've listened to your gibes long enough. Not another word about her in my presence, or you'll need the whole militia to stop my fists!" With that, he turned his back on them and strode off across the green.

Nate followed him. "Easy, Tom, easy," he said in his quiet voice when they'd passed out of earshot of the others. "No need to fall into a taking. We're your friends."

Tom took a deep breath to calm himself. "I didn't mean you, Nate."

"I know. But the others . . . they don't understand you. They don't know why you stand up for her. Neither do I, to tell the truth. She never has a soft word for you. And you know she's a damned Tory. With a tart tongue and a nature to match. And, on top of all that, from not having a man around to juice her, she's losing her looks. Pale and dried out she's getting. Everyone says so."

Tom peered at Nate for a moment, his eyebrows lifting. "Is that what everyone says?" He shook his head in disbelief, his lips curling in a pitying smile. "Then maybe you all ought to take a better look."

Three

Patience did not know why her father's mood at Sunday dinner was so cheerful, but she was certainly glad he'd learned nothing of the effigy. If he'd had even an inkling of it, the family would not have had the pleasure of a dinner free of bickering. But now the four of them—Peter Hendley and his three offspring—were able to sit down to dine in a spirit of unaccustomed good feeling.

Everyone, even Sally, their Negro house slave who was helping Patience serve the dinner, was aware of Peter Hendley's good spirits. He never once lifted his voice in anger. He didn't scold fifteen-year-old Benjy for the way he held his fork. Nor did he complain about the flavor of the soup or the toughness of the meat. This evening he actually praised Sally for the tenderness of the pork roast (which caused the black woman to throw Patience a look of sardonic amazement), complimented Barbara on the new way she'd tied up her wild red hair, and remarked to Patience that she was looking very well this evening.

Barbara blinked over at her older sister with surprise. "Indeed, you *are* looking well, Patience. There's color in your cheeks. One would think you'd found a new beau."

Patience shook her head in mock despair. "Tell me, Babs, what goes on in your fanciful head? Do you think of nothing but beaux?"

"Let the girl be," Peter Hendley said to his eldest daughter as he reached over and pinched the younger girl's cheek fondly. "She's too pretty to have to think of anything *but* beaux."

Papa's remark was true, Patience thought. Barbara was, perhaps, almost too pretty. Her looks brought her so much attention that Patience feared she was becoming spoiled. Barely seventeen, and just bursting into bloom, Babs still had the air of a mischievous child. Her unruly hair topped a full-cheeked face whose skin was still girlishly freckled and ruddy, whose huge brown eyes literally danced, and whose pointed chin gave her face its final touch of impish charm. But for her father to remark on her appearance was so unlike him that Patience and her sister exchanged amazed glances. And Benjy, the youngest of the three siblings, simply stared at his father agape.

It was clear to Patience that something special had occurred to put her father in this happy frame of mind. It was clear to Sally, too. "What's got into yo' papa today?" she asked Patience after the meal was over, when they were cleaning up in the kitchen. "He be sweet as the huckaberries in this pie."

"I haven't the slightest idea," Patience said, "but I intend to find out. Speaking of pie, why don't you give the rest of it to Aaron? Your boy's growing so fast, he needs more nourishment, or he'll be skin and bones like his mother."

At the mention of her son, Sally's eyes shone in her lean face. "He soon be tall as Benjy," she said proudly.

"Aaron'll overtake Benjy one of these days," Patience said as she took off her apron and started toward the passageway that led from the kitchen wing to the main house. "Give him what's left of the pork roast, too." She threw Sally a smile over her shoulder. "That boy'll probably stand six feet high by the time he's Benjy's age."

She hurried to join the family in the drawing room, expecting to find her father impatiently waiting for her so that he could begin the customary Sunday evening reading. (For several years now, it was her father's practice to read aloud to his offspring on Sundays. But not from Scriptures; one Sunday sermon was enough for him. Instead, he was slowly working his way through the books—all secular—in his "library." The library consisted of one tall bookcase holding about eighty volumes, but it was, as far as they knew, the largest collection of books in town. Papa was presently about halfway through Daniel Defoe's *A Tour thro' the Whole Island of Great Britain,* a book, describing the economy of England, that Papa found fascinating but that his offspring found dull as ditchwater, not that Papa gave a fig about that.) But Papa was not seated in his high-backed chair with the book on his lap. Instead, he was standing before the fire, leaning on his silver-headed cane and staring up at the painting that he'd so recently commissioned.

Patience stood for a moment in the doorway, studying him. It was strange, she thought, how that crude effigy had somehow caught his likeness. He was lean and tall, with his long gray hair tied back with a ribbon as frayed as the effigy's had been. His shoulders were slightly stooped with age, although he was not much beyond fifty-five years. Dear Papa! Seeing those stooped shoulders wrenched her heart. But she shook the feeling from her, determined not to spoil the pleasant mood that had permeated the air at dinner. "Aren't you going to read to us, Papa?" she asked, crossing over the threshold and taking a seat on one of the room's spindly chairs.

"Papa is studying his work of art," Babs said, throwing Patience a grin.

At the word "art," Benjy gave a hiccoughing laugh, and the two sisters did not dare to look at one another for fear of bursting into giggles. All three of them considered Papa's painting to be hideous. Benjy called it bilious, Barbara said it gave her nightmares, and Patience averted her eyes from it whenever she entered the room. To hear Papa call it art was too much. Even Patience gurgled deep in her throat.

Papa turned around, his brows knit. "Was that a laugh I heard? Don't you *like* the painting? Are you trying to tell me that it's *not* art?"

"I suppose, from some points of view it can be called art," Barbara said soothingly.

"If one views it standing well back," Patience gurgled.

"Very well back," Benjy amended. "Out the front door."

His two sisters choked back a laugh. Jocularity like this was commonplace among the three of them, but they did not often indulge in it in the presence of their father. Tonight, however, there was something special about Papa's mood that encouraged them to attempt a little teasing.

But Hendley did not see the humor. His admiration for his painting was too strong. "Come now," he admonished, "answer me seriously. You can't deny that this is a large, important, impressive piece of work, can you?"

"Oh, yes, Papa. It's important," Benjy said.

"And impressive," Barbara seconded.

"And if it were any larger," Patience said, "we could use it to replace the west wall of the barn."

That undid her brother and sister, who, throwing caution to the winds, burst into peals of laughter.

"That will be enough!" their father ordered. "None of you have an ounce of taste. Go along to bed, all of you! I've had enough of your jollity."

"But Papa, you haven't yet read tonight's chapter," Barbara objected.

"I'm no longer in the mood to read." He waved them off and turned back to his contemplation of the painting.

Benjy, relieved that the punishment was no worse, whisked himself out the door. Barbara and Patience followed. With the drawing-room door closed behind them, they gathered at the foot of the stairs, looked at one another and burst into loud guffaws.

"Replace the barn wall," Benjy repeated, hooting. "I must say, Patience, that was splendid!" He sank down on the stairs and caught his breath. "The shocking thing is that he took it all rather well. For Papa."

Barbara wiped her eyes. "I was certain he'd have an attack of apoplexy."

"So was I," Patience said, looking over her shoulder at the

drawing room door. "Something's made him mellow tonight. Go upstairs, both of you. I'm going back in there and find out what it is."

She tapped at the drawing-room door and went in. Her father was still studying his work of art. He threw her a glinting look over his shoulder and turned back to the painting. "Have you come to apologize?" he asked.

"Is there a need for apology? We were only teasing."

"I know that," he said without rancor. "Youngsters must be silly sometimes, I suppose. I didn't take your art criticism seriously."

This calm response was too unlike him. Patience, her eyes fixed on his back, sank down on her chair. "Something's happened, Papa," she said bluntly. "What is it?"

"I ordered this painting too soon," he said, his tone purposely, exaggeratedly mysterious. "It's out of date already. The north boundary of my property changed its shape today."

"Changed its shape?" Patience cocked her head at him. "Whatever do you mean?"

"Look!" With a broad smile of pride, he pulled a folded paper from the inner pocket of his coat, hobbled across the room to her and dropped the paper into her lap. She saw at once that it was a land deed. "It's a piece of riverfront property I just acquired," he chortled.

"Property," Patience murmured. "I should have guessed."

He went back to the fireplace and pointed to the area on the painting just north of the golden square. "This parcel here. Perhaps I can coax the next passing artist to gild it for me."

"The Betts parcel you've wanted for years!" Patience stared at the deed in astonishment. "Papa! How could you afford it?"

Hendley rubbed his hands together gleefully. "The price was a bargain for so valuable an acreage."

"A bargain?" Patience smiled in indulgent understanding of her father's excitement. She knew what the acquisition of land meant to him.

"It'll be worth double what I paid in two or three years," he bragged. But then a frown darkened his face. "This means, of course, that we shall be cash-poor for months. I wish I could have delayed the transaction till summer, when we'd have crops to sell. But the land would have risen in price by summer."

"We'll manage," Patience assured him complacently.

But Hendley continued to frown. "If we have a sudden need for money," he mused, "I suppose we could sell Aaron. He'd fetch a good price. He's grown strong as a man."

Patience felt a painful clench at her heart, as if it had been suddenly pierced by an arrow. "Papa!" she gasped, the blood draining from her face. "What are you saying? You can't *mean* that!"

Her father, hearing the abrupt change in her voice, turned and peered at her. The sight of her ashen face shamed him, and he immediately retracted. "No, of course I don't mean it," he hastened to assure her. "I was only blathering. Don't think on it."

"How can I not think on it?" She rose slowly from her chair, her knees trembling. "This is Aaron you're speaking of. Sally's only son, whom I held in my arms at his birth, and whom I helped to raise! He's part of the *family!*"

"Yes, of course he is. I've already said I didn't mean it." His eyes fell, and, leaning on his cane, he limped across the room. "You needn't give the matter another thought," he said before he left her. "Dismiss it from your mind."

She stared at the door as it closed behind him, her body atremble. How could she dismiss it from her mind? That her father could even *think* such a thing was revolting. By this year of seventeen hundred and seventy-four, civilization should surely have advanced beyond such barbarism. She had always believed, as did the Quakers, that the very *idea* of selling human beings was indecent. Any human being. But especially someone as dear to them as Aaron. Even if Papa did not agree with the Quaker views, he had to agree when it came to Aaron. To feel otherwise was unthinkable.

She walked out of the room, her emotions in turmoil. But by the time she undressed and slipped into bed, she'd achieved a measure of calm. There was no need to get in a state, she told herself. Papa had said he didn't mean it. Papa didn't lie. Papa was the person she most admired in the world. There was no reason why she shouldn't take him at his word. Was there?

Four

Later that night, Patience stood on a knoll overlooking Manhattan Island, staring at the sky that glowed with an orange light that was nothing like dawn. Flames! They lit the night sky low on the distant horizon, miles south of where she stood. It could be New York City burning, she thought. Or Haerlem Village. She was too far away to be sure.

She'd come out here because she couldn't sleep. The blow Papa had struck to her heart had been too strong. At last, when it was clear she couldn't put his remark out of her mind, she did what she often did in times of deep distress—she waited in bed till very late, when she was sure everyone was asleep, threw a cloak over her nightdress, slipped her bare feet into a pair of boots and crept out of the house. She crossed the south field and climbed the knoll, thick with trees and underbrush, to the very top where it overlooked the Spuyten Duyvil channel. It was her favorite place, her sanctuary.

As far as she could tell, no one else in Spuyten Duyvil had seen the flames. Probably no one else was awake at this late hour. Certainly no one else would be foolish enough to climb from a warm bed to venture out into a cold night, even to look at New York burning. But she hadn't come out to look at New York burning. The fire was a surprise.

This hill and the waters below had been named Spuyten Duyvil by the Dutch more than a century earlier. Legend had it that the name commemorated the death of a Dutchman who'd tried to swim the churning waters "to spite the devil" and had drowned in the attempt. Now it was Patience who came here to spite the devil—whatever devil was tormenting her at the time.

It was indeed a torment to remember Papa's words. How could she put them out of her mind? Aaron was Sally's only child. How could Papa think of Sally as a slave? Why, Sally was more of a mother to Patience than her own mother had been! Even as a child, she'd known better than to run to her hysterical mother with her troubles; it was to Sally she'd run—Sally, whose advice was sensible . . . Sally, who knew how to make her laugh . . . Sally, whose arms were always ready to offer the comfort of a loving embrace. Patience could never stand by and permit Sally to endure the pain of losing her son. That Patience's own father could even *suggest* such an act roused the demons of anger in her soul. That anger was what had driven her out to the cliff.

This was not the first time she'd stolen out at night to ease her spirit. It was something she did periodically, when her emotions threatened to explode. Since she was not the woman to resort to making scenes before others, even family, she'd found this means to air her feelings. Throwing tantrums or dissolving in torrents of sobs, as she had seen her mother do, was not her way. Emotions, she believed, were private things, too precious and fragile to be revealed to the disinterested or scornful eyes of others.

It was unseemly to steal out in the dark of night, but Patience didn't care. Whenever she stood out here on the promontory, feeling the wind whipping at her hair, hearing the plash of the water far down below, she would experience an inexplicable release. Here she could shout her anger into the wind or permit her tears to fall unchecked down her cheeks. Afterwards, she always felt a kind of triumph, as if she'd done something courageous. Perhaps there *was* something courageous in standing there alone and unprotected, facing the elements that buffeted her outside and in. On the other hand, it was probably a foolish and romantic aberration in a sensible, God-fearing woman of twenty-five years. Nevertheless, the experience was awe-inspiring. More than Sunday at church, it healed her soul.

Tonight she tried to calm her turmoil by swearing to the heavens that she would save Sally and Aaron from separation if it took her last breath. It was true that her father had denied that he had such an act in mind, but if it turned out otherwise, she would fight him tooth and claw. And she would win, because to lose was unthinkable.

But to oppose her father was unthinkable, too. All her beliefs had been learned from him. Peter Hendley was a good father and a man of strength and sense, quite the opposite of her mother, of whom Patience had often been ashamed. But her father had made her proud. She'd hardly ever found fault with him in her younger days. Whenever she'd felt it necessary to calm herself in this way before, it had been because of her husband, not her father. However, that business concerning her husband had occurred seven long years ago, not worth thinking about now.

Patience took a deep draught of the cold night air, letting the freshness of it seep into her lungs, and willed herself to think of something else. She tossed back the long, loose hair that the wind had blown across her face and looked about her. One of the things she loved about this place was the view. Natural wonders filled the eye in whatever direction one looked. Westward across the river she could see the New Jersey palisades on clear nights. They extended north to the horizon in unabated majesty. But the view she most enjoyed was to the south. From this vantage point on the Spuyten Duyvil promontory, her eyes could follow the silver breadth of the Hudson until, far down the river, she'd see lights. The lights of the village of Haerlem. She sometimes imagined she could see even beyond those, to the lights of New York City itself. It delighted her to believe she could see moving torches or candlelight in windows that might be more than ten miles away. The sight of the city tonight, however, was truly startling. The flames gave the southern sky a hellish glow. She wondered how many buildings had to be destroyed to create a light like that.

The wind was fierce, and, although there was a half-moon in the sky, its light was periodically obscured by the clouds that scudded by. But the flames glowing on the southern horizon were brilliantly clear. She watched them in frightened fascination, letting the sight erase from her mind the reason that had brought her here. The fire, enormous even at this distance, seemed as if it were being blown from one roof to another.

"It wouldn't surprise me none if an entire city street was burning down," a voice said at her ear.

She gasped and whirled around. It was Tom again. "Good heavens, fellow! You frighted me out of my boots!"

"Sorry, ma'am," he said pleasantly. "Didn't mean to scare you. I should've stomped up here with more of a clump."

She glared at him, her chest heaving. Not only was she still seething from the liberties he'd taken this afternoon, but now he'd intruded into her private place. "What are you doing here?" she demanded, embarrassed.

"Same as you. Watching New York burn."

She opened her mouth to deliver a sharp rebuke but stopped herself. She had no right to dress him down for wandering round the property at night. As far as she knew, there was no rule against it. But his presence here discomfited her. Hadn't he upset her enough for one day? And how had he managed to blunder upon her secret place? Had he ever done this before? Had he, deuced intruder that he was, been spying on her? "This is an ungodly hour to be up and about," she said in chagrin. "Do you do this often?"

He shook his head. "Hardly ever. I need my sleep. Do you?"

"That is a rude question, and none of your affair," she said in quick offense. But her tone sounded sour to her ear and filled her with shame. "If It be needful for you to know," she added in a softer tone, "I do come here at times. I like the view."

"You must like it mightily to wander out alone so late, and on such a night. 'Tis not the sort of behavior one would expect from the straitlaced Mistress Patience."

"Straitlaced!" Her eyes flew to his face, shooting sparks. "Do you think it your place, Tom Morrison, to make judgment of me in that insulting way?"

"Now, ma'am, don't ruffle your feathers. I was but rallying you. I meant no disrespect."

She dropped her eyes from him, feeling her cheeks burn. *Straitlaced!* How could he think of her that way after what had occurred that afternoon? She'd felt not at all straitlaced when he'd pressed her against him. Just remembering how his chest had felt against hers, how the sinews of his shoulders had felt under her hands, how her heart had hammered in her chest, and . . . and that terrible, frightening hunger in her innards . . . well, it was anything but straitlaced! She flicked a look up at him, wondering in a kind of panic if he could read her shameful thoughts.

But the faint moonlight revealed only the gleam of an apologetic smile on his face. "Besides, to be called straitlaced is none so terrible," he was saying. "I've heard people called much worse."

"I've no doubt of that," she retorted drily, covering her embarrassment with sarcasm. Besides, she'd heard the names he and his cohorts affixed to those they disliked. Who knew what worse names they'd given her in the tavern taproom? She was silent for a moment, thinking of the tavern rabble with whom he often kept company and whom she often suspected took pleasure in laughing at her behind her back. "I suppose," she said at last, "that my night wandering will supply you with *new* gossip to chew over with your tavern cronies."

He stiffened. "I'm not given to gossip, ma'am," he said, his voice suddenly cold. "I don't 'chew over' the business of your family with my cronies or anyone else."

She refused to let herself be rebuked. "Don't you?"

"No, ma'am, I don't. I and my friends have more important things to talk about."

"Yes, of course you do," she retorted tartly. "Sedition and treason."

He gave the accusation a moment of consideration. "Sedition, perhaps," he granted, "but treason, no."

" 'Tis too fine a distinction for me. I call all the rebel activity treason, from hanging effigies to dumping tea in the harbor, as those miscreants did in Boston two months ago. Even you would have to call *that* treason, isn't that so?"

"Not at all. I'd call it standing up for one's rights. And it wouldn't surprise me to hear that they do the same in New York harbor when the tea ships arrive here in the spring."

"Hummph! Dressing up like Indians and destroying property like naughty little boys! Very admirable, I must say. I suppose you'd be among them if you had the chance."

"Like a shot, ma'am. Like a shot."

They glared at each other for a moment. "Is that the sort of thing you say to each other at the tavern? And you claim it's not treason?" she accused.

He stuffed his hands into the pockets of his breeches and turned away from her. "Sedition or treason, call it what you like," he muttered. "At least you can't call it gossip."

She studied his back that was rigid with offense. Her assumption that he'd gossip about her had insulted him. She felt a twinge of sympathy for him and put out a hand to touch his arm, but withdrew it quickly. Instead, she made her next words conciliatory. "Perhaps it's a kind of disloyalty to the Crown for me to say this, but I think I'd rather have you talk sedition than to gossip about my night wanderings."

He gave a short laugh and turned around. He'd heard the apology in her voice and was quick to forgive. She could feel, rather than see, his grin. "On my honor, ma'am," he teased, "the story of your night wanderings will never leave my lips. I'll keep your secret until death."

"Humph!" was her response. But she noted for the second time that day that the fellow was much too impudent. "I suppose you expect me to thank you," she added proudly, attempting to reestablish her position of authority. Who was bondsman and who was mistress anyway?

He sensed her change of tone. "No thanks necessary, ma'am," he said with formal politeness, taking a backward step. "There's nothing to tell, after all. You came out but to see the view." He turned his attention to the fire. "And it's surely something to see tonight. Like a window in hell suddenly opened up and let out a spurt of fire. If the wind keeps blowing easterly, we might see the whole city burn to the ground."

The moon slipped behind a cloud, and in the darkness they stood together watching the distant flames, not speaking. But when the moonlight broke through again, she caught a glimpse of him, looking not at the fire but at her, his eyes alight with something that was not moonlight. She became conscious of the fact that she had nothing on beneath her cloak but her nightshift. "Tom Morrison, why are you staring at me like that?" she demanded, gathering her cloak more tightly about her.

"Sorry, ma'am. It's your hair."

"My *hair?*" She stiffened in offense again.

Tom Morrison, though an indentured man for most of his life, had an unquenchably lively spirit. And tonight he was indulging that lively spirit to the full. It excited him beyond measure to have encountered his mistress twice in one day in unexpected places and informal circumstances, and he couldn't stop himself from pressing his advantage. He looked down at her with undisguised admiration, taking in not only the hair (its dull-gold sheen now silvered over by the moon and floating, he thought, in bewitchingly tousled profusion over her high forehead) but the pale oval of the face he so admired. Then he quickly took in the rest of her: the graceful neck, the softly rounded shoulders, the small breasts that she was now protecting so carefully with her cloak, and the line of hip and thigh and long, long leg that showed through their heavy covering just enough for him to be able to enjoy. He couldn't help thinking, at that moment, that it was too bad the fellows at the tavern couldn't see her like this. But aloud he only said, "I've never before seen your hair hang loose."

"Oh." Patience felt herself redden again. The fellow was positively irrepressible in his tendency to take liberties! No wonder he consorted with rebels; insubordination suited his character. She turned her face away from him, one hand reaching up instinctively to pull her hair back into some semblance of order. "Well, you won't see it again, you can be sure of that."

"Never? That *would* be a pity."

Her eyebrows rose in disapproval. "That cheeky tongue of yours will get you a fardel of troubles, Tom Morrison."

"I know it, ma'am," he said without a hint of repentance. "It already has, time and again."

Patience shook her head helplessly. She knew she shouldn't be standing there, engaging in badinage with a bondsman. It made her feel disquieted, as if she were guilty of some sin. And she knew what the sin was. One could be sinful in thoughts, even if one were innocent in deeds. And her thoughts were in turmoil, stimulated by a disturbing emanation of powerful masculinity that she sensed in Tom's presence, an emanation she'd not been aware of before. She knew she should leave—a truly God-fearing, sensible woman would go back to her bed. But somehow, Patience couldn't bring herself to go. *I want to stay and watch the fire,* she told herself in excuse. *I only want to watch the fire.*

They stood for a moment side by side, not speaking, their eyes fixed on the distant flames. But she was unable to keep herself from speculating about him. "How long have you been with us, Tom?" she asked suddenly.

"Nine years almost."

"You were fourteen when my father bought your indenture, weren't you? That makes you twenty-three." *Younger than I,* she thought. She threw him a quick, appraising glance. He was manly in build, with broad shoulders and huge hands, but his face, though it had a strength beyond his years, was still boyish. "You look younger."

"I am, probably. Twenty-one, maybe. I was never sure. I made myself as old as I could when I came to this land."

"Did you?" She peered up at him curiously. "Why?"

" 'Tis a long story," he said, putting her off. "Look, the wind's changing."

It was true. The wind had shifted to the west; the spread of the fire would thus be contained. She let the subject of his age, which he'd so obviously avoided, drop. It was shameful and quite humiliating, she told herself, to have thoughts such as she was having about a man who might be as much as four years younger than she. But of course the thoughts would be shameful whatever age the man might be! So she ordered them firmly from her mind. Instead, she turned and watched the flames slowly dwindle to a reddish glow. "It seems the city won't burn to the ground after all," she remarked.

"No, ma'am, seems not." He looked downriver, his expression a bit rueful, as if he regretted the fire's demise. "Though if the city had burned, it would've been a sight to remember."

"Good God, fellow," she exclaimed, outraged, "think of the cost in lives and property! It would've been a terrible tragedy!"

"Yes, ma'am, that goes without saying." Utterly without shame, he threw her another of his brazen grins. "I didn't say I wished it. Only that, if it did happen, I'd enjoy being a witness."

"To enjoy others' pain is sinful in the extreme," Patience scolded with sanctimonious pomposity. The schoolteacherish tone of her scolding seemed a quite proper way to rebuff the cocky bondsman. And to restore her sense of herself. She started back toward the house with her head high.

Tom gave a low chuckle. "I swear, ma'am, you'd make a mighty fine preacher."

"Would I, indeed?"

"Yes, ma'am. There's not a man alive who wouldn't find pleasure in coming to your church. His ears could take in the lesson, and his eyes take in the hair."

"Insolent creature," she threw back at him over her shoulder as she strode on, glad that he couldn't see her blush.

"What a wonderment you'd be!" he called after her. " 'Twould give a glow to Sundays."

She pretended not to hear.

Five

At a little before nine the next morning, three women—Sally, Beatie McNab, a quiet little Scotswoman who came up from Fordham village mornings to help with the household chores, and Patience herself—bustled about the large kitchen, preparing the breakfast that would soon be served not only to the family in the dining room but to the servants and hands here in the kitchen. Patience, however, seemed not to have her mind on her work. She was beginning to sense that this meal was not going to be nearly as pleasant or peaceful as last night's dinner.

After removing the hot corn bread from the oven, she dropped it carelessly on the table, went to the kitchen window and looked out worriedly. "There's no sign of him," she said to the black woman bending over the fire, "and it's pouring."

"Them militiamen, they drill rain or shine," Sally said as she stirred milk into a pot of steaming oats.

The Scotswoman, who rarely entered into conversation, continued to knead dough, engrossed in her own thoughts.

Patience wheeled around to face Sally. "Is *that* what you think Benjy's doing? Drilling with the militia?"

Sally shrugged her thin shoulders. "What else?" She lifted the pot from the firehook carefully, a pad in each hand, and carried it to the work table in the middle of the room.

Patience turned back to the window. "Drilling with that rabble! What can he be thinking of?" She peered out again, searching through the rivulets of raindrops for some sign of movement on

the path that stretched in an oval curve in two directions from
the front of the house to the road. "If Papa gets wind of it, he'll
be livid! Especially today, when he has his big meeting on his
mind. That boy should be horsewhipped!"

"He be young," Sally said calmly, beating the milk and oat-
meal into a hasty pudding. "He dream a young man's dreams."

Patience stared at her over her shoulder. "Young man's dreams,
indeed! Foolish dreams, if you ask me."

Sally met her mistress's eye with a level look in her own.
"Benjy ain't askin' you," she said flatly.

"All the worse for him." Patience stalked over to the table and
picked up a serving spoon to help Sally load a platter with fried
potatoes and sausage. "He'll be one sorry lad if his father ever
learns of this."

"That's as may be," Sally retorted, "but don' bite my head off
'bout it. I ain't the one drillin'."

Patience's shoulders sagged. "I know, Sally," she muttered,
reaching across the table and squeezing Sally's hand. "I'm sorry."
She put down the spoon and went to the window once more.
"I'm out-and-out edgy this morning. I can't imagine what excuse
Benjy will have for Papa if he's late for breakfast."

Sally threw her a look of sympathy. "Benjy think of somethin',
don' you worry none."

Meanwhile, in the main part of the house, Peter Hendley stood
at the dining-room window, leaning heavily on his silver-handled
cane as he looked out over the west fields. His mood of the night
before had dissipated, for his leg was paining him more than was
usual. The bone had been shattered by a musket shell in the battle
of Louisbourg twenty-nine years before, and though it pained
him every day of his life, the ache was especially sharp on cold,
rainy days like this.

He'd come in from his workroom for breakfast, but no one
was yet at the table. It was the custom of the family to breakfast
at nine, though the entire household was up and at their chores
by six. A hearty breakfast at nine was appreciated after three

hours of labor, especially since they'd not eat again until dinner at four in the afternoon.

Hendley did not mind waiting a few minutes for his meal. It gave him time to enjoy the view. He loved looking out over his property from the rear windows; they faced west and offered a vista both beautiful and meaningful to him. Even now, with a heavy rain pattering against the glass, he could see down the slope through the branches of the leafless trees to where the Hudson flowed in serene majesty. Watching the rain making little pockmarks on the surface of the water, he let the pride of ownership sweep over him. This land was his, every bit of it that he could see—the orchard, the west acreage, the new barn that was built into a slope so that a hay wagon could drive into it from both the lower and the upper levels, the stable, the workshop, the smokehouse, the three storehouses and all the other outbuildings—all acquired and built by his own enterprise. (He also owned the fields to his north, an area so extensive it accommodated three tenants, but he couldn't see that from this window.) The sight of it filled him with the deepest kind of satisfaction.

His five-hundred acre holding was modest by comparison with the land patroons like the De Lanceys, the Phillipses and the Van Cortlands, and the buildings were not so grand as those his friend Josephus Lovell had built on his estate, Lovell Hill, on the other side of the Bronx river, but it was enough to give Hendley some importance in the area. And, with luck, he'd have more.

He knew he was obsessed. Too land-proud. He was not blind to the malformation of his character. The bastard son of a baron who'd refused to recognize him, Peter Hendley had grown up in the lowest ranks of London's class hierarchy, bitterly resenting the hopelessness of his lack of birthright. But here in America he had become landed gentry, and landed gentry was the American upper stratum. He'd achieved by his own ingenuity and labor what had been denied him by birth.

Yet there was nothing ignoble about his pride in his land. The best minds, both here and abroad, were agreed that political strength and personal virtue flowed from ownership of inheritable land. Landholdings guaranteed a man not only independence but power. Land title was the primary basis of social order, even in England. Peter Hendley was not alone in believing that to lose title to one's land was to lose not only a man's political influence but his personal identity.

Hendley could not understand the reasoning of some of the large landowners who showed sympathy to those idiots who preached independence of Britain. Didn't they realize that title to land was secure only if government was secure? A new government might wish to institute widespread land reorganization! Hendley, who a few years ago had won a battle over his own land title by the intervention of the British governor, knew only too well how important a stable government was to the integrity of property titles.

That was why he'd called a meeting of the local landowners for this very afternoon. He wanted to organize them into a Loyalist association. If he could get them to agree, their unified voice would be a strong influence in the county. And, what was more important, they could purchase a cache of arms—an arsenal—and be ready to assist the British troops if the rabble rose up to revolt, as they already had in Boston.

At that moment a flurry of movement caught his eye. Far to his left, on the path leading down to the barn, Sally's boy Aaron was leading a flock of geese to the barn for the quarterly plucking. The boy was not even thirteen, but he was almost as big as a man, and growing fast. One of these days, he'd be worth as much as eight hundred pounds in cash at the New York slave market. Hendley would hate to sell him—he needed all the hands he could get—but in a pinch . . .

Further up the path he could see Chester and Jeb carrying a load of wood to the workshop. He nodded in approval; this was a good day to rive shingles. Tom had probably set them to it. Tom was a good man; he ran the place better than an overseer. Chester, the first Negro Hendley had ever bought, was a good man, too, though getting on in years. But Jeb, an indentured man like Tom, was too often drunk. Tom always covered for him, but Hendley was no fool. He knew what was going on. That was the trouble with America, he thought with a sigh; land could be had if one had enterprise, but workers were in short supply. In past springs and summers he'd managed to find enough day hands to work the farm, but it was getting harder each year. If the day came when he couldn't purchase slaves or indentured men, he'd be in real difficulty. That was why he'd hold on to Aaron . . . as long as he could, anyway.

His ruminations were interrupted by the opening of the door behind him. "Good morning to you, Papa," said Barbara, prancing in and taking a seat at the table.

He grunted a response, hobbled to the heavy oak trestle table and took his place at the head. "Where is everyone?" he asked, reaching for the pitcher of birch beer that was the common morning drink and therefore already on the table. "It's a quarter past nine."

Barbara shrugged and held out her glass. "I, for one, stayed abed this morning," she admitted to her father saucily.

He threw her a mock frown while he filled her glass. "Abed all this time? For shame!" His remonstrance was mild, for he neither expected nor wished for Barbara to be anything but what she was, a charming, pretty flibbertigibbet whom it pleased him to spoil. "To stay abed half the day is an offense against God and nature!"

"Oh, pooh!" Barbara laughed. "God and nature didn't take the least notice." She put a graceful hand over her mouth and yawned. "What possible need is there for anyone to rise at the crack of dawn on a day like this?"

"Of course there's no need," said her sister Patience, just entering with the sausage-and-potato platter in one hand and a trencher with hot corn bread in the other. "No need at all, if you're willing to let others do your chores for you. Good morrow, Papa."

Peter Hendley merely made a dismissive wave in response. "I suppose Benjy is still abed, too. I won't have it, Patience, not from Benjy. He'll face my wrath when he comes down."

Sally, entering with the hasty pudding, threw Patience a quick look. Patience bit her lip. Papa's mellow mood was quite gone. It was too bad that such moods never lasted long. She knew that this meal would be a far cry from the last. Poor Benjy would have to face an angry father this morning. "You're too hard on the boy, Papa," she said.

"It ill behooves you to tell me how to treat my son," her father growled. "Sit down, Patience, and let us eat. We won't wait for him."

The platter had been passed around, and Sally had already served the pudding and returned to the kitchen, when the door opened again. Benjy stood on the threshold, his boyish face tense with unease. A handsome but slightly built fifteen-year-old, he hadn't yet learned to mask his lack of self-confidence, a lack that was revealed by his manner, his facial expression and even his posture. At this moment, it was obvious that he'd come in, not from bed, but from the outside. His dark hair was so wet with rain that it lay flat on his head, the shoulders of his coat looked soggy and his blunt-toed, buckled shoes were muddy. "Good morning," he said with a nervous smile.

"So, Benjy, you're not abed," his father remarked coldly, putting down his forkful of sausage. "Where have you been?"

"Out, sir," the boy said, hurrying across the room and sliding into his chair. "To the village."

"And what were you doing in the village on such a morning?"

Patience was troubled by her father's tone. He always spoke to Benjy with an icy impatience that wasn't deserved. "Here, Benjy," she interrupted, smiling at the boy, "have some hot tea. You look as if you need it."

Benjy threw her a grateful glance, but Peter Hendley glared at her. "I asked a question."

"Nothing untoward," Benjy said quickly, taking the cup from Patience's hand. "Just seeing friends."

"So early in the morning?" his father persisted suspiciously.

There was a moment of awkward silence. Barbara, who'd been too absorbed in spreading blackberry jam on her bread to take note of the tension in the air, remarked in her careless way, "Oh, he was probably dr—" Her tongue was stopped by her brother's sharp intake of breath. She looked up, realized she'd made a slip and immediately tried to correct it. "I mean, he probably has a . . . a draggletail in the village."

"Draggletail! Are you hinting that your brother is courting some female?" Hendley snorted. "Our Benjy? What nonsense!"

"Yes, it *is* nonsense," Patience put in. "Eat your sausage, Papa, before it gets cold."

But Hendley continued to peer at his younger daughter intently. "No, Benjy is as likely to go courting as you are to become a spinster. You were about to say something else, were you not, Babs? What was it?"

"Nothing, Papa," Barbara said, keeping her eyes on her plate.

Hendley slammed his hand on the table, causing everyone round the table and everything on it to jump. "Answer me, girl! What were you about to say?"

Benjy squared his shoulders. "She was going to say *drilling*," he admitted bravely.

"Drilling?" Hendley's face darkened ominously. *"Drilling?"*

Patience hurriedly reached for the trencher. "Sally baked her wonderful corn bread this morning," she said, cutting off a piece and reaching over to place it on her father's plate.

Hendley, his burning eyes fixed on his son's face, shoved her arm aside, causing the bread to go flying across the room. "Are you saying you were out there on the green, going through drills with those whifflers, noodles and loafers who have naught of use to do with their time?"

"It was just the . . . the r-regular militia drill," the boy stammered, his whole body tense.

"I told him he could go," Patience lied. " 'Tis only twice a month."

But her defense was ineffective. Her father raised himself to his feet. *"You damned jackpudding!"* he cursed. In what seemed like one motion, he lifted his cane high in the air and brought it smashing down on the table with a horrifying crack. It broke Patience's teacup and saucer into fragments and sent tea and splinters spraying over the table.

Barbara let out a little scream. Patience gasped as some of the tea spilled into her lap. *"Papa!"* she cried, jumping up.

He ignored her. "The town militia," he said to his son with icy scorn, "are a gaggle of do-nothings and misfits who'd be the first to turn on the King's men if trouble came, so don't try to pretend to me that they're regulars." He picked up his cane and hobbled to the door. Then he turned back and surveyed his three children, all of whom were watching him with expressions of shock and alarm. His eyes settled on his son. "If ever I hear of you drilling with them again, Benjamin Hendley, I'll whip you till you bleed." With that, he turned his back on them, left the room and slammed the door behind him.

No one moved for a long moment. Then Patience, trying in her mind to find excuses for her father's unreasonable rage, absently began to collect the pieces of broken crockery, her fingers trembling and her lips white. Barbara, who was unaffected by her father's tantrums, picked up her jellied bread. "I told you, Benjy, that your silly drilling would get you into trouble," she said, calmly resuming her eating.

"Damn you, Babs," the boy burst out, "if it weren't for your loose tongue, this wouldn't have happened. But I won't stop drilling, no matter what Papa does to me. I won't. Don't look at me that way, Patience. 'Tis more than a boyish whim to me. I won't give it up."

Barbara snorted. "You'd better, if you know what's good for you. And Tom, too."

Patience stiffened, cutting her finger on a shard of crockery. "Tom?"

Benjy looked at Babs in alarm. "Who told you about Tom?"

"I have my ways to learn things," Babs bragged, lifting her chin with annoying hauteur. "I hear that Tom's the one who puts you fellows through your paces."

Benjy pushed back his chair, jumped to his feet and, with fists clenched, glared down at Barbara. "You'd better keep that information to yourself, Babs Hendley. If you tell, I won't forgive you. Not ever, as long as I live."

"Pooh! Who cares? One would think we were at war or something, the way people are carrying on. This flagitious militia business is all nonsense anyway. Sit down and eat your breakfast."

"Naturally you think it nonsense!" Benjy sneered. "You're not capable of thinking a serious thought."

"That's enough, Benjy!" Patience ordered as she sucked a dot of blood off her finger. She eyed her brother worriedly. "I don't understand you. I know boys are drawn to guns and soldiering like flies to honey, but the Fordham militia is full of hotheads and rebels. How can you bear to associate yourself with them? Can't you see they're on the wrong side?"

Benjy ran a hand through his still-wet locks of dark hair. "I don't understand *you*, Patience," he said, his voice throbbing with boyish intensity. "All my life I looked up to you. To me you're a . . . a paragon. Always so kind and loving and . . . and wise. Yet in this matter, you've closed yourself off. How can you close your heart to the idea of liberty?"

"Liberty?" Patience shook her head and sighed. "What is it but a word? It has a fine ring, I grant you, but it will only be used by the rebels as an excuse to take what doesn't belong to them."

Benjy sank down in his chair and dropped his head in his hand. "That's Papa talking, not you," he muttered sadly.

Patience came round the table to him and put a hand on his shoulder. "Finish your breakfast, Benjy," she said, "and then go up and get out of those wet clothes. You won't do the cause of liberty any good if you come down with an inflammation of the lungs."

He put a hand on hers and looked up at her, his eyes moist. "I know I'm not clever or ambitious, like Papa wants me to be, but I'm right about this. Liberty doesn't mean what Papa says it does. Try to think, Patience, about how it sounds to someone else. Tom, say. Or Aaron. Think about it, 'cause one day you're going to see that the one who's on the wrong side is you."

Six

Patience watched Benjy climb the stairs, his shoulders sagging in defeat. Her heart ached for him. How could the poor fellow develop proper confidence in himself if his father was always disparaging him? It was no wonder Benjy put his heart in the cause of liberty; his father's attitude would push any boy to rebellion. If Papa would only show his son some respect, Benjy might surprise him. The boy might even get over his rebel leanings.

Throwing back her shoulders determinedly, Patience strode down the passageway to her father's workroom. She had to let her father know that she could not condone his treatment of his only son. She threw open his workroom door and planted herself in the doorway, arms akimbo. "Heavens to Holland, Papa," she demanded, "was all that rodomontade necessary?"

Peter Hendley, already seated behind his desk and engaged in cutting a quill to a proper writing point, looked up at her in annoyance. "I've said all I intend to on the subject," he said dismissively, "except to add that, if you don't wish me to have to carry out my threat to cane your brother, I expect you to keep closer watch on him in future."

"You would never cane him and you know it," she declared, stepping over the threshold and closing the door. "See here, Papa, I like his drilling no more than you, but you know how boys are drawn to guns and soldiering. They love parading about on the

green with muskets on their shoulders in front of all those gawking girls. Perhaps there's no great harm in his—"

"No great *harm?* Don't rattle on so foolishly! The town militia
is almost entirely composed of young hotheads. They'd foster a
rebellion merely for the excitement of it! Do you wish for your
brother to join the Sons of Liberty or some such abomination?"

"No, of course not, but—"

"Enough of this! I've more important matters on my mind. I
must prepare some notes for this afternoon's meeting." He got
up and limped to the window. "This damn rain! Do you think it
will keep some of the men home and ruin my meeting?"

So that's why he's so crotchety this morning, Patience thought
with a sudden wave of sympathy for him. "Don't worry, Papa.
Rain isn't likely to put anyone off who wants to come. I'll prepare
tea things for twenty, in any case. Be easy about the meeting.
'Twill surely be a success. Most will be in agreement with you.
There can't be much opposition to a plan that strives for peace
while preparing for war."

He turned and smiled at his daughter, the rare smile transform-
ing his lined face. "That's a good phrase. I think I'll jot it down."
He started back to his desk. "Have you given any thought to
where we might hide an arsenal?"

"I've no idea, except to use one of the storehouses."

"No," he said, sitting down and picking up the quill. "Too
obvious."

She shrugged and started for the door but stopped as an idea
struck her. If Papa would ask for Benjy's help with his arsenal,
it might make Benjy feel useful and bring the boy and his father
closer together. "Papa, I just bethought me . . . perhaps you ought
to ask Benjy's opinion on a hiding place for the arsenal."

His expression immediately hardened. "Good God, girl, no!
You mustn't even mention it to Benjy. The boy's irresponsible.
Besides, he has too many friends among the rabble. What if he
should let something slip? No, no, you and I must be the only
ones who know. Go along now, and let me work."

Patience knew it was useless to argue further. His mind was set. She looked down at his grizzled head and sighed in discouragement. "You underestimate Benjy, Papa," she said. "You always have."

His only answer was an imperious gesture of his hand that ordered her to be gone.

Seven

The meeting did not go well. Anyone watching the Hendley place could have guessed it. Although the rain had stopped by one o'clock, and everyone had come, crowding the gravel drive with every sort of conveyance from imposing landaus, coaches, and shays to little carioles and buckboards, less than an hour later only four vehicles remained. The diminished meeting was continuing inside, but it had obviously failed to generate any excitement. There was no sound from within the house, no touch of anticipation in the still, somnolent afternoon air. Even the few horses still waiting in the drive pawed the ground listlessly, as if they sensed failure.

Suddenly, from behind the kitchen wing on the north side of the house, the sound of high-pitched laughter broke through the afternoon stillness. The horses lifted their heads, whinnying in curiosity and turning in the direction of the noise.

The source of the laughter immediately appeared. Young Barbara Hendley, in a flurry of skirts, came dashing around the kitchen garden from the rear of the house. "You'll have to catch me first," she shrilled over her shoulder as she skittered over the drive and set off across the lawn.

Not three steps behind, a young man with very fair hair—and dressed somewhat too formally for this activity, in an elegantly embroidered, wide-cuffed, beruffled coat buttoned tightly over a protruding stomach—made a lunge for the girl. The two fell over on the grass, the boy on top. "Now will you kiss me?" he begged, pinning her arms at her sides.

"No! Let me up, you lummox! You're not a mere hundredweight, you know." The girl pushed him off and scrambled to her feet. "You oaf, I wager you've completely crushed my coiffure!"

"No, I haven't. You look lovely." He got up and brushed at the knees of his breeches without taking his eyes off the girl. "Lovely as always."

Barbara tossed her tousled curls and backed away a step or two. "Flattery won't win you that kiss, Henryk Bogaerde, any more than falling upon me did," she taunted.

Barbara Hendley did indeed look lovely. Even in her everyday gown of dark green homespun, she was noticeably womanly, for she'd pulled the neck of it so low that it revealed a swell of nubile bosom. It was the sight of that bosom, heaving from the exertion of the chase, that drove young Henryk Bogaerde wild. "You cheat!" he accused, stalking her. "You *promised* me! Have you no honor?"

"None at all," she laughed, letting him back her to a tree.

He confronted her, his hands flat against the tree trunk, one on each side of her face. "Come on, Babs, just one!" he pleaded. "You've been leading me a fool's chase for months."

"If I kiss you," Barbara asked, eyes glittering shrewdly, "what will you give me in exchange?"

The plump-cheeked fellow blinked. "In exchange? What do you mean? I haven't anything with me to barter . . . except perhaps one of the buttons of my coat. Will that do? They're silver."

"Oh, pooh!" she sneered. "I have plenty of buttons."

"What, then?" he asked desperately. "You know I'd give anything I had."

She lowered her eyes modestly. "How about . . . that ring you wear?"

His face fell. "The ruby?" He looked down at the red oval that decorated his little finger. "I *couldn't*, Babs. It was my great-grandmother's."

"So you've told me." She moved in a little closer to him, her breasts just grazing his chest, though her eyelids remained lowered. "It *is* a pretty bauble."

"You'll have it one day," he said, youthful passion making his voice crack, "when we're betrothed."

Her eyelids flicked up, revealing to the startled fellow a look of utter scorn. "Huh!" She thrust his arm away. "We'll *never* be betrothed, Master Bogaerde, never! I have other plans."

The young Bogaerde blinked. "Other plans?"

"I purpose to wed a duke. Or an earl at the very least. So there!"

Henryk had heard this before. Not at all discouraged, he grasped her by the shoulders and pushed her back against the tree again. "Time will tell about that," he declared with the sublime confidence that seventeen years of coddling by an indulgent mother and the prospect of inheriting two thousand acres of rich Westchester County land had nourished in him. "All I want now is one little kiss."

Barbara looked at him speculatively, the tip of her pink tongue making a frisky little pass along her upper lip. "All *I* want is one little bauble."

Henryk's knees turned to water. He twisted the ring quickly from his finger. "My father will murder me if he learns of this," he muttered. "There! It's yours." And he thrust the ruby into her hand.

Smiling in triumph, the girl slid her arms round his neck. "Here, then," she whispered, shutting her eyes and offering up her pursed lips.

Henryk emitted a trembling breath. "Och, Gott!" he groaned, excitement causing him to revert to the Dutch he heard at home. Slowly, very slowly, so that this hard-won moment could be properly savored, he lowered his mouth to hers.

"Stommeling! Dumkop!" came a sharp bark behind him.

Before Henryk's lips could actually touch hers, he felt a cruel hand seize his ear and pull him abruptly back from the very brink of ecstasy. *"Papa!"* the poor fellow cried, flailing about in agony. "Papa, let me go! I was only—"

"You vas only, you vas only!" the senior Bogaerde mocked, inexorably dragging his hapless son by his ear across the lawn to the drive where their landau stood waiting. "Not only I vaste my day at a useless meeting, but my son den I find behaving like a stupid bossloper! Henryk, your brains in your *knickers* you keep!"

"Babs!" Henryk wailed as his father shoved him into the carriage. "Oh, Babs!"

Barbara watched openmouthed as the coach drove off, but as soon as the coach was out of sight, she looked down at the the ring in her hand and shrugged. A slow smile suffused her face. Without giving the cheated fellow another thought, she skipped off toward the house. She was bursting to show her sister the ring. Patience, although as different from her as muslin from lace, would nevertheless have to be impressed by this prize.

In the kitchen, Patience heard the Bogaerde carriage crunch off down the pebbled drive. She ran to the front window and peered out. "Another one gone," she said in disgust.

Sally, at the other side of the kitchen worktable, grunted. "Which one this time?"

"Mr. Bogaerde." Patience wiped her hands on her apron and pushed a recalcitrant lock of dusky-blond hair into her cap. "I should have thought *he'd* be in sympathy with Papa's plan, even though most of the Dutch are Whiggish."

Sally shrugged. "Tom, he say y' can't tell these days who gonna turn out t' be Loyalis' an' who won't."

"Tom says, Tom says. I wish you'd stop repeating everything Tom says." Patience crossed the room to the fireplace, her skirts swishing impatiently. "What makes you think he knows so much? He's nothing but an ignorant indentured man."

"Not so ignorant as y're makin' out," Sally retorted, flipping her mistress a sassy look before lowering her eyes to the assortment of cakes and sweets she was arranging on a platter. "Do y' still want me t' slice this apple tart?"

Patience shook her head. "No, don't bother. I don't think there are enough—"

Barbara bounced into the kitchen at that moment. "You don't think there are enough what?" She struck a pose and waved her hand high in the air.

"I was trying to tell Sally, not you, that I don't think there are enough guests left at Papa's meeting to eat what we've already sliced." Patience eyed her sister with her usual glowering disapproval. "Did no one ever tell you that interrupting someone in the middle of a sentence is the worst sort of rudeness? And in addition, Mistress Slugabed, where have you been hiding all afternoon? We might have used your help here."

"Oh, pish-tush," Barbara retorted, "don't fuss at me about nothing. I was right outside in the kitchen garden. All you had to do was call." She waved her hand even more ostentatiously than before, wiggling the fingers.

Patience, turning to the fire to see to the kettle, took no notice of her sister's frantic arm motions, but Sally did. "What's that on your finger, chile?" the slave woman asked suspiciously.

Barbara beamed. "At last *someone's* noticed my ring."

Patience looked up. "Ring? What ring?"

"This one. Look, Sally, isn't it lovely?"

Sally looked. *"Lordy!* You ain't tryin' to tell us you foun' *that* growin' in the kitchen garden like a turnip!"

"Let me see!" Patience, hanging the kettle back on the hook over the fire, strode round the table and took Barbara's hand. "Good heavens, Babs," she exclaimed, her brow wrinkling with alarm, "that's the Bogaerde *ruby!* What on earth have you *done?"*

The girl snatched her hand away. "Nothing. The way you sound, anyone would think I *stole* it! Henryk gave it to me."

"In return for what?"

"For a kiss, that's all." Barbara's eyes fell in momentary embarrassment, but she immediately recovered her indignation. "And you don't have to scold about the kiss, because he didn't even get *that*. His father dragged him off before he could collect."

Sally laughed heartily, but Patience didn't find her sister very amusing. "Have you lost your *senses?*" she demanded. "This ring, besides being much too valuable to be exchanged for a kiss—even one of *yours,* Barbara Hendley!—has been given by the Bogaerde men as a betrothal gift to their brides for three generations or more!" She took her sister's chin in her hand and made her look up. "Is this your way of telling us that you've agreed to *wed* the fellow?"

"Wed *Henryk?*" Barbara squealed, shaking off her sister's hand. "Don't be crazy. He's only seventeen, he's a looby, and he's *fat!*"

"Then why on earth did you take his ring?"

"I didn't take it! I told you he *gave* it to me."

"Without any understanding between you?"

"He understands, all right. He understands I'd never wed a bumpkin like him. I told him so."

Sally clucked her tongue. "You calls him a bumpkin, an' he give you a *ring* for it? I'll never understan' white folks."

"Listen to me, Babs," her sister said firmly. "There's no use prattling on about this. There's only one thing that needs to be said: unless you want to become betrothed to the fellow, you must give that ring back."

Barbara's face clouded over at once. "I *won't* give it back!" She hastily hid her hand behind her. "He gave it to me, and it's *mine!*"

"Don't be childish," Patience said with finality, returning to the fire and lifting the kettle again. "I'll take you to the Dutch church on Sunday, and you can return it to him."

Barbara stamped her foot. "I won't! You can't make me!"

"Then I shall have to tell Papa you're betrothed. You will either return the ring to Henryk on Sunday, or Papa will tell our pastor to read the banns."

Barbara's face grew hot in fury, and her eyes filled with tears. "You *want* me to marry a dolt like Henryk, don't you! And I know why. It's so you can be the only one in this family to have caught herself an English lord!" Her pouting underlip trembled as she raised her voice in venomous fury. "Very well, *Lady Orgill,* if you must be such a stickler, I'll g-give it back!"

Patience did not alter her expression. She merely poured the boiling water from the kettle to the teapot. "Good, then," she said calmly. "Sunday." She picked up the tea tray and went swiftly from the kitchen.

Barbara glared after her for a long moment. Then she brushed the tears from her cheeks with an angry swipe of the heel of her left hand while she stared down at the ring on her right. "That woman's a damn interfering prig," she muttered sullenly.

"You watch yo' tongue, missy," Sally said, frowning at the girl. " 'Tain't no way to talk about yo' sister."

"I don't care," Barbara pouted. "She's a mean, frumpy old maid, despite having been taken to the altar by a peer."

"Is that so?" Sally demanded, her hands on her hips and her thin elbows akimbo. "Is that how yo' sister seem to you?"

"That's right. A jealous, mean, bossy old spinster."

Sally shook her head and began to wipe the cake crumbs from the table with a damp cloth. "One of these days, chile," she said, keeping her eyes firmly on her' work, "you ought to take yo'self another look."

Eight

Patience, setting the tea things on the dining-room table, put the altercation with her sister from her mind. Quarreling with Barbara was almost a daily occurrence, so dismissing it from her thoughts was easy. But dismissing the failure of her father's meeting from her mind was not.

She looked at the closed door of the drawing room worriedly. By her calculation, there were only three or four guests left. What were they talking about in there? She could hear their voices, sometimes rising angrily, but she couldn't make out the words. Were they quarreling? Why?

As she absently set up the cups and lined up the spoons, her thoughts returned to the remark that Sally said Tom had made about the difficulty of identifying loyalists. The fellow was right. It was all happening so quickly, this division of the population into loyalists and rebels; sometimes it was hard to know who was who.

One would think that those colonists who, like her father, were born in England would be strongly loyal to the Crown, but that was not necessarily the case; some English-born were among the forefront of the rebellion. On the other hand, people born on American soil were not necessarily rebels. She herself was a good example of the confusion. She loved her native American soil fiercely and would not wish to live anywhere else, but that did not prevent her from feeling an intense loyalty to the Crown.

It was infuriating. Why weren't the Loyalists loudly identifying themselves? Didn't they want to rally to the cause that would affect them all? She herself would shudder whenever she thought of the possibility of a rebel revolt. If all the notorious rebels—the Sam Adamses in Boston, the Patrick Henrys in Virginia, the Alexander MacDougals in New York—had their way, she might one day see her father tarred and feathered, their lands confiscated and their home destroyed. The prospect was terrifying. Yet the other Loyalists, in equal danger, did not do anything about it!

Unless her eyes were deceiving her, there seemed to be a great deal more support for the rebel cause than for loyalty to the Crown. One could see the rebel fever everywhere one looked. She could scarcely stroll through the town square without seeing signs of it. All that group that met at Peach's tavern—Jotham Dillard and Tom and the rest—they were all part of the growing wave of disloyalty. *They* were becoming more and more outspoken in their lawless arrogance; why weren't the Loyalists equally outspoken?

The same question was being discussed at that moment by the men who still remained at the meeting. In the drawing room, the three guests and their host sat sprawled among the dozen empty Windsor chairs. The four men, dressed for a formal meeting in wide-sleeved coats, lace-trimmed neckerchiefs, and curled or bound hair (except for the portly Josephus Lovell, who had actually taken the trouble to wear a powdered wig), stared at each other disconsolately. "I don't know why they can't see the danger," the gaunt Clymer Young of White Plains was saying glumly. "We're looking at the distinct possibility of treason, civil war and mob rule."

"And it *will* be civil war," Peter Hendley agreed, getting up and pacing about the room with his painful limp, "no matter what they choose to call it. What else is it, when all the colonies are split against themselves? There are rebel sons and Loyalist fathers already at each other's throats." Thinking of the morning's altercation with his own son, he sighed deeply.

"Pooh! Little storms! They'll never burst into outright tempests," said the bewigged Lovell, whose estate, Lovell Hill, lay just east of the Bronx River. "It won't come to war."

"Dash it, Lovell, you were ever an incorrigible optimist," Hendley snapped.

"Call me what you like," Lovell retorted cheerfully, "but believe me, the British militia can quell these minor skirmishes."

"I shouldn't be too sure of that," Clymer Young said, rising and fixing the other with his black eyes that were remarkably alive in his emaciated face. "My cousin, Jolley Allen, who is a tea merchant in Boston, bought two chests of tea of Governor Hutchinson's sons—two months before the villainous act in the Boston harbor, mind you!—and was from then on made miserable with threats on his life and property! Tar-and-feathering was threatened more than once. The poor man writ me that he expected his house to be pulled down and everything he owns destroyed. And neither his personal acquaintance with the Governor nor the British militia was any help. They had not the slightest effect on his tormentors."

"These are shameful, lawless times indeed," Lovell sighed, "but we shall weather them."

"Easy to say," Hendley responded, "but it won't be easy to weather a rebellion should we happen to find ourselves on the losing side."

"Are you suggesting that England will *lose* if there should be rebellion?" Lovell asked in disbelief.

"Your naïveté is amazing, Lovell," Hendley said bluntly. "In war there is always the possibility of losing."

Good-natured Lovell took no offense. "That is assuming there will be an actual uprising. I say it ain't likely. We have strong British governors in place, legal governments and strong laws. And there's General Gage and the British militia—"

Clymer Young snorted disparagingly. "It is foolish to depend on Gage and a small handful of British regulars—who can't even keep order in Boston—to keep the peace in all the colonies."

Carel Kuykendall, a blond, ruddy-faced man of Dutch descent, and holder of the largest estate of the four, leaned back in his chair, puffed at a long-stemmed clay pipe and spoke softly in an accent that made no secret of his ancestry and the fact that he and his family, after four generations in America, still spoke Dutch at home. "Dere vill be var. For certain."

"If you truly believe what you're saying, Kuykendall," Hendley growled, "you're pretty damn calm about it."

"I am alvays calm. My family has held its lands through Dutch rule and British rule. Ve'll hold it through vatever comes next."

"Perhaps you will . . . and perhaps you won't," Hendley muttered.

Lovell snorted. "What are you implying, Peter? That we'll be overrun with radicals and be stripped of our lands? That is too ridiculous."

"If it happens, who will be ridiculous then, eh?" Hendley sneered.

"You should be more calm also," Kuykendall advised his short-tempered host. "Lovell ain't far off. It ain't likely that a few roughnecks and radicals can overset the most poverful nation on earth."

"Nevertheless," Clymer Young argued, "I must agree with Hendley. It's at least a *possibility* that the rebels could be successful. Some believe that England is too distant from us. Truly it would be difficult to exercise control from across an ocean. And England is too busy with European troubles, some say, to exert itself to defeat a rebellion if it comes."

"He makes sense, Lovell," Kuykendall said, puffing his pipe thoughtfully. "Ve should consider all possibilities."

"You sound like a weathercock, Kuykendall," Hendley said.

"Veathercock? Vat is—?"

"Have you never heard the word? It's a Tory who turns Whig when the weather changes."

Kuykendall laughed. "Perhaps that's vat I am. 'Tis a sensible position."

"Huh!" Hendley dismissed such nonsense with a wave of his hand. "Let us speak seriously. I can't really believe that Britain will be defeated, but if it comes to war, she will need the help of all her loyal supporters. We must do something to prepare ourselves for a battle that begins to seem inevitable. We should begin to gather supplies—muskets, powder—"

"Do you mean . . . secretly?" Lovell asked, alarmed.

"What would be the point of making our actions known?" Hendley retorted.

"It all seems a bit hasty to me," Lovell muttered, lowering himself upon the nearest chair. He was frightened of danger, and it would certainly be dangerous if any of the local radicals discovered them hiding a cache of arms. Worse, the mere *thought* of muskets—and the prospect of having to use them—made him nervous in the extreme.

"Hasty!" Hendley slapped his forehead in impatience. "And what shall we wait for? For the rabble to make New York harbor a teapot like Boston's? For the colonies to hold a convention and threaten Britain with insurrection? For the local rabble to appear at our doors with barrels of pitch and feathers?"

"Calm, Hendley, calm," said Kuykendall gently. He broke off the top of his long-stemmed pipe that he'd already softened with chewing, threw the chewed piece into the fire and offered what remained of the pipe to Hendley. "Here, man, take yourself a puff. It vill do you good."

Hendley, refusing the offer with a curt shake of his head, turned and limped to the window, trying to ease his turmoil by looking again at his fields and orchards and the peaceful Hudson sparkling in the late-afternoon light as it flowed south to sea. "Be calm, you say, Kuykendall. But how can I be calm? I've come to my present position by dint of fierce determination, hard labor and much sacrifice. I can never be calm about retaining my land."

"You ain't alone, Peter," Lovell assured him. "We all care about our property."

Hendley turned around and shook his head. "Perhaps not in the way I do. Try to understand, Lovell. My own piece of God's earth is everything to me. My very own—mine, by God!—hard won and hard held. I've sacrificed everything for this acreage. I'll be *damned* if I surrender it to some rabble in the name of liberty or republicanism!"

"But, Peter," Lovell asked in confusion, "why would you have to?"

"Damnation, don't you understand? That's what a revolution *is!* It's nothing but a method of redistributing property. Underneath all the talk of ideals, of freedom, of colonial rights and wrongs, the real motivating force is *property.* Those on the losing side must give it up, those on the winning side take it!"

" 'Tis a cynic's view, Hendley," Kuykendall said.

"Perhaps." Hendley turned back to the window. He could mouth the platitudes as well as the next one, but when it came down to it, he knew one truth: everyone's politics depended on self-interest. But perhaps it would not do to press home so cold-blooded a fact. "Let me simply say this, gentlemen," he said, turning back to them. "I am loyal to king and country, to the death if need be, because I'm convinced it means I will thereby retain what is rightfully mine. The same should be true for all of you."

A heavy silence fell as the other three thought over his words. At last, Josephus Lovell, a kindly fellow who wished only to live in comfortable peace with his fellow man—so long as his fellow man made no claims on his estate, his purse or his dinner—rose, went to the window and clapped a friendly hand on Hendley's shoulder. "You worry too much, Peter," he said with his customary complacency. "Even if there is outright rebellion—which I don't for a moment believe probable—Britain will quell it in a moment."

"Damnation, Lovell," Hendley burst out in frustration, swinging round with the help of his cane, "has all this talk done nothing for you but to keep you in exactly the same state of mind as when you walked in here?"

"Calm, Hendley, calm," Kuykendall put in placatingly.

"I heard what you've said, Peter, but I still think you're being hasty," Lovell insisted. "Much too hasty, isn't that so, gentlemen?"

The others did not disagree.

Hendley gaped at them. "Good God! Don't you want to be prepared?" he demanded.

"How can ve prepare?" Kuykendall asked. "Twenty-two men ver here an hour ago. Now ve are four. The rest are not yet ready to decide vere they stand. It's easier to remain neutral than to declare oneself. As my friend Bogaerde said before he left, 'Better not to seek out trouble but to vait till it finds you.' "

"Aye, Peter," Lovell agreed eagerly. "Why worry about what *might* happen, when the odds are it won't happen at all?"

"It will happen," Clymer Young sighed, "but perhaps, Hendley, we're a bit premature to expect others to go racing into action. Let's hold back and await developments. When matters become critical—and they will—every man Jack of them, even the weathercocks, will be forced to take a stand."

Hendley stared at him for a moment and then shrugged. If even Clymer Young was reluctant to go into action, there was no point in continuing to argue. He would have to wait until events pushed them. And until then, he could begin to accumulate an arsenal on his own, at least as much as he could afford.

When Lovell saw that Hendley had capitulated, he jumped up from the chair, his jowly face breaking into a relieved smile. "So we are agreed, then, eh? We'll wait." He rubbed his hands together cheerfully, for postponement was his favorite kind of action. "I'm glad that's settled. We've plenty of time yet to organize ourselves. Meanwhile, Peter, did you not say something about tea?"

Nine

She is pushing her way against a cold, cold wind, although she is somewhere indoors. There are walls around her, and a steep stairway. Someone is climbing down. Goody Stephens, the midwife. Under one arm, Goody carries a shrouded bundle. "Let me see the poor creature," Patience says. But the midwife shakes her head. " 'Taint nothin' to see. Go up, she's waitin'."

Patience now hears loud wailing, full of pain. On the stairway Patience steps aside, for a man wants to go down. Her father. "Another one stillborn," he says. "Six out of nine birthings." His face is white as the shroud, and his eyes are two black hollows, like craters. "Make her stop crying," Patience begs. "I can't," he says as he goes limping down the stairs. "I never could."

Now Patience is in a room she recognizes. Her mother's bedroom. There is no more wailing, only a low moan. Sally, sitting in a corner, is holding a covered figure on her lap and rocking it like a baby. Patience approaches warily, her heart pounding. "Go on, look at her," Sally says. "Take a good look at what can happen to a woman on'y thirty-six." Patience pulls back the cover and stares down into the dead face of an old, old woman. "Mama!" she cries out in anguish, "Mama!"

Patience eyes flew open. She was in her own bed, trembling and soaked in sweat. That dream again. She'd probably cried out in her sleep and awakened herself. *Oh, God,* she thought, sitting up, *why am I still dreaming the same dream? Mama has been dead for nine years now.*

The dream always upset her, but tonight its effect was more intense than ever. She felt tears spring to her eyes. *Poor Mama,* she thought sadly, permitting herself to feel a sympathy for her mother's travails that she'd always kept buried. To feel for her mother was, in some strange way, disloyal to her father, so she'd tried all these years to avoid dwelling on it. Yet tonight, she couldn't seem to suppress—

"Patience?" came a voice outside her door, accompanied by a tapping. "Patience?

She climbed out of bed, hastily wiping the tears from her cheeks. Then, throwing a shawl over her nightshift, she went barefoot to the door. She opened it a crack, to find her father standing there, still fully dressed and holding a candle. "What is it, Papa?" she asked. "Why are you not abed? It must be very late."

"Only ten. I worked these past five hours on the accounts. I was on my way to bed when I heard you cry out. Are you all right?"

" 'Twas nothing, Papa, but a dream."

"You cried out Mama." He lifted the candle higher, to see her face. "Are you still having that old nightmare?"

Patience, suddenly aware that she was trembling, clenched her fingers. "It's not always the same," she said, trying to keep her voice steady. "In any case, 'tis naught but a dream. Not a matter to cause a to-do."

The candle flame trembled, for his hand was shaking, too. "You blame me for what happened to her, don't you? You think it was my fault."

She shook her head. "I don't think of it at all any more."

"You do in your sleep. May I come in, my dear? Perhaps we should speak of this."

She opened the door and stepped aside to let him in, but she felt a strong sense of misgiving. Some things, perhaps, should not be dwelt upon. Like her mother's suffering. And her own marriage. What good would come of chewing over the past? But her father was lighting her oil lamp with his candle, as if preparing for a long visit. "I don't know what there is to speak about, Papa."

"You were only sixteen when your mother passed on, so I didn't speak to you of her," he said, seating himself in her rocker and extending his bad leg. "But you're old enough now, Patience, to understand how things were. To understand that people have mostly themselves to blame for what they become. Your mother made *herself* old and ill, wishing for a life different from what she had."

"She had no liking for her life here, I know. She wanted to go back to England."

"Yes, foolish biddy that she was. Cried for England her whole life. Yet in England she couldn't have had a fraction of what she had here. We were nothing in England. Nothing. When I married her, I was a subaltern in a marine regiment. We had tiny rooms in a modestly stylish section of London, which I could barely afford. For her, I suppose, it was an amusing life; she was at the time a very young girl—only fifteen when I wed her. She liked the military society . . . the parties and balls and the excitement of the unexpected. But we had no prospects for the future, none at all. I had no title, no rank, no property. We would have become poverty-stricken nonentities when I retired, if life had gone on so. But chance brought me to America in '45. You know about that, I assume. About my military career?"

"Only a very little," Patience said, caught up in the story despite herself. She sat down on the edge of the bed and peered at her father intently. "I know you were a marine lieutenant on a British ship-of-the-line," she offered, "and that you distinguished yourself during the King George War."

"In but a very small way." He leaned back against the rungs of the wooden chair and rocked slowly, his thoughts sinking back into the past. "We were blockading the French at Louisbourg, in Nova Scotia. That's when I took a piece of shell in my leg and won my discharge. The misfortune was also my good fortune, for instead of mustering-out pay, they offered me a parcel of land. It was the Crown's way of paying off its debts and settling the colonies at the same time. I could have had a thousand acres in western New York. Instead, I chose two hundred acres here. I knew this property would be ten times more valuable than frontier land."

"And then you sent for Mama and settled down here?"

"Yes. I built her as fine a house as any in the neighborhood. I gave her position, dignity, comforts, even luxuries. She had house servants and gowns from England and silver goblets for her table and everything else a woman could wish for." He stopped rocking and his back stiffened. "And in return she gave me two daughters, one molly-coddle son, six stillbirths and an ocean of tears."

"Papa! That's not *fair!* Benjy is *not* a molly-coddle! And poor Mama couldn't help—!"

He put up a hand to stop her. "I know. I know. You purpose to say it was God's will."

"I did *not* purpose to say that!"

"What, then?"

"After two or three stillbirths, you should've *stopped*—!" She clamped her mouth shut, afraid that, in that outburst, she'd gone too far. Whatever had possessed her to say these things? She'd never before permitted herself to think of her mother's life this way. It was always Papa's viewpoint she'd shared. Why of late had she begun to question the ideas she'd accepted for so long?

Her father's eyes fell from her face. "A man needs sons in this land, Patience. Sons who care about the property. Sons who can work and enhance the value of the land. I have more than twice as much acreage as when I started, but only one son . . . a son who has no feeling or talent for farming or husbandry but only for sailing the dory and for drilling with his shiftless friends. I kept hoping for another son. A son more like you."

She was taken aback. "Like *me?*"

Leaning heavily on his cane, he got up from the rocker, crossed the room and took a stance in front of her. "Yes, my dear, you. You're not a whiner like your mother. You have strength. And you love this piece of ground, as I do. You are the only gift I've had from your mother that's worthwhile."

"I do not consider that a compliment," she said, unable to quell the flood of feeling for her mother that had welled up in her. "I . . . I loved Mama."

"So did I, until her everlasting tears drowned my affection."

She stared at him, aghast. Why had she never before permitted herself to understand her mother's tragedy? "If you had true affection for her, Papa," she said, choked with pain, "you should have taken her back to her England and stopped those tears."

"I thought of that sometimes," he said quietly, turning to the table where he'd left his candle. "But I could not give up the land. I shall never give up the land. I paid for it with my youth and my blood. Perhaps you must believe I sacrificed your mother's happiness for it, and yours, too, but some day you'll see, as I do, that any sacrifice is worth it."

She turned from him, a hand pressing against her mouth to keep from crying out in chagrin. An anger against him was rising up in her, an anger that was—well, what could one call it but rebellious? "How can *anything* be worth it?" she asked when she could speak.

He took up his candle and limped to the door. There he stopped and looked back at his daughter. She knew she should meet his unfathomable eyes with her own, but she did not. If he was asking for her understanding and forgiveness, she was not sure she could give it to him now.

He cleared his throat. "I can't prove its worth to you in words, Patience," he said, his voice revealing a touch of helplessness. "I can but say that you will understand one day. Perhaps you'll never live as a married woman because of me, or have children of your own. And by law I must bequeath the land that should be yours to Benjy. But I've written in my will that this shall be your home for life, and that any decisions taken in regard to its management must be approved by you. You'll be a woman of substance, of respect, even of power. You may not believe this now, Patience, but someday you will thank me. You'll see."

For some minutes after he left, Patience did not move, her mind dwelling on the legacy he'd just promised her. Substance, respect, power. What were they but words? They had not brought her mother a day of happiness. Something was amiss here.

She'd always accepted her father's beliefs about the ideals of womanhood, absorbing them so deeply into her nature that by this time she could hardly bring herself to question them. They had seemed to represent the best beliefs of her world. They made a triple litany: first, that a woman owed obedience to God, King, Father and Husband, in that order; second, that a woman's most admirable qualities were strength for labor, the absence of self-pity, and obedience without servility; and third, that people of sense valued property and protected that property by supporting stable government.

Good God! she thought, sinking down on her bed, overwhelmed by a shocking new thought. *Can it be that these ideals are all wrong?*

Ten

Shivering, Patience wrapped her shawl tightly round her shoulders. Her dream and her father's words had stirred up feelings she'd long kept dormant. His admission that he'd sacrificed her mother's happiness—and her own—to his need for property had been the lever that pried open the floodgate of memories that now overwhelmed her. Could the nagging unhappiness, the sense of failure that she lived with every day of her life and believed was caused by her ill-fated marriage, have another cause—her father's love of property? And was that love of property anything more than simple greed?

She rose slowly from the bed, went to the table and blew out the lamplight. Then she turned to the window. Below her, silvered by moonlight and February frost, lay the west fields and the orchards, stretching all the way down the slope to the river. She could see the silver-tipped ripples of the water glinting between the bare branches of the trees. Yes, she loved this piece of God's green earth for which her father had sacrificed two women's lives. She loved it, but was it truly a worthwhile exchange?

It was not a question she could answer. Her mother's life was over; there was no one now who could say whether Mama had made her own tragedy, as her father claimed. And as for Patience's own marriage—for which her father seemed to be taking all the blame—it had been her choice as much as his. Her father may have encouraged the original arrangement, but he had nothing to do with its eventual failure. Nothing at all.

Her married life had lasted less than a month, and it was something she'd tried, in the seven years since, not to remember. But now, in the darkness of her bedroom, with her father's words still ringing in her ears, it was, perhaps, time to think about it.

She had to admit that the episode had had a thrilling start. May of '67, it was. Patience was eighteen and unschooled in the art of dalliance She had had a suitor or two—local clods like Jotham Dillard for whom she had no liking—but had had few opportunities to test her skills at flirtation. Lord Orgill had been the very first.

The whole county had been agog at the arrival of Lord Orgill into their midst. The son of an earl, a not-too-distant cousin of the king himself, Walter Gordon, Lord Orgill, who'd come from England to tour America, was the most distinguished visitor ever to grace the county. Every landowner with a marriageable daughter and a desire to raise himself in society set out to engage his lordship's attention. Her father did not. Widowed, he needed his daughter Patience at home and therefore had no desire to marry her off. And as for his other daughter, Barbara, she was only ten.

Papa *did* permit Patience to attend a ball in his lordship's honor, held at Josephus Lovell's large estate, but only because Lovell's daughter Hannah was Patience's best friend. The ball was a very grand affair, almost like a fete in the city. The rooms blazed with the light of hundreds of candles, the tables groaned under the weight of dozens of delicacies: oysters, roast duck, and venison in profusion; mounds of potatoes, maize, peppers and butter beans; piles of biscuits, hot breads, cakes, pies and fruits. Champagne imported from France flowed as freely as if it were common ale. Four musicians filled the air with lively tunes. Hannah and all the other girls were dressed in their finest imported brocades and silks. But it was Patience his lordship singled out, Patience in her plain Sunday dress—twilled blue silk adorned with nothing more than a lace collar. He asked her hand for three dances! And he would have taken her up for a fourth, but she refused. More than three dances would have been quite improper.

All the girls were green with envy except Hannah, who had already set her heart on a local young man named Stuart Le-Grange and didn't share her father's longing to entice a nobleman into the family. After Patience refused Orgill's fourth invitation to dance, Hannah grasped her arm and dragged her out to the warming room. It was a place where nobody but the servants ever passed through and was thus the perfect place to talk over what had happened. "Whatever does he see in me?" the blushing, bewildered Patience asked her friend.

Hannah, a pretty if stolidly built brunette with a genial disposition and a sensible mind (except for a tendency—caused by overprotective parents—to worry overmuch about the state of her health) considered the question carefully. "It isn't that you're a beauty," she answered frankly, "but that you have such unadorned purity in your face."

"Purity?" Patience echoed in confusion. "Whatever do you mean by that?"

"You have a look about you that's very . . . very . . ." Hannah shook her head, unable to find the right words. "I don't know . . . as if you wouldn't ever lie, or accept dishonesty from anyone. I can't explain it. Pure, that's all."

"Are you trying to say virginal?" Patience pressed, not finding Hannah's explanation convincing. "Because all the girls at the dance look virginal, don't they?"

"No, I don't mean that kind of pure. All the others—and me, too—we're all dressed tuftafetty . . . tricked out in feathers and finery, simpering and flirting and fawning over him for all we're worth. While you . . . well, you're just yourself. I don't mean you're not lovely in face, for you are, in your special way. I suppose his lordship, after a lifetime with the overdressed, dissipated ladies of London, is charmed by your sort of purity."

"Oh, pooh," Patience said with a dismissive shrug. "If, to charm an English lord, it requires naught but a face of innocence over a plain blue dress, I can't believe he'd be worth charming."

Whatever the mysterious reason Lord Orgill had for his attraction to Patience, he continued to pursue her, remaining as a guest at the Lovells' estate and riding his horse over William Bridge to Hendley's house at every opportunity. There he would take a prominent place in the front room and hold forth, keeping the entire family spellbound with his tales of London society—of racing and gaming and the doings at court. His lordship, a large man with a booming voice, had an easy-come smile and a gift for innocuous conversation. Papa would listen to him with rapt attention while puffing away at his pipe; little Benjy would perch on the hearth and try to make sense of the stories that were quite beyond the grasp of an eight-year old; and Barbara, ten years old and already a flirt, would hang over his chair and ask all sorts of impertinent questions. Patience, however, would sit in her rocker, sewing, flattered at having won the attention of such a desirable nobleman but frightened at the prospect of having a real suitor. She'd seen her mother die in childbirth, and the prospect of courtship and wedlock was not entirely welcome.

The night Lord Orgill made his offer was one Patience would never forget. His lordship had maneuvered her outdoors by asking to see the Hudson by moonlight. When they strolled past the kitchen garden, out of sight of the house, he stopped and smiled down at her. "You are not very talkative, my dear," he said. "I believe you to be overly shy."

"Oh, no, my lord, I'm not shy. Only careful."

"Careful?"

She threw him one of her rare smiles. "You're what is known as a prize, you see. I've never before had to talk to a prize. I wish not to commit any gaffes, so I must be careful."

His smile widened. "Careful so as not to *lose* the prize?"

"That, my lord, implies that I might win it," she teased, "and I assure you that such an impossibility never crossed my mind."

He laughed, a great guffaw of a laugh that rumbled deep in his chest. "It must have, ma'am. Surely you didn't believe I've been riding across that deuced bridge every day just to exchange pleasantries with your father."

"That is just what I believed. Any break in the day's routine would provide you some relief from our dull provincial life."

"I find provincial life anything but dull. And if you don't guess why, you're not as clever a wench as I supposed. But tell me, my dear, how it is that so lovely and enticing a creature as you has not already captured a matrimonial prize?"

"We in the provinces are not richly endowed with gentlemen who can be called matrimonial prizes," she explained frankly. "Certainly we have none so spectacular as you."

He put his hand on her chin and tilted her head up. "Would you *like* to win this 'spectacular' prize?"

She felt her smile die. "I . . . I'm not certain," she stuttered, quite taken aback by his bluntness.

"Then let me help you become certain," he said, pulling her into his arms. He was very tall and broad in the shoulders and, in order to kiss her properly, he had to lift her off her feet. This he did with great assurance and aplomb.

Patience was both shocked and excited; she'd never before been kissed. She did not push him away, but neither did she let herself respond to the kiss, although her blood raced in her veins and pounded in her ears. "Is this considered polite behavior in England, my lord?" she asked breathlessly when he let her go.

"It is polite behavior anywhere, Mistress Hendley, if the gentleman's intentions are honorable," Lord Orgill answered smoothly.

Patience felt her heart leap up in her chest. She knew what "honorable intentions" meant. His words indicated that he was truly smitten, but she still found it quite hard to believe. "Honorable?" she murmured, temporizing. "I don't know what you mean."

He smiled down at her with all the cocksureness that wealth and breeding had supplied. "I mean, you little vixen, that I want to marry you," he declared and kissed her again.

She returned the kiss this time, but although she seemed to have somehow ingested a breast full of butterflies, her mind continued to function with its normal sanity. "But, my lord," she asked when her breath returned, "why?"

"Why do I wish to wed you?" His eyes gleamed in amusement. "That's a strange question. I don't really know why."

"Shouldn't you know why, my lord? Wedlock is an important step, after all."

"I'm not given to analysis of my feelings, my dear. That sort of thing is rather too feminine for me. But if you insist on reasons, I suppose I could say it's because you're quite . . . quite adorable," he said, taking her hand. "You're rather special, you know, Mistress Patience Hendley. So unspoilt . . . so untouched . . . so . . . so . . ."

"So pure?" she supplied drily.

"Yes, exactly. But reasons aren't really important, are they? The only reason that matters is that I've fallen quite helplessly in love with you."

"Oh!" She expelled a deep breath, sincerely overwhelmed. It was a heady victory for a provincial little nobody to have won an offer from a wealthy, titled Englishman who was sought after by every unmarried woman in the district. Her cheeks grew hot in both triumph and embarrassment, and "oh" was all she could say.

"My sweet child," his lordship objected, "you must know that 'oh' is not an answer."

Patience found herself not only bereft of words but trembling at the knees. "You'll have to ask Papa," she managed.

"Of course, my little innocent, of course. But in the meantime, can't you at least tell me if you find me to your liking?"

She studied him for a moment, hesitating. She hardly knew him, really. But he was very handsome, over six feet tall, with blond curls that fell over his forehead, a dimple in his right cheek, wide shoulders shown to advantage by a brocaded coat cut by the finest London tailor, slim hips and very good legs. Tonight he was wearing the most elegant silk stockings and a pair of dancing shoes decorated with rosettes. She'd never met a man half so fine. In addition to his looks, there was his voice. It was booming and hearty, always ready to burst into raucous laughter. And beyond those virtues, he had the good taste to find her charming and adorable and pure. How could she not find him to her liking? "I think you are the most fascinating man I ever met," she admitted.

He responded by sweeping her into his arms again. "You must let me show my appreciation for that," he said, pressing her to him in an embrace that was almost painful.

The embrace did not feel decent. She didn't like it. She lifted her hands to push him away, but then she stopped, letting her arms drop to her sides where they dangled in indecisive inaction. If she pushed him away, she asked herself, would he rescind his offer? She didn't wish him to do so. That would be too brief a triumph.

Just then, a noise from the underbrush made them jump apart. "Who's there?" Patience asked, feeling a flush of embarrassment at having been detected in this licentious embrace.

A figure emerged from the trees. "It's me, Tom."

Patience frowned at the intruder. He stood outlined in moonlight, his face shadowed, looking taller and more forbidding than any fifteen-year-old boy—and a servant at that!—had a right to look. Even through the distance and the darkness, she could sense his furious disapproval of what he'd seen. "What are you doing there?" she demanded, furious herself.

"Who *is* that?" Lord Orgill asked.

"It's our indentured man. Are you spying on me, Tom?"

"Going to the barn is all," came the gruff reply.

"This is a long way round, isn't it?" she asked in disgust. "Well, then, go on. Who's keeping you?"

The boy turned and took a couple of steps across the open field, but then he paused. "Sure you don't need me?" he asked bluntly.

"If I did, I'd say so."

Tom had no choice but to take himself off, though Patience

could sense his reluctance. Despite her annoyance at being spied upon, she felt a twinge of gratitude toward the boy; he'd created an opportunity for her to escape from what she feared were Lord Orgill's too-intimate embraces. "I think, my lord," she murmured shyly, "that we've permitted ourselves to remain out here in the moonlight a bit too long." And with awkward abruptness, she whisked herself off up the path to the house, leaving his lordship to recover from his surprise as best he could.

Patience had expected her father to refuse Lord Orgill's offer, and in the depths of her heart she was relieved at the prospect. She didn't feel ready for marriage. She didn't feel that she was well-enough acquainted with her suitor. And she didn't believe she would enjoy being removed from her beloved home, being taken across the ocean to London and being thrust into the dissipation of London social life. If her father refused Lord Orgill's very flattering offer, she would have her triumph without having to pay for it with the price of wedlock.

But to her astonishment, her father had said yes.

Now, seven years after these events, as she stood at the window of her unlit bedroom reflecting on the past, she was at last able to understand her father's reasoning. He'd sacrificed his daughter, as he'd sacrificed his wife, for property.

She could sympathize, in a way. She sensed in him the wounds that the humiliation of his ignoble birth and years of submission to onerous military servitude had wrought. Land ownership was the way to gain the power that his birth and his profession had denied him. Property made a man a gentleman in America. Property gave a man status, importance, power. He'd almost said as much tonight. And seven years ago, when Lord Orgill had chanced to enter their lives, Peter Hendley's claim to his property was in jeopardy.

Patience was now finally clear about the details. Putting together what her father had said tonight with what she'd known before, she at last could explain to herself what had happened. When the military government had awarded her father his deed after he'd fought against the French and Indians in 1745, there was no one more pleased with his mustering-out pay than Peter Hendley. He'd won the thing he wanted most: a chance to become a member of the gentry. As he'd cleared the land and planted orchards and laid out the fields and built a fine stone-and-brick three-story residence, he saw that his dream was coming true. But after the major work had been done, and the property had become truly his not only by deed but by dint of years of love and labor, he'd discovered that the title to the land was in question. A Dutchman named Betts, who held the patent to much of the land in the area, claimed the property was his, by an earlier deed signed by the eccentric Lord Cornbury, who'd been governor of New York some seventy years before.

Though her father managed to hold up the Dutchman's claim in protracted litigation, the matter was coming to a head just at the time of Orgill's arrival. Peter Hendley was feeling very nervous about the claim. The thought that the courts might, one day soon, decide that he'd been nothing but a tenant all these years made him sick in his soul. Patience had not realized it at the time, but she saw now that her father had viewed Lord Orgill as the means to his salvation.

As her father had sat in the front room smoking his pipe and listening to Orgill's tales, the plan must have taken shape in his mind. Lord Orgill had spoken often of his noble connections, in particular his intimate acquaintance with the Royal Governor of the whole New York province, Lord Dunmore. By what better way could her father be assured of the ownership of his property than by asking someone of Lord Orgill's importance to use his influence with Governor Dunmore to legitimize his deed? And in return for this favor, what would be more natural than to give his lordship his daughter's hand in marriage?

Patience now remembered that, within a fortnight of Lord Orgill's proposal of marriage, his lordship had extracted from the Governor an official document. Her father, ecstatic with triumph, had shown it to her. It stated that the Dutchman's claim to the land was obtained "in deceit of the Crown" and therefore invalid, and it reiterated the legitimacy of the later-dated British deed. The document was signed by three elaborate signatures—one the Governor's own—and decorated with an impressive gold seal. No one could possibly doubt its authenticity.

With his ownership of the property now assured, it behooved the overjoyed Hendley to make good his part of the bargain.

Patience had been too young and naive to understand fully that a bargain had been made. She only knew that she was to be wed. She was not entirely delighted at the prospect. Since dear Walter—as she was now enjoined to address his lordship—was as charming and amusing and as enchanted with his bride-to-be as ever, her reluctant feelings could not be explained by any deficiency in him. He was perfect. She was the luckiest girl in the whole of New York Province. Everyone told her so. The only reason anyone could find for her hesitation was that she did not like the prospect of being taken away from her home.

"It's quite true, Papa," she admitted to her father, "I cannot like it. All our lives will be overturned. Walter will take me back with him to London, and I'll be gone from the family forever. How will you do without me? Who will take care of Babs and Benjy? Who will run the household in my place? Have you thought of that?"

To give her father his due, he did seem stricken with remorse. He tried to explain to the eager bridegroom that there were good reasons for Patience's reluctance to be wed at this time. Lord Orgill came to her at once. "My dearest," he said, his hearty voice subdued with throbbing sympathy, "I quite understand. You are too young to be torn so abruptly from your roots. But you have me so besotted that I'll do whatever you wish. I'll even stay here in America with you, if that is your desire."

It was overwhelmingly generous of him. Patience was touched to the core by the kindness of his offer. It was only later that she realized why he'd made it. Orgill, whose wealth and good looks made him the richest of matrimonial prizes, had never before been faced with a reluctant female. That reluctance attracted and intrigued him to the point of desperation. It was that besotted condition, she belatedly realized, that caused him to agree to remain in America for the next six years, until Barbara's sixteenth birthday, to allow Patience to do her duty by her siblings and give her father sufficient time to find someone else to run his household. His lordship, in the meantime, would move into the Hendley household and live the life of a colonial gentleman.

With this sign of Orgill's generous nature, any lingering objection to him was swept away. The man was a paragon. The compromise was happily agreed to and a wedding date was set for June.

Patience, in a muddle of feelings she did not understand, passed her days in a fog. Everyone congratulated her and made much of her. Plans for the impending wedding ceremony were discussed over and over. She and Sally and a seamstress sent by Mistress Lovell began to work on a wedding gown fashioned from a ball dress her mother had brought from England. It was made of figured bellandine, a white tiffany silk glistening with silver threads. They trimmed the full-drawn, high-necked tucker and long sleeves with old Alençon lace they'd found among her mother's treasures. The older ladies, like Mistress Lovell and Goody Stephens, insisted that, as bride to a groom of such distinction, it behooved Patience to include a hip farthingale under her full skirts. Moreover, they declared, a full train was an absolute requirement. Patience agreed to a modest one. When she finally tried on the gown, she barely recognized herself. The lace at the neck, her tiny waist emphasized by the hip hoop, and the train that fell in a long sweep from the yoke at the back all combined to make her appear almost queenly. She'd never worn before—nor would she ever wear again—such a magnificent gown.

But her pleasure in seeing herself in the wedding gown did not assuage the little nagging doubts that kept making themselves noticed, little red flags waving at the edges of her consciousness. Then, a mere week before the wedding, she found Meg, Beatie

McNab's pretty daughter, who'd been hired as a housemaid during this period of increased social activity, weeping in the kitchen. The girl was upset by something Lord Orgill had done. On further questioning, Patience learned that her affianced bridegroom had assaulted the girl in the smokehouse. It was only because Sally had made a timely entrance upon the scene that a heinous act had not been consummated.

When Patience confronted him with the story, Orgill was not in the least embarrassed. It was nothing, he assured her with casual indifference. "Why, my dear," he chortled in hearty amusement, "in London, gentlemen have their way with serving girls all the time."

"Here, my lord," Patience retorted, trembling in distress, "such behavior is reprehensible in the extreme."

"It's Walter, my love. You must learn to call me Walter," he responded, chucking her under the chin. He went on to promise, in his heartily sincere way, that he would certainly respect the customs of the locality and never again indulge in such behavior, especially since she found it displeasing. "Besides," he concluded, bestowing on her a broad, amazingly guiltless grin, "once we are wed, I shall never feel the least desire to look with lust at another woman."

Not knowing what else to do, Patience let the matter drop. But her misgivings grew with every passing day.

Her recollections of the wedding itself, however, were as vague as memories of a dream. She recalled that it was a modest affair despite the importance of the bridegroom. There was a simple church ceremony, during which, she remembered, the pastor spoke endlessly of wifely duties and wifely submission. When Walter took her hand to place the ring on her finger, she remembered that her hand shook so badly he had to grasp her wrist to steady it.

Her father gave a celebratory dinner attended by fifty guests, including some friends of the groom who traveled all the way up from New York City to attend. A score of servants were hired from the village for the evening, some to cook, some to serve the meal, some to take care of the carriages, and even one assigned just to replace candles as they burned down.

Patience could not remember her wedding day with any feeling of gladness, for the day ended dreadfully. She'd gone up to her bedchamber early and dressed herself in her prettiest nightshift. Then she'd climbed into bed and waited with some trepidation for the consummation of her marriage. The trepidation came from inexperience, not ignorance. Years ago she'd received instruction from her mother on what to expect from this night, instruction that all girls received at the time of their first blood flux (what her mother called the curse of Eve). She believed she was fully prepared for what was to come.

But no one can be prepared for the errant feelings that attack the unfortified heart. Patience waited for her bridegroom with alternating eagerness and terror. Part of her hungered for the warmth of a masculine embrace, but another part feared the intimacy of marriage. What did she really know about this man she'd wed? Only that he was handsome and charming in company. What he was like in the recesses of his mind was a mystery to her. Should not a wife feel kindred to a man's thoughts? she wondered. Should not they exchange tender feelings? Or were these things that a woman could only learn with the passing years?

There's really nothing to fear, she kept assuring herself. *Everyone's told me often enough that he'll be the most desirable of husbands.*

So she waited, brushing her hair, dabbing her underarms with scent, pacing the room. But her roistering bridegroom did not appear for several hours. By the time he did, she'd fallen fast asleep. Suddenly she was rudely awakened by a drunken roar. Before she was fully aware of what the noise was and who it was who loomed over her, he fell upon her. Pulling aside her gown roughly, he spread her knees apart with his own and inserted himself inside her. It was done so quickly that to Patience it was more of an assault than an act of love. She gasped in fear and pain, the gasp becoming a pitiful, agonized cry. Her groom, however, taking the sounds as very satisfactory proof of her virginity, merely laughed his booming laugh and continued his activities with unwarranted vigor.

Patience thought she would be torn apart. She struggled to free herself from this overwhelming embrace, but the more she struggled the more her husband seemed to enjoy himself. At last she surrendered and lay still, although his every thrust gave her a stab of pain. It seemed an eternity before he sated his lust.

When eventually he rolled away from her and fell asleep, Patience slipped from the bed, burning with pain and shaken to her core. She was almost too weak to stand. Frightened by the blood dripping down her legs, she crept from the room and stumbled down the stairs to where Sally slept with her little boy, the five-year-old Aaron, in a tiny, low-ceilinged room above the kitchen. "Sally," Patience wept, "help me!"

Sally took one look at the ripped and bloody gown and knew what had happened. Quickly moving the deeply sleeping Aaron from her bed and putting him on a pillow on the floor in the corner, she drew Patience down on the bed beside her. She rocked the weeping girl in her arms like a baby until her sobbing ceased. Then she bathed her gently and dressed her in a clean gown. They lay silently side by side on Sally's narrow bed until the first light of day. "You mus' go back up," Sally said, rising reluctantly. "You a wife now."

"Yes, I know," Patience said, shuddering with revulsion. "It's my duty. But, oh, God, Sally, what have I done by marrying? For aught I know, I've ruined my life!"

She did her wifely duty every night for three weeks, hoping each time that the next time would be easier. But every time her husband reached for her, Patience's body tensed. The more tense she became, the more painful the intercourse. She endured the experience in teeth-gritting terror, like a monk submitting to flagellation. But she said nothing. It was something too painful and too private to speak of.

Although Lord Orgill continued to charm the populace, Patience no longer saw any charm in him. She found it harder and harder to speak cheerfully to him and soon was responding to his attempts at conversation with nothing more than monosyllables. And he, finding her cold and withdrawn, soon stopped trying.

It was no surprise, therefore, that his lordship became bored with provincial life in general and with his wife in particular. He began to speak openly of his longing for the sophistication of higher society, for flirtation and the sexual games of bachelorhood. After three weeks he packed a portmanteau and took himself off to New York. "You don't mind, do you, m' dear?" he asked his wife before he left. "I need a bit of excitement."

"I don't mind," Patience had replied, lowering her eyes to hide her feeling of relief.

"Good. Tell your father I'll be gone for only a fortnight."

But Lord Orgill didn't return at the end of the fortnight. Word came back a few days later that his lordship had, without bothering to inform them, boarded a ship bound for England.

Peter Hendley was furious, though he did his best to hide it. Lord Orgill had affronted his daughter and himself. It was an insult he would not forget, but from a practical viewpoint, he'd gotten what he wanted from the fellow. He now had his deed and his daughter, too. And, indeed, it was a relief to have the "dammed lumbering, haw-hawing fashion plate" out of the house.

Patience silently agreed.

But now, seven years later, as she stood at her bedroom window watching the glinting ripples of the Hudson down below, she felt a wave of resentment toward her father. His love of property had indeed cost her dearly. However, she tried to be fair. He'd not been completely indifferent to his daughter's feelings when Orgill failed to return. "I'll buy you passage to England if you wish it," he'd offered. "The man's a deuced worm, but if you want him, you can have him. Once you're in England, Orgill must surely acknowledge you. You're his true and legal wife. You have every right to live in his manor and be the wealthy and respected Lady Orgill."

"But Papa," she'd reminded him, "I never wished to go to England."

Patience had to admit that her father did consider the problem thoughtfully. "Some might say it's your duty to go," he'd mused. "It's usual to say that a wife's duty is to be at her husband's side, but this circumstance is not usual. Your duty is to be where you're most needed, and you're most needed here."

Patience had merely nodded, not wishing to reveal by word or manner the extent of the gladness that had spread over her.

But her father's brow had remained furrowed. "I don't mean to press you, Patience. You may speak your mind if you're not in agreement with me."

"I'm in full agreement with you, Papa."

"Are you? Speak up now, girl, while there's still time. If you're going to spend the rest of your days moping about the place with a long face, you may as well go to your husband."

"I want to stay here, Papa. Truly."

"Do you want to talk to the pastor first? His idea of your duty may be different from mine."

"I know my duty, Papa. It's here."

"Are you certain, girl? Can you face that your marriage is a standaway? I want you to be absolutely certain."

"Yes, Papa, I'm certain."

That had been enough to convince him. "Good," he'd replied. And he'd put the entire matter out of his mind. It did not trouble him that his daughter was barred from making another marriage as long as her absent husband lived.

And does it trouble me? Patience asked herself, turning away from the window and going back to her bed. *Do I mind being a married woman without a husband?*

She slid down under the covers and burrowed into her pillow.

Yes, I mind, she admitted to herself at last. She had no wish for Orgill to return, but her peculiar marital condition was not enviable either. She was accustomed to it now, of course, but she could still remember the pain of those first weeks after Lord Orgill's departure—the gossip in the neighborhood about the deserted bride, the whispering that ceased abruptly as she drew near, the snide laughter and the sarcastic greetings: "Good morning, your *ladyship!*" . . . "How do you do, *Lady* Orgill?" But she'd continued to hold her head up with dignity, and she'd faced them down, neither proud nor apologetic, and after a while it was "Good day, Mistress Patience," from all but the most snide, almost as it had been before.

But not quite as it had been before, she acknowledged glumly as she drew the covers up to her neck and shut her eyes. The experience had, of all things, turned her into a spinster. A dry, unloved, pitiable spinster. Yet in truth she'd rather have been a true spinster than a deserted wife. A true spinster, being virginal and untouched, could still dream of finding love, no matter how belated. She, however, could not. She was no more a maiden. Patience Hendley Gordon, Lady Orgill, was used goods. That was what her father's need for property had cost her: she could no longer dream.

Eleven

At breakfast on Sunday, an overcast but not an especially cold day for late February, Patience announced to the family that she and Barbara were going to take the cariole and drive north to Yonkers to attend services at the Dutch church. Benjy, though curious about so unusual a deviation of Sunday procedure, did not ask why. Papa was not even curious. "Take the landaulet," he said. "It smells like snow."

"Not very likely," Patience replied stubbornly. "Merely pope weather, rain at worst. One horse will do for us today. That way we shan't need to take a man with us to drive. We'll be fine. And after church, if you don't mind, we purpose to drive down to visit with Hannah. We'll be back before nightfall."

"Seems to me a great deal of foolish, unnecessary riding about," her father grumbled, "but suit yourself."

With that grudging assent to their plans, the two women climbed into the little two-wheeled, one-horse carriage and set out to the north on the Albany Post Road. Patience handled the reins, while Barbara sat beside her, pouting. The girl kept looking down at the ruby on her finger with such exaggerated longing that Patience could hardly keep from laughing. "You're gazing at that ring as if it were a kitten we were taking to drown," she teased.

"I wouldn't give a fig for a kitten," Babs retorted. "What value has a kitten? I wager I could trade a ring like this for a *hundred* kittens if I wished."

"Perhaps a thousand, if it were yours to trade." Patience guided the horse carefully round a turn before glancing back at her chap-fallen sister. "I hope, Babs, that when you give up the ring you are not going to embarrass us both by crying."

Babs threw her a burning glare. "I won't cry. Do you think me nothing but a common bunter?"

"A *bunter!* Really, my dear, where do you learn such words? You can't seriously believe I think you a vulgarian. In my eyes you're a lovely, lively, charming young woman with an unfortunate tendency to impulsive behavior. But tell me, Babs, when you return the ring to Mr. Bogaerde, what will you say to explain yourself?"

"I won't say anything to Mr. Bogaerde. He may not know that Henryk gave it to me. I shall give it back to Henryk himself."

"What will you say to Henryk, then?"

Babs sighed. "I'll say I was only teasing, and that I didn't mean to keep it." She twisted the ring off her finger and held it up to the gray sky. "Look, Patience, how it glows in the light. Isn't it beautiful? Perhaps it's worth becoming betrothed to Henryk just to be able to keep it."

Now Patience did laugh. "Do you really believe it's so beautiful as to be worth wedding someone you yourself described as silly and fat?"

"No, I don't, really. But even so, Patience, I shall never forgive you for being such a stickler and making me give it up."

Patience, who felt she needed no defense, gave no answer, and the two lapsed into an unfriendly silence.

They arrived at the church early and were immediately and warmly welcomed. Since the New York Colony's Dutch Reformed Church had instituted the use of English as their church language only two years before, visiting Anglicans or Presbyterians were a still a novelty, but now that the English-speaking visitors could worship among them with little difficulty, inter-visitation was much encouraged. Thus the Kuykendalls eagerly made a place for Patience in their pew, while Barbara went off to sit with the Bogaerdes.

By she time the service was over, Barbara's mood had undergone a complete change. She pranced up the aisle, waving and smiling at every familiar face, and when she joined her sister at the bottom of the church steps, her eyes glowed. "Patience, dearest, you'll never guess what's happened," she whispered excitedly into her sister's ear.

"It must be something remarkable to have you call me dearest again after being so furious with me about the ring. Did you return it, by the way?"

"Yes, of course I did. You were right, Patience, to make me do it. Henryk was very much relieved." She slipped an arm about her sister's waist and hugged it. "I'm sorry I behaved like such a wet goose."

Patience eyed the younger girl with suspicion. "You want a favor from me, don't you? What else can possibly explain this sudden effusion of affection and good spirits?"

Barbara made a moue. "Don't be miffy with me, Patience. I did what you asked, did I not? But I do want to ask a favor. Henryk's sister Ilse is going to visit her cousin in New York for a couple of days, and she's asked me to go with her! They are leaving *right now.* May I go, Patience, *please?"*

"On such short notice? Really, Babs, how can you ask? Before I could give you permission, we'd have to ask Papa, and pack up your clothes, and—"

"But my Sunday dress will do for two days, and Ilse says her cousin can easily supply me with a nightdress. And as for Papa, you know he always leaves such decisions to you. Please, Patience, don't say no!"

Patience frowned. "You are truly incorrigible. We agreed, did we not, that we were to pay a call on Hannah this afternoon?"

"Oh, pooh, you can go to Hannah without me. She's your friend, not mine."

The matronly Madame Bogaerde intervened at that moment

to add her entreaties to Barbara's, assuring Patience that the trip would be a rare treat for the girls, for a very elaborate frolic in honor of her niece's birthday was being planned. The girls would be carefully chaperoned and cared for, she promised, and Barbara would be delivered to her door by their coachman at the end of two days. Her eager supplication gave Patience little opportunity for objection. Not wishing to appear more old-maidish than she already did, Patience reluctantly gave her permission. Barbara, overjoyed, ran off to the Bogaerde carriage without a backward look.

Patience climbed up on the cariole feeling a strong resentment. Barbara, who had not a shred of consideration for others and who, everyone agreed, was much too self-indulgent, was given all sorts of privileges and opportunities for amusement, while she, Patience, was left to herself to perform the duties Barbara ignored. Her sister could drive off to a frolic, with never a thought for anyone else, but, after driving Barbara all this distance to the Dutch church so the vixen could do her penance for her foolishness (which had not turned out to be a proper penance at all), she, Patience, had to drive all those miles back the entire way to Hannah's *alone!* Hadn't Barbara promised to keep her company on this protracted trip? Of course she had, but after getting herself a more attractive offer, the girl had broken that promise without a second thought. Now Patience would have to spend hours in the deuced cariole all alone. And it was getting colder, too. It wasn't fair!

But after wallowing in this morass of self-pity, Patience caught herself up. Her resentments were unwarranted and unworthy of her at any time, but especially so on the Lord's day. This was not the time to indulge herself in ungenerous impulses. To make amends, she punished herself by repeating the fifty-first psalm three times . . . *Create in me a clean heart, O God, and renew a right spirit within* me . . .

By the time she'd purged her spirit, Patience had retraced her route back down the Albany road and had arrived at Fordham

Village, where she had to turn east on the Boston Post Road and cross the William Bridge over the Bronx River to reach Lovell Hill. As she rode past Peach's Tavern, she flicked a glance at the benches in front, wondering if she'd see Tom sitting there, as she knew he often did, with his arm about the voluptuous wench who worked within. But the benches were unoccupied today; it was too cold and gray for Tom and his loutish friends to be sitting outdoors.

Less than half-an-hour later she arrived at the Lovell household. Since she'd been on intimate terms with Hannah since childhood, she knew the place as well as her own. She drove her equipage up the long drive with the assurance of long familiarity, threw the reins to a waiting servant and ran across the wide, columned porch to the door.

Stuart LeGrange himself opened the door for her. Hannah had married Stuart shortly after Patience was wed, but the couple still lived in Hannah's father's mansion. Stuart, who owned a very successful lumber mill, could well have afforded to build for himself and his wife a home of their own, but Hannah's father had been widowed shortly after his daughter's wedding and prevailed upon the newlyweds to live at Lovell Hill. Patience at first had wondered if Hannah would regret her concession to her father, but she soon realized that it had been a good decision. Mr. Lovell was a peaceful sort, and Stuart—a portly, ruddy-faced, balding fellow who combined a good head for business with a kind heart—was as easygoing as his father-in-law. Thus they managed to live together in what Patience felt was enviable contentment.

Stuart ushered her into the high, imposing hallway and embraced her warmly. "Hannah can't wait to see you, Patience," he told her. "She's been watching the road all day."

Patience handed her cloak to a servant. "Is she well?"

"Well enough, I think, though she's jittery as a jaybird about her delicate condition. Go to her, my dear. I'll leave you two to be private. A talk with you is what she needs."

The Lovell drawing room, where Hannah was lying listlessly on one of the striped-satin sofas with a wet cloth over her forehead, was a large room with two tall windows that overlooked an expansive lawn and the hills beyond. Hannah turned her head to the door as Patience came in. "Oh, Patience, at last!" she cried weakly, putting out her arms. "You've no idea how much I need you!"

But Patience had a very good idea. That was why she'd come. In seven years of marriage, Hannah had not been blessed with offspring. Now that she was finally with child, she was terrified at the possibility of something going wrong. She needed soothing. Patience embraced her, and then sat down beside her. With Hannah's hand in hers, she spent the next two hours assuring her friend that there was no reason in the world why her baby would not be born hale. Hannah, who knew Patience was a woman of sense, took comfort from her words.

With that topic exhausted, Hannah turned the conversation to her husband. She was jittery about him, too. "He's still chortling over that Boston tea business," she confided to Patience. "He and Papa are forever bickering about it, though it's almost two months since Boston Harbor was made a teapot."

"But didn't you tell me that Stuart and your father never quarrel?" Patience asked in surprise.

"They do these days."

"Are you implying that your Stuart is a *Whig?*" Patience could not credit it, for Stuart had many qualities that were considered Tory: he was shrewd in business, old-fashioned in dress (even to the extent of powdering his hair daily), and conventional in manner. He seemed the last man in the world to have rebel sympathies.

"Too Whiggish for Papa, I can tell you that," Hannah admitted. "If I have to endure one more argument over dinner, with Papa ranting about wanton destruction of property and Stuart retorting with wanton Parliamentary taxation, I shall scream!"

"Stuart is probably only twitting your father," Patience said, unable to believe that sensible, good-natured Stuart could be in sympathy with the lawless, heathen rabble who'd made a mockery of the Crown in Boston Harbor.

"I don't know, Patience," Hannah said, chewing a fingernail worriedly. "Only yesterday Stuart said to Papa that he believed in his heart that when people have no right of consent to the laws under which they live, they live in slavery. That sounds very Whiggish to me. Does it not to you?"

It certainly did, but before Patience could reply, she heard a gust of wind shake the windowpanes. It was a north wind, bitter and angry, and it presaged a definite change in the weather. In almost no time, both ladies could feel the increased frost in the air. Within another hour an icy sleet was falling from the sky.

As soon as she saw the sleet, Patience announced her intention to set out for home. Stuart, who'd just come in to join the ladies for tea, added his voice to his wife's in begging her to spend the night. But Patience would not hear of it. She insisted that Stuart escort her to the door. "I have but to go three miles," she told him firmly as she tied her cloak at the neck and put up her hood. "They're expecting me at home."

But by the time she'd gone a mile, the world around her had changed. Ice glazed everything. Every twig on the trees, every pebble in the road, every blade of winter grass was embedded in what seemed to be a brittle covering of glistening glass. Even the sounds were like glass—the slightest breeze made a tinkling in the air, and when the wind gusted, her ears rang with the music of ice chimes. It was magic, as if the Snow Queen of legend had waved a wand and transformed the world into a frozen fairyland. If Patience hadn't had to worry about her horse's hooves slipping from beneath him or the cariole slithering sideways and toppling over, she would have found the view beautiful.

As it was, she had to concentrate too hard on holding tight to the reins to pay attention to the fairy-tale scenery. The horse had to be kept to a slow gait on a road that was only kept from being transformed into a sheet of glass by its numerous ruts and bumps.

When she got to the bridge, however, she found that the boards were much slicker than the road. The safest way to cross, she decided, would be to get out and lead the horse by the bridle. She pulled on the reins to stop the animal, but to her surprise, the horse suddenly bolted. The cariole wobbled crazily to and fro, tossing Patience like a ball from one side of the seat to the other. The reins pulled from her grasp. *"Whoa,* Caesar!" she cried in fright. *"Whoa!"*

But the horse, frightened by the slippery ground beneath his feet, paid no heed but galloped on, the equipage slithering and sliding behind. Less than halfway across, the little carriage veered into the wooden railing with a crash. The axle broke in two, causing the cariole to ricochet and topple over on its side. With a hideous, frightened whinny, the horse reared up, pulled himself free of his restraints and ran off. Patience, thrown clear of the carriage but tied to it by the reins which had wound themselves round her ankle, struck the iced boards of the bridge head first and knew no more.

Twelve

Barbara found the start of the journey to New York a great disappointment. A journey, to be interesting, must offer either entertaining companionship or exciting scenery, and this one promised neither. Her traveling companions, beside Ilse, were Ilse's chaperone and, of all people, *Henryk*. Never had Barbara found herself in duller society. Ilse bounced about on the seat in childish excitement. The chaperone, Ilse's great-aunt Augusta (called 'Tante Gusti'), was a flat-bosomed, forbidding, sharp-eyed woman who even while dozing in the corner of the carriage seemed to keep her eyes half open. It would not be possible to have exciting adventures with Tante Gusti's eyes always on them. And as for Henryk, his presence was the most provoking. How was she to attract the attention of any other young men with Henryk forever hanging about?

As for the scenery, she knew quite well that the view from the carriage window would be dull for most of the route down the length of Manhattan Island, but today, with the overcast sky and her disappointing companions, it would seem positively bleak. She would have nothing to attract her eyes for miles and miles but farms and untenanted land. They would have to drive through the half-a-dozen little towns before she'd even *begin* to see signs of city life. They would have to traverse the long length of the Boston Road, and then, below Greenwich Village, cut over to the Greenwich Road which ran along the west coast of the island. On that route there would be little of interest to see. There was, she belatedly realized, a long, tedious ride ahead of them. And what would she find at the end of it? Only a dull child's birthday party. Barbara was beginning to feel sorry she'd agreed to come.

But suddenly, after only half listening to the conversation between Ilse and her brother, she heard the word *ball*. Her attention was immediately captured. "Ball? What ball?" she asked. "Surely a child's birthday party cannot be called a ball."

"My cousin Tilda is not a child, Babs," Ilse laughed. "She will be eighteen." Ilse, a childlike fifteen-year-old who still wore her hair plaited and considered it grown-up merely to pin the braids up round her head, said the word *eighteen* with awe. "The party is something like what the English call a come-out," she explained. "With music and dancing, you know. I even think a betrothal will be announced. Tilda has been keeping company with a British officer."

"A *come-out* ball?" Barbara gasped. "With dancing? Why didn't you *tell* me? I can't wear this frumpy Sunday dress to a ball!"

"Girls!" Henryk sneered. "All you ever think of is gowns. Don't worry, Babs. You'll look lovely at the ball just as you are."

"Oh, pooh!" Barbara retorted with a toss of her head. "What do you know about what one should wear for a ball?"

"I know that a girl of seventeen shouldn't worry about what she wears, because she's too young to be asked to dance. However, Babs Hendley, if you are very nice to me, I'll prevail on Tante Gusti to let me take you up for a country dance or two."

Barbara stuck her tongue out at him, but Ilse threw her arms about his neck. "Me, too, Henryk, *please?*" she begged.

Henryk laughed. "You don't want to dance with your brother. I'll find a proper fellow for you."

Ilse glowed. "Will you, Henryk? Someone handsome?"

"It doesn't matter what he looks like, you goose," Henryk said importantly, feeling quite the rooster in this coop of hens. "What matters is his politics. You should always determine a fellow's politics before you involve yourself with him. His politics tells you a great deal about him."

"How do you determine his politics?" Barbara asked, leaning forward with interest.

"It's simple. If the fellow is a British officer or a traveler from abroad, he's almost always from a good family and is probably a Tory. If he's a local and seems well-to-do, he's probably a Loyalist. New York gentry are most always Loyalists; they believe it good for business. If he's Dutch, you can't always tell. They're often Separatists, because their ancestor, Peter Stuyvesant, had to give way to the British a hundred years ago, and some Dutch haven't yet forgiven them."

"Are you a Separatist, Henryk?" his sister asked.

"That's not any business of yours, my girl," he answered with a sidelong glance at the dozing Tante Gusti. "All you need to know is that Papa is a Whig, and the Whigs, though they want to have local rule, do not wish to be separated from Britain."

Ilse thought about that for a moment. "Do you think Tilda's intended is a Whig, too?"

"I don't know. Probably not. All I know is that he's a British officer, and that the family is pleased with the match."

Barbara was not particularly interested in cousin Tilda's intended. "What if a man tells you he's a Patriot?" she asked, returning the conversation to what she felt was a more interesting subject.

"In New York, if a man calls himself a Patriot, he's most likely a Whig, not a Separatist," Henryk explained. "In Boston, most likely he is a Separatist."

Ilse made an impatient gesture. "All those names! Whig, Tory, Loyalist, Separatist, Patriot, Rebel . . . and now you say they mean different things in different cities. It's too confusing."

Henryk shrugged. "It's the times that are confusing."

"But I'm confused also," Barbara said. "Isn't a Patriot a Separatist *wherever* he is, in Boston or New York?"

"In New York," Henryk explained, "it's the Sons of Liberty who are Separatists."

"Yes," Barbara agreed. "Those are the ones to look out for."

"Look out for?" Ilse asked. "Why?"

"Because, often as not, they're rabble," Barbara said. "Papa says that radicals and rebels get their numbers from the rabble. It's always the have-nothings, he says, who want to throw over the government and become the take-everythings."

Henryk cocked his head and eyed her curiously. "What does your brother say to that?" he asked.

"Benjy?" Barbara snorted. "He's a fool. He's besotted with liberty. But what can you expect from a sixteen-year-old boy?"

Ilse regarded her brother shrewdly. "I think, Henryk, that maybe you're besotted with liberty, too, else you'd have told us where you stand."

"And I think," he retorted, throwing another glance at his sleeping aunt, "that if you want me to provide a beau for you, you'd better say nothing more on that head."

The implication that Henryk could be as foolishly naive as Benjy on the question of separatism took Barbara by surprise. But at that moment, a tapping on the coach window diverted her attention. "Goodness," she exclaimed, peering out, "it's begun to sleet."

They were at the outskirts of Greenwich Village by this time, with New York City looming up ahead, so the mystery of Henryk's political leanings was forgotten. At last there was something to see outside the coach windows. To their right, the houses along the Hudson were becoming more numerous. Barbara pressed her nose against the window in order to see them better. The city houses were fascinating to her. Many of them had their own wharves, the householders preferring travel by boat to travel by carriage. The traffic on the river was often heavier than that on the road, and now, even in the sleet, a number of boats were sailing by.

The traffic on the road was heavy, too. The coach had to proceed more slowly now. All manner of carriages clogged the road—traps, shays, and buckboards wending their way among the larger two- and four-horse equipages. There were many people on foot, too, some protected from the sleet by umbrellas, others merely huddling their shoulders against the wind. A woman and her black slave were hurrying down the street sharing the same shawl held over their heads. There was even an Indian, Barbara noted. He was wrapped in a blanket and wearing a headdress of feathers; apparently unperturbed by the sleet, he sauntered along as calmly as if the sun were shining. Then, down the street, Barbara saw a group of redcoats running for shelter. "Mohairs," Henryk muttered scornfully, for that was the name New Yorkers gave to the soldiers they were forced to house. But Barbara watched them with eager eyes; they were young and handsome, and their uniforms were very dashing. *Oh, it's going to be so exciting to stay in New York,* she told herself joyfully, her eyes following the soldiers until they ran into a tavern.

On they rode, noticing how the neat brick houses were becoming more numerous and more close together, some of them three stories high. A number had railed porches on their roofs where, in summer, the inhabitants could sit and see the whole city stretched out before them. It was a lovely place to live, Barbara thought, much nicer than where she lived in Spuyten Duyvil, where nothing ever happened and where you could look out of your window all day and never see a passer-by. She knew that farther downtown, the street became narrow, crooked and dirty, and pigs roamed about freely, eating the garbage. But here the streets were very clean, wide and pretty, with trees planted between the paving stones. Most of the houses were in the old Dutch style, built of brick and stone, with the narrow, gable end facing the street. The roofs were very steep and the gable walls rose higher than the roofs in a series of steps. Each house had a good-sized yard, through which the travelers could see to the river and the wharves where the boats were moored. Even now in the sleet, the houses looked warm and welcoming.

"Oh, how glorious!" Barbara exclaimed as they pulled up before the neat abode of the New York City Bogaerdes, a house more than twice as wide as any of its neighbors. As soon as the carriage came to a stop, a black slave emerged carrying umbrellas. Tante Gusti, now fully awake, was the first one to be helped down. As she made her way up the walkway, followed by the servant holding the umbrella over her, she shouted loud greetings to her relations who stood waving at her from the Dutch-style front door whose upper half was open while the lower half remained closed until Tante Gusti reached it.

She was followed from the coach by Ilse and Barbara, who ran up the path arm in arm, disregarding the sleet. Henryk, carrying his own umbrella, brought up the rear.

There was much laughing, hugging and kissing inside the doorway, impeding Barbara's passage. Just as she was about to squeeze her way over the threshold, a young officer—as handsome a young man as Barbara had ever seen, and resplendent in a red coat and plumed tricorn—emerged from the doorway. He stepped aside to make way for her, smiled, tipped his hat and hurried off down the sleety street. "Goodness!" Barbara exclaimed in a whisper to her friend. "Who was *that?*"

"It must be Tilda's intended," Ilse managed to whisper back before being enveloped in her uncle's embrace.

Barbara, waiting to be introduced, looked out the door after the quickly disappearing officer. *Now, that,* she said to herself, her eyes glowing like a cat, *is exactly the sort of man I want!*

Thirteen

Lying in a black hole of semiconsciousness, Patience became aware of a growing irritation. Someone was shaking her, trying to wake her. "Let me sleep," she tried to say. "My head hurts." But her lips couldn't form the words. In the confusing blackness in which she was mired, she couldn't even seem to think. Then she noticed that she was very, very cold, much too cold to be in her bed. Unless her window had blown open in the night. Was that it? she wondered.

Slowly she opened her eyes. What she saw was so terrifying it froze her breath. It was a face . . . a man's face, glistening with droplets of ice and framed by tendrils of hair hung with icicles. It was a nightmare face, and it was horrifyingly close to her own. She opened her mouth to scream, but at that moment she recognized him. *"Tom!"* she gasped, her voice hoarse and unfamiliar to her own ears.

His hands tightened on her shoulders. "Where's Mistress Barbara?" He spoke tensely, with a chilling urgency.

"Barbara?" she echoed stupidly.

"She was with you. Where is she?"

Patience, utterly at sea, lifted her head and looked about her. She was lying on the bridge, a bridge that was, like Tom's face, both comfortingly familiar and bewilderingly strange. She knew where she was, but what had happened to transform everything? Then she turned her head and saw the wreck that was her cariole. In the blink of an eye her memory returned. "Oh," she breathed, relieved, "the ice storm. I remember now. I had an . . . accident . . ."

"But your sister," Tom pressed. "Where—?"

"She went with the Bogaerdes to New York. This morning after church. She's all right."

Tom's tight mouth relaxed. "Thank God. When I couldn't find her in the wreck, I feared she might have fallen into the river." He lifted Patience higher against his arm. "Tell me, ma'am, are you hurt?"

Patience blinked up at him. He looked like a creature from mythology with his icicled hair and his whitened eyebrows. A kind of Snow King. "How did you . . . happen to find me?" she murmured, still dazed.

"Caesar made his way back to the stable," he explained with a touch of impatience. "Are you all right, ma'am?"

She put a hand to her head, now aching severely. "Yes, I think so. Let me try to stand."

He helped her to her feet, but a stab of pain in her left ankle made her cry out. Without a moment's hesitation he lifted her in his arms and carried her to the landaulet that he'd evidently used to get here. "There now," he said, placing her on the seat, "let's get you home. Tomorrow, if the weather clears, I'll bring some men and take care of the cariole."

He threw a wool lap-robe over her and handed her the reins. Then he walked forward to the two horses. Taking hold of their curb-straps, he led them slowly over the rise of the bridge. Patience couldn't help noticing that he wore no coat. His loose jerkin was of thin leather that could provide no warmth, and his full-sleeved shirt was so thoroughly stiffened by the wet and cold that the fabric was rigid as glass. "Come up here, Tom!" she ordered. "You'll freeze to death down there."

"I'm all right, ma'am," he said over his shoulder. "I don't want to give the horses their head. 'Tis safer this way."

"Then put this robe over your shoulders."

He threw her a quick glance and then looked back at the road.

"No, thank you, ma'am You're the one had the accident. You might be hurt more than you think. You keep it over you."

They proceeded in silence over the bridge. Patience, pulling the lap-robe over her shoulders, was truly comforted by the warmth of the dry wool. Her shivering diminished, and even her headache began to ease. She wished there were another robe to offer Tom. He was undoubtedly chilled to the bone. Her eyes lingered on his frozen hair, the breadth of his shoulders under the glazed shirt, and the graceful way he moved. Most men seemed to swing their upper bodies when they walked, but Tom swung from the hips, keeping the rest of his body steady. It was an economical movement, yet rhythmical and sinuous.

She watched him move, unable to take her eyes from him. Since last week, the day of the effigy, he'd never been completely out of her mind. She could hardly believe, now, how little she'd noticed him before. Her view of him had undergone a complete change. She'd always thought of him as a boy, but suddenly he'd become a man, strong, good-looking and sure of himself, and, what was more startling, there was something about him that demanded to be noticed.

This quality was elusive—she couldn't put a name to it—but it had nothing to do with his appearance, though she'd always recognized that he was good-looking. Back when her father had bought his indenture, when Tom was about fourteen and she a young woman of seventeen, she'd recognized that his clever eyes, the strong line of his square chin, and his already sinewy frame were signs of handsomeness to come. And so they were, in spite of a too-prominent nose whose broad bridge had a bump in it where it was once broken, a pair of dark brows that angled down toward the nose, giving his face a fierce glower when he frowned, and a head of dark hair that was too long, too thick and always unkempt. Maturity had refined his features; he did not look coarse, like his friends at the tavern. Except for his wild hair, his face was quite gentlemanly. But why was she thinking of all this?

she asked herself. This preoccupation with a bondsman was utterly improper. She had to take herself in hand.

By this time they'd crossed the bridge and reached solid ground, so she ordered him again to get into the carriage. "You can guide the horses well enough from here. The ground isn't as slippery as the bridge floor."

He climbed up and took the reins from her. "Yes, ma'am," he said obediently.

"You seem unusually polite today," she remarked absently, wondering how she could offer to share the lap-robe with him without causing embarrassment.

"Yes, ma'am," he said again, his manner distant and forbidding.

"Here," she said, offering half the robe, "put this over you."

"No, I thank you. It's too small to cover us both. Better that one of us be warm than both be half chilled."

A wave of irritation swept over her. "Dash it, Tom, can't you ever do what you're told without argumentation? I'm quite capable of deciding what's better for us."

Tom never took well to being spoken to in that tone. "If you're so blasted capable, ma'am," he exploded, "then why the devil didn't you stay at the Lovells instead of dangering life and limb in an open shay in an ice storm?"

She stiffened in anger. "I'll thank you, Tom Morrison, to keep a civil tongue in your head! I don't care to hear your blaspheming curses. I'm not one of your tavern wenches."

"No, you aren't. My tavern wenches at least have the sense to stay indoors in a storm."

"I don't care to hear about your blasted wenches!" Furious, she pulled the robe closely about her and wrenched herself round on the seat so that she didn't have to look at him. " 'Tis a fine comment on these lawless times," she muttered, "that when a lady offers a man a kindness, she is rewarded with insults."

" 'Tis a fine comment on these lawless times," he retorted,

"that when a lady makes a tiny offer of kindness she expects to be rewarded with a large gratitude."

"A *tiny* offer of kindness?" Patience drew herself up in offense. "Tiny? Since when does one measure the size of a kindness?"

"Since the offerer started speaking of rewards."

She shook her head in utter exasperation. "Very well, then, sit there and freeze! If you fall ill with an inflammation of the lungs, don't blame me."

"No, of course I won't blame you," he sneered. "I'll blame the weather, not the person who didn't have the sense to come in out of it."

"That's enough! Have done! I misjudged. I'm sorry. But I didn't *ask* you to come out after me, did I?"

He stared at her in disbelief. "No. No, you didn't ask me. So when your animal came galloping into the stable, I should have ignored his wild eyes and the fact that he'd torn himself from the cariole, eh? I should have given no thought to the possibility that there'd been an accident. I should have gone to my bed and pretended nothing had happened. Is that what you're suggesting?"

Her eyes fell. He *had* come looking for her, after all. She'd have found herself in great trouble if he hadn't. Why did she always sink to this ill-natured behavior whenever she was in his company?

She twisted her fingers in her lap. "Look here, Tom," she said, keeping her eyes on her hands, "I'm not without gratitude for what you've done this afternoon. I had every intention of asking Papa to add five extra guineas to your account as soon as we got home. And I *still* intend to ask him, despite your incorrigible rudeness."

He was not softened. "Ah, yes," he said scornfully, "another of your tiny kindnesses, for which I'm supposed to be grateful."

To Patience, that was quite the last straw. "So now *five guineas* make a tiny kindness? Confound you, Tom Morrison, you are beyond all! Is there nothing one can offer you that you won't scorn?"

"Yes, ma'am, there is. But it has nothing to do with lap-robes or guineas, so it's unlikely you'd offer it."

She studied him curiously. He was looking straight ahead of him, his hands holding the reins tightly, his lips pressed together and his eyebrows knit in his most intense glower. Whatever it was he wanted to ask for he seemed unwilling to reveal. "Well, no harm in asking, is there?" she prodded. "What is it?"

"No, it's foolish. A whim of mine. Not worth speaking of."

It's something he thinks frivolous, like a coat, she thought, feeling an overwhelming pity for him. *He wants something costly and frivolous.* And he should have it, too, she decided. Why shouldn't he have a warm coat to wear on a day like this? She and Sally could alter that green worsted coat of Papa's that he didn't like and make Tom a present of it. The thought of giving the master's coat to the bondsman made her glow with self-satisfaction. *"Tell* me!" she urged, putting a hand on his arm. "Go on. Please."

Hesitating, he turned and stared down at her fingers curled on his sleeve. Then his eyes traveled up to her face. "Teach me to read," he said softly.

She did not think she'd heard him properly. "What?"

"I want to learn to read."

The request startled her. Not only was it unexpected, it was improper. A bondsman had no business reading. Reading only led to rebelliousness and sedition. Damn the fellow, why wasn't he asking for a coat? She snatched back her hand from his arm. "That's ridiculous," she said.

His mouth tightened, and he turned his face back to the horses. "I knew you'd think so. I shouldn't have asked."

"Don't you see that the request is . . . is inappropriate?" she asked, inexplicably troubled. "It's not the place of the mistress of the household to educate the farmhands in booklearning."

"I suppose not, ma'am."

"Besides, what can you want with reading? You're already quick with numbers. And you're a capable farmer; Papa says you're the best he's seen. You've less than a year left before your indenture is worked out, isn't that so?" She clenched her fingers, wondering why she felt this need to justify herself to him. "You'll probably have almost a hundred pounds in freedom dues, enough to buy some land of your own. Take my word for it, Tom, a few extra pounds to add to your reserve is your best reward, much better for you than reading lessons."

"Yes, of course," he said, his voice dripping scorn. "Again you know what's best for me. It's always the way of masters to decide what's best for their slaves."

They had arrived at the gate. Before Patience could answer, Tom jumped down from the carriage and strode over to open it. "Slave, indeed!" she retorted to his arrogant back. "What sort of slave speaks to his mistress as you do to me? And you only want to learn reading so that you can peruse those seditious writings out of Boston and Virginia. Oh, yes, I know you, Tom Morrison! I can recognize rebel leanings when I see them."

Not deigning either to respond or to return to his seat in the landaulet, he merely threw her a look of scorn. Taking up the bridles again, he led the horses on foot up the drive to the front door. Then he came round to help her down.

She waved him off. "I can manage without your help," she said proudly. But as soon as she put her foot on the ground her ankle gave way with an excruciating spasm of pain. She would have fallen to the ground, but he caught her up in his arms just in time and carried her up the steps to the front door. "Thank you," she said breathlessly. "I can manage from here."

He set her down at once and, without a word, tramped down the steps.

She watched him go, beset with guilt. He had done so much for her today, and she rewarded him with nothing but scolds. "Tom?" she called after him uneasily.

He neither stopped nor turned. "Yes, ma'am?"

"I . . . I'm beholden to you for what you did today."

"Yes, ma'am." He'd reached the carriage by this time. He took hold of the horses' curbs and began to lead them toward the stable.

"So if you really wish it," she went on, her voice made unsteady by a surge of eager excitement in her breast, "I'll teach you."

He stopped in his tracks and wheeled around, his eyes alight. "When?" he asked.

His reaction—and her own—filled her with confusion. "Damnation, Tom, you are the most provoking—!" she swore to mask her feelings. "Can you not give me a simple thank-you first?"

The corners of his lips twitched. "Are you saying you'll teach me even if, after I learn, I read sedition?"

She shrugged. "Yes, that's what I'm saying. One shouldn't give a gift with conditions attached."

"Then I truly *do* thank you, Mistress Patience." He took a step in her direction. *"When* will you teach me?"

"I don't know." She turned to open the door. "Papa would be livid if he ever learned of it," she muttered to herself.

"When?" the bondsman pressed.

She felt a pulse pound in her throat. "Soon."

He ran up the steps and, taking her shoulders, turned her to face him. "How soon?"

She stared up at him, captured by the burning eagerness in his eyes and frightened by her own. "Tomorrow," she heard herself promise. "We'll start tomorrow." Then, shaking off his hold on her and wincing to ward off the pain in her ankle, she limped over the threshold and shut the door on him.

Fourteen

Tom closed the door of his room above the stable and, shuddering, peeled off his frozen shirt. The room, having neither fireplace nor stove, was almost as cold as the outside. He could have had a bed on the other side of the stable's attic, where Chester, the always-inebriated Jeb, and Sally's boy, Aaron, shared a room that had a grate, but Tom had chosen this room. He preferred privacy to warmth.

Now, however, he would have liked a fire. His teeth chattered and his whole body shook as he leaned across his bed and pulled a ragged length of muslin from a hook on the wall. Hopping in place to keep his legs warm, he used the muslin to towel his back and shoulders. Then he rolled himself up in a blanket and threw himself on his cot. He was still shivering, but he felt wonderful. More wonderful than he'd ever felt in his life. So wonderful that he actually chuckled to himself. *She's going to teach me! Mistress Patience herself!* That promise was better than having a fire in the grate. It warmed his innards.

Since early boyhood, as far back as his memory could go, he'd wanted to learn to read, but there had never been anyone to teach him. There were two fellows at the tavern—Nate and Jotham—who could read, but he was quicker-witted than either of them, and it would have been humiliating to ask them to teach him. He wished he'd learned reading as a child. He had a vague recollection of his mother teaching him something from a book, but that was long ago in another world. No doubt that was where he'd learned his numbers. His skill with numbers was something he'd grown up with, a basic understanding of calculation he couldn't remember ever being without. But letters were another matter. He could look at whole columns of figures and make sense of them, but just let a word appear on the page and his brain froze.

Maybe his mother couldn't read either. He remembered very little of their life in London, where he supposed he was born. All he could readily bring to mind was his other name—Morris Thompson, it was. His mother called him Morrie, he remembered. And he had a dim recollection of a dingy room, with a pallet in the corner and a rickety chair by a window where his mother sat sewing, always sewing. The poor creature must have been a seamstress.

He also remembered the chandler's shop down the street from where he lived. He would sometimes be permitted to work there. He was probably only five or six years old, but they let him sweep the doorstep or polish the doorknobs for a few pennies. It made him feel important when he could put those pennies in his mother's hand.

But there were memories of childhood that were a good deal sharper in his mind than that time in London. The days on shipboard, for example, when his mother and he made passage to America. He couldn't have been more than seven or eight, he guessed. The memories were like a nightmare.

He recalled being in the dark underbelly of a sailing ship, bedding down in the same hold with what seemed to him hordes of other poor creatures. But the difficulties of crowding and poor sanitation did not dim the hope in their eyes. They were all on their way to a new life in America, his mother said. "You and I, Morrie, love," she told him repeatedly, "are going to a wonderful place called Mary Land." To the boy's ears the name sounded like Merry Land, and he was sure that a place with such a cheerful name would be wonderful indeed.

But from the day they'd come on board, his mother had been coughing. The cough worsened every day, and the other passengers kept their distance from her, as though she carried the plague. That final day of her life, she'd been so weakened that her poor frail body couldn't even let the coughs out. She could make only a horrid, rasping sound that racked her thin frame and brought up bloody spittle. He'd tried to help her by mopping her face with a piece of cloth he'd torn from his shirttail, but finally an elderly woman, trying to be kind, pulled him away from her, though he kicked and screamed in protest. They didn't let him near her again until the life had gone from her.

Even now he sometimes saw that ghastly white, lifeless face in his dreams. If he wanted to remember, he only had to shut his eyes, and he could bring to mind in all its painful detail the day of her funeral—how a small group of passengers gathered on the deck in a driving rain; how the captain of the ship said the prayer for burial at sea; how the grayish shroud that contained her body looked so small and flat; and how soft, how very soft the splash had been when the shrouded bundle slipped unresisting into the waves.

The ship docked in Philadelphia not many days afterward. The same elderly woman who'd taken charge of him when his mother died asked him where he intended to go. "What shall become of ye, poor child, all by yerself in a strange land?"

He'd already thought about it. "I'll find work with a chandler," he told her. "See, ma'am, I worked in a chandler's shop back home. Do you think, if I could've earned pennies from a chandler in London when I was practic'ly a baby, that I should be able to earn shillings in America, now I'm bigger?"

The woman sighed dubiously, but then she ruffled his hair and said, "O' course, lad, why not?"

This exchange did not do much for his confidence. But it was not to matter. Before he could disembark, a sailor came looking for him and took him by force to the captain's cabin. It was a very fine cabin, with polished wood paneling and a massive, carved desk that was so heavy it didn't need to be bolted to the deck. And there were two lamps hanging on brass chains from the rafters. They swung gently with the motion of ship, which still rocked even though they were in port.

But he didn't spend much time studying his surroundings, for he was uncomfortably aware that there were two men in the cabin, both of whom were observing him closely. One was the captain, who was seated at the desk. The other, standing above the captain and looking over his shoulder at some papers on the desk, was a heavyset man who didn't look like a gentleman even though he wore shiny boots and an elegant blue coat. The blue-coated man kept glowering at him, a look that frightened him to the marrow of his bones. "The brat ain't much of a bargain fer me," the man growled. "He's naught but a baby."

"All the more years of work ye'll get out of him," the captain retorted. Then he turned to the boy and smiled kindly. "So ye're poor Mistress Thompson's lad, are ye?" he asked.

"Yes, sir. Morris Thompson I be."

"Well, Morris, this is Mr. Gilpin, of Harford County, Maryland. He holds yer mother's indenture."

The boy blinked, confused. "Indenture?"

The heavy man snorted. "Don't play the fool, boy. Ye must know yer mother signed an indenture. How else do ye suppose she could've bought passage?"

The captain threw Gilpin a glare that ordered restraint. Then he looked back at the boy. "Mr. Gilpin means, lad, that yer mother signed papers that she'd work for him for five years in exchange for her passage money."

"And now I don't have the money nor the worker," Mr. Gilpin added curtly. "All I have is you."

The frightened child took a backward step. "M-me, sir?"

"Yes, you. An' how a scrawny little tadpole like you is goin' to do me any good is more 'n I can see."

"Ye'll have him till he's twenty-one," the captain said impatiently. "Instead of a houseworker for five years, you'll have a farmhand for—say, lad, how old are you anyway?"

Tom remembered how sharp his mind had been that day, tadpole though he was. He couldn't read, but he was far from a fool. He understood what was going on. The blue-coated man was taking him away in exchange for the passage money. *Ye'll have him till he's twenty-one,* that's what the captain had said. So the older he made himself now, the shorter would be his period of servitude. "Eleven," he said promptly, choosing the highest number he felt he could get away with.

"Horsefeathers!" Mr. Gilpin sneered. "He ain't a day more'n seven!"

The boy bravely stuck out his chin. "Eleven an' two months," he insisted.

Gilpin came storming round the desk, grabbed him by the ear and twisted it so painfully that he, skinny little fellow that he was, was forced to his knees. "Who'd ye think yer flimflammin', boy?"

"Ow!" he yelped. "Let me go!"

"Let the lad go!" the captain ordered. "This is my ship, Gilpin. Any more of that, and I'll have ye put ashore. Then ye can take this matter to the courts and see where that gets ye!"

Gilpin sent the boy sprawling across the deck. "The brat's a damn liar."

The captain shrugged. "Ye're a pair of liars, if I'm any judge." He studied the boy intently for a moment and then picked up a quill pen and dipped it in his inkwell. "I'll split the difference," he told Gilpin, "and put down nine."

"Nine!" Gilpin yelped. "He's nine like I got six fingers on this hand!"

"Come down from the high ropes, man," the captain ordered as he wrote a firm nine on the paper before him. "You'll get twelve years out of the boy, and that's more than double what you'd have gotten from the woman."

Gilpin grunted, stalked round the desk, took the quill from the captain's hand and brusquely signed the paper. Thus Morris Thompson's legal age became nine, and his life was turned over to a hardhearted stranger from a land that was beginning to seem very far from merry.

The captain looked over at the boy with an expression of sympathy. "It's settled, then, lad. Come here. Can you write your name?"

Tom—little Morrie that was—got to his feet. Reddening in shame, he brushed off the knees of his breeches. "No, sir," he mumbled.

"Then come and make your X," the captain said gruffly. "Don't look like that, lad. It's not the end of the world. The terms are fair enough. Ye work for Mr. Gilpin till January first of the year of yer twenty-first birthday, at which time ye get yer freedom and freedom dues of seventy pounds."

"Seventy pounds?" Gilpin cried in outrage. "Where does it say—?"

"Right here," the captain said, pointing to a paragraph on the second page. "I put it in myself. Ten pounds each year beyond the five years his mother was to serve. Fair is fair. Take it or leave it."

Gilpin took it. He was no fool either. He knew that many things could happen in twelve years. In all that time, he'd surely find a way to keep from having to pay so large a sum to an indentured man.

And as it turned out, he was quite right. The very first time the boy ran away from the Gilpin plantation in Maryland (an adventure he undertook when his legal age was twelve but when he was probably not much more than ten), he was dragged back in irons and—by a strange coincidence—was fined by the magistrate of Harford County, who happened to be Gilpin's brother-in-law, the amount of exactly seventy pounds. Since of course the indentured Morris Thompson had no such sum to his name, his master graciously accepted as substitute payment the striking-out of the seventy-pound clause from the indenture.

But that was not to be the last of his attempts to run away. Life was dreadful on the Maryland estate of Phineas Gilpin. Gilpin was a cruel taskmaster even to the farmhands he favored, and Morris Thompson was not favored. But little Morrie, who'd been a mild, soft-spoken child when he lived with his mother, now had other models from whom he could learn ways to shape his character—strong, stoic men, both black and white, who worked the fields with him. He soon developed a quick temper, a sharp tongue, a strong back and a pair of hard fists.

He fought stubbornly against every inhumane work requirement Gilpin instituted, once even stirring the other field hands to active rebellion. Gilpin found a reason to have him beaten almost every week. He was even given more than one treatment with the curry-comb, a particularly inhuman device by which the victim—usually a black slave—was scrubbed with the stiff horse-brush until his skin bled, and then rubbed with salt. It was very effective in ensuring obedience, but it did not work with Morrie. He ran away every chance he could—once making it as far north as Trenton. But each time he was brought back, and each time the magistrate added another year to his indenture. By the time he was fourteen, his indenture had been extended to age twenty-six.

But at fourteen, he ran off again, and this time he made it to New York. Phineas Gilpin and "Merry Land" had seen the last of him. He swore it.

When he saw the crowds milling about the cobbled streets of New York City, he was overjoyed. There was no possible way that Gilpin's agents could ever find him among those hordes of people. *I'm free at last!* he gloated.

But his freedom was to be brief indeed. Intending to look for work in a chandler's shop, he'd barely begun wandering the streets when a huge, greasy hand seized him by the scruff of his neck. He was lifted off his feet and, kicking violently, was carried into a nearby tavern and dumped unceremoniously onto a wooden bench in a little booth in the rear. The tall, pot-bellied red-faced stranger who slid into the booth beside him never once let go of his arm. "Now, then, boy," the man leered, "let's have yer name."

"What business is it of yours?" he retorted brazenly despite the frightened pounding of his heart.

"My business, boy, is to catch runaways like you."

Tom vividly remembered how his blood had run cold at the word *runaway*. "Wh-what makes you think I'm a runaway?" he asked, stiff-lipped in terror.

"I knows one when I sees one, boy. There's the rags you've got fer clothes, for one thing. And the way you was gapin' at the buildings, like you ain't never seen the like. I can always tell."

"Well, you told wrong this time." His mind was already busy planning how he might slide under the table and make a run for it if he could trick the fellow into releasing his arm. "I'm a chandler's apprentice."

"Sure, very likely. An' what's the name o' yer establishment, eh?" the man sneered.

"Jones's." It was a prompt reply. He could think quickly when he had to. "Jones's on . . . on . . . High Street."

"Jones's?" Hooting, the man slapped his hand on the table in sheer pleasure. "Pretty quick with yer tongue, ain't ye? So ye work for Jones on High Street, eh? This is New York, looby. There ain't no High Street. We got Wall Street, an' we got Broad Way, and we even got Smith Street, but no High Street. Good try, though. We've got plenty of Joneses."

"I tell you, I ain't no runaway," the boy insisted.

"I suppose, If I tore that shirt off you, I wouldn't see stripes on your back neither."

The boy knew he would. Desperate, he made a sudden jerk with his arm, shaking the fellow's hold, and dived under the table. But the large man was quick, too. He caught the boy by the hair, pulled him up and slammed his head against the wall. "Try that again, me lad, and you'll get worse."

Even now, so many years later, Tom could remember how his head rang with pain. "I ain't no runaway," he repeated helplessly, pressing his free hand against the back of his head where a lump was already beginning to form.

"See this, boy?" the man asked, pulling a newspaper from his coat pocket. "Looka here at this list of advertisements for runaway slaves and indentures. Let's just see, now. This'n could be you, right here. *Boy, sixteen, name George Trotter, thin, muscular, brown hair and eyes, escaped from Moresby Plantation, Roanoke, Virginia. Reward.* Is that you, boy? Is yer name George?"

"Would I tell you if it was?"

"No, you ain't George. Yer eyes is more black than brown. But it don't matter, 'cause I can do better by us both than sendin' you back to where you run off from."

The runaway eyed the pot-bellied flesh-trader suspiciously. "Oh? How's that?"

"I got these blank indenture papers here, see? What we do is, we think up a new name for you, you put yer X here, and then I sell you off to someone here in New York. We'll both get some good of it."

"What good?"

"I get a better price fer you than I'd get from a reward, an' you get a new master and new terms, an' you won't never have to go back to wherever it was ye run off from. So, what name should I put down, eh? Give yerself a name."

The boy sighed in defeat. Anything, he supposed, would be better than being dragged back to Maryland again. "Morris . . . son," he said glumly. "My name is Thomas Morrison."

The man thrust out his hand. "How do, Thomas Morrison?" he said, shaking the boy's hand cheerfully. Then after he filled in the name on the paper, he slapped Tom on the shoulder, leering. "Come on, Tommy lad, don't look so damn sulky. Meetin' me might turn out to be a lucky break fer you. A real lucky break."

"Sure," the newly named Tom Morrison said in utter dejection. "This is my lucky day."

In truth, Tom was already convinced by that time in his life that he would never experience a lucky day. He felt that he and luck were utter strangers, and this encounter with a corrupt New York flesh-trader did nothing to alter that conviction. He truly believed he was in some way cursed. Freedom was always just beyond his grasp.

However, the encounter did result in an improvement in his condition over what it had been in Maryland. His captor took him to the slave market at the foot of Wall Street, where black slaves were auctioned and indentures bought and sold every day. It was there that a Mr. Hendley, who was looking for able-bodied fellows to work on his farm upriver in Spuyten Duyvil, bought Tom's new papers. The terms were a ten-year indenture with a payment of fifty pounds at settlement time. Not a very large improvement over the terms he'd had in Maryland, he had to admit, but at least Hendley was no Phineas Gilpin.

In the ensuing years, Tom was never beaten, was fed substantial meals, and was provided with clean warm clothes and a dry, private place in which to bed down (all of which benefits had been denied him by Phineas Gilpin of Maryland). Peter Hendley had a quick temper, which sometimes drove him to inflict welts on his farmhands' backs with his ever-present cane, but he rarely used the whip and never the curry-comb. Tom, having stood up to a worse master, soon learned how to face Hendley down when he raised up his cane. Hendley hadn't used the cane on him for years.

After a while, Tom was even trusted to leave the property after working hours. He could meet with friends in the tavern. He could drink and sport and wench like any freeborn laboring man. But he knew he was not free. He hated being a bondsman. He wanted only to be his own man, free to live and work where he willed. Freedom was a dream that his few creature comforts could not dim.

Now, lying on his cot in his freezing little room, an elated Tom began to consider the possibility that he was becoming lucky after all. In the past nine years he'd done so well for Hendley's farmlands that Mr. Hendley (who was not known for his openhandedness) periodically promised him small increases in the amount of his settlement. By settlement time, if Hendley was true to his word, Tom would have close to one hundred pounds—enough money to buy some land. And settlement time was only one year away from becoming a reality. His servitude was almost over.

He didn't often let himself dwell on the ending of his indenture. The anticipation of it had the power to twist his gut. He'd waited so long and wanted it so badly that he now had only one fear—that it wouldn't happen. That something would occur to prevent it. It was better, he believed, not to celebrate good fortune in advance; it might turn out to be like a beautiful butterfly that crumbled to powder in your fingers when you caught it. It was better not to think about it at all.

But today he couldn't help himself. He felt excited, alive, happy almost. He couldn't keep the feeling down. He'd done it! He'd asked her, and she'd said yes. He was going to learn to read! It was the one thing besides his freedom that he'd ever wanted. Reading could make a free man really free. It was the best of tools for making one's way in the world. To be able to read the news in the *New York Gazette,* to decipher a map, and to make out what was said on the notices posted in front of the tavern—those would be benefits enough. But to be able to study history and philosophy and the thoughts of great men—those could be achievements to make life a triumph! If he could read, he'd be able to accomplish anything.

He wasn't used to feeling happy. It filled his chest so full it almost hurt. But it was too rare and precious a feeling to push away. He clutched his blanket to his chest like a lover and rolled back and forth on his cot in a kind of ecstatic trance. Could it be that luck was making friends with him at last?

No! he thought, sitting up abruptly and wrapping his blanket tightly round him. *Only a fool lets himself be carried off to cloud-cuckooland.* There was danger in this premature euphoria, the danger of dashed hopes. If one's dreams took one too high, and those dreams failed to materialize, the blow of the fall could be devasting to the spirit. He had to guard against that blow.

But it was hard to keep from feeling euphoric after what had happened today. Mistress Patience was going to teach him . . . Patience herself! Patience with the shiny hair and the glowing eyes. Patience who moved like a goddess despite the prim restraint of her dark dresses and high starched collars, who trailed an aroma of peach blossoms, who bit her underlip when she was upset and dropped her eyes when she was embarrassed so that her dark-gold lashes brushed her cheek, and who, when her soft shoulder accidently brushed his, could set him trembling like a rabbit. She would be alone with him every day, bending over him and speaking in her honeyed voice, her breath brushing his ear!

It was something he'd daydreamed about since the first day he'd laid eyes on her, when he was fourteen years old. And now it was going to happen. He could hardly believe this good fortune was within his grasp.

But there was danger in this, too. Though the prospect of spending a bit of every day with her made him crazy with excitement, he wasn't so crazy that he couldn't see the danger. His friends, if they knew, would tell him not to do it. None of them liked her. Jotham called her Mistress Prissface, and Freda, the tavern wench who gave herself to Tom every time he had the hunger, described her as a skinny, sanctimonious, stiff-necked prude. Even Nate had said she was drying into an old maid. But they had no eyes—no eyes at all. Tom knew better what Patience was.

That was the trouble. She was the embodiment of all his dreams of womanhood. If he spent time so close to her, he could lose his head. She could never be for him . . . or for any man except that British fool, Orgill. Could he bear to have her close to him and never touch her?

Yes, he could manage it, he told himself. He had to. He'd waited too long for his freedom to endanger it now, when it was so close. No woman could make him endanger it, not even Mistress Patience. He would concentrate on the reading, nothing else. Having her teach him reading was luck enough. No man, not even one a great deal luckier than he, could expect to have everything.

Fifteen

The New York Bogaerdes were overjoyed to see the weather clear next morning, for it presaged success for their daughter's birthday frolic. The prosperous household at the very top of Vesey's Street was abuzz with activities. Two of the servants were clearing the outdoor walks and windows of all remaining ice, while the others were polishing silver, clearing the center of the drawing room for dancing, hanging festoons on the stair-rails and setting the table for a bountiful buffet. Mistress Bogaerde, Tilda's mother, impressed her sister-in-law, Tante Gusti, to help in the kitchen, where the two women and three servants would spend the entire day busily preparing all sorts of delicacies. The buffet would include a number of Dutch dishes, of course, like little cheese truffles called *kaastruffels,* stewed pears, *karnemelk* pudding made with buttermilk, and Tilda's favorite pancakes, *flensjes,* which could be eaten with powdered sugar or jam. In addition to these were several purely American dishes, like apple turnovers, sweet-potato biscuits and tapioca pudding. These treats, when combined with rum punch, white Madeira, or Mr. Bogaerde's favorite drink, a liquor made from honey called metheglin, were certain to make the ball a gastronomic success.

Barbara, keeping herself aloof from the preparations, remained in the guest bedroom she shared with Ilse, a bedroom very different from hers at home, for here the beds were built into cupboards, Dutch style. During the day, the cupboards were closed, making the room seem like a sitting room. Fortunately, however, there was a dressing table in the room. Barbara spent the morning sitting before the dressing-table mirror staring glumly at the top of her too-modest, dark blue Sunday gown, wishing for a fairy godmother to wave a wand and transform it to a proper costume for a ball.

To her delight, a fairy godmother (in the person of the good-hearted Ilse) did appear. Ilse dashed into the room just before noon with a green velvet gown over her arm. "Look at what I persuaded Tilda to lend to you!" she clarioned. "Shall we see if it fits?"

It was a lovely gown, the fabric soft and shimmering and the style, a sacque that buttoned tight at the waist and then fell open to drape over a full petticoat, was quite fashionable. It had a cream-colored satin embroidered stomacher that would go well with her own off-white petticoat, a low-cut bodice stiffened with whalebone, and half-sleeves with turned-back cuffs and ruffles of lace below. The bodice, to fit tightly, would have to be taken in, and the skirt shortened. In addition, Ilse had been ordered to give strict instructions to the wearer that a row of modesty lace would have to be inserted at the décolletage. But Barbara was not troubled by the prospect of alterations. She had all afternoon to take care of those details. As she pranced around the room showing Ilse how the dress looked, she was beside herself with joy.

Her high spirits lasted through the afternoon, for she convinced Ilse to do the sewing for her by exaggerating her incompetence with the needle and praising Ilse's ability to the skies. While Ilse toiled away with her needle, taking in the seams of the bodice, turning up the hem and tacking on the modesty lace, Barbara slipped out of the house and took a stroll around the neighborhood. She returned to the house an hour later with cheeks glowing from the wind and eyes shining with excitement, for she'd discovered, on her walk, a linen-draper shop in which were displayed a row of dolls dressed in the latest London fashions. She'd examined these "fashion babies," as the storekeeper had called them, in minute detail and thus learned a new way to dress her hair.

The glow remained on her cheeks and in her eyes despite the fact that she'd had to be dragged back to Vesey's Street by Henryk, who'd been ordered by the eagle-eyed Tante Gusti to run out and find her. "How could you be so foolish as to walk about the streets unescorted?" he scolded when he came upon her. "When we get back to Spuyten Duyvil, Tante Gusti is bound to report this to your father."

"Oh, pooh," Barbara retorted flippantly, determined not to let anything spoil her mood, "what is there to report? Nothing untoward has happened to me."

But her mood was somewhat dampened that evening, when she and Ilse were dressing for the ball. That was when she discovered that the strip of modesty lace hid the part of her bosom that only recently had developed its ravishing swell. "I'm going to rip this lace off," she declared, frowning at herself in the mirror. "It spoils the entire effect."

"No it doesn't," Ilse argued, studying her friend with sincere admiration. "The green is perfect with your color, and I've never seen your hair so pretty. You look very grown up with your hair pinned up that way."

Barbara fingered her tresses smugly. She'd spent more than an hour on her coiffure (piling most of her wild ringlets on the top of her head and brushing the rest into one long curl that she permitted to fall over her shoulder) and knew it looked charming. "Thank you, Ilse," she said to her friend's reflection in the mirror, "but though my hair may look grown up, the dress looks childish with the lace covering me like this."

Ilse shrugged. "Tante Gusti won't permit you to remove it," she said flatly as she urged Barbara to the door, "so you may as well make the best of it. Come now, or we shall be late."

When the two girls reached the bottom of the stairs, Barbara was surprised to find that most of the guests had already arrived. "We Dutch," Ilse said proudly, "are always prompt."

Barbara looked about her in fascination. She saw a varied crowd that included turbaned matrons, elderly gentlemen in wigs, younger men who, in the newer fashion, wore their hair uncovered, elegant young women (who, in Barbara's opinion looked far more fashionable than she with their jewels and elaborate coiffures), and a sprinkling of children who darted about in unsupervised glee. The guests crowded all the rooms of the lower floor—the large hallway, the dining room where the food was already laid out, the spacious drawing room, and the back room that the Dutch called the parlor. The many voices, and the music of three fiddlers scratching away on their instruments from their place on a platform in the drawing room, made a very lively noise.

Barbara had barely taken in the scene when Henryk emerged from the crowd and grasped her arm. His eyes bulged ludicrously in admiration of her appearance. "You are the prettiest girl here," he whispered in her ear.

She smiled in self-satisfaction. That remark was as good a start to the evening as a girl could expect.

As Ilse ran off to fill herself a plate of treats from the buffet, Barbara continued to examine her surroundings. The guests stood about in groups, eating, talking and laughing, but the largest crowd—gathered in the center of the drawing room and made up entirely of men—was the one that caught her attention. The men in that group were not eating or laughing; they were listening attentively to a small, round-shouldered man with a sharp nose, heavy lips and a high forehead topped with elaborately curled and powdered hair.

"Who is that?" Barbara asked Henryk, who was still gawking at her in infatuated awe.

He turned his eyes away from her reluctantly and focused them on the man she indicated. "Oh, that's Oliver De Lancy, the brother of the head of the New York Assembly. He's one of the most influential men in the city." He threw her a look of pompous self-importance. "The New York Bogaerdes are very well connected, you see."

"So it would seem. What are they speaking of so intently?"

"The latest news of the British tea ships, I imagine. Mr. De Lancy is very worried about the mood of the populace if the ships should dock here."

Barbara moved closer to listen. "I've noted a fearful undercurrent of violence," Mr. De Lancy was saying. "One might even call it a threat. It's not only the mechanicals, but the merchants, too, are itching for a reason to riot, ever since that fellow from Massachusetts rode in, trumpeting the news of the Boston resistance. What was his name, Cortland?"

"Revere, I think," another man answered. "Paul Revere."

"Yes, that's the name. He certainly stirred up a storm. Governor Tryon is so worried about the unrest that he's sent a message to England requesting that the tea be sent back."

"Will England agree?" someone asked.

But Barbara was not interested enough to remain to hear the answer, for at that moment her eye was caught by the appearance of red coats moving about in the hallway. Tilda's handsome suitor had just arrived with a handful of friends.

With Hendryk following adoringly behind her, she made her way to the hall, just in time to see Tilda's soldier kiss the hand of the girl to whom, tonight, he would become betrothed. Tilda blushed, smiled happily, and, tucking her arm in his, took him round to introduce him to the guests. Barbara, while waiting her turn, looked him over carefully. She'd not been mistaken in her appraisal yesterday; he was indeed just the sort of man she admired. To say he was handsome would be an oversimplification. One might not be able to make much of his individual features, she admitted to herself, for if described separately they would sound unremarkable, but somehow, in combination, they enhanced each other. For example, though of no more than average height, his carriage and the breadth of his shoulders made him seem tall, especially in that breathtaking red-and-gold dress uniform. And though his hair, tied back with soldierly neatness, was an ordinary brown, as were his eyes, and though his skin was weathered to a definite swarthiness, his features—a fine nose, square chin, and cheeks that showed dimples when he smiled—when seen together were in beautiful balance, making his face seem manly and immediately likable. Barbara could not take her eyes from him.

When at last Tilda brought him to meet her, Barbara felt bereft of breath. "Babs, I'd like to present First Lieutenant John Pilkington," the young woman said, giving Barbara a wink to indicate her approval of the way Barbara looked in her gown. "Jack, this is Ilse's little friend, Barbara Hendley. Doesn't she look adorable in that gown?"

Barbara wanted to scratch Tilda's eyes out. Little friend, indeed! Adorable, indeed! The fellow would think she was ten years old! She took a deep breath to make her breasts stand out, and, offering her hand, favored him with her most brilliant smile. "I'm *so* pleased to meet you, Lieutenant," she said seductively.

The officer, barely glancing at her, bowed over her hand. "Delighted," he murmured and moved on.

Lieutenant Pilkington's utter indifference was only the first in a series of disasters for Barbara. Determined to win his notice, she spent the evening trying all sorts of stratagems, to no avail. First, when she saw him chatting with another redcoat in the parlor, she went in, passed right in his line of vision and smiled at him enticingly. He, however, was so engrossed in his conversation he looked right through her. Another time, she brazenly went up to him and asked if he liked the *kaastruffel*. He peered down at her blankly. "I haven't tried it, Mistress . . . er . . . er . . ." he mumbled.

"Hendley," she reminded him. "Babs Hendley."

"Yes, of course," he said awkwardly, "Mistress Hendley." And he immediately turned to speak to a gentleman behind him.

On a third occasion, when she saw him lead Tilda onto the floor to dance the High Betty Martin, Barbara seized Henryk's arm and forcibly dragged him onto the floor. "But we haven't got Tante Gusti's permission," Henryk protested, "and besides, I don't know the steps of this dance."

"You don't have to know them," she hissed in reply. "Just frisk about in time to the music." She pushed and pulled him across the floor until they were right beside the lieutenant and his lady, at which moment Barbara began to laugh and frisk about as if she were having the time of her life. But if her behavior had any effect on its target, she could see no sign of it.

And so it went all evening long. Soon it would be midnight, Tante Gusti would force her to go up to bed, and all hope of making an impact on the beautiful lieutenant would be gone forever. Quite desperate by this time, she conceived a last, madly impetuous plan. All she had to do to prepare for it was to get herself a glass of fruit punch, stand near the dining table and wait for him to come. But first she whisked herself into the dimly lit, small sitting room at the side of the hallway, where all the cloaks and outer garments were stowed, and ruthlessly ripped the modesty lace from the neck of her gown.

When in due course the lieutenant appeared in the dining room and headed for the punch bowl, Barbara was ready. Holding her full glass of punch carefully before her in her right hand, she brushed by him, jiggled his elbow with her right arm, and gave a little cry as the punch spilled, not quite accidentally, over the bodice of her gown. *"Look out!"* she cried, letting the glass fall to the ground with a crash.

The officer wheeled about. "Good God!" he exclaimed, gaping at the broken glass and the splattered girl standing before him. "Did I do *that?* I'm so dreadfully sorry. I didn't see you."

"Oh-dear-oh-dear," Barbara murmured, letting her eyes fill with tears. "I've spilled it! The g-gown is *ruined!* And it isn't even m-mine!"

The lieutenant, red-faced in embarrassment, pulled out a pocket handkerchief. "I'm truly sorry, ma'am, truly. Perhaps I can—"

She turned a pathetic face up to him and shook her head. "No, not here. It's so . . . awkward. All these people . . ."

"Yes, of course," he agreed, looking about helplessly. A servant came up at that moment to sweep up the floor. "Shall we ask this man to find a housemaid—?"

She pretended not to hear. "This way," she said, taking his hand and hurriedly leading him out of the room. "We must be quick, before the stains set. I don't want Tilda to see."

"Tilda?" he asked, following her in confused obedience.

"The gown is hers. She let me wear it for the ball. I shall be devastated if I've rewarded her kindness by ruining it." She led him into the little sitting room. "Here," she said, closing the door, "we can be private. I'll take your handkerchief now, if you please."

If Lieutenant Pilkington wondered why she'd taken him, instead of just his handkerchief, to this little hideaway, the question soon left his mind. As the red-headed girl dabbed uselessly at the stains on the bodice of her dress, he began to notice that the bodice covered a very luscious bosom. In fact, his first impression of this girl was undergoing a radical adjustment. Even in the dim light provided by a banked fire and two meager candles on the mantel, he could see that she was not a child at all, but a very appealing young woman. "I'm afraid my handkerchief is not doing much good," he said, taking it from her and using it to wipe away a drop of red liquor that had lodged itself in the cleft of her bosom just above the edge of her enticing décolletage.

"No, it isn't." Emitting a tremulous sob, Barbara let her head drop on his shoulder. "Oh, God! What am I to do?"

He slid a comforting arm about her waist. "Don't cry, little one," he said softly. "I'll tell Tilda it was all my fault."

She lifted her head and looked up at him, her eyes aswim with tears. "I can't let you d-do that, Lieutenant. Not tonight."

"Tonight?" he repeated absently, for he'd heard what she said with only a small part of his mind. The rest was preoccupied with studying this girl he was holding so lightly in one arm. He was a soldier, well-traveled and experienced in dalliance, but she was like no girl he'd ever seen. A little slip of a creature, with a waist he could span in his two hands, she was more than just pretty. The skin of her bosom, where he'd wiped off the spot of punch, was so smooth that his fingers itched to touch it. And the face looking up at him was luminous despite a spattering of freckles. Her lips, blurred and swollen from her tears, were ripe for kissing. Did he dare? She was only a little provincial from the colonies, after all. These colonials liked people to take liberties.

"It's your betrothal night," Barbara reminded him, her heart beginning to pound in triumph. She'd recognized that look in his eyes. "Tilda would be angry with you, and we can't let that happen. Not tonight."

"She won't be angry," John Pilkington assured her. "It was an accident, after all. And Tilda's not the sort who angers easily. She has a very even temper."

"Has she?" Barbara glanced up at him with a flutter of lashes. "How fortunate for you."

"Yes." He drew her closer, for he too could recognize a look . . . a look of invitation. "Very fortunate." He lowered his head to hers and kissed those eager lips.

It was, Barbara realized with a start, her first real kiss, but she must not let him know that. She did not want him to think her a naive child. She pressed hard against him and let her arms creep round his neck. It was the most pleasurable feeling she'd ever experienced, and from the way the lieutenant's arms trembled, she was sure he felt the same. But his first words, when he released her, were, "What a naughty little child you are, ma'am. What did you say your name was?"

She wanted to stamp her foot. "I'm not a child!" she exclaimed. "And you ought to remember my name. You heard it twice."

He wrinkled his brow. "Yes, I seem to remember that. Something with a B. Betty, is it?"

"Babs," she pouted, pulling herself from his arms. "Babs Hendley."

"Yes, now I recall. Ilse's little friend. But not a child, I admit." He drew her back into his embrace and smiled down at her warmly, the dimples appearing in his cheeks. "Has anyone yet told you, Babs Hendley, how very lovely you are?"

"Yes, many," she said, tossing her head. "Dozens and dozens." Her abrupt movement caused a few curls to come loose and fall over her forehead.

He tucked them back. "I'm not at all surprised. You've quite taken my breath away, you know. I do believe you're the prettiest creature I've ever laid eyes on."

"Prettier than Tilda?" she asked saucily.

"Naughtier, anyway." He pulled her closer. "Very much naughtier. And for that you must pay a penalty." He lifted her off her feet until their faces were level, and, holding her tightly against his chest, kissed her again.

It was a heady kiss, utterly dizzying. She had to cling to his neck for dear life. She thought she might swoon in ecstasy, but before a swoon became a real possibility, the door to the little room burst open. It was Henryk. "Jack?" he asked, peering into the dimness, "Are you here? Uncle Willie is about to announce— *Babs!*"

The lieutenant set her down at once and adjusted his coat. "Is it time?" he asked casually, though he couldn't hide his struggle to catch his breath. "Then let's go. I'm ready." Throwing a last, somewhat longing glance at Barbara, he strode quickly from the room.

But Henryk continued to gape at her, aghast. She turned away from his disconcerting stare, flushing in shame. After a moment, his shock turned to fury, and he stomped across the room to confront her. "What did *he* give you for that kiss?" he asked nastily. "One of his medals? Whatever it was, I doubt it can be worth more than a ruby ring."

"Don't be disgusting," Barbara muttered. She pushed by him and walked out of the room with her head high.

In the drawing room, on the platform in front of the fiddlers, Mr. Wilhelm Bogaerde stood between his daughter Tilda and Lieutenant John Pilkington, with the guests crowded in front of them and looking up at them eagerly. Barbara took a place at the back of the crowd and watched.

Mr. Bogaerde smiled broadly. "Here on my right," he said loudly, "is my Tilda who on this night celebrates the eighteenth *verjaardag* of her birth. And on my left, one of the finest specimens of British manhood, the son of Sir Matthew Pilkington of Sussex, England, First Lieutenant Jack Pilkington." He took each of their right hands and joined them in front of him. The two young people smiled at each other, Tilda turning bright red.

"Well, go on, Willie," someone in the crowd shouted. "Let's hear it already!"

The crowd laughed. At the back, Henryk leaned over to Barbara and muttered in her ear, "His father's only a baron. I thought you wanted a duke or an earl."

She paid him no notice. On the platform, Mr. Bogaerde was placing his arms around the shoulders of the pair. "It's my pleasure," he said, "to announce their betrothal."

There was a loud cheer and much applause from the crowd. Mr. Bogaerde pushed the newly betrothed couple together and left them alone on the platform. The lieutenant smiled down at the girl beside him and lifted her hand to his lips. This brought more cheers, which the couple acknowledged by smiling and nodding to the throng. With his hand clutching his betrothed's, the officer surveyed the crowd. Barbara, at the back, waited patiently, her lips curled in a slight smile. She knew whom his eyes were seeking.

His gaze met hers at last, and though his expression did not change, their eyes locked. His smile seemed to freeze.

Henryk threw Barbara a sneer. "Well, he's betrothed," he mocked in Barbara's ear. "Too late for you now."

Barbara, her eyes not moving from those of the man on the platform, ran the tip of her tongue slowly along her upper lip. She could almost feel Jack Pilkington's intake of breath. "Perhaps so," she murmured softly, waving Henryk off with a flip of her hand, "and then again, perhaps not."

Sixteen

While Barbara had been strolling the streets of New York City, excitedly anticipating her ball, life on the Hendley estate was proceeding as usual, except that everywhere one went on the grounds, one could hear the drip-drip of melting ice. The mid-afternoon sun was doing its work despite the cold. Aaron, dressed in a duffel-wool coat, with a shabby muffler pulled over his head to protect his ears from the icy wind, loped down the path from the barn to the kitchen. He gazed at the glistening world delight-edly, aware that his ice-glazed surroundings were a rarity that would not last long.

He whistled as he walked around the smokehouse and across the frozen kitchen garden. Aaron's nature was almost invariably cheerful. His round face, an unexpected contrast to his thin, gan-gling limbs, shone with good humor. The natural wonders of the world fascinated him. His eyes drank in the otherworldly glow that the slanting red rays of the sun gave to the diamonded land-scape. To him it was a magical fire-and-ice kingdom. He stopped along the way to look at an ice-imbedded oak leaf here and a gleaming black stone there. When he arrived at the kitchen door, he paused to admire a row of long icicles that had formed along the lintel. Grinning, he broke one off and licked the point as if it were a confection. He kept sucking on the icicle as he knocked on the door.

His mother opened it, took one look at her son and knocked

the icicle from his hold. "What you think you doin', chile?" she demanded.

The boy laughed, his teeth gleaming white in his black face. "Ain't no harm in suckin' ice," he said.

Sally rolled her eyes as if asking heaven for understanding. "What you doin' here? Ain't you got no work to do?"

"Come to see Miz Patience. I got a message fo' her."

Patience appeared behind Sally, wiping her hands on her apron. "Yes, Aaron, here I am. What is it?"

"Thanks for the apple tart you give me the other day, Miz Patience. It was the best tart I ever did eat."

"Of course it was." Patience smiled at the boy. "Your mother made it."

"I knows it. My mama's the bes' baker in the colony," Aaron said proudly.

Sally snorted. "Huh! Is *that* what you come all this way for? To tell Miz Patience you like the tart?"

"No, that ain't why. I has a message from Tom, ma'am."

Patience's smile faded. "Oh?"

"He say to tell you that the sun'll set pretty soon."

"The sun'll set?" Sally glared at the boy. "What kin' of message is that?"

"I understand it, Sally," Patience said with a sigh. "Tom's reminding me that he can't take reading lessons in the dark." She looked at Aaron as she untied her apron. "I hoped he might forget."

"No, ma'am," the boy said, shaking his head. "Not Tom."

"Tell him I'll gather up some books and be right there."

"Yes, 'm. But where, ma'am?"

"The barn, I suppose. Upstairs, in the loft."

"Yes, ma'am," the boy said, turning to go.

"Aaron?" Patience stepped over the threshold and caught him by the arm. "You won't say anything to anyone else, will you?"

"No, ma'am, I knows better. Tom a'ready made me promise."

He gave her his white-toothed grin. "After he learn, he promise to teach *me!*" With a wave, he ran off down the path.

Patience came back into the kitchen. Sally closed the door behind her and eyed her mistress with raised brows. "Readin' lessons?"

"Don't say it, Sally, whatever you're thinking. Just don't say it." Patience took off her apron and started for the passage to the main house. "Just come and help me find that green coat we made for Papa that he didn't like."

"I don' have to fin' it. I knows where it is," Sally retorted, following her. "An' what make you think I p'poses to say somethin'? It ain't no skin off my nose if a loony somebody want to get a good tongue-lashin' from her papa for givin' away coats an' readin' lessons. I wasn't goin' to say nothin'. Nothin' a-tall."

Patience and Tom found a barrel and a stool and set up the schoolroom in a corner of the barn loft that faced west, where the setting sun shone in through a broken slat in the barn wall. The light had an amiable, pale yellow mellowness, giving the shadowy corner of the loft a benevolent glow, as if Heaven were bestowing its approval on this secret, illicit endeavor. Tom, wearing the green coat that was too small for him but that kept him deliciously warm in the chilly barn, sat astride the stool, leaning his elbow on the barrel and peering in furrow-browed confusion at the book in front of him, a confusion brought on as much by the nearness of Mistress Patience bending over him as by the mysterious markings on the pages before him.

The book was an old primer, copied by a Philadelphia printer from an English primer by John Newbery, that all the Hendley children had used to learn their letters. It was called *The Royal Primer Improved,* with a subtitle declaiming: *Being an Easy and Pleasant Guide to the Art of Reading.* But it proved to be anything but easy.

Patience opened the book to the first page. "This is the most important page in the book," she explained. "It's the alphabet. Can you read the alphabet?"

"No, ma'am."

"Can you just say it, then?"

"No, ma'am, no one ever taught me the alphabet," he admitted, reddening.

She sensed the depth of his shame. "It's not so very difficult," she said comfortingly. "There's a little rhyme that will help you remember." And slowly, firmly, she repeated the familiar childhood alphabet-rhyme until he'd memorized it and could go down the list in the book and say the letters in their proper order. But when she asked him to recognize the letters *out* of order, he stumbled and failed. "No, it's a D, not an O," she corrected. "The O is a circle, you see? But the D is only a half circle."

Tom's fingers tightened into fists. "Half circle, yes," he muttered.

As the minutes passed, he grew more and more humiliated. The N's and the M's confused him. The O was easy, but sometimes it had a little tail, and he forgot the name for that one. Then he confused the U and the double-U, the Z that was a backwards S, the F and the E, one of which had two protrusions while the other had three, but he couldn't remember which was which.

What was wrong with him? he wondered. *Little children* were able to do this! Why couldn't he? Mistress Patience would think him an idiot!

When he called a P an R for the third time, and she reminded him for the third time that the R stood on two feet while the P stood on only one, he reddened to his ears. *"Damn* me for a stupid blockhead!" he burst out in agonized frustration, sweeping the book off the barrel with an angry swing of his arm. Then, with head lowered, he leaped to his feet, fled across the loft and down the ladder out of her sight.

"Tom!" she called after him. "Come back! It's only a small error. You're learning."

But he was gone. She could hear his footsteps stomping down the path to the stable. She sank down on the stool feeling defeated. What had gone wrong? Tom Morrison was far from a fool, she knew that. His cleverness with numbers was sufficient proof. Reckoning was a difficult skill even for people with years of fine education, yet he'd taught it to himself. So his inability to learn the letters had to be her fault, not his. Had she tried to encompass too much at once? Had she pushed too hard? Had she corrected too harshly, or neglected to praise? *She* was to blame for his humiliation, she told herself, and she didn't know how to make amends.

She sat on the stool with her head lowered, awash in abject misery. But why? She should feel *relieved*. If he'd really given up, she wouldn't have to come here any more and do this illicit thing. But the truth was she wanted to do it. It was exciting to meet him secretly like this, more exciting than anything she'd felt for years. Her father would explode in fury if he knew, but, in all honesty, that threat made the meeting even more exciting. She'd enjoyed the past hour more than she'd dreamed possible. Sitting near him, their shoulders touching, she'd felt her heart race and her blood bubble in her veins. Once he'd reached over to point to something, and his hand had touched hers. He'd quickly snatched it away, but the touch had sent tingles right up her arm. Worse, she had a terrifying urge to take his hand and press it to her breast.

Remembering the feeling, she winced in shame. *No,* she thought, *that just won't do!* She couldn't live with herself if she felt such shameful feelings every day. If he hadn't run off, she would have had to back away herself, promise or no promise. She could not endure a daily dose of such exquisite, degraded, agonizing feelings. It was fortunate the man had given up. Very fortunate indeed.

Of course it was *un*fortunate for Tom. She'd been deeply

touched by his need to learn. He'd been so achingly *eager,* and she had failed him. But it couldn't be helped. He'd been too impatient, and she'd been too . . . well, there was no point in going over all that again.

Several minutes passed while she remained immobilized by painful guilt. At last, reminding herself that she would be missed at home, she slid off the stool and knelt down to pick up the primer. As she was about to rise, she heard a sound on the ladder. Her heart bounced in her chest. *"Tom?"*

His head appeared at the edge of the loft floor. "Yes, ma'am, it's me." He climbed the remaining rungs and crossed the floor to where she still knelt. Bending down, he took hold of her elbows and raised her to her feet. "I'm sorry, ma'am," he said, dropping his hold and lowering his eyes to his wet boots. "I'm a great fool."

She wanted to take his face in her hands and soothe his wounded vanity with kisses, but of course she did not. "Only if you give up so easily," she said gently.

Tom lifted his head and met her eyes. "I never intended to give up. If you let me take that book to study over night, I'll try to learn those damn letters by tomorrow."

She let out a long breath. *Tell him,* she ordered herself. *Tell him you cannot—!* But the words that came stumbling off her tongue were, "I have no doubt you'll learn them." And she handed him the primer.

He slipped the little book into his coat, nodded, and went to the ladder. Before descending, he looked back at her, his eyes pleading. "You'll be here again tomorrow?"

That look in his eyes caught her breath. If only he'd been arrogant, as he'd been yesterday, she might have been able to refuse, to save herself, to stay away, to protect herself from feelings she knew were shockingly debased. But at this moment all she could see was a boy, hurt and shamed by a weakness he was powerless to correct without her help. He needed her, and that need tore away the weak defenses she'd tried to build against him. His moment of humiliation, this brief exposure of his one deep shame, had utterly disarmed her. She smiled a weak, wavering smile of surrender. "I'll be here. Tomorrow and whatever other days we'll need."

Book Two

Liberty and Lies

Spring 1774

Dearest Hannah,

    We are all delighted to hear that your little son Caleb was born Hale and Healthy and that you are doing well. It was the happiest News of this very happy Spring! I have attached blue ribbons to the Cap and Shift I knitted for him, and Chester will deliver them with this note. I myself shall follow in a very few days, for I cannot be Content until I lay eyes on the handsome fellow.

    Your little Caleb seems to have brought good Fortune to all the world. At the very moment of his birth, the East India Company tea ships turned back to England instead of docking in New York Harbor, thus causing the threat of revolt to subside. Tell Caleb I hold him responsible for bringing Peace!

    Things in the Hendley household are also much more cheerful these Days, what with Benjy going less often to his ridiculous "drilling" and Babs singing about the house like a girl in Love. Ever since her return from her trip to New York with the Bogaerdes, the chit has been blessedly Abstracted and Contemplative instead of Impulsive and Argumentative. I suspect that she had a Flirtation in the city and is busily turning over in her mind Ways and Means to get back there to continue it. But I don't trouble myself over the matter; if I know my Sister, she will find a new Interest soon enough.

    With all this cheery News, I myself feel like singing about the house! But of course I shan't. Instead I will continue to behave in my usual Sensible fashion and go to help prepare

Dinner. But even though I don't sing, Hannah, I'm sure you know that my Heart is rejoicing at your happy News. With fondest affection, I remain yours, etc.,
Patience.

Letter from Patience Hendley
to her friend Hannah LeGrange
Spuyten Duyvil, New York,
15 March 1774

Seventeen

Spring came slowly to the Hudson valley in 1774. For most of March the only signs that it was on its way were the little shoots of green that pushed up through the brown earth, mere beginnings of what would soon become a rich palette of wild-flowers: luscious strawberry plants, white daisies, deep-hued violets, Queen Anne's lace, and clover. By April the maples, whose buds had already begun to show a faint reddish cast back in February, were brightening and enlarging despite the cold, as were the yellow-green buds of ash and birch. But the blooms of the walnut and cherry were not yet visible. The wind still blew cold and wet from across the river, and the ground remained hard and hoary with frost. Nonetheless, Patience found it a joy to throw open her window in the morning; though it was still early in April, she believed she could really smell spring in the air.

On this particular April morning, when she went to her window in the dimly-glowing hour just before dawn, it occurred to her that she was in an unusually cheerful frame of mind; never in all her years had the advent of spring found her more eager to greet the day. But there surely was more to account for this elevation of her spirits, she suspected, than the mere anticipation of spring. Was it caused by the anticipation of this afternoon's reading lesson with Tom?

Although she still felt a secret shame over the enjoyment she took in his company, she was nevertheless proud of the success they'd achieved. The fellow, once he'd become familiar with the

letters and learned how to turn them into sounds, had made remarkable progress. He was already complaining about the child-
ishness of the primer, and he was quite right; he was ready for
more advanced texts. Patience derived much satisfaction from
this achievement, but the satisfaction troubled her, too. The time
she spent with Tom in the barn loft—was it *too* great a pleasure?

But Tom's reading did not account for all of her good spirits.
Best of all for their sustenance was her conviction that her father
had forgotten his threat to sell Aaron. He'd said not one word
about it in all these weeks. As each day had passed with no renewal of that threat, the knot in Patience's chest had eased. She
was now convinced that her father's remark had been naught but
idle words. He hadn't meant them, she assured herself, and she
needn't feel any further concern about the matter. It was no wonder her sprits were high.

But a few minutes later, when she came striding into the
kitchen, those high spirits evaporated as if they had never been.
The fire hadn't been started. That small detail was all that was
needed to fright her—a warning, as alarming as a bell, that something was amiss. Sally *always* started the fire before sunup.
What—?

The sound of a low moan drew her eyes to the corner. There
in the shadows, sitting on the hearth ledge with her knees drawn
up and her head lowered between them, was Sally. At the sight
of her, Patience's insides twisted in terror. Sally was motionless,
her back bent over, her arms limp, her skirts drooping over her
thin legs that had sagged apart, and her head hanging heavily
between. She looked like a work of sculpture—a representation
in ebony of utter despair.

Patience gasped. "Sally?" She knelt down beside the black
woman and touched a bony arm. "What is it? What's happened?"

Sally turned her head and looked at her mistress with one eye.
The white of it was enlarged, the pupil distended and wild. "Yo'
papa," she whispered hoarsely. "He say he gon' sell Aaron."

"No!" Patience felt herself stiffen, legs, fingers, lips. It was as if every part of her body had hardened to protect itself from a blow. Except the blood that raced through her veins and pounded in her ears. "No. No. He doesn't mean it. He can't. It's a mistake."

"No mistake." Sally lifted her head. Clenching her fists, she put them to her mouth as if to stifle her inner screams. "Nex' month. He takin' my boy to the slave market down in New York nex' month. He tole me to ready the chile." With a cry that seemed wrenched from her very soul, she began to rock herself back and forth in pain. "How can I ready the chile for the slave block? Oh, Lord, le' me die!"

Patience took her in a tight embrace, holding back the agonized rocking. "No, no, Sally, don't! We won't let it happen. Mama talked him out of it once, didn't she? This time I'll do it."

Sally threw Patience a look in which terror overwhelmed the glimmer of hope. "When yo' mama did it, Aaron was on'y three. Not worth much. Now he thirteen. Big shoulders. He bring a good sum on the block."

"Sally, listen to me! Aaron will not be taken from you, I promise you."

Sally only shuddered and began to rock again.

Patience clung to her and rocked with her. "I swear it, Sally. I won't let him take Aaron away. As God is my witness, I swear it."

Patience ran to her father's workroom, her knees trembling, and pounded rather than knocked at the door. His voice from within ordered her away. "I don't wish to be disturbed," he said.

She disregarded the order and pushed open the door. He was bent over some papers that she could see were not the account books he usually labored over. From the way he hastily shoved them into a drawer when he saw her, she guessed they had something to do with his scheme for an arsenal. This was not the first time she suspected he'd gone ahead with the scheme, but he'd not discussed the plans with her. For some reason he was keeping those plans secret from her. At some other time, when she could think about those things, she would ask him why. But the arsenal and all the other Loyalist concerns did not interest her now. "What I want to see you about is too important to wait," she said, her voice shaking.

He eyed her furiously. "And what makes you believe that your interests are more important than mine."

"You may take my word that they are," she said, meeting his eyes bravely.

His eyes fell. "Well, you're here, so say your say," he muttered.

She stepped over the threshold and closed the door, taking a breath to calm herself. "Papa, you cannot have been serious when you told Sally you intend to sell Aaron."

A flush of red began to color Peter Hendley's neck. "I was indeed serious. And I want no discussion of the matter."

"Papa! This is not *right!* How can you *think* of doing such a thing? Did you not promise Mama, years ago—?"

Hendley banged his hands on the desk. "Didn't you *hear* me, woman? I said *no discussion!"*

"But we *must* discuss it! To sell the boy is an offense against God! 'Twould be a *vile sin* to break up a family! And one we've harbored in our home for so long. What can you be thinking of?"

"It's ready cash I'm thinking of! The sale of a strong black boy will bring me enough cash to pay six day-workers from now till harvest and still leave a profit for . . . for other things!" The look of shock on his daughter's face darkened the flush on his own. "Times are not easy, you know," he muttered, dropping his eyes. "We cannot afford to be ruled by sentiment."

"Sentiment? Can you equate a mother's love for her son with mere sentiment?" She came round his desk and knelt at the side of his chair. "Papa, please! If you are feeling financial pressures, let us find other ways to practice economy."

"There aren't other ways."

"There must be. If you must sell something, sell a piece of

land. The riverfront acreage you recently acquired. Don't you think you were doing well enough before—?"

"Well enough?" His lips tightened in an angry scowl. "Are you to say what's well enough? I will never sell land. Do you understand me, Patience? I will *never* sell my *land!*"

She winced in pain. "Is land more precious to you than *people?*"

"Do you *dare* to reprimand me?" he shouted furiously. "Is *this* how a God-fearing female addresses her father? Get up, woman, and cease this indelicate harangue! You know nothing of economy, so don't presume to instruct your father in these matters. I said I will not discuss this and I mean it."

Patience whitened at his tone. "Papa!" she gasped, pulling herself up. "Papa, we *must* discuss it. You cannot—!"

"The subject is closed," her father said between clenched teeth, his neck and ears apoplectically red.

"But, Papa, I gave Sally my *word*—!"

"You had no right to give it, so you have only yourself to blame. Now get out of here and leave me in peace. Did you *hear* me, woman? Out of my sight! *Go!*"

The last words were spat out with such venom that Patience was shaken. Her father had never taken such a tone with her before. She stumbled from the room, her emotions in turmoil. While seething with fury at him, she was filled with disgust at herself, too. Her head was bursting with all the arguments she hadn't been permitted to express. Her father had been unreasonable and overbearing about a matter that could end in human tragedy. Sally and Aaron were not objects to be wantonly traded but human beings whose hearts could break! But her father did not see it. And she had not been strong enough to make him listen. Her mother had done it once. Why couldn't she?

After a while her passions cooled, but her determination remained strong. She had given her word to Sally before God. Whatever it cost her, she would keep it. She had to find a way.

Her mind wrestled with the problem all night and the next day, but she could think of only one solution: Sally and Aaron had to run away. But running away was dangerous. It would be almost impossible for a Negro woman with a boy. Unless . . . unless . . .

Her whole being trembled with the enormity of her idea. But in order to carry it out, she needed help. Legal help. She racked her brain to think of someone who might help her . . . someone who knew the law and might have sympathy for a tortured slave. Then, as if all her faculties had sharpened to help her accomplish this one aim, the answer burst upon her. Stuart LeGrange! She remembered her friend Hannah saying to her, that day of the ice storm, that Stuart was showing himself to be Whiggish. Patience, who'd considered herself a dedicated Tory as long ago as yesterday morning, realized that no Tory of her acquaintance would be in sympathy with her plight. In this case a Whig might be just what was needed. She remembered the words Hannah had quoted her husband as saying: *I believe in my heart that when people have no right of consent to the laws under which they live, they live in slavery.* At this moment those words had a fine ring. In fact, they were words of deep meaning and great beauty. Perhaps there was a modicum of elevated principle embedded in the rebel cause.

But it was not the rebel cause Patience wanted to embrace, only that part of it that would help Sally. *Yes,* Patience thought with a sigh of hope, *perhaps Stuart LeGrange will be the very man I need.*

Eighteen

"I purpose to pay a visit to Hannah this afternoon, to see the baby," Patience announced at breakfast the next day.

Her father, who had not exchanged a word with her since their quarrel, looked over at her uneasily. "I'll drive you," he said brusquely. "I've a mind to discuss something with Lovell."

"I'll go, too," Barbara said promptly, her whole face lighting up. "I'd love to see the baby."

Patience winced. She had counted on going alone, to attempt to speak privately with Stuart. This sudden expansion of the travel party disconcerted her. "How about you, Benjy?" she asked drily. "Shall we make it a family outing?"

Benjy, who was already roguishly plotting ways to take advantage of his father's and sisters' absence by taking out the dory for a pleasure sail, grinned and shook his head. "Not me, Patience. I beg to be excused. I don't care to coo over babies. But please convey my congratulations to one and all."

The trip to Lovell Hill was awkward, for Patience and her father exchanged only the most necessary words, and Barbara, surprisingly, failed to fill in the silences with babble. The girl was too absorbed in her own concerns to chatter; she was busily plotting a strategy to accomplish a purpose of her own.

Barbara had spent the three weeks since her New York adventure dreaming of her lieutenant and hoping she would receive some word from him, but no word had come. This silence, instead of causing her to forget him, made him seem even more desirable. She was convinced that she would die of a broken heart unless she could lay eyes on him again.

With this problem on her mind, she heard Patience announce her intention of seeing Hannah. Babs immediately conceived the idea of coaxing Hannah into holding a ball in honor of Tilda's betrothal, with Tilda and her lieutenant as guests of honor! It could be a combined celebration for both Tilda's betrothal and the birth of the new baby. What better reasons could there be to have a frolic? And, since she herself was bound to be invited to any ball that Hannah held, she would have the opportunity to see her love again.

The only problem with this scheme was that Hannah had no close connection with Tilda and the New York Bogaerdes. Barbara had to provide Hannah with a reason to wish to honor them with a ball. It was her attempt to solve this problem that kept Barbara silent on the trip to Lovell Hill.

The Hendley carriage arrived at the Lovell estate just before teatime. After the newly born infant had been brought down from the nursery and duly admired, the hosts and their visitors gathered round the tea table in the Lovell drawing room. Hannah poured the tea. "It's only Holland, I'm afraid," she apologized. "There's no English tea to be had for love or money."

"Not for long," Lovell declared airily. "Parliament will order the East India Company tea ships back to New York soon enough, and we'll have English tea aplenty."

"And you don't think we'll see a repeat of Boston in the New York harbor?" Stuart LeGrange asked.

"No, I don't. New York ain't Boston. New Yorkers have more sense."

"It's not a question of sense but of ideals," his son-in-law said between sips of his Holland tea. "Ideals of honorable men holding fast to their principles—that taxation without fair representation is a violation of the rights we were born with."

"Principles, balderdash," Peter Hendley growled. "Drowning the tea was not instigated by ideals but by lawless self-interest. It's the American tea merchants, who stand to be run out of business by low English tea prices, who are behind all this."

Stuart looked up from his cup. "That may be true in part," he said mildly, "but you can't believe that there are no *idealists* who oppose British stubbornness. Don't you think there are some men of honor and principle in the opposition?"

Patience's attention was riveted to Stuart's admirable remarks, but her father was not impressed. "Honor and principle, ha!" he snorted. "Then where were these idealists in the last three years, eh, the years of peace and quiet? I'll tell you where they were. They were to be found in Boston and Virginia and everywhere else, quietly paying duties on tea and molasses without a word of objection, because they didn't feel it in their pocketbooks! Damned hypocrites!"

"One can look at it another way, you know, Hendley," Stuart pointed out quietly. "One can say they were quietly paying their duties in the hope that Parliament would appreciate their restraint and reward them for it by recognizing that we colonials have some rights. But with this *new* tax—minor though it is—Parliament is telling us *again* that we in the colonies have no rights at all. Perhaps these honorable men feel that the time for meek acceptance is over."

Hendley drew in a breath to make a sharp reply, but Hannah put a restraining hand on his arm. "My husband loves to play devil's advocate," she said laughingly. "Don't waste your energies arguing with him. I don't think he believes a word of what he says."

"Hummph," Lovell grunted, eyeing his son-in-law dubiously. "Devil's advocate or not, he can certainly set up a loyal Englishman's hackles. Come, Hendley, let's leave these youngsters to their senseless chatter. You said you have some business with me. We'll talk in the library."

As the two older men departed, Hannah shook her head at her

husband in disapproval. "Dash it, Stuart," she chided, "you seem to have driven away half our company. I hope you're satisfied."

Stuart calmly filled his pipe. "We still have Patience and Babs with us. Much the best half."

Patience studied the plump fellow with an intent curiosity. "Tell me truly, Stuart, do you believe what you say, or are you, as Hannah claims, merely a devil's advocate?"

"I hesitate to answer you, ma'am," he said with a mischievous twinkle, "knowing full well your Tory sympathies."

Patience nodded. "That in itself is an answer," she said. "I was certain you were sincere. No man can espouse a cause with such conviction and fluency without believing what he says."

Stuart's brows lifted in pleased surprise. "That sounded almost like a compliment, ma'am. I hope it means that I may continue in your kind regard despite our political differences."

"Politics!" Babs interrupted impatiently. "That's all one ever hears in conversation these days."

"How right you are," Hannah seconded. "I wanted to talk about *household* matters, not politics. For instance, Patience, I have found a bolt of that pillow ticking you wanted."

"Ticking!" Stuart hooted. "Is *that* what you want to talk about? My dear wife, do you call that *conversation?"*

"I do," Babs declared in immediate support of her hostess. "If you and Patience wish to continue talking politics, I wish you will go for a stroll on the portico and leave Hannah and me to speak of ticking, of the baby, and of other really *important* things!"

Patience could have kissed her. "What a very good idea!" she exclaimed. "If Hannah has no objection, I wish you *would* take me for a stroll, Stuart. I rarely have the opportunity to argue politics with a Whig."

With Hannah's good-natured approval, Patience threw a shawl about her shoulders, Stuart took his beaver hat, and the two went outdoors. Barbara watched them go with relief. Here was her opportunity at last, and she seized it. "Did you hear, Hannah, that I've been to New York? Ilsa Bogaerde invited me to a frolic for her cousin Tilda's betrothal—"

Hannah looked up from her jam tart with interest. "Is Tilda Bogaerde *betrothed?* How lovely! I met her when she was a child, you know. I remember her very well. She had the silkiest hair."

"She remembers you, too," Barbara chirped, leaning forward eagerly, to make her lies sound more sincere. "And her mother asked after you."

"How very kind of her," Hannah murmured, refilling her teacup. "Is Tilda's intended a Dutchman?"

"No. He's a British soldier. A lieutenant, I think."

"Really? Dashing and handsome, I suppose."

Babs shrugged. "Nothing out of the ordinary." She reached for a raisin cake and nibbled at it for a moment before going on. "I told Tilda and her mother about your baby. And I described this house to Tilda. She was most impressed. Though the New York Bogaerdes have a lovely, large house with many fine amenities, living in New York City, you know, they can't really duplicate the elegance of a country home like this." She looked down at her cup and casually swirled her tea. "Tilda said she would very much enjoy seeing Lovell Hill some day."

"Did she?" Hannah looked about at her luxurious surroundings with a complacent satisfaction. "I must invite her some time soon."

"And her mother, too, of course," Babs pressed brazenly. "Madame Bogaerde is very knowing on the subject of carpets and draperies. She would take much pleasure in seeing yours."

"You goose," Hannah laughed. "Naturally, I'd ask her mother, too."

"And you could show them the baby. They'd all be enchanted with your adorable baby. You should have them *all* come to see him, the New York Bogaerdes and the Westchester ones, too." She widened her eyes as if a wonderful idea just dawned on her. "You should have a party and have *everyone* come to see the baby!"

Hannah blinked at the girl. "What a wonderful idea, Babs! I haven't given a party in ages."

Barbara beamed at her hostess with shining eyes. "A party!" she gasped, the picture of pleased surprise. "It *is* a splendid plan! The New York ladies could see your house, you could meet Tilda's betrothed, and everyone could see your baby! How utterly delightful!"

Outside, Patience suggested to Stuart that they stroll the pathways instead of the portico. When they were far enough away from the house for her to be certain no one could see or hear them, she broached the matter that had not left her mind for a moment in the past two days. "Stuart," she began, her heart beating, "I took you out here for a reason. I need your help. Desperately."

Stuart stopped walking. "My help?"

"Advice would perhaps be a better word."

"Advice?" He looked both astounded and uneasy.

"Yes. Legal advice. I don't know where else to turn."

He did not hide his surprise. "I, ma'am? But you know I'm not a lawyer."

"Yes, but I hoped . . . that is, I thought that, being a man of business, you might have some knowledge of . . ."

"Of what, ma'am?"

"Dash it, Stuart," she burst out nervously, "stop *ma'aming* me! I need you as a friend!"

Her outburst drew a smile from him. "A self-confessed *Whig* to be friend to Toryish Patience? Has the world turned topsyturvy?"

She laughed. "Your Whiggishness will be an asset in this case, I think."

The little exchange relaxed them both. He drew her hand in his arm and continued to stroll. "I've always been your friend,

Patience, and will continue to be. You may count on that, whatever mischief you're up to."

"Then, tell me . . ." She drew in a breath before proceeding bravely. ". . . what is the procedure for freeing a slave?"

His jaw dropped. *"Freeing a slave?"*

"Yes."

"What on earth are you *saying?"* he asked, gaping at her. "You own no slaves. Are you speaking of one of your father's?"

Her eyes fell. "I cannot answer that. Would it be better if I said this is a hypothetical case?"

"Yes, perhaps it would." He continued to peer at her for a moment quite as though he'd never seen her before. "You are asking, hypothetically, what steps must be taken?"

"Yes. What information can you give me, Stuart?"

He paused before replying, steering her slowly along the gravel path toward the gateposts. "The procedure for freeing a slave is simple enough," he said at last, keeping his tone businesslike. "One makes out a writ of manumission and has it signed by two witnesses."

Patience threw him a look of alarm. "A writ of manumission?"

"Don't let the word fright you. It's merely a form full of legal phrases. '*This writ, made on the tenth day of* et cetera—you know the sort of thing—*doth hereby covenant, promise and grant full freedom from servitude* et cetera *from the party of the first part to the party of the second part* et cetera.' Any lawyer will fill one out for a small fee."

"Yes, of course," Patience murmured abstractedly. They walked a few more steps in silence. Then she turned a worried face up to him. "I can't go to a lawyer, Stuart."

He stopped and took her by the shoulders. "Dash it, Patience, what are you up to?"

"I can't say."

He stared down at her, the eyes in his round, cheerful face wary. "If you're thinking of doing what I *think* you're thinking of doing, it's a very dangerous business. The penalties for aiding a runaway are severe."

"I know that. But there are two lives at stake."

"As vital as that, eh? Very well, say no more. I think I understand." He dropped his hold on her and rubbed his brow thoughtfully. "I may be able to get you a form from my lawyer, with any luck at all."

Her breath caught in her throat. "Can you? Oh, Stuart, if you only could!"

"I don't see why I couldn't. He wouldn't have to know why I wanted it. Besides, he's not the sort to ask questions."

She grasped his arm, her eyes glowing. "Stuart, that would be so good of you! God bless you! You can have no idea what this means to me."

"I think I can," he responded, peering at her with a new respect. He took her arm, and they started back toward the house.

"Do you think . . . is it possible to do it soon? Within a week?" she asked hesitantly. She'd already asked so much of him.

"I don't see why not."

"Truly? Oh, *dear* Stuart, you are a good, kind man!"

She expelled a breath of relief. There was hope now, hope that she could save Sally and Aaron. She would get the writ from Stuart, fill it in with false names and set Sally and her son on their way to freedom in Boston! Her earlier tension turned into elation.

But almost at once her elation faded. "I just thought of something. How can you get the writ into my hands without anyone discovering us?"

His eyebrows rose. "As bad as that at home, eh?"

Patience nodded, her mind racing. Then she caught her breath. "The ticking! You heard Hannah say she has a bolt of ticking for me. If I forget to take it with me tonight, she'd have to send it."

Stuart did not follow. "I don't underst—"

"If . . . couldn't you slip the form into the bolt? Without her knowing it, of course. I know you won't want Hannah involved in this."

"Yes!" He could follow her now. "I think it can be done without involving her. The ticking is a good idea. Leave the details to me."

They came up to the portico. She took hold of his hand and pressed it. "The words are inadequate, but *thank you,* Stuart."

He looked down at her ruefully. "I shall not be worthy of your thanks if I don't warn you again that you're embarking on a dangerous enterprise. I shall send the form to you, my dear, but the filling it out is up to you. I suppose I needn't remind you that forgery, too, is against the law."

"You needn't remind me."

"I pray I shall not come to regret what I've agreed to do this day. I dread to think of what they'd do to you if—"

"Then don't think of it, Stuart." She ran up the steps, and then turned and beamed down at him. "Think only that, whatever chances, I shall be grateful to you till my dying day."

"Don't be so grateful," he retorted as they prepared to face the others, "for till *my* dying day, I shall deny that this conversation ever took place."

In the library the third tête-à-tête was under way. Peter Hendley, expecting to have to expend a great deal of energy and all his verbal powers to convince Lovell to contribute both support and money to his plans for an arsenal, was surprised by Lovell's prompt agreement. But Lovell, still embarrassed by the signs of his son-in-law's Whiggish propensities, acquiesced to the request quickly. Although the prospect of violence still made him nervous, he promised to contribute generously toward the purchase of a cache of powder and muskets. "One hundred pounds," he offered, "so long as you handle the matter and leave me out of it." And with that reluctant agreement he hastily made for the door.

"Stay a moment, Lovell," Hendley requested, getting up from his chair with the help of his cane and hobbling over to the fireplace, where the fire was burning down. "I want to ask your advice about something."

Lovell paused in the doorway. "If it's about military supplies, I shan't be of much help. You know more about the subject than I'll ever learn."

"No, this has nothing to do with military matters. It's about indentures. You've a good number of bondsmen working your land, so you've more experience than I. There's that fellow of yours, Blackwell, for instance. He's almost thirty, ain't he? How long have you had him?"

"Going on twelve years, I think. Why?"

"It's a goodly period of time. Most indentures end after five years or so."

"He signed for ten. But he tried twice to run off, so the magistrate added four years." Lovell came back into the room, closed the door again and threw Handley a wide grin. "He's toed the mark pretty closely since then, I can tell you."

"He seems a good worker. Who'll replace him when his time's up?"

Lowell shrugged. "I'll offer him a good wage and a bit of land. He'll stay."

"Mine won't," Peter Hendley said glumly, kicking a log of the fire and sending up a shower of sparks. "He has a hundred pounds due on settlement. He'll surely want to go off on his own."

"You're speaking of Tom Morrison, I take it. You're right about that one. Too damned independent, if you were to ask me."

"But he's shrewd, and a good worker. And the other men look to him and take his orders. I'll be hard pressed when he goes."

"Yes, I can see that." Lovell sat down on a wing chair near the fire and looked up at his guest. "When's his settlement? Soon?"

"This summer."

Lowell shook his head sympathetically "Too bad. He'll be

hard to replace. Why don't you try making him a good offer. He may take it."

"No, not Tom," Hendley said, discouraged.

"Then there's only one other way." Lovell leaned forward and lowered his voice. "Catch him doing something illegal and haul him to court. At least you'll get a couple of years more from him that way."

Hendley turned from the fire and peered down at him, brow wrinkled. "But he doesn't do anything illegal," he muttered, considering the matter.

"They all do, I warrant you. Keep a close watch. You're bound to discover something." He got up and clapped Hendley on the shoulder. "Just keep your eyes open, man. Keep your eyes open."

The two men walked slowly to the door. "Catch him doing something illegal, eh?" Hendley's eyes suddenly brightened with a gleam of cunning. "Yes, indeed. That's *just* what I'll do."

Nineteen

Catch him doing something illegal, Lovell had counseled. Peter Hendley was impatient to follow the advice, but there were two problems to solve before he could take action. The first was to determine what illegal act Tom Morrison might indulge in. And the second was to catch him at it.

In mid-April all of New York and its surrounding counties were abuzz with the news of New York's very own tea party. Two tea ships, first the *London* and, two days later, the *Nancy,* had arrived in New York, though Governor Tryon wisely prevented them from entering the harbor. A band of "Mohawks," the same sort of false Indians as those in Boston, had sailed out, boarded the *London* and made a tea party of their own. So decisive was the act that the *Nancy* had immediately turned about and made for England. When Peter Hendley heard of the affair, he wished he could accuse his bondsman of taking part, for that would surely be considered a punishable act of sedition, but in truth Tom had not even heard about the tea party until Hendley himself told him the news.

By that time Hendley had been watching Tom for four days but could find no fault with him. Tom's only questionable act was his making off for the tavern of an evening, but it could hardly be considered an illegal act, since Hendley had given Tom tacit permission by not forbidding it all these years. However, Hendley had no idea what the fellow did there. Perhaps that was the answer. Perhaps he should find out just what went on at that deuced tavern . . .

The very next time Tom took off for Peach's tavern, Hendley followed him. He stayed well back in the shadows all during the long walk from the farm. By the time they reached the tavern, it was almost nine, and dark.

Tom, having not the slightest suspicion of being followed, went immediately to a small, private room behind the taproom where his friends regularly met. He greeted them with his usual cheer. His best friend, Nate Cluett, was already sitting at a long trestle table (which, with the two benches on either side of it, was the room's only furnishing) reading the New York newspapers by the light of two smoky oil lamps. Looking over his shoulder were the innkeeper, Samuel Peach, and three other tavern regulars, Jotham Dillard, Daniel Styles and Charley McNab, the husband of Beatie, the Hendleys' Scottish housemaid. Something in the newspaper had so captured their interest that they took no notice of the tankards of ale at their elbows. And they certainly took no notice of the man who was spying on them from outside the mullioned, many-paned window at their rear.

"Ah, there you are, Tom," Nate greeted. "We've been waiting for you to settle an argument."

"An argument about what?" Tom asked, sliding onto the bench beside his friend.

"About this committee they're goin' to organize in New York. See, the paper says so, right here."

Tom took the newspaper and started to read the item, feeling a glow of pride that he was now able to do so. He'd learned how in two short months of lessons. In two months he'd gone through the child's book that Mistress Patience called the primer, he'd learned to write his name and the whole alphabet, he could read the newspapers (though still slowly and haltingly), and this very day he'd started on a real book. It was called *The Vicar of Wakefield,* and he could hardly wait to get back to it. Reading had changed the world for him.

He'd barely begun to read the item, however, when the door opened and the barmaid came swishing in. Freda, who'd been fighting off the attentions of the patrons of Peach's Tavern for six years, was confident of her charms. Every swing of her hips, every toss of her long, unkempt hair, every shrug of her almost-bare shoulders revealed her contempt for the men who so consistently leered at her. But her feelings for Tom were different. For Tom she had a special affection that she took no pains to hide. Her face brightened at the sight of him. "There you are at last," she exclaimed, coming up behind him and winding her arms round his neck. "I was afraid you weren't coming."

He did not look up from the paper as he pried himself loose from her arms. "Do this a bit later, eh, Freda? I'm trying to read."

"Well, la-di-da! Someone's become very bookish all of a sudden." She ruffled his hair fondly. "Ain't you thirsty for a pint?"

"Aye, that I am." He threw her a grin. "Hurry up with it, will you, lass?" he begged, patting her rump as she moved off.

By the time she returned with the tankard, he'd finished reading. "Is this what you're all arguing over?" he asked, looking up at Nate. "That they're going to organize a committee of fifty, in disregard of the governor's council, to meet in May? What's in this to argue about?"

"Committees, committees," Freda said, putting the tankard down in front of him. "It's all you ever speak of."

"If the subject bores you," the innkeeper said to her pointedly, "you can take yourself off. I suspect that there's plenty to busy you in the taproom."

Freda tossed her head scornfully. "I took care of the washin' up," she said. "There ain't much more to do." Nonetheless she picked up the empty tankards from the table and flounced out.

When she'd closed the door behind her, Samuel shook his head in disgust. *"Idlers never lack for excuses,"* he muttered and then added for good measure, *"Idle hands do the devil's business."*

"Aye, Sam'l, we know," Charley the Scotsman said indulgently, "but let's return to the subject at hand, if you please." He turned to Tom. "The argument is about who'll be elected to the committee," he explained. "Jotham says—"

Jotham slapped his hand down on the table angrily. "Jotham can speak for hisself," he snapped. "And I say they'll fill that committee with Tories." He was decidedly annoyed, having been defending his unpopular opinion since early evening. The more the others had argued against him, the more he'd become entrenched in his point of view.

"The rest of us say it'll be full of rebels, like the one in Boston," Daniel said in his high voice, always startling when coming from a man with a barrel chest that measured forty-four inches around. "What do you think, Tom?"

"Aye, Tom," Samuel seconded. "We want to know what you think."

"What Tom thinks, what Tom thinks," Jotham muttered in disgust, taking a swig of ale from his tankard. "Does nobody here hold an opinion till he hears what Tom thinks?"

"Hey, are you saying we ain't got minds of our own?" Daniel demanded, leaning across the table and pulling Jotham to his feet by his neckband.

Jotham, a good six inches taller than Daniel, was not intimidated. "Aye, that's what I'm sayin'." He pushed Daniel off without spilling a drop of his drink. "Want to make somethin' of it?"

"Aye, I want to make something of it!" Daniel retorted, bringing his face nose to nose with Jotham's.

"Come now, boys," Nate said placatingly, "no need to get belligerent."

"Aye, Joth," Samuel put in. *"A short temper makes long trouble,* as they say."

"Another sayin' from that collection of homilies you learned at yer mother's knee?" retorted Jotham witheringly. The loud laugh that followed his gibe soothed his temper somewhat, and he sat down with a shrug. "But I suppose I won't have any peace till Tom has his say. Go on, Tom. Speak up."

"I thank you for your permission," Tom said drily, raising his tankard to Jotham in salute. "If you truly want to know what I think, gentlemen, it's that New York is a far cry from Boston. New York has more Loyalists per acre than any other place on the Continent. If you ask me, Jotham has the right of it."

Jotham whooped. "Aha! Did ye hear that?" he chortled, pounding the table in delight. "I have the right of it! Tom said it hisself! If I told ye once I told ye a hundred times—Tom Morrison's a lad with a head on his shoulders!"

This brought another round of laughter from everyone at the table, but when it died down, Tom pointed out that his view was nothing to feel merry about. "If the committee *is* Loyalist, as I predict, it means that any sort of active rebellion is bound to be put off."

The others nodded glumly. "For how long, do you think?" Nate asked.

Tom shrugged. "Until they feel the pain in their purses. We'll see a goodly lot of turncoats then."

A silence fell over all of them, and they reached for their tankards, their faces sober.

But the man outside the window was smiling in triumph. Peter Hendley had been listening to every word, and there was no question in his mind that his indentured man had been speaking sedition. It was sedition if he'd ever heard it.

Later, when the friends had drunk and argued their fill and said their good-nights, Tom found Freda waiting for him. She drew him to the inn's back stairway and leaped up into his arms. "I ain't seen you all week," she whispered in his ear, tickling it with her tongue. "My insides are starvin' for you."

"I've been hungering a bit myself," he laughed. He lifted her more securely against his chest and carried her up the stairs to the little dormered room she called home. On the way up, she kissed his cheek and neck, fondling him with one hand while undoing the laces of her bodice with the other. By the time they crossed the threshold, she was naked to the waist, her girdle dangling from her fingers and her bodice lying somewhere behind them on the stairs.

Freda's room was not much larger than his own, but it contained a real featherbed, which, to Tom, was a voluptuous addition to the luxury of lovemaking. He fell upon it at once, with the girl still in his arms. She immediately began to undo his breeches, while he struggled with her skirt and petticoats. In another moment he was upon her, her legs raised tight round his waist, and he was penetrating her, listening to her little animal squeals that he knew would soon become loud gasps of arousal.

But he was not to hear those gasps. At that moment the door banged open, and, as the pair on the bed pulled apart in alarm, a cold voice ordered, "Get up, you pawn of Satan, and pull up your breeks!"

The light of a single candle flickered in from the doorway. Freda screamed. Tom blinked into the light, his heart pounding. He could make out three figures—two standing in front of the light and therefore indistinguishable, and the third holding the candle and plainly identifiable. But he almost doubted his own eyes. *"Samuel?"* he asked in disbelief. "Is that *you?"*

"I'm truly sorry, Tom," the innkeeper mumbled miserably. "He made me—"

"Never mind these questions," the shadowed figure barked. "Tom Morrison, on your feet!"

Tom recognized the voice. "Mr. *Hendley!* What in hell *is* this?"

"Cease your damned blaspheming! Get up, I say!"

Tom's eyes were becoming accustomed to the light. One of the shadowy forms did indeed belong to Mr. Hendley, and—again Tom could scarcely believe his eyes—the man was actually brandishing a pistol. It was an enormous old dueling pistol, and it somehow made the whole scene ludicrous to Tom. "Good God, sir," he said, more amused than frightened, but holding up his hands nevertheless, "you surely don't intend to *shoot* me, do you?"

The touch of amusement in his voice did nothing to soften Hendley's resolve. "I intend to bring you before the magistrates in the morning, you godless miscreant, but if you don't follow my orders, I *will* shoot. I have the sheriff here beside me, so you needn't doubt that it would be legal."

"That's right, boy," the sheriff said, his voice not unkind. "Up, now, and dress yourself. You're under arrest."

Twenty

The sheriff tied Tom's hands behind his back before giving him over to the custody of Mr. Hendley. Then Hendley marched him home. While they walked, Tom tried to reason with him, asking what he'd done to bring this about. "You've never before objected to my going to the tavern after work," he pointed out. "I've been doing it for *years!*"

"That admission will make it all the worse for you," was all the answer Hendley made.

By the time Tom, still trussed, was thrown onto his cot and left alone, he understood what was going on. *It's the settlement,* he realized with a sinking heart. *He doesn't want to give me my settlement and let me go!*

The realization made him sick. He'd tried to prepare himself for just this sort of disappointment, but all his preparation failed him. The reality of his predicament fell upon him like an avalanche of stones, and he was crushed.

By morning an overwhelming lassitude had taken over his body and killed his spirit. He felt nothing but a terrible hopelessness. If anyone had asked him how he'd arrived at court that morning, he could not have answered. Nor could he have described the place in which his hearing was held, for in the twenty minutes of the hearing's duration, he sat impassively in his place, unseeing, unhearing, unfeeling and unmanned.

Since the case was too insignificant to be brought before the Court of General Sessions, which met in Westchester only twice a year, the matter fell under the jurisdiction of the local justice of the peace, who was empowered to try minor cases without benefit of a jury. The justice in question was a cold, very British gentleman named Hugh Forster, who reveled in the title Squire. Squire Forster had been appointed to the post by a member of the powerful New York De Lancy clan, to whom he was related. Never having studied law, he masked this substantial inadequacy by observing to the letter all the superficial rites and customs practiced by the magistrates of Britain to give dignity to the office. He held court whenever he deemed a session was warranted in a large room at the rear of the first floor of his Fordham residence, where he presided with great formality in red robe and wig, taking enormous pleasure in acting as both judge and jury.

The bailiff read the charges aloud. Peter Hendley's complaint against his indentured servant fell under the rubric of contempt of authority, in three separate counts: absence from his master's property without permission; making seditious remarks against the authority of the government; and engaging in fornication outside the sanctity of wedlock in direct opposition to the laws of God and the rules of his servitude. To all these accusations, Mr. Hendley told Justice Forster, there were reliable witnesses: to the charges of absence and sedition, there was Samuel Peach, the innkeeper of the Peach's Tavern; and to the charge of fornication, there was the sheriff himself.

Samuel Peach, who'd seated himself in a dim corner of the large room in the hope that no one would notice him, turned white at the sound of his name and threw an agonized look across the room at his friend, the accused. But Tom did not return the glance. He remained impassive. Samuel's presence as witness against him failed to shake him from his lethargy.

The justice, seated behind a baize-draped table on a raised platform, required the witness Samuel Peach to stand and be sworn. Then, without permitting the witness to sit, he commenced the questioning. "Was the accused present in your tavern last evening?"

Poor Samuel nodded tearfully.

"A nod is not sufficient, Mr. Peach," the Justice said nastily. "A yes or a no is needed."

"Yes, Your Honor."

The squire sighed. "Is that a yes to my explanation or a yes to the question?"

Samuel shifted his weight nervously. "To both, I suppose, Your Honor."

"Good. Then we can proceed. Did the accused visit your tavern often?"

"Once in a while, yes."

Squire Forster's expression began to show disgust. "What do you consider 'once in a while'—once a month? Twice a week?"

"More like twice a week," poor Samuel mumbled.

"Yes, I thought so," the Squire said with some satisfaction. "And on those semiweekly occasions, did the accused say that he had permission from Mr. Hendley to be there?"

The Justice's sarcastic tone riled Samuel. "He didn't have to say," he said with sudden spirit. "He's been coming to the tavern for *years* without no objection from Mr. Hendley."

"Isn't it possible that Mr. Hendley had never given permission and didn't know the accused was not in his own bed?"

"No, I don't think it's possible," Samuel maintained firmly. "Tom never acted secret about it."

"But Mr. Hendley says he didn't know. Are you calling Mr. Hendley a liar?"

Samuel, taken aback, blinked. Then his eyes slid from the judge to the accused and back again. "No, Your Honor," he mumbled miserably.

"That, at last, is a satisfactory answer." Justice Forster looked down at the papers before him. "Let's go on to the second charge. Did you ever hear the accused express opinions of a seditious nature?"

"No, Your Honor. At least, I don't think so, not knowing what the word means."

The justice glared at him. "What word?"

The bailiff leaned over to the squire and whispered in his ear, "I think he means seditious."

Squire Forster put a weary hand to his forehead. "Let me try to make the question simpler," he said with barely disguised impatience. "Did you ever hear the accused express, for example, the wish for a New York Committee of Correspondence to be made up of rebels?"

Samuel hesitated. "I don't think so."

"That's no answer," the Justice snapped. "Either you heard or you didn't!"

"It's said, Your Honor, that a *man should hear twice before he speaks once.*"

Peter Hendley jumped to his feet in irritation. "Damnation, Peach, forget your deuced proverbs! I heard him and you heard him."

"You are out of order, Mr. Hendley," the Justice barked, banging his gavel. "Sit down!"

"Sorry, Squire," Hendley muttered, sitting.

"Well, Mr. Peach?" Squire Forster turned to the witness with a glare. "Did you or did you not hear the accused speak those seditious words?"

"No, Your Honor, not exactly."

The Squire's patience was rapidly evaporating. He glowered forbiddingly and raised his voice. "Are you saying that you *never* heard the accused speak sedition?"

"I'm saying, Your Honor, that *for bad words, deaf ears.*"

"Yes, or no, Mr. Peach," the squire snarled, "yes or no."

"Well, then . . ." Samuel faced the questioner courageously. "Then I say no, I never did."

"What?" The Justice threw up his hands in exasperation. "You featherwit, if you never did, then your answer should have been yes!"

The trembling publican looked up at him in bewilderment. "I should've said yes?"

"I asked if you're saying that you never heard him speak sedition. If you never did, you must answer, 'Yes, I never heard him speak sedition.' "

"Well, your honor," Samuel mumbled, backing down, "I . . . er . . . I wouldn't say that neither."

His honor groaned. "Then what *would* you say, dammit! No, don't answer that. I don't want to hear another of your blasted adages. Let me give you a question that will get us to the essence. To your knowledge, does the accused harbor rebellious feelings toward the Crown? Yes or no."

Samuel pondered the question for a moment before lifting his head bravely. "No, Your Honor," he said with utmost sincerity, "no more 'n anyone else I know."

For Squire Forster, that answer was the last straw. "I will interpret that answer to be as much an indictment of your acquaintances as of the accused," he shouted. "Get out of my sight, man! You're excused."

The interrogation of the sheriff on the charge of fornication went more smoothly. As soon as it was established that the sheriff had actually seen the accused with his own eyes, unclothed in the bed of the unnamed barmaid of the inn, that was enough evidence for the justice. And after the accused refused to say anything in his own defense, the squire promptly found for the plaintiff on all counts, settling the matter by levying a penalty of one year and twenty-five pounds for each offense, thus adding three years to Thomas Morrison's indenture and reducing his settlement sum to a mere twenty-five pounds.

The severity of the penalty surprised the few onlookers. Even Hendley hadn't expected quite so harsh a judgment. As he and Tom rode back to the farm side by side on the buckboard, Hendley threw the servant a number of surreptitious, guilty glances. After several minutes of silence, he said, "It will pass, Tom. Three years will pass. And I'll reward you for your good work, just as I promised before. I shall not let you go to settlement impoverished. I'll pay you all the freedom dues you deserve."

But Tom did not answer. He didn't even look at his master. He'd already made up his mind that he would flee.

Later that night, tossing on his bed in an agony of frustration, the icy numbness that had frozen his feelings began to melt. He, who had not shed a tear since boyhood, found himself weeping for the dreams that had been so close to being fulfilled. He hated the farm now. He hated Hendley for the trick he'd played. He hated the prospect of three additional years of servitude. He hated his work, and his life, and himself. He hated this room, this house, and everyone he knew. He hated Samuel, who'd done him in, and Freda who'd tempted him, and even Nate, merely because he was free. There was only one person he didn't hate. Patience. Patience, who every day was teaching him to read.

He sat up and wiped his eyes, letting the image of her face drive the rest of the day's images from the forefront of his mind. He dwelt on every detail of the vision—her hair that shone a rich gold in the sunlight, her eyebrows that turned up just a bit at the outer ends, her lashes that seemed so dark when they brushed against her cheeks, the full lower lip that made her seem stubborn or angry until she smiled, the strong yet softly-rounded chin, the line of her neck that curved with such grace into her sloping shoulder, the other curves of breast and hip and thigh . . .

He shut his eyes and let himself wallow in the vision of her. Maybe he would stay around a little longer and let her finish her teaching. The torment of his slavery could be borne if he could still see her each day. He could always get away afterward, when the teaching ended. He expelled a long, weary breath. Yes, he would remain here in this prison yet awhile.

Twenty-one

In a town where people knew each other's lives intimately, surprisingly few heard about Tom's misfortune. Samuel was too ashamed of his part to speak of it. Tom himself confided the details to no one but Nate, who knew how to hold his tongue. Hendley, whose instincts told him that his family would not approve of what he'd done, kept silent on the matter. Thus Patience learned nothing of what had happened.

In happy ignorance of her pupil's pain, Patience continued with the reading lessons. The teaching hour had become the time of day she most enjoyed, especially now, when waiting for the delivery of a certain bolt of pillow ticking made every moment of the day rife with almost unbearable suspense. At least for the brief duration of the lesson, she could banish the writ of manumission from her mind.

The day after the hearing that Patience knew nothing of, she stood in the barn loft listening to Tom read aloud, as she always did. But today she was aware that something was different about him. The hayloft was usually a pleasant hideaway, the arc of red sunlight that managed to shine in through the broken slat in the barn wall giving just the perfect light for reading while bestowing a residue of glow to the air around them. It had been an hour of the day in which they'd both found peace and pleasure. But today Patience noticed that Tom felt neither peaceful nor content. His brows were knit, his eyes bloodshot, his manner surly. She won-

dered if she'd done something to anger him, but she felt it unseemly to ask.

Tom sat on the little stool, reading aloud. Standing behind
him—hearing the confidence in his voice as he carefully enun-
ciated each word—Patience was filled with pride. He'd learned
so *quickly.*

She'd been afraid, at first, that a man who hadn't learned to
read by the age of twenty-one (or whatever the fellow's real age
was) would have too hard a time of it. But now, after two months
of schooling, Tom was reading remarkably well. She stared at
his bent head as he sat huddled over the book she'd stolen from
her father's meager collection, his arms surrounding it protec-
tively. It was an old, leather-bound volume, *The Complete Poeti-
cal Works of John Dryden.* Patience, when she'd surreptitiously
removed it from her father's bookshelf, had feared it would prove
too difficult for her pupil. But Tom had again surprised her with
his quick mastery, as he'd done consistently since learning to
decipher the letters. As soon as he'd conquered the primer, he'd
moved quickly. He'd scorned the childish tales she'd brought him
next, but the novel *The Vicar of Wakefield* immediately captured
him. He now carried the book about with him hidden in his vest,
reading it by himself at every spare moment. And she was certain
he was regularly reading newspapers in the tavern. She'd even
seen him smuggling pamphlets—revolutionary ones, no doubt—
into his room. Well, he'd warned her he would. It was part of
their bargain.

She suspected that he probably knew enough by this time to
continue his education without her, but, strangely, neither one of
them had ever said a word about discontinuing the lessons.

She looked down at him, her eyes warm with admiration for
the sureness of his reading. The shaft of light haloed his dark
hair—thick wavy hair, appealingly unkempt. She had a sudden,
inexplicable urge to touch where it curled over the collar of his
homespun shirt. The urge was an itch in her fingers. She had to
tighten them into fists to keep from surrendering to it. She

couldn't permit herself to touch him, for if she did, she feared that something dreadful would happen. What that dreadful thing would be, she didn't permit herself to guess.

If Tom didn't arouse these improper feelings in her, she would have felt less guilty about this entire enterprise, less ashamed, less fearful of discovery. What *could* she say in her own defense if her father caught her? *Kindness. Charity. Those were my motives, Papa.* But perhaps it would be best not to dwell on her motives. She wasn't at all sure, herself, what they were.

She turned her attention to his reading, suddenly caught by a change in the tone of his voice. She recognized the tone. It was an intensity of voice, a throatiness, that indicated he'd been impressed by some new idea. That was what she was proudest of in his education—his fascination with the *meaning* behind the words he was reading. She bent over him to see what it was that had stirred his mind.

Tom's finger pointed out the passage for her:

Happy the man, and happy he alone,
He who can call today his own;
He who, secure within, can say,
Tomorrow, do thy worst, for I have lived today.

As she read it, he watched her intently. Then he looked back at the book and asked quietly, "What does it mean, to call today your own?"

"I'm not sure. It's a good question. The words are simple enough, but the meaning isn't. Think you it means that a man, to be happy, must appreciate the present moment?"

"No." He shook his head, unsatisfied, and stared at the page. "I think you can appreciate something without owning it. To *own* the day must mean something more. A man must've had . . . must've had some sort of *triumph* to feel he owns the day."

"Yes, you may be right. It's very perceptive of you, Tom. But do go on."

As if he didn't hear, he continued to stare at the page, silent.

"Is something the matter?" she asked.

He pushed back the stool. "To call today your own," he said in a voice that was strangely husky, "must be a rare good feeling."

"I suppose it must be. I hadn't thought about it."

He turned away. The gap in the wall was just at the level of his eyes, and he gazed out where, far below, he could see glints of the Hudson flowing quietly by, not quite obscured by the afternoon haze. *"Tomorrow do thy worst, for I have lived today,"* he muttered.

"Something *is* the matter," she insisted, sensing a deep trouble in him.

"No, ma'am, nothing. The words just saddened me somewhat."

She looked down at the book again. The words were illuminated brilliantly in the reddening sunlight. "Saddened you? I don't see why, Tom. 'Tis not a sad poem."

His voice was low. "It is to me."

Twenty-two

Another day went by without the delivery of the bolt of pillow ticking. It was now more than a week since Patience had talked to Stuart about the writ. She lived in terror that something had gone wrong. As she watched Sally go about her work in a silent daze, her heart clenched. Every moment of the day was an agony of suspense for both of them.

The following morning dawned sunny and too warm for April. By ten, Patience, bending over the work table in the sewing room sorting goosefeathers for pillows, was sorry she'd begun this task; it was too hot a day for feathers. She loosened her collar and dabbed at her neck with her handkerchief. Summer weather in spring. It wasn't good for people or plants. They'd all flag by afternoon.

"Mistress Patience?"

Someone was calling her name from the front room. She jumped up, her blood freezing in her veins. Perhaps the ticking had come at last!

Forcing herself to stay calm, she brushed a few of the sticky little feathers from her dress and walked across the hall with as little hurry in her step as she could endure. If it was the ticking, she must not appear unduly eager to receive it.

But it was not the ticking. Hovering in the open doorway stood Tom, with Chester right behind him. Both of them fidgeted worriedly.

She knew at once, by the look of them, that something was

wrong. "What's amiss?" she asked, tense with disappointment and fear.

"It's not serious," Tom said, his voice strangely tentative. "A slight accident."

"Accident?"

"It's Benjy."

Patience stared at the bondsman blankly for a moment, trying to collect her wits. Then she winced in understanding. "Oh, my Lord! He's hurt!" She took a hurried step toward the door. "Where is he?"

"Right outside here, ma'am," Chester said.

Tom stopped her from dashing out by taking hold of her shoulders. "Now, don't fall into a taking," he said quietly. "It looks a lot worse than—"

But Patience, looking past him, gasped. Chester was leading the boy in. Benjy's step was unsteady, his expression dazed, and one side of his shirt gory with blood. Tom, fearing Benjy might faint, dropped his hold on Patience and ran to the boy. Scooping him up in his arms, he carried Benjy to the sofa and laid him down. Patience bent over him, her pulse pounding in fear. Benjy looked up at his sister's pale face and tried to grin. "It's just a small wound. Don't tell Papa."

Patience, white-lipped, knelt beside him and unbuttoned his shirt. She located the source of the bleeding just below his right shoulder. Someone had tried to stanch the wound with a folded cloth that was now completely blood-soaked. She removed it gingerly and, with shaking fingers, wiped the blood away and took a look. It was only a flesh wound, she saw at once, but it was deep enough to make her shudder. "Get Sally," she said over her shoulder to Chester. "Tell her to bring a basin of water and some toweling."

Chester nodded and ran from the room.

"I'll get the spirits." Tom strode across the room to the cabinet where Peter Hendley stored his rum and brandies.

"What need have we for spirits?" Patience asked, trying to

stanch the still-bleeding cut by dabbing at it with her handkerchief.

"Applied on the outside, liquor keeps the wound from infection," Tom answered, pouring two fingers of rum into a glass, "and applied on the inside, it brings the boy back to his full senses. The sight of the blood made him a little squiffy."

Patience passed the back of her hand over her forehead. "It's made me a little squiffy, too."

"Then you sip first." Tom knelt beside her and held the glass to her lips. She sipped and choked, but the liquor did make her feel more able to cope. Meanwhile, Tom took the handkerchief from her, folded it to the thickness of a pad, soaked it with the spirits and pressed it firmly against the wound. Benjy cried out from the burn of the liquor. Tom handed him the glass, which still contained a finger of rum. "Drink it down, boy. It'll help."

Patience sat back on her heels and breathed a sigh of relief, silently thanking God that the wound was but a superficial one. "How did this happen?" she asked her brother.

Benjy, revived by the drink, sat up and cast Tom a nervous glance. "Well, y'see, I was drilling, and—"

Patience stiffened. *"Drilling?"*

Benjy's mouth turned sullen. "I told you, Patience, I *have* to," he muttered defensively. "All the fellows drill."

"Since when is that an excuse?" Patience's relief was rapidly turning to anger. "How dared you go drilling when Papa expressly ordered you not to have any part of that foolishness? And you, Tom! How dared you encourage him?"

"Here, press this tight," Tom said to Benjy, taking the boy's hand and pressing it on the pad in place of his own. Then he stood up and looked down at Patience. "He's right, you know. All the fellows drill."

"And you see what comes of it!"

Tom shrugged. "Nothing so terrible came of it. The truth is, ma'am, that he was only pricked with a bayonet."

"*Only* a bayonet? Do you permit *boys* to drill with *bayonets?* Are you daft?"

"The drills are not dangerous, ma'am. This was just a small accident—"

Benjy sank back against the sofa pillows. "You don't have to cover for me, Tom. It was all my own stupid fault." He threw his sister a sheepish grin. "I feel such a fool. I tripped over my big feet when we were doing a face-about, and I pricked myself with my own bayonet."

" 'Tis an insignificant wound, Miss Patience," Tom said with kindly calm. "He'll be good as new in a week if we keep it free of infection."

Patience, already on edge from the tension of the past week, was overly shaken by this accident, and she lost her temper. "I don't need any advice from you, Tom Morrison!" she snapped. "I blame you for this whole thing!"

Benjy blinked up at her in surprise. "Damn it, Patience, what are you ripping up at *him* for?"

"Be quiet, you idiot! Don't think I won't rip up at you, too!"

But before she could fully vent her spleen, Sally came running in, with Chester at her heels carrying the basin and cloths. Sally shoved everyone aside, knelt down beside the invalid and took a look at the wound for herself. Then, with a relieved sigh, she looked up at Patience. "Seem like he'll live," she said with a little twist of a smile. "Now yo' all step aside an' le' me get him bandaged proper."

"Can't we do it upstairs, Sally?" the boy begged. "Babs may come in, and even Papa. I don't want anyone else to know about this."

Sally nodded. "You, Chester, take the basin an' these other things. Tom, le's you an' me help Benjy up to his room."

Benjy got shakily to his feet. "Leave me be. I can walk without any damn help."

"I don't see why you must add blaspheming to the rest of your crimes," his sister said, following Chester, Sally and the wounded boy to the stairs. "You, Tom, wait right here," she flung over her shoulder. "I haven't finished with you."

Tom didn't answer.

Patience climbed three steps before becoming aware of his silence. She turned about sharply. "Did you hear me, Tom?"

Tom's eyes blazed in fury. "Yes, Mistress Patience, ma'am," he said between clenched teeth, "I heard you very well."

It was half an hour before she returned. Tom spent the time prowling the floor, cursing under his breath. *Oh, yes, your lady-ship, I heard you very well indeed,* he muttered savagely. *Talking to me as if I was scum on the edge of a pond. Is it my fault your brother is a clumsy fool? I work for your damned father from sunup to sundown, pruning his orchards, plowing his fields, cur-rying his horses, keeping his cattle, striking his bargains, and who knows what else . . . and all for naught! For him to trick me out of what is mine! I should've run off after that farce of a trial. I only stayed in the hope of a kind word from you. What a fool I am! I should have run off years ago. I'd be a man of substance by now. I only stayed because I . . . because you . . . oh, never mind! I'm the biggest sort of fool. And you . . . sometimes I think you're a bigger one. Yes, I know, you give me lessons. But you don't see me. You never even look.*

When she returned, he was standing at the window, staring out as if something important was happening out there. But from the way his fingers clenched and unclenched, she could tell he was not seeing the noon sun on the greening maples outside the window; he was only trying to get hold of his temper. "Tom," she said, her voice low and restrained, but with an edge, "turn around, please. I wish to speak to you."

He neither moved nor answered.

"Very well, I can speak to your back, if you prefer it." She sat down on the sofa, determined to be firm. She turned away from the sight of his angry back and folded her hands in her lap. "You've been a good and useful man on this farm, Tom, and for that reason I didn't want to stir up trouble for you with Papa, so

I closed my eyes to your various activities with that farcical militia and the other rebel groups with whom you choose to waste your time. But today's . . . episode, I'll call it . . . has made it plain that I must act. I've no wish . . . that is, I don't purpose to report this matter to my father . . ." She glanced at him uneasily, but he gave no perceptible reaction. "I see I've won your undying gratitude for that," she added dryly.

There was still no reaction.

Patience sighed and went on. "I won't speak to Papa about what happened," she went on, "but in return you must promise me to give up all such activities completely. There must be no drills and no meetings. I want your word on it."

"No," he said, not turning.

"What?" It was she who turned. She stared at him, astonished.

"No."

She couldn't believe her ears. "What are you saying?"

He wheeled around. "I'm saying no. You will *not* have my word. I shall go to meetings if I wish and to drill if I wish."

Patience rose magisterially from the sofa. "How dare you speak to me that way! We hold your indenture, remember? In this household you are but a . . . a . . ."

"Say it," Tom sneered. "A slave."

Her eyes fell. "I was going to say servant."

"A man who earns wages can be called a servant. I am a slave."

"Is *that* what's been eating at you of late? Wages? Money?"

"It's easy to sneer at money when you have it," he retorted.

Patience shook her head impatiently. "What need have you for wages? You eat the same food I do. That shirt you wear I sewed for you myself. And with the very same linen I used for my own petti—" She caught herself in time. "—garments," she concluded lamely.

He smiled wryly. "I'd rather have wages and purchase my own shirts. Even if the linen were not the same as you use for your petti-garments."

She felt outwitted . . . helpless. "It's nothing but male pride," she muttered, sinking down on the sofa. "But I'll not bandy words with you. You know you'll have the equivalent of wages when you get your freedom dues."

"*If* I get my freedom dues," he muttered, unable to resist, although, deep within himself, he was glad she knew nothing about his humiliation in court and the romp on the featherbed that had brought him there.

"What do you mean?" she demanded, puzzled.

"Never mind. It's of no importance. Freedom dues will make no difference now."

"Why not? I don't understand."

"I'd not give up my meetings and drillings in any case."

She jumped to her feet in exasperation. "Tom, you fool, you're selling your future for a wild and doomed adventure."

"That may be."

"Why won't you understand? This is a wonderful country in so many ways. In a few months you'll have your freedom and enough money to buy some land. A man could . . . could make something of himself."

He grimaced bitterly. "Make *what* of himself?"

"Why . . . why, he could make himself a prosperous man . . . a useful man . . ."

"An equal?"

She blinked up at him in bewilderment. "An equal to whom?"

"To you."

"I . . . I don't know what you mean," she stammered, taken aback.

"Yes, you do."

His piercing look and his words discomfited her. They were too true, too blunt for her to know how to deal with them. Ruffled, she turned away. But he, embarked on this heady path, couldn't stop himself. He grasped her shoulder and pulled her round to him. "Well?" he demanded. "Answer me!"

"You forget yourself, Tom. Let me go."

"You mean I forget my *place*." He took his hand from her and walked away in disgust. "No matter how many acres I might someday buy, you'd still keep me in my place."

She lifted her chin proudly. "No man may maul me about, whatever his station."

"That's not true," Tom said bitterly. "It was acceptable for Orgill to maul you that night in the orchard, before you even knew him a week. Oh, yes, I remember it! My lord Orgill was not out of *his* place, was he? A peacocky lecher with an embroidered waistcoat, rosettes on his shoes, and a haw-hawing laugh to cover his venom. But he had his father's title and thousands of pounds a year, so he was an acceptable equal. Equal enough even to *wed* you!"

The color drained from her cheeks. "That is none of your business! And, ancient history that it is, what does it say to our purpose, pray?"

"It says much to our purpose! England is full of his like. And the king sends them here to rule me and those like me! And we must obey their stupid and selfish laws and bow down to them and call them our betters!"

"So that's what your precious rebellion stems from!" Patience retorted. "Petty jealousy!"

"Jealousy!" He slapped his forehead in frustration. "Oh, but I'm a jackass to try to discuss politics with a woman!"

"Well, listen to *you,* Tom Morrison!" she said in offended dignity. "How independent and clever you've grown in such a short time. It seems only yesterday that this ignorant woman, with whom you cannot discuss politics, sat you down and taught you to write your own name!"

That stopped him in his tracks. "That's the truth, at least," he said ruefully. "Don't think I'm not beholden to you for it."

"I want no thanks. I only want you to be sensible. If you keep up this seditious talk, the day will come when you find yourself—along with your Sam Adamses and your Alexander Mac-Dougalls and the rest of your rabble-rousers—rotting in an English gaol. Or hanging from a yardarm."

"I'd rather be hanged with them than live like this," he declared, adding nastily, "At least my rabble-rousers know better than to believe a *title* makes a *man.*"

"That's enough, dammit!"

The blasphemy shocked them both into silence. She clapped her hand to her mouth. The shrill curse echoed round the room, its reverberations hanging in the air like a reproof from God himself.

Patience had to pace the floor twice to get hold of herself. "This is a loyal household, Tom," she said at last. "There will be no person here who speaks sedition against England or the king."

"Good, then, I'll go," he retorted promptly. "And let the king do the spring plowing."

"It won't solve our problem if you waste time making idle threats."

He took a deep breath. "It's not an idle threat, ma'am," he said, suddenly aware that he'd truly come to a decision. "I *am* going. Today."

"Tom!" Her eyes widened in sudden fright. "You can't mean it."

"Yes, I do."

"You can't," she cried, her throat tight with panic. "The law forbids!"

"British law!" he said scornfully, striding to the door.

"Tom, *no!*"

He paused in the doorway and looked back at her. The frightened look in her eyes drained his anger from him. "I can't stay, ma'am," he said gently. "It was bound to happen, soon or late. I'm sorry."

"Tom, please, don't act the fool!"

"I want you to know, ma'am, that I'll always be grateful to you. Every time I read a word."

She took a step toward him. "Don't do it, Tom! Not with your freedom so close!"

He drank her in with his eyes one more time. "I shan't forget you, Patience Hendley. Not ever."

A cry of anguish welled up in her throat, but she choked it back. Her pride would not let it out. Besides, there was no use to cry out. He was already gone.

Twenty-three

Tom believed, after his recapture, that the fault was not in his escape plan but in Mistress Patience's treachery. There had been nothing wrong with the escape plan. The strategy was simple and logical, even if his emotions were in turmoil when he concocted it. He intended to set off by foot to the city, where he could melt into the anonymous crowds on the streets before Hendley would discover he was missing. If he left at nightfall, he would not be missed till morning. That would give him a seven-hour lead. Seven hours would be enough. In seven hours he could reach the docks and might even manage to stow away on a ship bound for Boston.

But he did not get the seven hours. The town sheriff, on horseback, caught up with him in two. He'd barely reached Haerlem Village. Someone had given him away. Patience . . . who else?

He was taken to Justice Forster, where his indenture was lengthened again, and he was given a fine that cost him what remained of his freedom dues. This did not surprise him; he expected to be fined.

But he was also given a public beating, a punishment he did not expect. Only a few of the townspeople watched, and no one cheered or laughed. Nate openly wept.

The beating did not bother Tom very much. He'd had worse. Besides, all the while he was being lashed, he made his mind concentrate on his next escape. He swore that nothing and nobody would hold him now. He'd get away, for good next time.

He'd plan better. He'd head not for the city, but north. He'd follow the river, not the road, and never leave the shelter of the trees. He'd make it the next time. And nobody would know when or where. He'd not tell a soul.

There would be nobody, next time, who could betray him.

Twenty-four

Everyone on the farm spoke in whispers about Tom's failed escape, so of course Patience knew that he'd returned. But she didn't learn of the beating until she overheard Aaron asking his mother for an unguent for Tom's back. After eliciting the details from Aaron, she ran out of the kitchen, hid herself in her bedroom and wept bitterly for Tom, for his pain and humiliation. *Papa shouldn't have punished him,* she sobbed into her pillow. It was painful to realize that her father could be cruel. And it *was* cruel of him to drag poor Tom to face the magistrate. There was no necessity for it. The bondsman had been brought back. Wasn't that punishment enough?

Before her anguish had even begun to subside, she heard Barbara call her name excitedly from outside the front door. It took real effort to stifle her sobs. When she was able to control her breathing, she wiped her eyes and went to the window, just in time to see the Lovell carriage pulling away down the drive. She gasped. The ticking had come!

She ran to the stairs but forced herself to make a calm descent. At the bottom she met Barbara, who was waving an envelope excitedly. "It's come!" the girl exclaimed in breathless delight. "The invitation's come!"

"What invitation?" Patience muttered, her heart sinking in disappointment.

"The invitation to Hannah's ball! It's to be held on the tenth! I don't think I can *bear* to wait so long!"

Patience put a shaking hand to her forehead. "Is *that* what the coachman brought? An invitation? Wasn't there . . . something else?"

"Just a bolt of cloth."

Patience would have liked to throttle the girl. "Where is it?" she managed to ask quietly.

Barbara shrugged indifferently. "I told Beatie to take it." She ran up the stairs with her precious invitation, adding over her shoulder, "She probably took it up to the sewing room."

As soon as Barbara disappeared, Patience whisked herself upstairs to the sewing room. She spied the long package at once. Silently, she closed and bolted the door. Her hands shook as she tore the string and carefully removed the paper wrapping. There lay the striped fabric, but no document was visible. She had to unroll the cloth till almost the very end of the bolt before she found it. She picked up the single, printed sheet and eyed it eagerly. There was no mistake; the words *A Writ of Manumission* were printed in curlicued letters right across the top. Her relief at actually having it in her possession made her clutch it to her breast. *Thank you, God!* she breathed. *Thank you, Stuart Le-Grange.*

She read it over carefully. Stuart LeGrange had been right in assuring her that a writ of manumission was simple to fill out. All Patience had to do was fill in a few blanks. With lies.

Now that she had the form in her possession, there was no time to waste. She swung immediately into action. First she folded the writ and slipped it into the bosom of her dress. Then she went upstairs, took a quill and inkpot from her desk and hid them in her laundry basket under the soiled linen. Finally, picking up the basket, she went quickly from her room, down the stairs and out to the kitchen.

She found two women in the kitchen—Beatie, sitting at the work table dreamily stringing beans, and Sally, sitting on the hearth listlessly stirring a soup. "Sally," Patience said, "I need your help with the laundry. Beatie can keep on eye on the soup."

Sally looked at Patience questioningly. Patience gave a small nod. Sally, eyes suddenly alight, got up from the hearth, wiped her hands on her apron and followed Patience out the door. Beatie, as usual, did not look up. When daydreaming, she never paid any mind to the goings-on around her.

Patience led Sally across the gravel path to the smokehouse. With a quick look around to make sure no one was observing them, she opened the low door and slipped inside, Sally at her heels. Once inside, Patience put down her basket and bolted the door. Then she turned to Sally and grinned. "I have it!" she said, her voice triumphant though she tried to keep it low.

"Oh, Lord!" Sally breathed.

The two women embraced for a long moment, not saying a word. Then Patience pulled the document from her dress. "Your freedom!" she said tremulously.

Sally took the document in her hand. She handled it gingerly, as if it were an ancient artifact that might crumble at her touch. "Jus' a piece o' paper," she whispered, examining it with awe. "Jus' a piece o' paper!"

Later, with both women seated on barrels among the hanging hams, the slabs of bacon and the dried fish, Patience read the writ aloud, explaining those parts that Sally didn't understand. There was, for instance, the phrase decreeing that freedom from servitude be awarded "to the above-named and all heirs and assigns in perpetuity." "It means, Sally, that freedom is guaranteed not only to you but to all your children and your children's children and their children for ever and ever."

Sally asked to hear the words over and over. She wanted to learn the document by heart. By the time she did, tears were flowing down both their faces.

"Now we have to fill in the spaces," Patience said when they'd dried their eyes. "We have to give you and Aaron new names, so Papa can never find you." She bent over the laundry basket and fished out the pen and ink. "What do you want to be called?"

Sally thought for a moment. "Can I be Mary Craig, like yo' Mama?"

"You can be Mary, of course. But the last name must have no connection to us. How about something commonplace, like Jones or Smith?" Then she shook her head. "Though perhaps those are a bit *too* commonplace."

"Baker," Sally said with decision. "Baker, 'cause that's what I's gonna be."

"Good, Sally," Patience approved. "It's inventive. I like it."

Sally proved to be even more inventive in the naming of her son. "Le's call him Dee," she said.

"D-E-E?" Patience asked. "Why?"

"I was thinkin' he should dress up like a girl when we run. They won't be lookin' for a woman with a girl. If anyone stop us to ax what the Dee stan' fo', it can stan' fo' Dee-*bor*-ah. But he can't be Deeborah when we light somewheres fo' keep, so, then, the Dee will be short fo' Andy."

"Yes, I *see*," Patience exclaimed, embracing her in admiration. "You've done some thorough thinking on this, Sally. Dressing Aaron up as a girl is a wonderful idea! I'll get one of Barbara's old dresses for him. He's so slim at the waist, I'm sure 'twill suit."

Patience looked about for a surface on which to write. She chose the top of a pickle barrel, and it was there that she committed her criminal act. She filled in a false date (making Sally's freedom retroactive by a year and two months), she chose the fictitious name Robert Muncey as the party of the first part, and she wrote in the names Mary Baker and her offspring Dee as parties of the second part. And at the bottom she forged three signatures: first for the fictional Mr. Muncey and then for two imaginary witnesses. The whole task took five minutes. But when she finished, her hands were trembling.

When the form was completed, the two women sank to their knees among the preserved foods and prayed. Sally prayed for aid on this most frightening undertaking. Patience prayed for forgiveness. She had done sinful things this day, and before she went to sleep that night she would do worse. She had lied to her family, she had signed false names, she was stealing valuable property from her own father. She was a liar, a forger and a thief. She prayed, but she knew the prayers were tainted. Deep in her heart she could not feel shame. In truth, she'd felt an enormous and strange elation when, a moment after they'd risen to their feet, she handed Sally the writ, with the ink on it scarcely dry, and whispered, "Tonight, Sally. You go tonight, an hour after dark. We'll meet in the stable. Be ready."

Twenty-five

Just before sunset, at the hour when she usually gave Tom his reading lesson, Patience stole out of the house. She knew he would not come to the barn for the lesson, not any more. But she had to see him. She hurried around the kitchen garden, ran down the path to the stable and climbed up to his attic room. In answer to her knock, he opened the door. "Mistress Patience!" he gasped, dumbfounded. In all the years he'd lived there, she'd never come to his door.

"Don't say anything," she whispered nervously. "Just, please, let me in."

He stood aside, and she stepped over the threshold. There she stopped short. The bareness—the sheer poverty—of the room astounded her. It was a narrow, skimpy place, with one uncurtained, dirty window. The only furnishings were a cot with an uncovered mattress, a pillow and a ragged blanket, and, beside it, a small table that had been roughly fashioned from unmatched boards. The table held all his worldly possessions—a pile of books and pamphlets, a pail, and a razor for shaving. A few articles of clothing hung from pegs on the wall. And that was all. "Oh, dear God!" she murmured.

He read her mind. "Yes, it does look shabby," he said dryly. "You must excuse me, ma'am. I'm quite humiliated. Not expecting company, I had the draperies and carpets taken out for cleaning."

She was too upset to take offense at his sarcasm. She turned her face up to him, her eyes wide with pity and shame. "You have no *sheets!*"

"Sheets?" He blinked down at her blankly and then burst into a guffaw. "Sheets! Farmhands don't have sheets, ma'am. I haven't slept on sheets more than a dozen times in my life. But surely, ma'am, you didn't climb up here to talk about sheets."

Her eyes fell. "No, of course not. May I sit down?"

"Certainly, ma'am, if my unsheeted bed will do."

She perched on the edge of it, pulling her skirts close. She felt ashamed of the luxurious look of the printed muslin of her dress against the dingy drabness of his bare mattress. "I've come to ask you a very great favor, Tom," she explained, looking down at her fingers that were nervously twisted in her lap. "It's something very dangerous, and illegal, too, which makes it even more dangerous for you since . . . since you've so recently broken the law. So you are free to refuse me if you're reluctant to chance it. I shall understand."

"Well, out with it, ma'am. I can't accept or refuse until I know what we're speaking of."

"It's Sally and Aaron. I must get them away from here, for Papa threatens to sell the boy. I've given her a paper saying she's free—"

"A writ of manumission?" he asked, astonished.

"Yes." She threw him an admiring glance. "You know of such things?"

He shrugged. "We slaves have a keen interest in the legalities of freedom."

"Yes, of course. I should have realized." She dropped her eyes, disconcerted by his closeness. He seemed to be looming above her, huge and unfriendly, and in this tiny closet of a room she could put no distance between them.

The silence became too lengthy for comfort. "Go on about Sally and Aaron," Tom urged.

"Right. You see, if they could get to New England, where no

one would know them, and the writ could be accepted as genuine, they'd have a chance."

"There are more free Negroes in Boston than anywhere else in the colonies, I'm told," Tom said, leaning back against his table, considering the prospects. "They could make a life in Boston."

"That is what I hope for them. That's why I thought . . . if they could reach New Rochelle tonight . . ."

He shook his head. "New Rochelle is too great a distance by foot to—"

"I hoped you might take them by horse."

"By horse?" His brows lifted in surprise. "I?" He peered at her, his mind rapidly evaluating the possibilities. "Yes, I could do that in three or four hours. It would give them a very good start."

"And in addition, if they had tomorrow—if their absence went undetected tomorrow—they might be able to make it. But for that to happen, you must get yourself and the horse back here before dawn, so that everything will seem ordinary to Papa tomorrow morning."

"I see. They would leave tonight, you say."

"Yes. I told them to meet me in the stable an hour after dark."

He rubbed his chin, thinking. "It would take, at most, four hours to get there, less than three back. It can be done. It's a good plan. No one would guess they started on horseback."

She held her breath. "You'll do it then?"

"Yes, of course I'll do it. With the greatest of pleasure."

She studied his face, half reluctant to accept his generosity. "Have you given this enough thought, Tom? If you're caught, it might put off your own freedom for years. I've heard whisperings that you've already lost . . ." Her voice petered out for a moment as her throat tightened in pity for him and in shame for her father's part in his loss. "And you'd lose some of your freedom dues too, most likely," she added, her eyes lowered.

He laughed mirthlessly. "No need to fret about that, ma'am."

"What do you mean? Of course I need to fret about it. It is your future."

"Well, never mind. It's of no great moment now. We haven't much time. You should go and tell Sally to dress in dark things. No white collars to catch the moonlight. I'll see to Aaron."

"Yes, please, do go to help the boy." Patience gave him a sudden smile. "Though Aaron's appearance may surprise you."

She stood up and took a step toward the door but, overwhelmed with gratitude, could not leave. She turned back and put her hand on his arm. "I'm much obliged to you for this, Tom," she said shyly. "Someday, somehow, I shall make my thanks tangible."

He snatched his arm from her as if her touch were lethal. "No need for that, ma'am," he said in tones of ice. "I'm not doing this for you. To help Sally and Aaron get their freedom is all the reward I need."

His coldness hurt and puzzled her. Something she'd done had angered him, but she feared to ask what it was. She was very much aware that there was already too much intimacy in this room. "Well, whoever you do it for, you have my gratitude," she said, opening the door. "May God be with you tonight."

"Wait!" He reached out and caught her arm. "Before you go, ma'am, tell me one thing. Just one thing." He drew her back into the room and shut the door behind her. "I shall go mad if I don't ask it. How is it that you are so generously clearing the way for Sally and Aaron to escape from this place, yet you blocked the way for me? Am I not as worthy of freedom as they?"

She stared up at him in bewilderment. "What are you talking about?" she asked. "How did I block your way?"

"You needn't play the innocent, ma'am. I know who betrayed me when I ran off."

"Betrayed you? How could I have betrayed you? It's true that I didn't believe you should have run off—after all, your situation and Sally's are quite different, and, besides, your indenture is . . .

was . . . almost at an end—but I did nothing that could be called betrayal."

"That, ma'am, is nothing short of a lie!"

"A lie? *Tom!* How *dare* you—?"

"How would your father have known I was not in my bed that night unless someone informed him?"

She gasped in sudden comprehension. "Are you suggesting that I told Papa? *I?*"

"You were the only one who knew my intentions."

She gaped at him, unable to believe her ears. "Are you saying . . . can you really believe that I betrayed you *then* and am lying to you *now?*"

She was looking up at him, her dark eyes so sincere and artless that he almost believed he'd wronged her. And the fragrance of her . . . the smell of peach blossoms that wafted from her hair . . . set his blood rushing wildly through his veins. But he was not a man to be easily culled. Not even Patience Hendley, eyes and fragrance notwithstanding, could make a fool of him. "That is precisely what I believe," he said tightly.

A tidal wave of fury rose up from deep inside her and choked her throat. When she thought of all she had done for him—the trouble she'd taken to give him lessons, the tears she'd shed over his punishment, the agony she'd suffered over his pain—the injustice of his accusation infuriated her. "You dastard!" she raged, lifting a hand to strike his face. "How *dare* you say such things of me?"

He caught her hand in the air. "Think you that your anger will be more convincing than the facts?" he sneered. His own fury made him brazen, and he twisted her arm behind her, pulling her against him. "Or that a slap across the face can turn a lie into truth?"

Locked in this furious embrace, they glared at each other for a long moment, both breathing heavily. For a heartbeat or two, her anger kept her from feeling anything else, but almost at once she became aware of his closeness, of his arm pressing her breast against his, of his face so near to hers that she could feel his breath on her cheek. Something clenched inside her, a spasm of desire so strong and urgent that it paled all the other feelings this interview had aroused. *I want him to kiss me,* she thought with a shock. *More than anything else in the world I want him to kiss me!*

If she had said the words aloud, her desire couldn't have been clearer to him. And there was nothing he would have wanted more than to oblige. How many times had he imagined holding her like this, bending over her, pressing his mouth to hers? His eyes glowed in expectation of the realization of his dream. What had he to lose? He'd already lost everything. What was he waiting for?

But no, he would not permit himself to do it. She had betrayed him, and he would not reward that betrayal by showing her what he'd once felt for her . . . what he *still* felt for her. He would not set himself up to be betrayed twice.

She saw the burning look in his eyes grow cold, but she didn't understand the desire in him nor his conquering of that desire. She only understood that she'd been rejected. He believed she'd betrayed him to her father, and nothing she did or said would change that belief.

She wrenched herself from his hold. "Damn you, Tom Morrison, I deserve better from you," she said in a shaking voice, completely unaware of having uttered a curse. "I've given you my time, my skill, my attention, my friendship, even my . . . my . . . even more. To convince yourself, after all that, that I would betray you, is the greatest insult!"

"I'm well aware of what you've done for me, ma'am," he muttered. "That does not excuse—"

"No more!" she cried, covering her ears. Then, having silenced him, she dropped her arms and turned to the door. But before leaving she looked back at him one last time. "In spite of my gratitude for what you're going to do for Sally tonight, I'll never, *never* forgive you for what you said today!"

Twenty-six

There was no moonlight that night, after all. The stars and moon were obscured by a thick cover of clouds. This would have been considered fortunate by the conspirators, except that the air smelled decidedly of rain.

When the four of them gathered in the stable after dark, Tom stood apart from the others. Patience took her leave of Sally and the boy but did not look at him. Neither she nor Tom wished to show forgiveness for the quarrel of a few hours earlier, so neither acknowledged by so much as a nod the presence of the other.

The leave-taking was marked by whisperings and tears. Patience and Sally hugged each other as if they would never see each other again, which was indeed likely. Even Aaron cried when Patience embraced him. It wasn't until Tom coughed to remind them to hurry that they pulled apart.

Tom led the horse quietly out of the barn, Sally and Aaron following behind. Aaron—walking clumsily in his long skirt, with his boyish head covered by a bandanna—would have been laughable had the situation not been so fraught with danger. Poor Sally, beset with an avalanche of conflicting emotions—exhilaration at the prospect of freedom, heartbreak at leaving her closest friend and the only home she'd ever known, and terror at the dangers ahead—kept looking back and waving at Patience, who stood watching them from the barn door and trying not to cry.

Tom did not let himself look back once.

Not until after they'd passed the gate and had crept several yards down the road did they mount the horse, Aaron sitting in front of Tom and Sally clinging to him behind. About an hour after they'd started, the rains began to fall. Nervous, damp and depressed, they remained silent for all four hours of the ride. It was only when they arrived at the outskirts of New Rochelle that Tom offered his one bit of advice. "Ask for wages, Sally," he urged. "Whatever work you do, you must get wages. You're free now, and freemen work for wages."

There were more tears at parting. Tom watched them walk away down the Boston Post Road until they were swallowed up by the rain and fog. Then he turned his horse about and started for home.

But why go home? he asked himself. He should run away now, too. This very night, in fact . . . for didn't he have a horse under him? Never on any of his previous flights had he had a horse. Having the animal might make all the difference.

But of course his disappearance would make it worse for Sally and Aaron. If he returned tonight, and the horse was put back in his stall, their absence might not be noticed for a day or so. But if he did not return, the whole scheme would become obvious right away. Therefore he *had* to go back. He had to give them the extra time. They would need it.

The trouble was that he had nothing to draw him back. Before, there'd been Patience. She'd been the enticement that made the return to imprisonment bearable. Now he'd lost even that. He didn't understand her. She'd been so kind to him of late, teaching him to read and write. When she'd bent over him to see what he was reading, or when she'd taken his hand to help him shape a letter on the writing pad, he could feel her affection. He was not the sort of peacock who could make himself believe in affections that were not there. But what had happened to her affection when he'd run away? She'd stopped his escape in the most treacherous, harmful way—she'd told her father. Didn't she realize what that would cost him?

But then there had been her visit to his room. He'd seen the look in her eyes when he'd pinned her arm back. He couldn't be mistaken about that, either. Could she truly be drawn to him in that way, or was it a pretense to convince him of her innocence? Perhaps the enticement of solving the riddle of Patience could be the object of his return to servitude. If he could solve the riddle of her, it would all be worth it.

The night was wet and dark, and the hours in the saddle passed slowly. After a while, Tom found himself nodding off. This was dangerous, and he tried whistling under his breath to keep himself awake. The rain soaked his thin coat and dripped from his hair and neck down his back, but even that didn't keep him from feeling the pull of sleep. He longed to get home, to pull off his boots and his wet clothes and fall on his cot for one blessed hour of sleep. One hour would be heaven. If he could sleep, he could forget . . . forget the angry words they'd thrown at each other . . . forget the look of innocence in her eyes . . . forget how she'd felt in his arms, the lovely softness of her, the intoxicating smell of her hair . . . forget that she'd . . . betrayed . . .

He woke with a start. The rain still fell, but the sky showed the gray light of dawn. A shock of alarm shot through him. He'd fallen asleep so deeply that daybreak was upon him! Where was he? Where had he let the horse take him? How far was he from home? Was he lost? He surely was late! Good God! Had he ruined everything—for Sally, for Patience, and for himself?

He shook himself awake and looked about him. He was at a crossroad; that was why the horse had stopped in indecision. It was the ceasing of motion that had awakened him. Now he, too, was undecided. Judging from the faint light in the sky, east was behind him. He turned the horse south and spurred him ruthlessly forward. He was not at all sure where he was or where he was going. He could only pray he'd chosen the right fork.

It was another quarter hour before he saw another human being. A rickety cart with a bearded driver was coming toward him. "Where am I?" he shouted anxiously.

The driver laughed. "Drank all night, did ye?" the old codger asked as they drew abreast of each other. "You young'uns ain't got the sense you was born with. That way's Yonkers, less'n a mile ahead."

"Yonkers! Thank God!" Tom waved to the old fellow and spurred ahead, breathing a sigh of relief. His horse had had better sense than he. He'd be late, but by not more than an hour. All might not be lost.

When he reached the gate, he slid from the saddle and led the horse up the path to the stable. Now he blessed the rain, for it was keeping everyone indoors. He reached the stable without meeting another soul. Relieved, he pushed the stable door open and led the horse inside. He'd made it!

He checked with all the other hands and learned that Hendley had not yet been seen that morning. Evidently all was serene. Tom could go about his business as if nothing was amiss. There was plenty that he could do, even on a rainy day like this. The others had done the milking already, but there were tools to be mended, seedlings to be potted, stalls to be swept, wood to be chopped. He ought to get to work.

But his clothes were damp, his bones weary, and his brain exhausted. It was raining. It would probably rain all day. There'd be no harm in postponing his chores for an hour or two while he went back to his room and stole a few winks.

As he stumbled up the stairs to his room, his sleepy brain lingered on Patience, picturing her face as it had looked when he'd held her in his arms. That's how he wished to fall asleep— with the feel of her pressed against him. In an almost-blissful fog, he clumped across the passageway toward his room, pulling off his damp coat as he walked. He threw open his door with a sigh of relief. Sleep. One more moment and he could fall upon his cot and close his—"

His eyes popped open in surprise. Had he stumbled into the wrong room? He stood stock still in his doorway, blinking in astonishment. Then he burst into a hoarse laugh. He leaned on the doorjamb, laughing until his sides hurt, until the tears ran down his cheeks. "Patience, confound you!" he gasped, lurching to the cot and falling down on it, burying his face in his pillow as his hands—like those of a lover fondling the soft, bare shoulders of his beloved—slid slowly, caressingly, down the sides of the bed.

For his bed had been completely made over—with sheets.

Twenty-seven

Tom slept away most of what was left of the morning, though he'd intended to nap for only an hour. He woke with a start, his heart pounding in alarm. He'd slept for a good bit longer than an hour, he was sure of that. He peered out the window to get a sense of the time, but all he saw was a leaden sky and an empty landscape. The still-falling rain had driven all human inhabitants indoors. Without the sun to give him a sense of the time of day, and with no timepiece to call his own, he couldn't be certain how long he'd slept. Had he been missing from work too long? Would Hendley notice he was not at his chores and start asking questions?

To rid himself of the nauseating grogginess brought on by a sleep that was both too short and too long, he splashed his face with water from the pail on his table, all the while berating himself for oversleeping. It hadn't even been a good sleep. He didn't feel at all rested, and, worse, he'd had a troublesome dream in which he hungered mightily for a luscious pear that kept rolling out of his reach, tantalizing him. The blasted fruit rolled round and round a wide table (spread with a white, smooth cloth), repeatedly but narrowly eluding him. Finally, with a desperate lunge, he grabbed hold of it with both hands and bit into it, only to find that it wasn't a pear at all but a nettle with sharp burrs that cut his tongue, its juices bitter as gall. The bitter taste still lingered in his mouth.

Since he'd fallen asleep in his clothes, he didn't have to dress.

He ran down from his room and out the stable door, where he paused and looked around. Still no human being in sight. Everything else seemed quiet enough. Perhaps no one had noticed his absence. If that were the case, all he had to do was to get busy in the stable, and all would be well.

He began to shovel out the dirty hay from the horses' stalls with a vigor born of guilt. But the activity did nothing to lift his spirits. He was deeply depressed. Nothing in his life gave him a reason for cheer. His present was as bleak as the weather, and his future promised no improvement. And it was all Patience's fault. She'd betrayed him and destroyed his hopes.

A few hours ago, when he'd seen his bed made up with sheets, his heart had lifted with pure love for her. But now the memory of her ruthless tale-bearing overshadowed that little act of generosity. *Can you really believe, you miserable, lying traitor,* he asked her, in imagination, timing every word with an angry thrust of the shovel, *that sheets on my bed can make up for your unforgivable act of betrayal?*

He'd just started to pitch fresh hay into the horses' stalls when Chester came into the stable from the barn. "So, you come back," the Negro slave said, flashing Tom a grin. "I thought you run off for good this time."

"Don't know what you're talking about, Chester," Tom countered with bland innocence.

"No? Did you think you could disappear for mos' twen'y hours an' me not notice?"

"I just overslept, is all."

"Don' try to diddle me, Tom Morrison," Chester said flatly, taking up a rake to assist Tom with his chore. "When Aaron didn' come to bed las' night, I went lookin' for you, to ask if you knowed where he was at. An' when I saw you was gone too, I didn' need no knock on the noggin to figure out what was goin' on." He leaned on the broom handle and threw Tom a knowing wink. "I knows you helped Sally an' the boy get away. But don' you worry none. I didn' say nothin' to nobody."

"Thanks, Chester." Tom expelled a long, relieved breath. "So no one at all came looking for me? Or them?"

"Only Miz Patience, early this mornin'."

Tom stiffened. "She did?"

"That ain't nothin' to trouble about. I played real dumb. I didn' want to give you away twice."

Tom nodded and turned his hand to shoveling the stable dirt into a barrel, but something in Chester's words belatedly caught his attention. He lifted his head with a start. "Twice? What do you mean, twice?"

"You know, like the las' time you run off. It was me gave you away then, you know."

"I don't know. What are you talking about?"

Chester frowned at him. "It's the plain truth, though it was you's own fault, that time. You shoulda tol' me your plan, Tom. I woulda made up an excuse to tell ol' Hendley, if I'd knowed."

"Are you saying that the night I ran off, Hendley asked you about me?"

"Yeah. He come here lookin' for you."

Tom gaped at him, the pulse in his temples beginning to pound. "Here, to the stable? That very night?"

"Sure. How else could he find out you run off? If he hadn'a come, you woulda had till mornin'."

"*You* told him?"

"Well, I had to, didn' I? He told me to go up an' find you, an' you wasn't there, so—me not knowin' you run off—I told him you mus' be out somewheres walkin' about. Well, that's a pretty lame excuse, so right off he gets suspicious, an' the nex' thing I know he's makin' me run for the sheriff."

Tom goggled at him, his mouth agape and his pulse pounding. It was *Chester,* not Patience. Chester! *Oh, God,* he thought, *what have I done?*

As he and Chester continued the stable chores, Tom's mood swung wildly between elation and despair. Patience had not betrayed him. He'd called her a liar and a traitor, but she was neither.

This discovery changed everything. She was now as pure as the angels, while he . . . well, he was an unspeakable cad!

Now his mind was completely occupied with the problem of finding a way to apologize to her. *I'm sorry, ma'am,* his mind declared to an imaginary Patience, *I should have known. I'm a cad. A churl. A blasted idiot. While you are beautiful, gentle, wise, and kind. Forgive me. I was crazy with hurt, but only because I love you so. I'll never think evil of you again, never. I love you. Forgive me.*

Of course, he'd never have the courage to say those things aloud. But he'd find something to say. He had to. She deserved an apology. After all, even after she'd endured his unmerciful slanders, hadn't she made up his bed with sheets?

Twenty-eight

Sally and Aaron walked steadily northward for three days, keeping as much as possible in the shelter of woods. But when they crossed into Connecticut without having once been accosted, they began to believe they were safe. Aaron even took off the despised dress that had been hampering his stride. By the dawn of the fourth day, however, the weather turned bad, their feet were sore and their food gone. They had to seek work. It was time to be bold.

At the outskirts of Stamford, they left the cover of the trees and tramped openly up the road. They could see, in the distance, the chimneys of the town, but just down the road stood a lone building, a large structure of white clapboard topped with a slate roof. A sign, with the picture of a sailing ship painted upon it in bright colors, hung on a post in the front yard. Sally came to a halt in front of it and stood studying it. "What's the trouble, Mama?" Aaron asked, puzzled.

"What's that house?"

Aaron, who'd taken a few reading lessons from Tom, could make out the words on the sign. "Old Anchor Arms," he read aloud, slowly and laboriously. "We Serve Publick Breakfast, Afternoon Tea and Dinner."

"A tavern, eh? Maybe we can work here for a day. We need a meal. An' a good sleep."

"We be takin' a big chance."

"Our whole life be a big chance."

Cautiously, they skirted the building and found the kitchen door. Sally knocked, her heart pounding. They had not faced another human being since they'd said good-bye to Tom.

The door was opened by a stout, middle-aged woman. She started at the sight of two unkempt Negroes. "Yes?" she asked, narrow-eyed.

"Mornin', ma'am. We lookin' for a day's work," Sally said.

The woman raised her brows. "For a *day?*"

"Yes, ma'am. See, we on our way to Boston."

The woman studied them closely. "Are you runaways?" she asked bluntly.

Sally did not panic. "We's manumitted," she said firmly. "I got papers."

The confidence in Sally's manner was convincing. "Well, we always can use some extra hands," the woman said with a shrug. "Wait here, I'll get my husband."

As they waited, Aaron fidgeted. "I didn' like how she look at us, Mama. Let's go."

"We has to face people some time," his mother said. "Might as well be now."

The tavern keeper appeared at the door, a stocky, big-shouldered, ham-fisted man with a rubble of beard. "What's your name?" he asked Sally coldly.

"Mary Baker," Sally answered promptly, "an' this is my son Dee. What's yours?"

The show of spirit caused the man to grin, revealing several blackened and misshapen teeth. "Spunky, ain't ye?" he chortled. "Eben Simpson's my name. I own this here tavern. The missus says you want work." He looked them over closely. "What can you do?"

"I can cook, an' my boy here can do stable work.

The man nodded in approval. "Well, we got plenty for you to do. Martha, show this here Mary Baker what's to be done in the kitchen. An' you, boy, come with me."

Sally threw Aaron an uneasy glance but began to follow the woman.

"Wait a minute, Mama," Aaron said. "What about wages?"

"Wages?" Mr. Simpson echoed, eyebrows lifting forbiddingly.

"The boy's right," Sally said, remembering Tom's last instruction. "We mus' have wages."

"Well, of course you get wages," the innkeeper snarled.

"How much?" Sally persisted.

"Two shillings for you, if you work till closing. An' another for the boy."

"Three for me," Sally said brazenly. "Two for the boy. An' supper an' a place to sleep."

The man hooted. "You don't think much of yourself, do you!" he exclaimed.

"I'm a real good cook. An' my boy know horses."

Mr. Simpson shrugged. "All right, agreed. But only on liking."

"You'll like us good enough," Sally said and, with head high, followed his wife into the kitchen.

The tavern, situated at a junction not far from Stamford, where the road from Danbury joined the Boston Post Road, was a busy place. Martha Simpson first set Sally to doing the washing up, but when the place grew crowded in the afternoon, she let the black woman assist with the cooking. It wasn't long before Martha recognized Sally's talents. The Negress could handle three pots at once, and her way with spices filled the air with delicious aromas. When Martha tasted Sally's boiled turkey soup, she could hardly believe that her ordinary ingredients had been transformed into this culinary masterpiece. "Delicious!" she exclaimed. "Wherever did you learn the receipt?"

"Ain't no receipt," Sally replied. "It's all outta my head. I been doin' cookin' for a long, long time."

By evening, Martha had let Sally completely take over the preparation of the dinner. At the height of the evening rush, after overhearing one of the travelers praise to the skies a dish that the new cook had called beef collops, Martha remarked to her husband that she'd hate to see the black woman go.

"Who says she has t' go?" her husband said with a leer.

Martha Simpson opened her mouth to question what he meant, but something in his eyes made her hold her tongue. If her husband was up to something nasty, she didn't wish to know what it was.

When, close to midnight, the tavern keeper at last closed his doors, Sally approached him with her hand out. "Miz Simpson says my cookin' was much to her likin', so can I have the wages now, please?" she asked.

"No hurry, is there, woman?" Mr. Simpson asked. "I'll pay you in the morning. Didn't you say you wanted a place to sleep? You can use the stable loft. Martha'll give you blankets."

"Thank ye kin'ly," Sally said, "but my boy 'n me aim to be leavin' early, so we like our wages now."

The tavern keeper eyed her speculatively. After a moment, he put his hand in his pocket and handed her five shillings. "There," he said, turning away. "No one says Eben Simpson don't keep his word. A bargain's a bargain. Have a good night's sleep."

Sally found Aaron waiting for her in the stable. She showed him the five coins. "Our first wages," Aaron said, looking at them in awe.

"Yeah, but I don' trust that man," his mother whispered, her brow knit worriedly. "You too weary to set off now?"

"Without sleepin'?" Aaron asked, his face falling.

"We can sleep somewhere else. I got a doomful forefeelin' we oughta get far away from this place."

Aaron knew better than to quarrel with his mother's "doomful forefeelings." They quickly bundled up their meager belongings and slipped out the stable door. But they hadn't gone three steps when the light of a lantern flashed in their eyes. Sally, shading her eyes with a shaking hand, made out Simpson's hefty form. "Mr. Simpson, is 'at you?" she asked, trying to keep her voice steady.

"Yeah, it's me," came a mocking reply from the shadows. "Goin' somewheres?"

"We purpose not to stay the night after all," Sally mumbled, her stomach knotting.

"Oh, is 'at so?" The heavy man waved the lantern in their faces and backed them toward the stable. "What if I was to tell you that you'll stay the night and a lot more?"

"We g-got to get to Boston," Sally said.

"Yeah? Why?"

"We . . . has work there."

"Ye don't say. Work, eh?" With a threatening leer, he advanced upon them slowly, backing them over the threshold and into the stable. "Why go all the way to Boston, when you can have work right here?"

"We's . . . promised," Sally insisted.

"Who's to care? If you don't show up, do ye think they'll come lookin' for you? Never in this world. Two Negras disappear, so what? Happens all the time."

"You can't make us stay," Aaron said bravely. "We's free."

"So you say. That's what all you runaways say. Why should I believe ye?"

"It's true," Sally cried nervously. "I'll show you!" She reached into the bosom of her dress and pulled out her precious paper. Here! See? We's manumitted."

Simpson held the lantern aloft and looked at the paper. "Seems like a writ, right enough. Mary Baker and offspring Dee. Those could be your names, I s'pose. But it's only a piece of paper. What if it should accidentally catch fire from this lantern and burn up? Who'd believe you then?" And he reached out to pull the paper from her.

"No!" Sally cried, clutching it to her breast. "No!"

"Gimme that!" Simpson muttered, advancing on her.

"You leave my mama alone!" Aaron shouted, leaping on Simpson's back and trying to pin back his arms.

The lantern fell to the ground. Simpson swung around, pulling

Aaron's arms from him and elbowing the boy hard in his chest. Aaron grunted in pain, fell to his knees and doubled over, clutching his chest with both arms. Simpson, meanwhile, snatched up a shovel that was lying nearby. Holding it like a cudgel, he moved purposefully toward Sally. "Gimme that paper," he demanded again.

With a cry, Aaron leaped to his feet and started toward Simpson, his eyes wild. The tavern keeper wheeled around, swinging the shovel toward Aaron's head. Sally grabbed at the tavern keeper's arm with the strength of desperation, but her grasp only slightly blunted the force of the blow. The shovel struck Aaron on the side of the head. The boy, stunned, staggered back. Blood spurted down over his left eye. With his brain reeling, he shook his head, trying to steady himself.

Simpson, seeing that the boy was dazed, turned back to the mother. "Gimme the paper or I'll give you a taste of the same," he threatened, lifting the shovel and moving toward her.

Aaron, now almost beyond fear, brushed the blood from his eye and charged toward the assailant, head lowered like an enraged bull.

"No, Aaron!" Sally ordered from between tight lips, her eyes fixed on Simpson. "Take this and *run!"* And quick as a snake's tongue, she thrust the writ into Aaron's hand.

Simpson turned and lunged for the writ, but Sally flung herself at him, one arm thrusting the shovel aside and the other wrapping itself round his neck.

"Mama, I *can't—!"* Aaron cried, gaping in confusion from the writ in his hand to the struggling pair before him.

Sally, though locked in a bearlike tussle she would soon lose, managed to throw her son a look of fierce authority. *"Run, I says!"* There was no mistaking the teeth-gritting determination in her tone. Aaron knew he had better obey. With one last look at his mother wrestling for dear life with her hefty assailant, he turned and stumbled from the stable.

Although dizzy and in an agony of despair, he made his way

across the courtyard toward the road. His chest was heaving with sobs. He ran almost blindly, head throbbing, forehead cut and dripping blood, and one eye swollen shut. He did not see the carriage that had just turned into the courtyard until he almost ran into it. A passenger who was climbing down—a tall gentleman in a long black coat—caught him in his arms. "Whoa, there, boy," the man said, kneeling down and patting Aaron gently on the shoulder, "thou hast no need to be in such a hurry. The horses can stand in the air for a mo—" Then he gasped. "God save us, boy, thou'rt bleeding!"

"Lemme go," Aaron burst out between choked sobs. "We's manumitted, see?" And, trembling with hysteria, he held the paper up to the stranger's face. "Free!"

"Yes, boy, I see," the man said kindly. "Does someone try to say thou'rt not?"

Aaron dashed the blood from his eye and looked up at the stranger's face. It was a round face edged by a short, thick black beard and topped by a wide-brimmed, flat-crowned hat. The boy, reading a gentle warmth in the man's eyes, clutched at his arm. "In the stable!" he croaked urgently. "He be killin' my mama!"

The stranger stared at the boy for a moment and then rose. "Take me there," he ordered.

When they arrived at the stable door, the sight that met the gentleman's eyes appalled him. The light from the fallen lantern threw huge, angular shadows across the partitions of the stalls and up the walls of the stable, but the tavern keeper, disheveled and bleeding from the nose, was standing in full light, busily tying a gaunt Negress to the post of a stable door with a thick rope. The woman's hair was wild, her cheek swollen with battering, her mouth bruised, and her head lowered in despair. Her hands and feet were already bound to the post, and Simpson was now adding a final cruelty—twisting the rope round her neck.

"What in God's name art thou *doing*, man?" the stranger demanded.

Simpson whirled about. "Who the hell're you?"

"Refrain from blaspheming in my presence," the man thundered in a voice that resonated throughout the stable and echoed in the rafters. "Untie that woman at once!"

Aaron, meanwhile, had run to his mother's side. "Mama!" he sobbed, lifting a shaking finger to her bruised cheek.

Sally raised her head and uttered a heart-rending groan. "I tole you to run," she moaned.

Simpson, eyeing the stranger nervously, picked up the shovel he'd discarded. "Why should I untie her?" he asked curtly. "I can do what I like with my slave."

"She ain't his slave!" Aaron cried in fury. "We jus' worked here a few hours! An' we got the wages to prove it!"

"Yeah? Then where are they, eh?" Simpson sneered.

Aaron's eyes widened. "Mama?"

Sally shook her head. "He took the money back," she said through bruised lips.

The stranger strode up to Simpson and glared down at him. Though slender of build, he was a full head taller than the stocky tavern keeper. "Untie her, I said."

Eben Simpson, awed by the other man's stern dignity, backed away. "You ain't got no right to interfere," he muttered. "The woman's my property."

"Is she, indeed? Then can thee explain away the woman's writ of manumission?"

"The writ's a forgery. I heard her call the boy Aaron. But his name is Dee on the writ. See for yourself."

"I have no need to see. 'Tis evidence enough to see her battered face, and the boy's. Untie her, I say. *Now!*"

Simpson hesitated, studying the stranger closely. What he saw in the man's fiery eyes and preacherish demeanor convinced him that this man—obviously a Quaker and obviously prosperous—might be a person of some influence who could very well make trouble for him. He therefore decided to follow his orders. He laid down the shovel and made quick work of untying the rope.

The stranger put a supporting arm about the tottering Sally.

As he helped her toward the stable door, he instructed Aaron to tie Simpson in his mother's place. Then he turned to the chastened tavern keeper. "Thy wife will find thee soon enough," he said. "In the meantime, leaving thee languishing in thy bonds will permit us to take our leave in peace."

"Should I tie his neck, too," Aaron asked, setting about his task with vigor, "jus' to let him see how it feels?"

" 'Twould be simple justice," the stranger replied, "but no. 'Tis not the way of the Friends to seek revenge."

Outside the stable Aaron and his mother faced the stranger. "I don' know how to thank you, sir," Sally said.

The man smiled down at her, his full cheeks shining in the dim night light. "No need for thanks."

"Yes, sir, there mos' surely is. If it wasn't for you, I'd 've lost my boy an' my freedom. An' you ain't even ast us 'bout the name on the writ."

"The writ means little to me," the gentleman explained while he removed a handkerchief from his pocket and tied it over Aaron's wound. "You see, I belong to the Society of Friends."

"Friends?"

"Some call us Quakers. We of the Society do not hold with the enslavement of any human souls, whether they have a writ or no." Having completed the bandaging of Aaron's head, he turned to Sally. "I am Jonathan Myers of Marblehead, Massachusetts. If thou art going north, I would be happy to take thee up in my carriage."

Aaron and Sally exchanged looks. "Yes, we's goin' north," Sally said, her bruised mouth twisting into a grateful smile. "We'd be mos' beholden for a ride."

Later, riding through the night in the kind gentleman's conveyance, Sally surreptitiously smoothed out the crushed and bloodied writ, folded it and tucked it back in her bosom. It might not mean much to Mr. Jonathan Myers of Marblehead, but it meant the world to her. *Freedom from servitude to the above-named and all heirs and assigns in perpetuity.* The document containing those words was the most precious thing she'd ever owned. Though one man had ignored it, another had tried to burn it. That attempt alone was proof of its value. She pressed her hand against where it lodged between her breasts. Her writ. She would keep it safe if it meant her life.

Twenty-nine

For the next few days, Peter Hendley did not miss Aaron's presence in the barn or the fields, for he left the supervision of the hands to Tom. Nor did he pay mind to the fact that Sally was not serving his meals. So long as his food was placed before him at the proper time, he did not much care who served it. By increasing the hours Beatie spent in the kitchen, Patience was able to serve those meals with her usual efficiency and promptness. She explained Sally's absence by a simple, "She's probably feeling poorly." Hendley accepted the black woman's absence without question. It was a remark of Barbara's that finally jogged his curiosity. "Sally must really be sick," Babs said at dinner on the third day after Sally's departure. "She's missed six meals in a row."

Patience (who'd not said a word to her brother or sister about Sally and Aaron, not wishing to involve them in the affair) tried to silence the girl with a warning glance, but it was too late. Her father looked up with knit brows. "Yes, Patience, what's wrong with her?"

Patience shrugged. "I'm no doctor," she muttered, not meeting his eyes.

"Then perhaps I should have a look at her. I don't want the woman malingering."

"Sally ain't the sort to malinger," Benjy said in quick defense. "She's never stayed in bed before, not once that I remember."

"That's true," Barbara agreed. "She must be very ill."

"Perhaps so," Peter Hendley said, pushing away his plate. "I'd best go see to her at once."

Patience, heart sinking, knew she'd come to the time of retribution. "Papa, forbear a moment," she requested, rising from her chair. "I must speak to you in private first."

"Later," Hendley said, also getting up.

"Now, Papa, please. It's important."

Hendley felt a twinge of irritation. He did not like to be contradicted. "I've already said later," he snapped, heading for the door.

"Very well, Papa," Patience said, lifting her chin. "I'll be waiting for you in your office. After you find Sally's room empty, you'll undoubtedly wish to speak to me."

Hendley whirled round, balancing himself on his cane. "Empty? What do you mean?"

Patience walked past him out the door. "In the office, Papa, if you please. We need to be private."

Hendley glared at her as she moved away from him down the hall, her skirts swishing and her back rigid. *The girl's changing,* he noted in annoyance, *and not in a way I like. She's becoming too forward. Too independent by half.* But her manner suggested that there was serious trouble, so he swallowed his irritation and followed quickly after her. Benjy and Babs, also sensing trouble, jumped up from the table and ran after their father. They reached the office door in time to have their father slam it in their faces.

Patience stood at the side of his desk, bravely erect. "Sally and Aaron have gone, Papa," she said quietly. "Gone for good."

Peter Hendley's neck reddened, the color slowly rising into his face. "Gone? Run off? Is *that* what you're telling me?"

"Yes."

"Damn!" He took a turn about the room to vent his spleen. After a few steps, he turned back to his daughter. "When?"

She met his eye but did not answer.

He shrugged. "You don't need to tell me. I can guess. More than two days since." His mind began an immediate calculation of times and distances—in two days, they could have got as far as New York and hidden themselves in the crowd. Suddenly, however, another thought struck him. His eyes narrowed. "Damnation, woman, was this *your* doing?"

"Yes. Yes, it was."

His expression darkened. "I should've known," he muttered bitterly.

She put up her chin. "Yes."

A pulse in his neck began to throb. "You purposely disobeyed me! What's gotten into you, Patience? You never before—"

"You never before threatened to sell Sally's son."

"And that threat was enough to make you cast aside all sense of duty to your father?"

"In this one matter, yes."

"When did it become your right to question my decisions? Have you lost all sense of . . . of respect for me?"

"Papa, I haven't—"

"You have! *You* . . . the one person in the world for whom I care! And a black woman means more to you than I do!"

"Papa, try to understand. She was a mother to me."

"And I am your *father!* It is *my* blood runs in your veins! Does that mean nothing?"

"It means a great deal. But can't you concede that it's possible you're wrong this once?"

"Be still!" His anger deepened to rage, a rage made more virulent by his own deep-seated, unrecognized guilt. "Damn you, first you take it upon yourself to oppose me, and now you *judge* me! Who do you think you are, you . . . you *bitch?*"

Patience gasped, and her cheeks turned white as chalk. The word was bad enough, but the venom in his tone chilled her blood. "Papa!"

He hobbled over to her. "Where did they go?" he demanded through clenched teeth.

"I don't know."

"Tell me where they are!"

"I don't know."

He grasped her by the shoulders. "Don't add lying to the rest of your sins! Where are they?"

"Papa, p-please . . . !"

"Tell me, you blasted mismanaging female!"

"Papa, you're choleric," she said, trying to keep her voice calm. "You'll make yourself ill. This matter is not so important that—"

"Not important? They are *property!"*

"They are human beings! I *begged* you, Papa—"

"And I said no! Who is the master here?" He shook her violently. "When did they go? The day before yesterday, wasn't it? Was it at night? When?"

She tried to steady her head that was bobbling about from his shaking. "Please, Papa, let me go! I have nothing more to say."

But he wouldn't give up. His daughter had betrayed him. He loved her, and she'd rewarded that love with this betrayal. He was beside himself. "Where did they go? The city? Down toward Philadelphia? Up north toward Boston?"

"It doesn't matter," she said, wrenching herself from his grasp. "You'll never find them now."

The answer enraged him even more. His face purpled. He lifted his arm and struck her a blow, backhanded, across her face. The force of it thrust her back against the wall. She struck it with a crash and slid, dazed and shocked, slowly down to the floor.

Outside the door, Barbara and Benjy heard the crash. "Papa, open up!" Benjy shouted, pounding the door.

"Papa," Babs screeched, "what are you *doing?"* And she burst into frightened tears.

Hendley, not so crazed by his uncontrollable anger that he could look at his fallen daughter without feeling remorse, took a step toward her. She stared up at him, eyes wide with shock, as a dribble of blood dripped down the side of her chin from where he'd split her lower lip. "Don't look at me like that," he muttered.

But she continued to stare. This man, her father, seemed a monster, unrecognizable to her.

Clenching and unclenching the fist that was free of his tight hold on his cane, Hendley struggled against his urge to kneel down beside her and tend her wound. This was his daughter Patience, the one member of the family for whom he felt both love and respect. He would not have believed, a few moments ago, that he could ever strike her. Shame welled up in him as if from the overflow of a long-suppressed underground river. *Patience, my beloved girl, I didn't mean it! I'm sorry!* The words trembled on his tongue.

But he could not open his mouth to say them. He could never apologize. What she'd done—her betrayal of that which he held dearest, his property—was too great a sin. Stemming the flood of shame and regret with a wall of residual anger, he tensed his muscles and froze his face. "You can't shame me with that look," he mumbled. "You deserve worse."

She didn't respond. With her tongue testing the cut on her lip, she struggled to rise. He held out a hand to help her up, but she brushed it aside, got to her feet and, without looking at him, strode across the room and out the door past her astonished siblings.

Benjy and Barbara, having glimpsed her bruised and bleeding face, turned their wide-eyed, horrified gazes on their father. He hobbled across the room to the door but took no note of them. He shut the door in their faces and leaned against it, giving way to a wrench of pain that suddenly sliced across his chest. It was a cutting pain, knife sharp. It constricted his heart so tightly that the blood in his veins stopped flowing. He had to double over. It was the worst pain he could ever remember experiencing. Breathing hard to keep from crying out, he wondered if he was dying. But whether he was dying from an actual heart attack or a terrible spasm of fatherly guilt, he could not tell.

Thirty

Patience sat huddled on the floor in the corner of the dark barn loft, moaning and rocking herself in misery, as she'd seen Sally do. It was late to be out of the house; she should be home, preparing supper. But she'd had to get out, away from Babs's and Benjy's inquiring eyes. She'd chosen the barn loft instead of her secret place overlooking the river because she wanted not to look at the world but to hide from it . . . to huddle in a corner and nurse her wounds. Here, hidden away in the loft, she hoped she might find ease from her turmoil. Only one other person knew of the existence of this little hiding place, and he was not likely to find her here at this hour.

She'd never been so confused and unhappy in her life. Nothing made sense. Her own behavior had been wicked and disobedient, but it seemed right. Her father had been lawful and within his rights, yet his behavior seemed cruel and ungodly. How different life had become since her girlhood, when Papa's views had been her gospel, and she hadn't felt the need to question them. These days, it seemed, she did nothing *but* question them. How could perceptions change with such sudden—?

"Mistress Patience? Are you there?"

The urgently whispered question came from down below, the voice belonging to the very person who she'd believed was not likely to come. She didn't answer. She needed to be alone. Her emotions were stretched too thin to handle anything more tonight. If she sat still and didn't breathe, Tom wouldn't know she was there, and he'd go away.

But Tom didn't go away. He climbed up the ladder. She saw the light of the candle rise higher and higher until the flame became visible, held in Tom's hand. "Go away, Tom," she mumbled, the words hurting her bruised underlip.

He heaved himself onto the floorboards and came toward her, holding the candle out in front of him. "Forgive me if I'm intruding," he said, peering through the shadows at her huddled form. "I've been trying for two days to speak—" Suddenly he spied her swollen cheek and bruised mouth. "My *God*," he exclaimed, dropping to his knees beside her, "what happened?"

"Nothing," she answered stiffly. "Go away."

He studied her through narrowed eyes. "It was your father, wasn't it? He knows about Sally and Aaron."

She shook her head. "Please, Tom, this has nothing to do with you. Go away."

"Did he do this to you?" Tom put the candle down and took her face into both his hands. "I could kill him!"

"It's n-nothing s-serious," she stammered, feeling sobs welling up within her. The gentleness of his fingers on her face and the look of pained concern in his eyes undid her. Unused to tenderness, she collapsed upon his shoulder and wept, the sobs hiccoughing up from deep inside and racking her frame.

He held her in his arms as if sheltering a child, his cheek against her hair, murmuring soft words like "Hush, my sweet, hush," and "No, no, don't cry."

The gentle, unexpected haven of his arms eased her pain. It was comfortable and safe in his embrace, and for a long while after her sobs ceased she did not move. But slowly, despite a strange reluctance to face the fact, she admitted to herself that her behavior was, to say the least, unseemly. She inched herself out of his hold and wiped her cheeks with the back of her hand. "Thank you, Tom, 'twas kind of you to soothe me," she said with embarrassed formality. "I'm quite myself now. You may go."

But the tearful embrace had had an effect on him, too. He smiled at her with a confidence he'd never before felt. "Go? Not on your life. I've been trying to talk to you for two days."

It was then she remembered she was furious with him. "Do not take advantage of my momentary weakness," she said, making her voice aloof and cold. "Please go away. I don't wish to talk to anyone just now, and especially not to you."

"You don't have to talk. Just listen." He sat back on his heels and took her hand. "You see, I have to apologize to you for what I said the other day. Calling you a traitor and a liar. I was very wrong."

She snatched the hand away. "Indeed," she said icily. "You don't have to tell me that. I know quite well how wrong you were."

"It was Chester, not you, who informed on me. When he told me, I wanted to cut my tongue out."

"It would've been too drastic a punishment for so minor an impertinence. I paid your silly insult no mind.

He grinned. "No *mind?* You were ready to slap my face."

"You exaggerate your importance to me, Tom Morrison. I care nothing for what you think of me."

"You must care a little, ma'am. Else why did you so kindly cover my bed with sheets? And a pillow slip, too."

Patience felt herself blush. "Well, it isn't *decent* for a man to sleep without sheets."

"Then Chester should have them, too. And the rest of the hands who live in."

"I have every intention to see to that. As soon as I have time to hem enough sheets."

He sat down beside her and made himself comfortable by leaning back against the wall. "Well, ma'am," he said cockily, stretching out his booted legs and crossing them at the ankles, "the fact that I'm the first must mean something."

"It means nothing of any purport," she snapped.

He put his hands behind his head and sighed contentedly.

" 'Tis a wonder, sleeping on sheets. So smooth and silky, like a woman's skin. It drives me wild sometimes. I run my hand along the pillow and imagine it's your shoulder."

"Tom!" Her voice was a sharp reprimand.

"It's nothing but the truth, ma'am. Every night, when I curl up on my bed under my blanket, I imagine myself holding you in my arms. I imagined it even before you gave me the sheets." He turned on his side and peered brazenly into her face. "Do you ever imagine me that way?"

"Tom Morrison, you go too far!"

"I know. I've lost my mind. Ever since Chester told me it wasn't you who betrayed me, I've been like a man possessed. I make speeches to you in my head. All day long. It's become a habit, talking to you in my head. And now that I'm here with you, saying these things aloud, it's like . . . well, it's like wine. I'm drunk with it."

"Then go and put your head under the pump!" she said with asperity, struggling hard against that part of her that was finding his ramblings fascinating.

"No, I can't go yet. I haven't told you half. Don't you want to hear the words I've yearned to tell you all these years?"

She couldn't help herself. "What words?"

"Oh, commonplace words, though I've never said them aloud before. Words to tell you how very beautiful you are."

"Are you making mock of me, Tom? I'm not in the least beautiful."

"Making mock of you? How can you ask it? You are so lovely that I get a knot in my gut just looking at you. You've been beautiful to me since the first time I laid eyes on you, when I was a mere boy. The first time I ever saw you, you were sitting under the big elm, reading. You were wearing a white dress, with the skirts spread all around you. And your hair was plaited and hanging down over your shoulder. To my eyes you seemed a creature from heaven, unearthly and untouched by the dunghill that filled my world. I wanted to fall on the grass beside you and rest my head on your lap and lie there forever just looking up at your face."

"Oh, Tom!" She expelled a long, tremulous breath. It was not a tale that a woman could listen to unmoved. But then she shook her head. "It's no more than a boy's romantic nonsense," she said, her voice sweeter than her words. "You've surely grown up by now."

"No, not much," he admitted. "I loved you then, and I love you still."

A pulse began to throb in her throat. "No!" she said in a frightened whisper. "No! You mustn't—"

"I mustn't?" He sat up abruptly, his lighthearted mood turning to anger, for 'mustn't' did not strike him as a satisfactory response to a declaration of love. "Is there a law that forbids love to creep into a man's heart? And if there were, how is such a law to be enforced, ma'am? Is there a magistrate somewhere who can order the feeling whipped out of me? It's a whipping I'd willingly endure. This love, I tell you true, is a damned hellish pain. I'd gladly rid myself of it if I could."

She reached out a hand to comfort him but quickly snatched it back. "It's improper of us to be speaking so. I am . . . married."

"Do you think I need reminding? Not a day goes by that I don't think of it." He leaned toward her and peered closely at her face. "How could you do it, Patience? How could you wed that damnable Orgill? Peer though he is, he was never worthy of you. I knew it even before he was fool enough to leave you."

"Wedding him was a grievous error," she murmured sadly. "I admit it."

He groaned and gathered her in his arms, nestling her head on his shoulder in an instinctive gesture of sympathy. "If I were given my freedom, I could overcome every obstacle that looms between us but that one."

"Could you, Tom?" she asked, wide-eyed with awe.

"Could I!" Dreamily, he rested his cheek lightly on her hair.

"If I were free . . . and you were free . . . I'd win you somehow. Whatever it took to make you love me, I'd do it!"

She didn't know if it was the comfort of his arms that made her say it, or the way the candlelight outlined his hair, or the pungent masculine smell of him, or merely the sheer joy of the moment, which seemed to have pushed her earlier pain into some dim recess of memory. Whatever it was, the need to express out loud the feelings she'd so long kept hidden even from herself became overwhelming. "You wouldn't have to do anything, Tom Morrison," she whispered, her voice choked and her throat stinging, "for I . . . I love you already."

The arms that held her trembled. Tom could not believe what he'd heard. He was probably distracted, holding her this way. He tilted up her face, looking for substantiation. Reflected candlelight flamed in her eyes and tinged her translucent skin with an amber glow. And her mouth, swollen from the bruises and the sobs, was irresistible. All he could think about was kissing her. To kiss her was as necessary and right as breathing. Besides, he told himself, this was all a dream, anyway. It couldn't be happening. In real life, he would never have had the courage to say what he said. And surely she could not have said those words he thought she'd said. In a little while he'd wake and find himself on his cot. So, he decided, he might as well draw her up a little tighter in his arms, lower his mouth on hers and do it. Kiss her.

He did it gently, the merest brush of lips, for her mouth was hurt. Despite the softness of it, the kiss felt very real to him. No dream, this. The gentle pressure was quite thrilling enough for him; he didn't demand more. But after a moment her arms crept up around his neck and clung tightly, and, with a little cry from her throat, she cast off whatever restraints had held her feelings captive. Her lips pressed his with the urgency of passion.

Her kiss—and it had truly become hers—cut off all his powers of thought. From that moment on, all was instinct. Her passion ignited his, and they kissed wildly, abandonedly . . . mouths, eyes, ears, throats, until their lips and tongues were familiar with every part of the other's face and neck, until they were dizzy and the walls of the barn whirled around them and he lifted her up and carried her a few steps to the nearest mound of hay and laid her upon it and himself upon her and undid the buttons of her dress and slipped it from her shoulders down and down, all the while kissing and kissing, and she unlacing her stays, unbuttoning his shirt and pressing her bared breasts against his chest, feeling his shoulders and the sinews of his arms, moaning and panting and wanting more and more, feeling wet with wanting and then his hand on the wetness, the touch sending electrical shivers through her body and he on her closer and closer and then . . .

. . . and then her body remembered *before*—the cruelty and pain of it—and she stiffened in terror.

Though it was outwardly the slighest of stiffenings, he felt it. She'd suddenly withdrawn from him. Dismayed, he lifted himself away from her. "Oh, God," he whispered, "I've frightened you!"

She blinked up at the face so close to her own, barely visible in the light of a guttering candle too distant to be of help. But even in the dimness she could see the loving concern in his eyes. "No, not you," she murmured, and she wound a bare arm about his neck and drew him to her again.

He kissed her eyes and mouth and let his hands slowly roam over her, learning with his fingers the shape of her breasts and the curves of her back, until her breath became rapid and she wrapped her legs tightly around him. It was time. He moved inside her gently, advancing and withdrawing with the rhythmic restraint of a dancer of a gavotte. He held himself back until he felt her body lift itself after him, lift with him, pull him in to her, deeper and deeper until restraint was no longer necessary. He felt her arch and tremble and moan, and he knew it was right. She herself did not know anything but that she was very gradually being overwhelmed with a desire to press closer to him. The desire grew stronger, and she pressed closer and closer until it seemed to her that their two bodies could not be pried apart. This was not in any way like the couplings she'd known in her marriage. She was burning, twisting, past all restraint, and if there was pain, it was too insignificant to be noticed in the flood of all-enveloping, unutterable ecstasy that was washing over her—"

"Patience, are you up there?" came Barbara's voice from down below.

They broke apart at once. "Damnation!" Tom muttered hoarsely.

Patience sat up, her pulse throbbing wildly as a great wave of shame overwhelmed her. *"Babs?"* she managed.

"You'd better come home right away," Babs called up to her. "Something is very wrong with Papa."

The nightmarish encounter with her father returned to her consciousness with the force of a blow, draining away the last of the heat of interrupted passion. "Is there something wrong with him indeed?" she asked coldly.

"I know that he quarreled with you, Patience, and that you must be very angry, but he's *sick*. Really sick. Come quickly."

Tom helped Patience to her feet, and she hurriedly pulled on her dress. "I'll be right there, Babs. You go on ahead." She threw Tom a quick look, then lowered her eyes and did up her buttons with shaking fingers.

"Please, Patience, be quick," her sister shouted from below. "What on earth are you *doing* up there anyway?"

"I said I'm coming," Patience snapped, "so stop asking questions and just run along!"

"Very well, I'm going. But *hurry!"*

Patience stood listening until her sister's retreating footsteps could no longer be heard. Then she turned to him. "We must forget this, Tom," she said quietly. "It was a momentary lapse. I wish we . . . but we can't. Everything . . . what was said . . . what we did . . . it mustn't become . . . significant."

He paused in the act of buttoning his shirt. "No?"

"It was sinful. An act of copulation committed by a married woman outside the sanctity of wedlock. It will *not* happen again." She forced herself to turn away from the warmth in his eyes and went to the ladder. With a foot on the first rung, she looked back at him. "I mean it, Tom. In future, we shall go on as we always have, as if this night never happened."

To her surprise, he smiled. It was a very small smile, turning up only one corner of his mouth. But small as it was, there was a definite gleam of triumph in it. *"Tomorrow, do thy worst!"* he said.

Book Three

Impatience

Fall 1774 to Spring 1775

Dearest Hannah,

Thank you for the Invitation to your "Frolic" next month. I wish we could accept, for I have not seen Anything of you since our visit in March, but Papa seems unwilling to Trust himself to make the trip, this despite the Doctor's assurance that he is Well Enough. I know you have repeatedly postponed the Date for his sake, and I love you for being so Considerate, but if he remains reluctant to make the Journey, it would not be Proper for Barbara and me to go without him, even with Benjy's escort.

In strict Confidence, Hannah, I will admit that Papa is not taking his Illness at all well. Although the Doctor has assured him that he has made a Remarkable Recovery, his mind dwells much on Death. Last month he called in Clymer Young to design for him an enormous Mausoleum on the northern corner of the estate. Hannah, I do not exaggerate. Such a Monument is more suited to a British Nobleman than to an American farmer! The ground has already been broken on the Site, and the Stonemasons are at this moment busily at work. I wish I had the Courage to point out to Papa that it is more admirable, after one dies, for the Living to regret that there is no monument than to wonder why there is one. But even if Papa and I were on better Terms than we are these Days, I would not have the Courage to express this Sentiment. Nor would Papa listen. He is as obsessed with the Project as he is with his other obsession, the Political Situation. The approaching Congress of the American Colonies in Philadelphia is making him wild. I do not think the Delegates to the Congress want to start a war—they would be foolish to do so, for an American Rebellion would surely be a Lost cause and would result in bringing about worse Reprisals than we have yet experienced—but Papa insists that the aim of the Congress is Warmongering.

However, I speak too much of Papa. I would much rather be speaking of your baby. Please write and tell me how Well your little Caleb is doing. I suspect he's grown Several Inches since I saw him. Has he already outgrown the little Cap I knitted for him?

Well, my dear, the sun is lowering. It is time for me to put up my pen. I need not tell you how very Disappointed I am, not to be able to be with you at the Party. Poor Barbara, who has been looking forward to the Affair with real Impatience (and has made herself a new gown, quite lovely despite a shockingly low Décolletage, sewing every stitch herself with a Diligence and Meticulousness she has never before shown), is utterly Desolated. She says to tell you that she Pleads with Papa every day on this matter; she is determined to make him Change his Mind. If she succeeds, you can be certain we shall be there.

I remain, as always, your affectionate Friend,
                                   Patience

Letter from Patience Hendley
to her friend Hannah LeGrange
Spuyten Duyvil, New York,
20 August 1774

Thirty-one

Despite the late-August heat, a large, excited crowd had gathered along the road at the approach to the King's Bridge. The crowd, mostly men but with a sprinkling of women and boys, were craning their necks northward. It was midafternoon, a time when most of them would usually have been more usefully employed. But, obviously, something very special had drawn them here.

Samuel Peach, carrying a small keg on his shoulder, stood with a group of his tavern regulars at the very edge of the roadway. "Any sign of a dust cloud?" Nate Cluett asked Jotham, who was almost a head taller than he.

Jotham Dillard shook his head. "Nothin' yet. But look yonder!" He pointed across the road. "Comin' down the hill. It's *Tom!*"

Nate, surprised, ran across the road toward the indentured man. "Tom, you fool! Have you gone and taken French leave?"

Tom grinned and threw an arm over the shoulder of his best friend. "You didn't think I'd miss this, did you?"

"But if Hendley finds out you've made off without permission, he might haul you before the magistrate as he did last spring," Nate worried as they joined the others at the roadside.

Tom shrugged. "I'll take the chance. The worst they can do is beat me again. They've taken everything else."

His friends greeted him noisily. Tom noticed the keg Samuel was bearing on his shoulder and the mugs hanging from his belt.

"Samuel Peach, you gudgeon, have you brought your tavern out here?"

The innkeeper took no offense. "Tease all you want, but I ain't no fool. *He that prepares for the worst may hope for the best.*"

"What 'worst' do you prepare for on so happy a day?" Tom asked.

But just as Peach started to answer, a loud cheer from the crowd interrupted him. A dust cloud had appeared on the horizon. *"They're coming!"* the young boys shouted, jumping up and down. Suddenly it seemed as if everyone in Fordham was joining the throng, shouting and waving.

Tom looked about him in some surprise, for he hadn't expected so great a crowd or the show of so much enthusiasm. Yet he knew that the town of Fordham was not the first to be in an uproar. Every village and town between Boston and Philadelphia was— or would be—in a similar uproar, for the approaching coach was carrying a famous entourage from Boston. The renowned Samuel Adams, and Boston's other delegates to a newly called congress in Philadelphia, were travelling south. Of all the delegations gathering in Philadelphia, the one that most stirred up the emotions of the populace was the group from Boston.

In Tom's opinion, the man most responsible for stirring up those emotions was Sam Adams himself. Ever since May, when London's angry reaction to the Boston Tea Party became known, all the colonies were in turmoil. The punishment that Parliament had devised, the Port Act, seemed to every colonial but the most avid of Tories to be an act of the nastiest sort of revenge. Boston was being made the whipping boy. Unless and until the Massachusetts city made abject apology to the Crown and paid for the damaged tea, Parliament ordered that their town meetings be curtailed, that the Provincial government be moved to Salem, that a large contingent of British soldiers be quartered in town, and that the port of Boston be closed to all traffic, even to the ships carrying basic necessities. In effect, the Port Act meant the destruction of Boston as a center of trade and politics. "Little wonder," Tom had declared to his cronies, "that everyone's calling that damned legislation the Intolerable Acts."

What most delighted Tom was the swiftness and strength of the reaction in the colonies. In response to Sam Adams's circular letter declaring that Boston was "suffering in the common cause," every colony sent foodstuffs and other necessaries by land routes to assist the beleaguered Bostonians. He read in the newspapers of the outpouring of letters of support from the various committees of correspondence. Moreover, the colonies were taking action to protect themselves from possible British excesses. Committees of Safety were springing up in all the provinces, unsanctioned legislative bodies were being elected, and local militias were on alert. As soon as word spread of Parliament's action against Boston, angry demonstrations were held as far south as the Carolinas. In Virginia, June first was declared a day of fasting and prayer "to implore the Divine Interposition for averting the heavy Calamity, which threatens Destruction of our Civil Rights." In New York City, a mob carried the effigy of the British Prime Minister, Lord North, through the streets and burned it. Tom only wished he'd been able to be there.

For Tom, whose only hope of *personal* freedom now lay in the possibility of *political* freedom for the American colonies, these events were soul-stirring, for they were the best portents yet of impending revolution. And most stirring of all to his soul was the news that a Continental congress, with representatives from almost every colony on the continent, was about to be held. As he watched the dust cloud grow larger, he said aloud what he'd been thinking. "The fact that this congress is going to be held at all is almost a *miracle.*"

"Why a miracle?" Jotham grunted in his usual argumentative style. "It's on' y a meetin'."

"When did you ever before hear of all the colonies on the whole Continent holding a meeting?" Nate demanded.

"Especially since they ain't never come to no agreement about anything else," Daniel added.

"That's right," Tom said, "Even a simple thing like non-importation makes the members of our assemblies come to blows. So the fact that they could all agree on holding a congress seems like a miracle to me."

"They didn't all agree," Jotham muttered truculently. "Georgia ain't sendin' a delegation."

"That's only because they're having Indian troubles and they need the redcoats to help them," Nate pointed out.

Jotham shrugged. "Anyway, Tom's makin' too much of it. Nothing much'll come from a congress anyway but a lot of jawin'."

"Jotham's prob'ly right," Daniel said. "It'll be run by the Loyalists, and they won't do anything."

Nate had to agree. "The New York Assembly suggested such a congress back last May, and you, Tom, would be the first to admit they're full of Tories."

"Yes," Tom allowed, "but both the Whigs and Tories going to the congress are agreed that they're meeting to find a way *how* to respond to Parliament, not *whether* to respond. That's a good start. And what's more, I hear that the delegations, like the one from Massachusetts, are more Patriot than Loyalist. After all, it took the hotheaded Whigs of Virginia to make this Congress happen."

The others nodded, for it was quite true. Neither Samuel Adams nor the New York Assembly had been able to arrange a Continental Congress. It was not until those fiery young Virginians had cried for it—men like Patrick Henry, Thomas Jefferson and Richard Henry Lee—that the miracle had come about. Tom was convinced there was every reason to hope that most delegates were in sympathy with the Patriots.

Meanwhile, the delegates to this unprecedented Continental Congress were already gathering in Philadelphia. And now the delegation from Boston was on its way south. And its route carried them right through Fordham!

The word of their coming had preceded them, and as the Bostonians rode south in a splendid coach and four (led by two out-riders in front and four in the rear), they were met with eager crowds all along the way. Every town rang bells and shot cannon. Cheering men and women stood waving in doorways, lined the roadways or hung from upper windows to see them pass. Now the town of Fordham was about to see them, and they would do no less.

In another moment, the carriage itself could be seen through the dust. Closer and closer it came until it was almost upon them. But as it trundled past the curve of the road leading to the bridge, a huge groan rose from the crowd, for it did not appear to be slowing down. The people along the roadside began to fear that all they would see of the five men seated within were their shad-owy outlines.

But at that moment, Samuel Peach, endangering his life and limb, stepped right into the path of the conveyance. Pointing to the keg resting on his shoulder, he shouted at the top of his voice, "Stop for a cool drink, gentlemen! Cold cider, compliments of Samuel Peach of Peach's Tavern, yonder!"

To everyone's delight, the coach came to a stop, and a be-wigged head topped with a gold-trimmed tricorn leaned out of one of the windows. "We shan't say nay to a cold drink," the gentleman said. "Not in this blasted heat."

The crowd cheered. By the time the drinks were poured, the coach was encircled by a happy mob. Then the door opened and out came a wiry young gentleman who leaped from the steps and turned to hand down from the coach an older man in a red cape. The man in the cape, an imposing gentleman of about fifty, with a strong nose and chin and wearing an unkempt wig under his cocked hat, said to the younger man, "Thank you, Cushing, I *would* like to stretch my legs." He then inclined his head to the crowd and slowly strolled round the carriage, the dignity of his bearing causing the mob to clear a way for him.

A moment later the three remaining delegates climbed down from the coach. One of them, quite tall and handsome, immediately began to shake hands with the onlookers. The second discreetly asked to be directed to an outhouse. The last, a stocky man in his late thirties, with very full cheeks accentuated by a wig that was profusely puffed over his ears, merely leaned against the carriage and sipped his cider with obvious pleasure.

Jotham studied the travelers with interest. "Do ye think the hand-shaker is Sam Adams?" he asked Tom in a voice much too loud for good manners.

"No," Tom muttered, embarrassedly aware that the stocky man leaning on the coach could hear them, "Sam Adams is the one in the red cloak. Haven't you ever heard of the famous red cloak?"

"Cain't say as I have," Jotham said, craning his neck to get a better glimpse of the notorious Bostonian. "He looks very grand, don't he, in that coat with the gold buttons?"

Tom nodded. "I must admit I didn't expect his red cloak to look so very fine. I'd heard it described as ragged."

The gentleman leaning on the carriage smiled wryly. "That's because it's new," he said to Tom in a confiding way. "An unknown benefactor provided him with a complete wardrobe for this occasion, to replace the disgracefully shabby attire he usually wears."

"Oh, I see," Tom smiled back. "I hope that a change of wardrobe doesn't mean a change of views."

"Oh, indeed not!" the gentleman exclaimed with sincere conviction. "Mr. Sam Adams has not changed his views for more than thirty years, and I can assure you he will not change in the next thirty. The man has the best grasp of the meaning of liberty—and the strongest love for it—of any man I know."

"Can you tell us, sir," Nate asked him, leaning over Tom's shoulder, "which one is Mr. *John* Adams?"

"John Adams?" The gentleman's eyebrows rose. "I'm surprised you've heard of him."

Tom grinned. "Nate, you jackpudding, you're *speaking* to him."

John Adams—for it was truly he—broke into a pleased guffaw. "How on earth did you guess that?" he asked Tom. "I surely cannot be very well known here in Westchester County."

"You're too modest, sir," Tom said. "We've known of you ever since you defended Captain Preston in the Boston Massacre trial in '70."

"Tom, here, reads your writings wherever and whenever he can find them," Nate put in, blushing at his own temerity in speaking so freely to a famous man, "and that's the truth, sir."

"I'm very pleased to hear it," John Adams said, reaching out and shaking Tom's hand warmly.

"I read ye, too," Jotham lied, grabbing the Bostonian's hand as soon as Tom released it.

Then, as Nate took his turn to be so honored, the other travelers began to return to their conveyance. Jotham, unwilling to let the moment end, told John Adams eagerly, "We're drilling our militia just like you wrote in the last circular letter. Tom, here . . . he's the one puts us through our paces."

"Good for you, lad," Adams said, clapping Tom on the shoulder. "Keep it up. One of these days you'll discover it's not for naught."

Another moment, another lusty cheer from the crowd, and the coach was on its way. The people began to disperse, but Tom and his friends lingered, gazing after the disappearing carriage in awe. Jotham, however, shook his head in disappointment. "I wish we'd a shook hands with *Sam* Adams instead of John," he sighed. "Who's John anyway? On'y Sam's cousin."

"Never mind, Joth," Tom said in consolation. "You'll brag about shaking that man's hand one day. I have a feeling we'll be hearing a lot more about cousin John in time to come."

Thirty-two

Peter Hendley was still too weak to venture far from home, but he would not have joined the mob at the King's Bridge even if he'd been well. He felt nothing but scorn for the meeting in Philadelphia and for all its participants. "They call themselves a congress," he ranted to Barbara, who'd come into his bedroom with a bowl of bright blue asters, "but they're nothing but a collection of upstarts and hotheads. Those damned delegates'll spend their time bickering—just see if they don't!—and they won't come to agreement on a single matter of importance."

"Yes, Papa, I know," Barbara said with a teasing smile. "You've said it often enough."

Hendley, though fully clothed, was taking his daily bed rest. As he leaned back against a mountain of pillows, he frowned ruefully at his pretty young daughter. "It's just too bad, Babs, that you have no interest in politics," he grumbled, pulling out one of the pillows behind him and thrusting it under his left leg. "You're nothing but a flibbertigibbet."

"So I am," the redheaded girl agreed cheerfully, in full awareness of the affection behind the gruffness of his tone. She'd always been his little pet, and she knew it. "But at least you have Patience to talk to. She takes a great deal of interest in the stupid Congress."

Hendley's expression clouded, and he dropped his eyes. "Patience doesn't discuss these things with me anymore."

"Give her time, Papa. She's been sorely blue-deviled since Sally left. But she'll get over it, wait and see."

"Hummph," he grunted, picking up the newspaper that was lying beside him.

"I'm sorry I'm too flighty to understand politics, Papa, but one can't help one's nature." She picked up a folded coverlet and spread it over his legs, but he kicked it away. She shrugged and refolded it. "Speaking of flighty matters," she went on, "I hope you've decided to escort us to the Lovell's frolic. The doctor says you're well enough now."

Hendley lowered the newspaper and glared at her. "What does the doctor know? I now better than he how well or ill I feel."

"Sorry, Papa, I didn't mean to get your dander up. But think about it, will you? The frolic will be good for you. You'll be able to curse the Congress with Mr. Lovell to your heart's content."

"Won't do you a bit of good to ride rusty in this matter," her father said flatly.

"I won't stop riding rusty about this, Papa. I can be as obstinate as you. I want to go to the party more than anything, but since we won't go without you, *go you will!*"

His only response was another grunt.

Babs, encouraged by his mild response, pranced out of the room happily, but in another moment poked her head round the doorframe. "Oh, Papa, I almost forgot. Patience said to tell you there's a man waiting to see you. From New York. A Mr. Barlow."

Hendley's face brightened. He thrust the paper aside and swung his legs over the side of the bed. "So he's come. Good! Have him wait in my workroom. I'll be right down."

When Babs delivered her father's message downstairs, Patience herself led the visitor from the front room toward the passageway to her father's office. She did not exchange many words with him, for he did not appear to be the sort with whom a gentlewoman should converse. He was a burly, unkempt fellow with beady eyes set in a ruddy, pock-marked face, and his thickset body was carelessly swathed in clothes that, like his fingernails, were none too clean. From the look of him—and because she knew her father—Patience had already guessed who he was: an agent whose vocation was the recovery of runaway slaves.

At the foot of the back stairs, she and the visitor came face-to-face with Hendley, who was making his painstaking way down with the help of the banister and his cane. Patience, her lips pressed together and her back stiff with disapproval, strode ahead of the men through the passageway and threw open the workroom door. Then she stood back and, without giving her father so much as a glance, allowed the two men to pass in front of her. As soon as they stepped inside, she closed the door on them just loudly enough to indicate to her father how she felt.

Hendley frowned at the door for a moment. Then, with a sigh and a shake of his head, he looked up at the man from New York City and offered his hand. "Thank you for coming, Barlow," he said. "I'd have come to you, but I've been ill."

"That's all right," the fellow answered. "I'm used to travelin' great distances—follerin' leads, y' see. From New York to here ain't no great distance to me." He shook Hendley's hand enthusiastically. "Artemas 'Black Hawk' Barlow at your service."

"Sit down, Mr. Barlow. Would you like a drink? Porter? A bishop?"

"No, thank you, sir. Slaked my thirst at the inn at the foot o' the bridge. Peach's Tavern, I think it's called."

"I'm sorry you did that." Hendley frowned as he took the chair behind his desk and motioned his guest to another. "That damned inn's a hotbed of upstarts and rebels. I suppose you heard all sorts of seditious talk there."

The agent shrugged. "I didn' pay any mind. Just had a mug o' cider is all."

In truth, Mr. Artemas Barlow had no interest in politics. He was the sort who could cadge a living with his wits or with his fists no matter who was in power. He'd advertised himself in the newspaper as *"a Factor of Inquiry, having much Experience and Success in the Discovery and Recovery of Runaways, both*

Slaves and Bond-slaves." Hendley, who'd been wondering all through his convalescence what action to take to recover his "property," had seen the advertisement and had written to the agent a week earlier, requesting an interview. And, with impressive promptness, here the fellow was.

Barlow took a shrewd look about the room before taking his seat. "No, sirree," he declared as he settled into the chair, "I don't claim to know much about politics. What I *do* know is my trade, so let's get down to business, if you've a mind. You have a runaway slave you want found, right?"

"Two slaves," Hendley corrected. "Two." He leaned back against the slats of his wooden desk chair and studied the agent closely. His illness, though severe, had not in any way affected his judgment. Although he'd suffered what the doctor diagnosed as a severe paralytic seizure brought about by an apoplectic stroke, he had by this time almost completely recovered. The fact that the stroke had been caused by a blockage of the blood in the brain did not seem, fortunately, to have affected his mind. And although the paralysis of his left side had lasted almost a month, his use of his limbs was now almost fully restored. Yes, his mouth was slightly twisted (the left corner frozen in a downturn, making him look perpetually cross), and the left half his tongue was bereft of feeling and the ability to taste; but he was otherwise much as he'd been before. He was, therefore, quite capable of taking the measure of the man in front of him.

Artemas Barlow, with his narrow eyes and coarse features, was not someone to inspire admiration. But Hendley knew that the fellow's rough appearance did not necessarily signify that he wouldn't be good at his job. Searching out runaways was not an occupation that required delicacy.

"Two, eh?" the agent was saying. "That makes it easier." He leaned forward, his expression hardening. "But easy or hard, my price is the same. Fifteen percent o' their value."

"I won't haggle," Hendley responded, having convinced himself of fellow's ability by the blatant self-confidence of his manner. "I don't grutch you a good fee, Mr. Barlow, so long as you find them."

"I'll find 'em. I ain't called Black Hawk for nothin'."

"I don't believe it will be as easy as you think," Hendley warned. "They've been missing since April." He handed the agent a closely written sheet of paper. "Here, I've written down full descriptions, but I haven't any other information to offer. I don't even know the direction they took."

The agent shrugged. "North. You don't find many nigras goin' south these days."

"Well then, I'll leave it all in your hands. Find them and take them to New York. Don't bring them here—I'll meet you in the city. I calculate they'll fetch at least eight hundred the pair, but even if they bring less, I guarantee you one hundred twenty pounds minimum."

Barlow eyed him curiously. "You sure you want 'em brought to New York? I'm willin' to bring 'em here and save you a trip."

"No, I don't want them here. It would be too upsetting to my . . . but never mind. You don't need explanations. And I don't want you bothering me with details. Just get on with your job and keep the details to yourself 'til you have them."

With the terms agreed on, the two men shook hands, and Black Hawk Barlow took his leave. Hendley stood at the window and watched him ride off on horseback, feeling a satisfying sense of relief. It was done. He could put the matter out of his mind for a while. Now if only Patience would put the matter out of *her* mind . . .

Patience's attitude toward him was indeed troublesome. It was easy for the doctor to warn Hendley not to let himself become agitated, but how could he remain easy in his mind when Patience was still distant to him?

Of course, the doctor would not believe such a thing of Patience. He'd often repeated to Hendley that his illness could have been fatal had it not been for his daughter's devoted care of him. And Hendley had to admit it was true. Despite the hideous scene that had preceded his attack, despite the fact that he'd actually struck her across her face, Patience had done her duty. She'd been the mainstay of the household and the estate. But he could not ignore the stiffness in her verbal exchanges with him, the rigidity of her back whenever she came to his bedside, the look of reproof at the back of her eyes. She had not forgiven him, and he feared she never would.

Perhaps she didn't understand that he was changed. The experience of severe illness had left an unerasable mark on him. The onset of the stroke had been terrifying, and he lived in constant fear that it might happen again. He had a distinct memory of how he'd felt . . . the pain, the frightening paralysis, the abnormal pounding of his pulse, the laborious breathing and the overwhelming certainty that death was about to seize him. Then there had been the blackness of unconsciousness followed by the smell of sal volatile under his nose and the ludicrously painful effect of the horrid sneezing powders that the doctor had used to bring him round.

But that was only the beginning. The recovery period had been just as nightmarish. Not only had he been forced to endure the imprisonment of enforced bed rest, but the doctor had bled him much too often, he'd had great difficulty voiding, and, worst of all, he'd had to face weeks and weeks of torture as Patience and Benjy, under the explicit orders of the doctor, had walked him about the room, pushing and prodding him to use his legs, in their daily attempt to revive his paralyzed muscles.

There was no denying the success of their combined efforts. They had been tireless, the two of them. (Babs, the pleasure-seeker, had been too overcome by the pain in his face to participate in the exercises.) As a result, he could now climb up and down the stairs without assistance, work in his office for a few hours a day, take short walks outdoors, and down his food without revulsion. In other words, he'd finally returned to life.

But the doctor had warned him that things could not proceed

as before. "You'll have to be calm," the doctor said. "Excitability can undo you. And you'll have to stay away from strong drink."

Hendley had laughed bitterly. "I can easily refrain from drinking," he'd retorted, "but how can I stay calm while this colony reels with unrest?"

He did not add, *and while my daughter views me as a monster.* But, whether the doctor would believe him or not, Patience's distantly dutiful bearing toward him did not contribute to a feeling of calm well-being.

Fearful of a recurrence of stroke, he was sincerely trying to insulate himself against excitement. Not only had he rid himself of the runaway slave problem, he'd enlisted Clymer Young as well as Josephus Lovell to assist him in the buying of munitions for the cache of arms he was accumulating in a secret hideaway at the northern corner of his estate. He'd known even before he became ill that he could not build his arsenal without help. He'd hoped that Patience would assist him in this endeavor, but the girl no longer seemed receptive to his plans. Lovell was helpful in supplying funds, but Clymer Young was more willing to take an active role. Hendley was grateful that Young's Loyalist feelings were as strong as his. Clymer Young, the only one in the world beside himself who knew the site of the secret cache, was overseeing the details of his plan with energetic enthusiasm.

Nevertheless, there were still real obstacles to his serenity of mind, the worst of which was his ruined relationship with his daughter Patience. That blasted scene over the slave business—in particular the moment when he'd struck her face—had ruined his health and cost him his daughter's affection. True, he had hurt her badly. But she'd hurt him, too, more than she knew. She'd shown that she felt more love for Sally as a parent than for him. It was humiliating to find oneself second in one's daughter's affection to a Negress! He had feelings too. Didn't she have any respect for them?

Sometimes he tried to put himself in her place—to look at the incident through her eyes. At those times, he permitted himself to wonder if he'd been wrong to have tried to sell Aaron. But he always answered no. Slaves were property, and if Patience could not accept that principle, she was in the wrong, not he.

But right or wrong, he wished he could find a way to restore the former good will between them. *Perhaps,* he thought suddenly, turning away from the window and hobbling toward the door, it *might be helpful to go with my daughters to the frolic at the Lovells.* Parties and such fripperies were always pleasing to the ladies, and his company at such an occasion might be the way to warm Patience's heart. In any case, he couldn't think of a better plan.

He threw open the door. "Babs," he shouted down the passageway, "I've changed my mind! I'll escort you and Patience to the Lovells after all."

Thirty-three

Beatie must have overslept, Patience thought in surprise as she entered the deserted kitchen. The morning sun, though not yet showing itself above the low-lying clouds, was already lighting the underside of the leaves outside the kitchen's east window with a pale, autumnal glow—a good indication that the time was well past six. Since the taciturn Scotswoman was remarkably reliable—almost always well started in her chores by the time Patience came down—her absence this morning was not only unexpected but troublesome. No fire had been started in the hearth, and the room was chilly. A cold wind, unusually sharp for September, had blown in from the north and was rattling the shutters and sending draughty messages down the chimney that summer was over.

Patience bit her lip in anxiety as she piled up the logs on the grate and lit the kindling. But her distress was not caused by Beatie's having overslept or by having to perform this particular chore; it was the prospect of having to go to the door to get the milk when it was brought round from the barn, a chore she'd avoided since spring.

Avoidance was how she was dealing with Tom. Not that Tom usually delivered the milk himself—it was Chester's job to do the milking and bring round a fresh pail of it to the kitchen—but lately Tom had taken to doing the delivery more and more often. He'd stand in the doorway peering over Beatie's shoulder to try to catch her eye, but Patience would not let herself look his way.

Just as, when the servants came for their meals, she'd manage not to be present. But this morning, if Beatie didn't arrive soon, and if Tom decided to bring round the milk himself, Patience might have to face him.

It had not been easy to avoid him all these months, especially when the weather was warm and she was out of doors. If she were working in the kitchen garden or simply taking the air, Tom would somehow manage to pass her way. But she'd held him at a distance by keeping communication to a mere nod. She'd not indulged in any conversation beyond a simple "Good day." Sometimes, before she turned away from him, she'd catch that look of hurt and longing in his eyes—a look that would cut through her heart like a knife through butter—but she hardened herself to it.

She'd managed to avoid him, but it was harder to avoid her own thoughts and longings. The nights were the worst, when she'd lie sleepless, feeling that sinful ache for him. Every moment of their time together in the loft was imprinted on her memory . . . every spoken word, every whispered endearment, every touch of his fingers and pressure of his body. If she permitted herself the indulgence, she could recreate from memory the overwhelming passion of that night. Sometimes, to drive the memories away, she'd have to get up and prowl about the room, making herself say the seventy-first psalm: "In thee, O Lord, have I taken refuge; Let me never be ashamed." She'd say it over and over until overcome by weariness. Often afterwards, her sleep would be troubled by fearful, erotic dreams that she was glad she could not remember when she woke.

She couldn't forgive herself for permitting herself to love him. She was a married woman and a Loyalist; he was a bondsman and a rebel. She was, despite her recent erratic behavior in the matter of Sally and Aaron and in her single act of adultery (an act for which she prayed daily for the Lord's forgiveness), a dutiful, properly behaved woman who was heart and soul for God and king. He was heart and soul for rebellion, ready to sacrifice anything for what he felt was his cause. She'd seen the seditious pamphlets he carried in his pockets. And she was well aware that he often stole away from his duties to drill with the militia or to attend rebel meetings. Only last week he'd disappeared from the orchard, where he'd been desperately needed to oversee the harvesting of the crop of yellow pears, to go down to Fordham to watch Sam Adams pass by. Sam Adams, a rabble-rouser who constantly twisted the facts to make his case, who would not balk at outright lies to advance the cause of liberty for the colonies— that was the sort of man who was a hero to Tom! How, knowing they were divided by these moral and political differences, had she permitted herself to fall in love with—?

A knock at the kitchen door stopped her thoughts. Pulse racing nervously, she went to the door and opened it. Of course it was he. She was not surprised. There he stood in his shirtsleeves, his cheeks reddened by the wind and his tousled hair haloed by the early morning sun. He seemed not a bit disconcerted at finding her in the doorway. "Good morning," he grinned.

She reached for the pail. "Thank you. I'll take it."

Tom held it out of her reach. "I'll put it on the table for you," he said brazenly, brushing by her and stepping over the threshold.

She remained holding the door open. "Thank you," she said again, pointedly dismissive.

"You may as well close it, ma'am. I'm not going yet awhile."

She drew in a breath, and her back grew rigid. "Yes, you are, Tom. Right now."

He strolled to the doorway as if he were obeying her order, but when he came abreast of her, he lifted her off her feet and into his arms in one swift movement, kicking the door closed at the same time. Then he heaved her up on his chest and swung her round and round in delight. "At last!" he chortled.

"Tom, have you gone mad? Put me down!"

"I will. As soon as you kiss me."

"Stop this! I thought we'd agreed—"

"I never agreed."

The reeling and the height made her dizzy but not less dismayed. "Tom, put me down at once! Beatie will be here any minute now!"

"No, she won't," Tom said, his eyes gleaming in triumph. "She's waiting in the barn till I give her word."

"You mean you *arranged* this?"

"What else was I to do? You're so damnably clever at avoiding me."

"You . . . you *trickster!* Put me—!"

He lowered her just enough to bring their faces close. "Kiss me."

"No! Tom, please, you *mustn't*—"

He did not let her finish but set her on her feet so that he could hold her tighter. Before she could take a breath or recover her equilibrium, he pressed his mouth on hers. She struggled against him for a moment, but she could not free herself. After that moment, she didn't wish to. She felt dismayed at herself, but her arms crept up round his neck and her body sagged against him quite against her control. For an unmeasurable breath of time they clung together, but then she forcibly broke from him, turned away and burst into tears.

Her reaction startled him. "Damn me," he cursed under his breath. He came up behind her, stricken with remorse. "Don't, cry, Patience, please! I'm sorry. I never intended to upset you."

"If you d-didn't intend it, you w-wouldn't have done it," she stammered through her sobs, not turning round.

"Yes, I would. I . . . I had to."

"H-had to?"

"Yes, to prove to myself that what happened last April wasn't a dream. It's been more than four months . . . and not a day has passed that I haven't wanted—"

"In this world," she cut in, her voice choked, "we don't often get what we want."

"You don't have to tell me that," he retorted. "I know it better than you."

She dashed her tears away. "Then why do you insist on making matters harder for yourself . . . and for me?"

"Is it hard for you? It surely doesn't seem so."

"Can you not see that it is?"

"I can't see anything when you turn your face from me every time I come near you!" he burst out.

She would not turn her head, but the effort to keep from doing so sent a shudder through her body. "What you want of me, Tom," she said brokenly, "is the greatest of sins."

"Patience! I didn't . . . I don't . . ." He stared at her bent head, trying to find the words to do battle with hers. None came to mind. His love for her *was* sinful, he supposed, to everyone in the world but him. How could he argue against the *Commandments?* He put a gentle hand on her shoulder, but immediately withdrew it. "Very well, ma'am," he sighed, "I won't do this again if it upsets you so."

At those words she looked over her shoulder at him. "Is it a promise, this time?"

There was a pause while his eyes searched her tear-streaked face. Then he nodded, defeated. "Yes, yes, blast it, I promise!"

He went to the door. She followed, to close it after him. On the threshold he paused and looked at her. "I *didn't* dream it, did I?"

She dropped her eyes. "Let's agree that it *was* a dream. It's better so."

"Not for me." He grasped her shoulders angrily. "Damn it, woman, tell me it wasn't a dream! Give me that, at least."

She could not look him in the face. " 'Twould be an empty gift," she said in a small, choked voice.

"Tell me!"

"Oh, Tom, my *dear,*" she whispered, meeting his eyes at last, "if it *was* a dream, I dreamed it too."

Thirty-four

It was apparent from the first that Hannah's party, so long anticipated and so carefully prepared for, was going to be a disaster, but no one could have guessed how huge a disaster it would turn out to be. First of all it rained, a devilish downpour that was worsened by an angry wind. The umbrellas that the servants carried out to protect the arriving guests on their dash from carriage to doorway proved of little use. The New York Bogaerdes (who, because of the distance they had to travel, had been invited for the weekend) entered the hallway of Lovell Manor with not only their cloaks but their bandboxes and nightcases dripping wet.

Barbara had dressed for the party in an alamode-silk gown of pale lavender that she'd designed and laboriously stitched all by herself, but it was so heavily sprayed with raindrops by the time she reached the doorway that she almost burst into tears. "Look at me!" she wailed to Patience as soon as they found themselves alone in the room set aside for the ladies to remove their outer garments and repair their coiffures. "The skirt of my gown is *drenched,* and the silk is *certain* to pucker!"

"You look perfectly lovely," her sister assured her, "and, moreover, you won't be the only female whose hem is rainspotted. Besides, with the boldness of your décolletage, no one will be looking at your hem."

This was cold comfort to Barbara, who'd planned and worked for months to ensure that her appearance would be perfect for this longed-for night. But she was to learn that puckers on her gown would be the least of her troubles.

Her first encounter with the man of her dreams was her next blow. As the guests gathered in the Lovells' huge drawing room, Hannah ushered the New York Bogaerdes (accompanied by Tilda's red-coated betrothed) round the room to make the introductions. When she brought the group to Barbara, Lieutenant Pilkington bowed over her hand as if he'd never met her. Poor Barbara was appalled. "But we've already m-met," she cried, her lower lip trembling. "You *must* remember!"

"Yes, of course, I remember," the officer murmured with a false smile, just as anyone might who was mouthing a polite lie, and he turned away to greet Hugo Bogaerde and the other members of the Westchester Bogaerde clan, who had just made a noisy arrival.

Barbara was quite ready to die. Quivering on the edge of tears, she lowered her head and moved surreptitiously across the room to where her brother was engaged in a boyish attempt at flirtation with Ilse Bogaerde. On her way, she passed Henryk, who did not greet her but turned coldly away. This in no way improved her state of mind.

Barbara hurried her step and tugged at her brother's arm. "Benjy," she muttered tensely, "get me out of here."

Benjy had been feeling very grown up and dashing in his first real evening coat (the lace-trimmed sleeves of which young Ilse was obviously admiring) and was not happy at his sister's interruption. But before he could give Babs a proper set-down, he noticed something about the way her head was bent—something that warned him she was in distress. "Please excuse us," he said to Ilse with a quick bow. With his brows knit worriedly, he took Barbara's arm and led her from the room.

They hurried down the corridor to the next room—it proved to be Mr. Lovell's library—and went in and closed the door. "Goodness, Babs, what's amiss?" the boy asked in alarm, peering at his flushed sister from across the long table that occupied the center of the room.

"He *can't* have forgotten me!" Barbara exclaimed, tears beginning to spill from her eyes. "He *can't!* He made *love* to me!"

"Who?" Benjy asked, wide-eyed.

"It's some sort of pretense, that's what it is!" The girl dashed the tears from her cheeks and began to pace around the table furiously. "It must be a pretense! But what can he mean by it?"

"What on earth are you talking about?" Benjy asked as he followed behind her bewilderedly. "Did someone take liberties with you?"

"I haven't forgotten *one little thing* about *him!*" she ranted on, ignoring her brother's alarmed concern. "I could slap his *face!*"

"Whose face, dash it! *Whose?*"

She wheeled on him. "Lieutenant Pilkington's, that's whose."

Benjy stopped short. "Matilde Bogaerde's Lieutenant? *He* made love to you?"

Barbara barely heard him. "How dared he pretend not to know me! How *dared* he!"

Benjy's cheeks grew hot in anger. "He made *love* to you? That . . . that *redcoat?*" He stormed round the table to the door. "I'm going to call him out!"

Barbara heard him at last. "Benjy," she ordered, *"stop where you are!"*

"Why?" He turned to his sister in frustration. "The fellow's a bounder!"

She slapped a hand on the table with determination. *"Listen* to me, Benjy, I never meant to—! You must forget all this. You didn't hear anything of what I said, do you understand me?"

Benjy blinked. "What do you mean? Of course I heard—"

"Then please forget it. It was all . . . foolishness. Nothing important. Do you hear me?"

"I hear you, but I don't understand. If the fellow manhandled you, he ought to be punished."

"He didn't manhandle me. Forget all about it." Forcing a smile, she came round the table to him and patted him on the cheek. "I'm feeling much better now, truly I am. Let's go back to the party."

Benjy thrust her hand away. "I say, Babs, you don't have to be afraid for me. I know how to shoot. I can handle this."

"Benjamin Hendley, you will not handle *anything*," his sister said firmly. "If a *word* of what you heard just now ever leaves your lips, I will never, ever forgive you."

"Dash it, Babs, are you just going to let the fellow get away with his dastardly deed?"

"I tell you there was no dastardly deed. And if there was, you may take my word he won't get off unscathed. I can deal with Lieutenant Pilkington very well myself." She put out her hand. "Agreed?"

Her brother rolled his eyes heavenward. "Girls! I'll never understand them." Reluctantly, he shrugged in capitulation. "Very well, agreed," he muttered, shaking her hand.

"Good. Now that's settled, Benjy, will you please take a good look at me? Do I look passably well? I don't want anyone to see me with red eyes."

With her brother's assurance that her eyes were hardly red at all, the two returned to the drawing room.

No one noticed their return because an argument had arisen that had captured everyone's attention. Mr. Wilhelm Bogaerde of New York, who had not met Peter Hendley before and thus had no idea of the extent of his Tory convictions, had innocently remarked that he hoped the Congress, now meeting in Philadelphia, would be a success. In response, Hendley had snapped, "What would you call a success? Declaring a war over a boatload of tea?"

"Nobody wants war, Hendley," Stuart had said gently. "That is not the goal of the Congress."

"Massachusetts wants it," Hendley insisted.

"That ain't so," Wilhelm Bogaerde argued. "I heard from my

cousin—cousin Jan, you know, Hugo, who's just returned from Philadelphia—that the Adamses are being, how you say, restrained."

"Ha!" Lovell sneered, forgetting his role as polite host, "Sam Adams, *restrained?* Never!"

Hendley's misshapen mouth twisted into a mocking smile. "Right you are, Lovell. And even if the Adamses are not shouting, you can wager your trews that they're doing plenty of manipulation behind the scenes."

"The Massachusetts contingent will not propose war," Stuart insisted, his voice calm but firm. "They know as well as anyone that in a military struggle with England we would likely lose, and then we'd have to face a despotism much worse than anything we face now."

Hendley did not like Stuart's interpretation one bit. *"What despotism do we face now?"* he demanded belligerently.

Stuart's eyebrows rose. "Do you not call the Intolerable Acts despotic?"

"No, I don't. I call them a just punishment. Let Boston take its lumps and leave the rest of us alone."

"You can't mean it, Hendley," Stuart remonstrated. "Parliament cannot treat American landholdings like medieval fiefdoms. Our holdings were founded by free men exercising their natural right to—"

"Natural right?" Hendley leaned forward and brandished his cane. "What natural right? The right to oppose our true government?"

"Papa," Patience warned softly, "you are getting excited."

"Ach, who cares about politics," said Madame Bogaerde, "ven ve can see a baby. When shall ve see your little Caleb, Hannah?"

"The nurse will bring him down when he wakes for his late-night feeding," Hannah promised, smiling proudly at the prospect.

But Peter Hendley did not care about babies. He promptly returned to the argument. "I take a real dislike to the phrase 'natural rights,' LeGrange. When I hear those words I always assume, and usually correctly, that it is coming from a revolutionary."

Stuart reddened and opened up his mouth to reply, but Hugo Bogaerde intervened. "Now, now, Peter," he said placatingly, "you can't call LeGrange a revolutionary. He's a businessman who doesn't vant a distant monarchy to interfere vit his trade, is all."

"Thank you, Mr. Bogaerde, but I am quite capable of speaking for myself," Stuart said, his usual calm good nature giving way for the first time to a show of irritation. "As for your accusation, Mr. Hendley, it is completely unfounded. One needn't be a revolutionary to believe that Parliament and the Crown are two separate entities. Allegiance to the latter does not mean one has to be obedient to the former."

"Hear, hear!" chortled Wilhelm Bogaerde.

"Right you are!" Henryk Bogaerde burst out with enthusiasm, but he subsided immediately as his father threw him a forbidding glare.

Hendley banged his cane loudly on the floor and, with all eyes turned to him, prepared to make a loud rebuttal. Patience drew in a breath, alarmed at her father's rising color. Hannah, looking from one to the other, knew this altercation had to end. She jumped up from her seat and announced loudly that she was certain the butler was about to open the doors to the dining room for the buffet. Then, throwing her husband a glower of rebuke for his part in the argument, she asked Peter Hendley for his arm to escort her to the table, thus effectively cutting off further discussion, at least for the moment.

In the dining room, Barbara, dinner plate in hand, edged up to the buffet as close to her lieutenant as good manners allowed, and reached out for a slice of roast beef at the same moment as he. She even jostled his arm. He responded with a cold stare and promptly walked away.

Disconsolate, she took her plate (on which, for appearances' sake, she'd placed a piece of smoked fish and a spoonful of string beans that Hannah insisted on calling "harico") to the window of the drawing room and poked at the food with her fork. From the corner of her eye she saw Lieutenant Pilkington bring a mug of mulled cider to his affianced bride where she sat on one of the sofas between her mother and her aunt, delicately eating a spoonful of Hannah's famous ragout'd lobster. When Tilda rewarded her lieutenant with a glance of loving gratitude, Barbara had to turn her eyes away from that tender display.

She almost jumped, a few seconds later, when a voice said in her ear, "You might find it more comfortable in the next room, Mistress Hendley."

"What?" she gasped, her heart pounding as she looked round to see if it was really he. It was.

"I was only suggesting that you might find a more comfortable place for eating in the next room," Jack Pilkington said, his expression impassive and his tone distantly polite. "There's a table there, I believe. I intend to make use of it myself in a moment or two."

"Oh?" Barbara asked stupidly, blinking up at him.

He merely bowed and moved off to the punch bowl.

The bewildered girl stared after him, gathering her wits. His words were an invitation, that much was clear. Once she realized it, the girl did not hesitate for long. Taking a deep breath, she forced herself to stroll across the room with a casual lack of speed, but once out of the eyesight of the others she raced down the corridor to the bookroom. There she carefully placed her platter on the table, sat down in front of it and tried to calm herself.

An endless few minutes went by, but he did not come. Her nervousness and anger increased with every passing second. When she could bear it no longer, she rose from her chair, intending to stalk out of the room. It was at that moment the lieutenant, holding a heavily loaded plate before him, appeared on the threshold.

They stared at each other for a moment, not moving. Neither said a word. Then Jack Pilkington tore his eyes from hers and glanced up and down the corridor. Satisfied that no one was about, he whisked himself over the threshold and, carefully balancing the plate, closed the door behind him. Keeping his eyes fixed on her face, he set the food down on the table. *"Egad,"* he breathed at last, his eyes alight, "you're even more beautiful than I remembered."

Something exploded inside her, emotions made up partly of fury and partly of joy. "You *bastard!*" she cried, throwing herself upon him and beating his chest with her fists. "So you remembered me after all!"

He laughed, caught her fists in his hands and held them tight. "Remembered you? You little baggage, you haven't been out of my thoughts for one hour since I last laid eyes on you."

"Oh, *Jack,*" she exclaimed, misty-eyed, "really?"

"Oh, yes, really. You've been quite real in my mind. I had only to close my eyes and there you'd be. It's your mouth, I think, and that way you have of running the tip of your tongue along your upper lip. You put a curse on me, didn't you? I've been under a spell ever since I saw you do it."

"Silly!" She gave a gurgling laugh, but it died in her throat. "Then why did you never come," she asked petulantly, "nor even send me word?"

"Vixen, you know why. I am a man betrothed. There is such a thing as honor."

She wound her arms around his neck. "Oh, pooh! Honor be hanged."

"Yes," he sighed, pulling her to him, "when your mouth is so close, honor be hanged."

He kissed her hungrily, and she responded with fervent, if innocent, passion. He lifted one hand and let his fingers trace lightly over the line of her cheek and jaw and down her neck, aware of the little tremors that followed in the wake of his touch. But when his fingers reached the cleft of her breast, he himself trembled. "I didn't believe my memory of this," he murmured, ". . . that your skin could be so soft . . . so incredibly soft . . ."

A wave of desire welled up in him so powerful that he found it startling. It was a desire strengthened by months of abstinence during his very proper betrothal. Mathilde, he'd discovered, had neither a sense of humor nor a spirit of adventure. More to the point, she showed no taste for what she called the "bundling and huggermugger" that many other betrothed couples indulged in. She invariably would reject his attempts at sexual foreplay with a firm withdrawal, softening the rejection by smiling and wagging an accusing finger in his face. "You naughty boy," she'd say in her soft voice, "you must stop trying to play these wicked little games." Thus Barbara's uninhibited passion, which in other circumstances might have struck him as vulgar or even indecent, now seemed to him youthfully exuberant, attractive and wildly exciting.

Aware only of the burning in his loins and the warm responses of the alluring creature in his arms, he lifted her up with one arm and, sweeping aside the plates of food with the other, laid her on the table with himself on top, all the while kissing her throat and the curve of her shoulder. She did not resist, for every bone and muscle of her body seemed to have turned to quivering jelly. "Jack, the door . . ." she managed to gasp. "Someone may come . . ."

But he was beyond caution. And when he slipped the shoulder of her gown down her arm, and she felt his lips on her bared breast, she too lost her sense of time and place. She could only moan in an agony of passion. When she felt his tongue caress her nipple, she was not aware of her response. She had no consciousness of twisting her fingers tightly in his hair and gasping out the ecstasy that was welling up within her.

But the sound froze in her throat, for something *did* finally penetrate her consciousness. Someone was opening the door.

"Oh, my *Lord . . . !*" came a cry from the threshold.

The lovers did not need to look to know who was standing

there. Mistress Mathilde Bogaerde, stunned, stared at them, her
cheeks slowly turning white. Then, either because the shock was
so great or because she couldn't think of what else to do, she
fainted dead away.

Out in the corridor Madame Bogaerde and Tante Gusti, who'd
been strolling a short distance behind Tilda carrying their tea-
cups, saw the girl fall to the floor. Madame Bogaerde screamed,
dropped her teacup and ran to the book-room doorway. Inside,
the lieutenant and the red-haired temptress, who'd not yet had
time to gather themselves together, still lay upon the table, Barbara's breast with its rosy, hardened nipple plainly visible, and
Pilkington, on top of her, gaping over his shoulder in wide-eyed
guilt.

Madame Bogaerde's scream brought the entire household
swarming into the corridor. In another moment the doorway was
crowded with horrified onlookers, babbling, gasping and shouting questions in unison.

"Vat has happened? Vat?"

"Oh, no!"

"Is that *Pilkington?*"

"Step aside and let me through!"

"Babs? Iss dat sveet little *Babs?*"

"Not *Jack!*"

Jack, his moment of paralysis over, leaped up and helped Barbara to her feet. The girl, more benumbed than embarrassed,
hurriedly pulled her gown up on her shoulders, while Jack
stepped in front of her in a defiantly brave attempt to shelter her
from the glares of shocked disapprobation.

Pandemonium followed. Tilda's mother, with another cry,
knelt down beside her daughter and began to chafe at her wrists.
Tante Gusti hovered over Madame Bogaerde's shoulder mutter-
ing curses in Dutch. A humiliated Peter Hendley cursed in English.

"Look at them!" someone muttered. " 'Tis beyond *belief!*"

"Odious behavior!"

"Odious? It's positively *flagitious!*"

Henryk stalked angrily down the hall and slammed out the front door. Wilhelm Bogaerde shouted for his carriage, declaring firmly they were going home at once. Hugo Bogaerde echoed those sentiments in a voice as angry and loud as his brother's. Stuart turned from one guest to another trying to placate angry tempers. Benjy made a move toward Pilkington, determined to challenge the fellow to a duel, but he was restrained by a hissing order from Patience to behave himself.

Soon Tilda was lifted to her feet. Held firmly under each arm by her tight-lipped parents, she was led, still swooning, to the door. Terse good-byes were exchanged, and, their luggage retrieved, the entire New York party made for their carriages and drove off into the night.

The Westchester Bogaerdes followed their example, their carriage trundling hastily off in the opposite direction.

Meanwhile Peter Hendley, his twisted mouth accenting the icy fury of his eyes, threw Barbara's cloak over her shoulders and dragged her to the carriage without a word, followed by a frustrated Benjy. Patience, throwing an apologetic look to her friend Hannah, was the last to board the Hendley equipage. Off they rode in a spray of rain and shame.

The last guest to take his leave was the red-coated lieutenant, who, having been left behind by the betrayed family that had brought him, had to borrow a horse from Stuart in order to make his way back to the city.

Hannah and Stuart stood in the lighted doorway of Lovell Hill watching Pilkington ride off in the rain. The sight of his red coat receding in the distance marked the dismal finish to the "frolic" the hostess had been so long anticipating and preparing. It was the final straw. Poor Hannah burst into a flood of tears. "Oh, Stuart," she wailed, throwing herself into his arms, "what a catastrophe! They never even had a chance to see the *baby!*"

Thirty-five

Barbara wept all the way home, but not from shame or unhappiness, for she felt neither. Her tears were mostly a defense against her father's fury. Hendley had never before taken her to task for her behavior, but tonight he'd been deeply humiliated. "To see my daughter behave like a *wanton*," he sneered as soon as the carriage was under way, "is something quite new in my experience. Did you not sense your actions were those of a common *nightwalker*? If you had no care for your own good name, could you not give a thought to mine?"

"It wasn't her fault," Benjy said in brave defense of his sister. "That blasted redcoat is the—"

"Silence!" his father barked. "I need no bullyrag from a mealy-mouthed tadpole who knows nothing of the world."

"Papa—!" Patience remonstrated.

"Nor do I want words from *you*," he snapped at Patience. "In fact I want no discussion at all. But *you*, Mistress Easy Virtue, are not to imagine that you can have a flourish with a fellow—and a betrothed fellow at that!—and not pay a price."

"Flourish!" Patience exclaimed, appalled. "That is a *dreadful* word to use. Her skirts were not raised!"

"If it was not a complete leap, it was close enough as makes no matter," the father said in disgust. "Her skirts would have been raised, I have no doubt, if a witness had not happened along."

"They would not!" Babs declared between sobs. "And I don't . . . even know . . . what 'f-flourish' means!"

"It's a quick roll in the hay," Benjy muttered in her ear.

"I'm glad to know," Hendley said with icy scorn, "that my son and my eldest daughter are so well versed in the language of the tavern."

"You're the one used the word first," Benjy muttered, too angry with his father to guard his tongue.

His father leaned forward and struck his son a blow across the cheek. "I told you to keep still!"

All three of his offspring cried out at the blow, but Hendley silenced them with a gesture of restraint. "Not another word!" he gasped, falling back against the seat. "My pulse grows too rapid. We shall speak of this tomorrow, when we are calmer."

But they did not speak of it the next day. Hendley merely ordered his daughter to remain in her room until further notice and would not allow another word to be said on the matter.

Babs chaffed under her imprisonment. She could not go down-stairs for her meals nor outdoors for an airing. Nor could she think of any way in which to get a message to her love—the matter that troubled her more than any other. When Patience brought her meals to her on a tray, Babs repeatedly begged her sister to smuggle out the letter she'd written to Lieutenant Pilk-ington, but this Patience refused to do. "It is not seemly for you to write him," the elder sister explained patiently. "Your behavior has been quite rash enough. If your lieutenant truly loves you, he will find a way to reach you."

"Thank you, Mistress Too-Much-Patience," Babs seethed.

"You, my dear, are behaving as if you ought to have been named *Im*patience," her sister pointed out mildly.

"What do you know about true love anyway?" Babs muttered in angry rebuttle.

Thus the sisters fell at odds with each other, making the atmosphere of the household even more glum. Three long days went by, during which Babs's frustration grew unbearable. She could only get through the hours by concocting complicated plans to run away, plans (like climbing from her window at night by means of a rope made of torn sheets, stealing a horse from the stable and riding bareback through the darkness to New York to confront Lieutenant Pilkington in his barracks, the location of which she had not an inkling of) that she knew were too impractical to offer any hope of success.

In the wee hours of the fourth night of her imprisonment, however, she was awakened by the sound of pebbles pattering against her window. She drew aside the curtains and discovered, to her overwhelming delight, her redcoated lover standing below, bathed in moonlight. "Jack!" she squealed. "How did you find me? How did you know which window—?"

"Hush, girl," he hissed, "do you want your father to hear? Come down and let me in! I must speak to you."

She motioned for him to go round to the kitchen door. Then, throwing a shawl over her nightshift, she flew barefooted down the stairs and over the cold floor of the passageway to the kitchen. As soon as she admitted him, he swept her up in a wild embrace. They kissed with all the passion that enforced separation had stored up in them. But the lieutenant soon pulled himself away and held her off. "You must keep your distance and not distract me," he said firmly. "We have no time for this."

Babs, picking up her shawl that had slipped to the floor, giggled happily. "Oh? Not even for one little *flourish?*"

He shook his head in mock disapproval. "Babs Hendley, you *are* a naughty puss! What a chase you will lead me after we're wed!"

Babs gasped as the shawl slipped unheeded to the floor again. *"Are* we to be wed?" she asked, wide-eyed.

"Yes, if you'll be still for a moment and let me explain." He picked up the shawl and wrapped it over her arms and shoulders, holding it tightly around her as if to protect her from both the cold night air and himself. "My colonel has dispatches that must be delivered to London, and I've convinced him to make me his envoy. I've booked us passage on the *Nancy,* but it—"

"Us?" Babs squealed. "Do you mean to take *me?"*

"Of course. Did you think I could sail away without you? If I couldn't bear keeping Manahattan Island between us, how could I bear an ocean between us?"

"Oh, Jack!" she whispered, overwhelmed.

She tried to throw herself upon him but he held her off. "Behave yourself, vixen, and hear me out! The ship sails tomorrow—today, actually, for it is well past midnight I suspect—so we must be quick. Go up and dress yourself at once in something warm. Pack only those things you will urgently need on board ship. Hurry, girl, for we haven't much time. I have a carriage hidden in a clump of trees behind the house, and the air is too cold for the horses to be kept standing for long."

Barbara could scarcely believe her ears. Until this moment everything that had occurred between them had seemed like a game, full of excitement and danger but not quite real. Now, however, something had changed. Her breath caught in her throat as the enormity of what was happening fully burst upon her. "Do you mean . . . are you suggesting . . . an *elopement?"*

The sudden hesitancy in her voice struck him like a blow. "Oh, my *dear,"* he murmured contritely, "I am a boor! This is all too fast and wild for you, I know. We've met only twice in our lives, and now I come to you, in secret and without warning, in expectation of spiriting you away from everything you've known. You deserve better. You should have been properly courted; I should have spent months calling on you regularly, and then I should have sought your father's blessing—"

"You'd never have got it anyway," she said, "not after—"

"I know. But even if I could, I haven't time for all that now. I must go back to England. But at least I should have done *this* properly. I haven't even *asked* you . . ."

Her eyes fell. "No, you haven't."

He grasped both her hands and sank to one knee. "My beautiful, sweetest love," he whispered, "you know as well as I that from the moment we met we weren't strangers. We knew each other's thoughts right from the first. You knew at once that I wanted you much more than I ever wanted Tilda. And I knew that you, vixen that you are, wanted me. That's why I assumed you guessed my intentions . . . that we be married on board ship by the captain as soon as we are out to sea. But a man should not assume such things. So I ask you, Mistress Barbara Hendley . . . please, my dear, will you come away with me and be my wife?"

The moonlight streaming into the kitchen windows silvered his face and shone in his eyes. Never in all Barbara's sixteen-and-one-half years had she laid eyes on anyone so magnificently knightly or heard words so thrillingly romantic. This was the stuff of Arthurian legend, and she was Guinevere. It did not suit a Guinevere, when embarking on a voyage, to trouble her mind about the familial responsibilities she might be leaving behind, or to wonder about what might lie in store for her when the voyage ended. When a romantic adventure beckoned, Guinevere would run toward it without a backward look!

Shivering in sheer joy, Babs slipped down to her knees and took her knight's face in her hands. "Yes, my love," she breathed. "Oh, *yes!*"

And there on the cold stone floor, with the pots and pans gleaming eerily from the walls around them, and with the moonlight shedding its benevolent approval on them both, they plighted their troth . . . with a flourish.

Thirty-six

Dawn was just inching up on the eastern horizon as Tom, obeying a summons from the master, made his way up the path from the stable to the house. He walked quickly, with hands stuffed into the pockets of his breeches, and shoulders hunched against the early morning frost. A thin mist floated up from the river, softening the brilliant autumn colors of the leaves of the maples and oaks that lined the path, like a painter smearing a thin white wash over the too-bright colors of the painting below. But Tom didn't notice the tender opalescence that the combination of mist and morning light had created with the leaves. He was on his way, he guessed, to one of Hendley's periodic tongue-lashings, and he was bracing himself for it.

He did not know what particular transgression Hendley had in mind to berate him for, but whatever the crime, real or imagined, the scolding was certain to be unpleasant. Hendley was bound to be in a foul mood. Everyone on the estate knew by this time about Mistress Barbara's transgression at Lovell Manor, and everyone who'd had any contact with Hendley since that night—and had felt the sting of his tongue—knew that his temper had not abated. *No,* Tom thought, digging his hands deeper into his pockets, *this is not likely to be a pleasant interview.*

He found Hendley waiting for him in the workroom, seated behind his desk. The master did not waste a moment on greetings or niceties. "Didn't I tell you to keep the field workers away from the north field?" he demanded as soon as Tom had closed the door.

"The north field?" Tom asked, eyeing Hendley with puzzled mistrust.

"Yes, the north field!" Hendley snapped. "Where Clymer Young's men are working. And you needn't look that way at me, as if I were speaking Greek."

"I just don't understand. You've never ordered us to keep off the north field before."

"Well, I'm doing so now. Mr. Clymer Young is working on my burial vault, and he wants to use his own workmen for the task."

"No one's stopping him," Tom said reasonably. "Our men only wander over there occasionally, to take a look—"

"Who gave them leave to look? They have work to do, don't they? Then see that they do it and not hang about where they've been forbidden to go!"

Tom shrugged. "Whatever you say. But Mr. Young's men are doing a strange job of it, if you ask me. The hole they're digging is deep enough to bury half the population of Fordham."

"Well, we're not asking you. So mind my orders and keep yourself and all the rest of the hands out of Mr. Young's way. Is that clear?"

"As a bell," Tom answered shortly and turned to go.

"Drat you, fellow, hold still! I've one thing more to say. Is it true, as I've heard, that you're drilling the rabble of the town in soldiering?"

Tom looked over his shoulder warily. "If you're speaking of the militia, yes, it's true."

"I thought you understood that I ordered you to cease and desist."

"I do it on my own time."

"You have no such time, except as I give it to you."

Tom wheeled about. "I have the Lord's day by law, don't I? That's one thing, at least, that you can't steal from me."

Hendley's angry glare wavered, but only for a moment. "Are you saying you drill on Sunday?" he asked with caustic disdain.

"No, but I make up the work, even if sometimes it means doing it on Sunday."

"I gave you no such right! I won't have it. There's to be no more—"

"The militia is a legal body, and they have to be drilled. Even the magistrate will agree on that. And I'm the only one who knows—"

Hendley snorted in scorn. "You? What do you know of soldiering?"

Tom shrugged again. "There's a manual. I studied it."

"Oh, you did, did you? Since when did you learn how to read?"

"I learned."

"By yourself? A likely tale."

"I had help."

"Had you indeed? From whom?"

"A friend."

"One of your rabble co-conspirators, I have no doubt."

Tom merely shrugged.

"Well, if you steal out again for that purpose, I shall have a talk with the magistrate, and you'll discover that the law is not as loose as you think It. I'll have you taken from militia duty faster than you can blink."

"Go ahead. The militia can get along without me," Tom said indifferently. "It won't matter much in the long run."

Hendley's mouth twisted contemptuously. "You're right, it *won't* matter much. As if such a rabble as your so-called militia could make a mark against trained British musketeers."

Tom smiled at Hendley pityingly. "I meant that one little militia company won't make much difference when one takes into account all the thousands of men the colonies can muster when there's a need."

"What nonsense is this?"

"It's no nonsense. Did you not hear that Connecticut alone

was able to muster four thousand men *in one day* last month, when they heard a rumor that the bloodybacks had shot a man in Boston? Those Connecticut volunteers made a line of march that had the Boston redcoats ashiver, despite all their splendid British training."

"Balderdash! Four thousand, indeed! Where did you learn this foolishness? In one of Sam Adams's lying circular letters?"

"It's no lie. There were four thousand at the least. Some say the number would have been double if the rumor of the shooting hadn't turned out to be false."

"Even if that count were accurate, which I don't for one moment believe," Hendley sneered, "what does it prove?"

"It proves," Tom retorted, "that the colonies can muster up an army if they're provoked too f—"

He was interrupted by the abrupt opening of the door. Patience stepped over the threshold, her face pale. "Papa, something dreadful has—" But at that moment her eyes fell on Tom. "Oh," she gasped, flushing and paling in quick succession, "I didn't know—"

Tom, seeing her distress, stepped back toward the door. "Good morning, ma'am," he murmured politely. "I was just leaving."

"No, stay," she said, getting hold of herself. "We may need you." She crossed the room quickly to her father's desk. "Papa, I don't know how to say this but to say it. Babs has run off!" She handed him a letter that she'd had clutched in her hand.

Hendley, whitening, stared up at his daughter in stunned disbelief. Then he spread the letter on the desk before him, his fingers trembling. His eyes rapidly took in the scrawled words on the single sheet of paper. As he read the note over again, his expression changed from alarm to anger. Then he slowly crushed the paper in his hand. His eyes clouded, and he stared out in front of him without seeing.

Patience broke the silence. "Tom can saddle Caesar and ride to the city after them, Papa. Perhaps he can catch them before the ship sails."

Hendley's face hardened. "No," he said, slowly rising from his chair. "No."

"But, Papa, she's only a child—"

"*No!* She's old enough to have made her bed. Now let her lie in it." He grasped his cane and hobbled to the door. "Don't speak of her to me again. Ever." He crossed over the threshold and then turned back. "I'm going to lie down for a while. Call me for breakfast."

Tom and Patience said nothing until his footsteps could no longer be heard. Then Tom took a step toward her. "I'll ride after her without his permission, if you wish it, ma'am. Where did they go?"

Patience shook her head sadly. "No, it was a foolish suggestion. The ship will surely have sailed by the time you'd reach the New York pier. Besides, I suppose Papa is right. She must lie in the bed she's made."

"Your father is hardly ever right," Tom said in disgust. "The girl is not a bunter. She eloped, to wed a man she loves. It was an act of bravery. Rebellion. You should admire her for it."

"*Admire* her?" Angry tears spilled from her eyes, which she dashed away with the back of her hand. "Her rebellion has torn this family apart. We shall probably never see her again! What is so admirable about that?"

"The separation from her family is a high price to pay, I admit," Tom said quietly, suppressing a powerful urge to take Patience in his arms and comfort her, "but what is admirable is that she's won her liberty. Her freedom. There's no price too high for that."

" 'Tis natural, I suppose, for *you,* in your circumstances, to think so," she said, turning away from him, "but can you truly call what she's won freedom? Is it freedom to follow whatever whim possesses you at the moment, no matter the cost to others? That is not liberty but *license!*"

"Can you really believe that's what freedom means to me?" Tom pulled her round to face him and frowned down at her. "License to indulge in one's *whims?*"

"What else can I believe? To wish to be free of those who love and protect you is self-indulgence at best and arrant disloyalty at worst."

"Spoken like a true Tory," Tom retorted. "That is exactly how the Tories view the mother country—the parent who loves and protects us. What utter rot!"

"Why is it rot? Why?"

"Because the parent, no matter how benevolent—and neither your father nor England is particularly benevolent at the moment—the parent who is unwilling to give his offspring freedom when that offspring is strong enough to fend for himself stifles that offspring's normal growth and thus becomes a tyrant."

"My, my, Tom Morrison," she taunted, throwing off the hand he'd kept on her shoulder, "what a glib tongue you've developed all of a sudden."

"Is that your answer—to belittle what I say merely by calling it glib? Liberty is no glib concept to me. It is the one goal I've been striving for since boyhood."

"Yes, I know." She sighed, her anger falling away as she remembered how very many years he'd been a bondsman. When she spoke again, it was with a softer voice. "But Tom, can't you see that freedom . . . liberty . . . they are but words? You value them because you feel the lack. I understand that. But no matter what you call yourself—bondsman or free man—your life will not *substantially* change. The reality of life is that you'd still have to till the soil and chop the wood, isn't that so?"

"Yes, but for *myself*. When and how it suited me. Can't you see how different the very same work can be when a man is free to do it for himself?"

"But if, for the mere satisfaction of calling yourself free, you must have rebellion, I don't know if it's worth it."

"You *do* know it's worth it. You do! You gave it to Sally and Aaron. Freedom was more than a word for *them*, was it not?"

"Yes, but—"

"Damn it, Patience," he burst out, taking her roughly by the shoulders as if he were going to shake the Tory out of her, "this is something in you that I shall *never* understand! You put aside your scruples for their freedom—you *rebelled* for them. You wished for them to be free. Why do you not wish the same for me?"

She stared up at him, wide-eyed. "I don't know. I never thought—"

"Think, then, damn you, think!"

But she couldn't think. Her mind seemed frozen, locked into a pattern of thought to which she was so accustomed that it was difficult to break out. Certainly Tom was right to say that freedom was more than a word in regard to Sally and Aaron. Why was it less significant for him? She tried to find an excuse for herself— for what she was beginning to realize was her own callous inability to understand the deep humiliation he suffered from his condition of servitude. "Perhaps . . . perhaps I don't fully understand your need for freedom. I admit that. But surely your need cannot be as great as it was for them . . ."

"Why not as great? Freedom is a human need. Am I less human?"

"Not less human, but less needy. Don't forget, Tom, that your servitude is a temporary thing. It will soon end."

He stared at her, wondering if he should spill out the truth about his servitude—his conviction that it would *never* end, that Hendley would keep finding ways to extend it as long as he was of use.

But Patience took his silence as a sign that she was succeeding in making her point. "So, you see, you don't need my help, as Sally and Aaron did. Yes, I rebelled against my father at that time, but rebellion remains an anathema to me. I've paid dearly for it. I shall never see Sally again. Nor Barbara either. Rebellion is a force that divides and kills, that tears people apart, that breaks countries apart. I hate it!"

"Yes, I know," he sighed ruefully. "You've been your father's daughter for too long."

She put up her chin. "That's not true. My views are my own."

"No, I don't believe that," he said, going to the door. "But I *do* believe that one day something will happen to force you to think for yourself. When that day comes, Patience Hendley, you'll discover that freedom is to the spirit what air is to the body: without it you won't be able to breathe. Some instinct in you made you give breath to Sally and Aaron, but you stopped there. When you yourself take a deep whiff of it, that instinct will burst into bloom like a fruit tree in spring, and then, my girl, this house will rock on its foundations with your rebellion!"

Thirty-seven

Barbara, clinging to the ship's railing for dear life, gazed out at the seething ocean in despair. To the horizon in every direction nothing could be seen but the great, ugly, heaving mass of dark gray turbulence that appeared to have no purpose but to smash itself against the fragile vessel that carried her. How the ship kept itself whole was both a mystery and a miracle to her.

It seemed to her that this beastly voyage would never end. The *Nancy* had been ploughing through rough seas for days and days, its decks tilting frighteningly, sometimes at angles almost perpendicular to the horizon and awash with icy water, its sails flapping in the wind and its masts groaning so loudly that she was certain they would crack. She shouldn't have come up on deck at all, but to remain below was even worse, for the tiny cabin that had been their honeymoon abode now reeked dreadfully of vomit.

At first, life aboard the *Nancy* had seemed enormously romantic. The weather had been fair the first week of their voyage, and she'd not minded that the cabin (the best on the ship except for the captain's quarters) was dark and barely furnished with two uncomfortable bunk beds and a crude table and chair. The mate had miraculously unearthed the one article of furniture she absolutely required—a mirror. With that, and with the service of the captain's own steward to do the cleaning up, she'd been content with her surroundings. Besides, being a married woman was great fun. All the men from the captain down had smiled indulgently at the bride every time she passed. She preened with pleasure at hearing herself addressed as Lady Pilkington. And she doted on being the only woman dining in the officers' mess, the center of attention of half-a-dozen men. Best of all, she and Jack had had plenty of privacy and had spent it deliciously. They'd made love half the night and strolled the deck by day, arms about each other. Jack, when not whispering wickedly intimate things in her ear, would tell her about the pleasures of their future life in London. Married life as the wife of an English nobleman was promising to be even better than she'd dreamed.

But the weather had changed the second week out, and Jack had become seasick. This drastically altered the honeymoon atmosphere, which rapidly changed from heavenly to nightmarish. The poor groom hadn't had a good day since. By this, the third week of this endless journey, Jack was so weak he could barely lift his head from the bunk. He could not summon up enough energy even to speak; all he could manage were occasional hoarse groans between bouts of retching.

Barbara tried hard to give her husband a full measure of wifely support in his illness. During that first, blissful week of their marriage, she'd fallen more deeply in love than ever. She could hardly believe how close they'd become, how easily they'd learned to please each other, and how soon they'd become comfortably yet thrillingly intimate. It was not Jack's fault that he'd fallen ill; he deserved her devotion in bad times as well as good. For that reason she forced herself to spend hours sitting at the side of his bunk, holding his head while he sipped a bit of water, smoothing back his matted hair, rocking him in her arms when a fit of coughing took hold of him. But the long days in that confined space were hard to endure. The captain's steward tried to keep the place habitable for Barbara, but even his herculean efforts could not purify the stagnant air.

Despite Barbara's valiant attempts to stay at her husband's side, sometimes, when his retching made her queasy or when the stench of the room threatened to overwhelm her, she had to run out for a while. To breathe the ocean air, even in its present turbulence, was the only way to clear her lungs. She would plait her unruly tresses in a tight braid, pull on a stout pair of boots borrowed from one of the seamen, wrap herself round with her heaviest cloak and clump up the stairway (the mate repeatedly reminded her that "it's called a ladder, ma'am. Not a stairway, a ladder.") to the quarter deck. There, following the mate's strict instructions, she would take hold of a rope, one end of which was tied to the top rung of the ladder, and, tying the other end round her waist, would slosh across the deck to the railing. As much as she despised the wet, the cold and the bleakness of the view, she found that the wind whipping at her hair and the spume spraying her face were somehow invigorating and restorative. After a few deep breaths she felt healthy again.

It was there on the quarter deck on this stormy afternoon of the twenty-second day of the voyage that the captain found her. "What are you doing up here, ma'am?" he shouted, not angrily but merely to be heard above the wind.

"It's more open than our deck," she explained, but since the wind whipped the words out of her mouth, he could not hear. "I like it up here," she shouted, "better than either of the gun decks."

He shook his head and gestured to his ear, indicating that he hadn't heard a word. Then, untying her from her bonds, he took a firm hold of her arm and, with what she thought was admirable surefootedness, pulled her along the heaving deck to the doors that led to his cabin. Once inside the passageway, he loosed his hold on her. "Didn't mean to be rough with you, ma'am," he apologized, "but that wind makes movement difficult and con-versation impossible. Come along with me to my quarters. I wish to speak to you about your husband's condition."

The captain's quarters were large and surrounded on three sides with windows, but even here the atmosphere was dark be-cause of the heavy sky. The captain lit a lamp that swung over his work table by a chain from the ceiling beams and told his guest to settle herself on the window seat. "You're a brave little lass," he said, perching on the edge of the table and studying her with kindly eyes, "to venture out on deck in this blow."

She shook her head. "Not very brave. It's just . . . the cabin gets so . . . stifling sometimes."

"Yes, I know. It's a damnable shame. But I warned your husband that a voyage in this season would not be a tea party. November on the Atlantic is always stormy, I've discovered. And for a young woman on her very first sailing . . . well, I warned him. But he insisted that you're a hardy little puss. And, as it happened, he's the one took sick, not you. You've turned out to be hardier than any of us expected."

"Thank you, Captain," she said, eyeing him worriedly, "but you didn't bring me here to tell me how hardy I am, did you?"

"No, ma'am. It's about Lieutenant Pilkington. His condition worries me somewhat. He should have recovered his sea legs by this time, you see."

"Should he? Even though the sea is as rough as ever?"

The captain shrugged. "I can't say for sure. Some cases of seasickness can last the voyage through, I suppose, though I've never seen one myself. I don't wish to alarm you unnecessarily, but I'll tell you frankly, ma'am, I've never seen a case of seasickness quite like this one—with feverishness, and coughing."

Barbara's heart sank. "Yes, he *is* feverish. I've noticed that myself. Do you think he's suffering from something other than seasickness?"

"I'm not a doctor, nor is there anyone aboard to consult. The only thing to do is wait and see. I suppose it's possible he'll recover when the weather turns. But if he doesn't—"

"Oh, God!" Barbara gasped, turning pale. "I never thought of such a possibility."

"Perhaps you should think of it, my dear. Best to be prepared. We dock at Plymouth in less than a week, and—"

"A week?" Her face brightened at the prospect. "Only a week?"

The captain smiled back at her. "These winds are good for

omething. We've made excellent time." But the smile quickly
aded. "When you disembark, ma'am, if Pilkington remains ill,
ou'll find yourself in a difficult situation, having to make all
he arrangements yourself."

Babs stared at him. "Arrangements?"

"Yes, my dear, arrangements. Hiring a carriage, getting the
aggage seen to, locating lodgings, perhaps finding a medical
nan to look at him, if he doesn't seem better." He threw her a
ook of fatherly sympathy. "I know this is a bit frightening to a
ride as young as you, my dear. Dealing with a new marriage in
new country is not easy even in the best of circumstances—"

Barbara felt her chest constrict. A new marriage in a new coun-
ry . . . and with a sick husband. The prospect was terrifying. For
he first time since she'd run off from home, she regretted having
loped in such haste. She should have been better prepared to
eal with the serious problems of life. Never before had she felt
o completely alone. She needed her sister. *Patience, oh, Pa-
ience,* a voice within her cried, *what have I done?*

The memory of Patience brought a sudden lucidity to her
nind. If Patience were in this situation, she'd know what to do.
*atience was good at dealing with problems. Patience was strong
nd decisive and did not give way to fear. Babs remembered how
vell Patience had dealt with the problem of Orgill's abandon-
nent. She'd put up her chin and carried on.

Well, I can do that, Babs told herself bravely. *For Jack's sake,
f not my own, I can be strong and decisive, too.* There was noth-
ng so difficult about hiring a carriage or finding lodgings. She
vas a married woman now, not a child. She could put up her chin
nd carry on.

With that resolve she got to her feet. "Thank you for your
oncern, Captain," she said, striding to the door with a sure-
ooted step despite the heaving of the floor beneath her, "but
ack will be fine once we're in port. You'll see."

The captain looked dubious. "And if he's not?"

"Then I'll handle the arrangements," Babs answered with an

assurance she was far from feeling. "Don't worry your head about me."

To her immense relief, the sea became calm the very next day permitting Jack a few hours of the first restful sleep he'd experienced in weeks. When he woke, he was able to sit up. By the next day he was managing to hold down his food, and by the time the ship docked, he was on his feet. His uniform hung loosely from a frame much diminished in girth, and his cheeks were still white as chalk, but with the steward's arm supporting him, he made his way down the gangplank on his own still-shaky legs.

Barbara, standing beside the captain, watched her husband go down. "See? I told you he would do it," she said with pride.

"Yes, ma'am, so you did." The captain patted her shoulder but his eyes were dubious. "Nonetheless, I'd have him see a doctor if I were you," he cautioned. "And soon."

Later, standing on the busy dock and apprehensively surveying the crowds that bustled about them, Barbara suggested to Jack that they find lodgings in Plymouth. "Would you not like to rest for a few days before embarking on the carriage ride to London?" she asked solicitiously.

Jack shook his head. "No, I'll rest better at home."

They hired a carriage right there at the dock and started at once for London. Barbara had eagerly anticipated her first sight of the greatest city in the world, but she barely caught a glimpse of it, for the ride was long, and the sky had darkened early. Besides, Jack occupied all of her attention. He seemed listless, and he began to cough with a frequency Babs found worrisome. The rocking motion of the carriage was very much like that of a ship and by the time they drew up at the doorway of Pilkington House in Upper Seymour Street, Jack was looking green.

Despite his weakness, he threw Barbara a wan smile as the carriage drew to a stop. "It's been a devil of a honeymoon, Babs my love," he said, taking her hands in his, "but now that we're n firm ground—and home—I'll soon be back to my old self. Then I'll make it all up to you, I promise."

Barbara lifted one of his hands and rubbed it against her cheek. "Oh, Jack," she whispered, "I don't think it was a devil of—"

But before she could finish, someone pulled open the carriage door. "Welcome, sir," came an eager voice from outside. "It's good to have you home!" Barbara looked up to see a tall, elderly man smiling up at her husband.

"Jeffers!" Jack exclaimed, climbing down from the carriage and shaking the man's hand. "I'm glad to see you!"

By the time Barbara realized that the man was the butler, other servants had appeared. A pair of liveried footmen had hurried out of the door and were taking charge of their meager baggage. And a third was paying off the driver of the hired hack.

Meanwhile, two elegantly clad ladies appeared in the doorway. The elder of the two, small in size and very wrinkled of skin, threw out her arms and ran down the three stone steps that fronted the door. "Jack!" she cried. "Oh, my *darling!*"

While Jack enfolded the lady—obviously his mother—in a fond embrace, Barbara peered out of the carriage window at her new home. By the light of the amazing number of lamps that lit the doorways of every house in the street, she could see that Pilkington House was the widest in a row of fine-looking town residences. The houses were more crowded together than those in New York City but more impressive in architecture. All the houses lining the street were of stone rather than brick, the doorways topped with fanlights and ornamented with porticos and pilasters, and the windows tall and gleaming with light. All the facades exuded importance, permanence, solidity and wealth. *But,* Barbara thought pridefully, *Jack's family home is the largest and finest of them all.*

"Ma'am?" the butler murmured, offering her a hand. She stepped down and, heart beating excitedly, followed Jack and his mother up the curved steps and into the front door where Jack was immediately embraced by his sister. As a veritable army of servants bustled about, Jack's mother and sister clung to him, laughing and crying and kissing his cheeks. "Your father is, of course, at his club," his mother apologized. "How sorry he'll be to have missed your arrival!"

Barbara stood alone, watching the scene and feeling, for the first time in her life, neglected and unimportant. But soon Jack extricated himself from the double embrace and smiled at her. "Babs, this is my mother, Lady Olivia Pilkington, and my sister Henrietta. Mama, Hetty, this is Babs. My wife."

The two women turned to her at once, their smiles fading. "*Wife?*" Jack's sister, Hetty, exclaimed in a tone that sounded to Barbara very much like horror.

Lady Olivia merely stared at her.

Jack gave a snorting laugh. "Surprised you, eh? Yes, this delightful creature is my treasure from America, my wife. And a terrible honeymoon I have given her, so, Mama—and you, too, Hetty—must make it up to her by giving her the warmest possible welcome into the family."

Lady Olivia raised to her eyes a pair of glasses that had been hanging round her neck by a jeweled cord. "How do you do?" she asked coldly, peering through her spectacles as if at a specimen of insect life in a glass jar.

Barbara felt her chest clench. "How do you do, my lady?" she mumbled, bending her knees in an awkward curtsy.

Jack's sister made a sound in her throat that might have been a greeting but was utterly unintelligible to Barbara. Hetty Pilkington was a woman of at least thirty years, with a long, horsey face sitting incongruously atop a fore-shortened body, the incongruity emphasized by the ruffles and rosettes that decorated her gown and by her profusely curled dark hair that was only minimally covered by a lace spinster-cap. This unappealing woman continued to regard Barbara with an expression that could not in any way be described as welcoming. Such unexpected coldness froze Barbara's tongue, but before her silence could become truly embarrassing, Jack broke in. "Forgive me, ladies," he said

s voice suddenly hoarse, "but the trip has quite undone me.
et me leave you to get acquainted. Jeffers, help me upstairs. I
ust get into bed."

The three women watched silently as Jack slowly mounted the
airs on the butler's arm. Even when he disappeared round the
nd of the stairs they remained motionless. But as soon as they
eard the sound of a door closing above them, Hetty expelled a
embling sob. "My *God,* Mama," she cried, "he's nothing but
kin and bones!"

Jack's mother wheeled round to Barbara, her eyes flashing
enomously. "You . . . you damned provincial *strumpet, "* she
issed into her face, *"what* have you done to my *son?"*

Thirty-eight

For a long moment, the atmosphere in the entryway was tense with an antagonistic silence. Barbara did not know how to defend herself against her new mother-in-law's insulting words. She was not prepared; she'd never given a moment's thought to the subject of in-laws. And even if she had, she would not have expected Jack's family to take her in such instant dislike. With a sinking heart, she realized that this was but another in the series of blows that were destroying her happy expectations.

Meanwhile, Hetty whispered in her mother's ear to guard her tongue. "Jack might not like you to offend his bride," she warned. Then she turned to Barbara and tried to ease the tension by changing the subject. "I suppose your abigail didn't wish to leave America," she murmured, her voice lifting at the last word to make the statement a question.

"Abigail?" Barbara echoed in bewilderment.

"Maidservant," Lady Olivia explained coldly. "You *did* have a personal maidservant at home, did you not?"

"Well, I . . . I don't know if I'd call her 'personal,'" Barbara answered. From the disdainful expressions on the others' faces, she knew she'd made some sort of *faux pas,* but she didn't understand just what it was.

"Perhaps young women in the colonies are permitted to travel about unaccompanied," Hetty suggested.

"But I didn't travel unaccompanied," Barbara pointed out. "I had Jack."

The two other women exchanged pitying looks. "Here in England, my dear," Hetty explained, "a lady doesn't travel without her own maid. It is simply not done."

"Oh, I see," Barbara mumbled, humiliated.

Lady Olivia, meanwhile, stared at the two pieces of luggage—one her son's military trunk and the other a straw bandbox carelessly tied with ship's rope—lying on the floor at the foot of the stairs, awaiting deployment. "Is this *all* your baggage?" she asked in amazed disdain.

"Jack didn't give me much time, you see," Barbara apologized, flushing. She was only too conscious of the shabby appearance she made, with her hair plaited like a housemaid's, her cloak deplorably tattered by the sea air, and her sturdy gown bedraggled by a month of continuous wear. "He said I should take only what I'd need on shipboard—a heavy cloak and a change of underclothes. If I'd have taken anything more from home, I would've had to go searching about for a proper portmanteau and would've waked the whole household."

"Are you saying that you made a *runaway* match?" Hetty asked in horror.

"Well . . . yes." For the first time it occurred to Barbara that not everyone would consider elopement a romantic way to be wed. Blushing more deeply, she launched into a labored explanation. "There was no time, you see. And even if there were, Papa wouldn't have forgiven . . . that is, it was only three days since Tilda—she was Jack's betrothed, you know, until she realized . . . well, in any case, she'd given him back his ring only days before. Besides, the ship was due to sail—"

Lady Olivia held up a hand to stop her. "You needn't explain," she said, her voice resonant with revulsion. "If Jack found so hurried an arrangement necessary, he must have had his reasons."

"Necessary?" Hetty gaped at her mother as a dreadful new idea dawned on her. "Mama! You can't mean—?"

Her ladyship's eyebrows rose. "Good *God,*" she exclaimed, gasping, "I never thought of *that!*" Then bluntly fixing her eyes on the waist of the strange girl her son had brought home, she demanded loudly, "You—Mistress Whatever-your-name!— you're not in the *family* way, are you?"

Barbara did not immediately understand what her mother-in-law was asking, but when she did, her redheaded temper flared up like a firecracker. "In the first place, ma'am," she declared furiously, "my name should be easy to remember. It is Lady Pilkington, just like yours. In the second place, if you are imply- ing that my being 'in the family way' is the reason your son married me, you are mistaken on both counts."

"Well, you needn't fly into alt," her sister-in-law said in quick defense, throwing her mother another warning glance. "You can't blame us for wondering."

"After all," the mother-in-law added, relief making her more willing to relent, "we had no word of the marriage. You, a chit from the colonies, were thrust upon us without warning. We can- not be expected to know how you colonial girls behave."

But Barbara would not be placated. "In the colonies, your ladyship, we would find your manner of greeting quite inhospi- table," she retorted. "And as for your questions and the assump- tions behind them, well, we colonials would be too generous to *think* them, much less to express them aloud!" With her chin high, she stalked up the first few stairs. "And now, if you don't mind, I'd like to be shown up to my room. Like Jack, I find myself too tired to remain in company."

Her room, Barbara soon discovered, was small, draughty and depressing. She couldn't even see a view, for the windows were too high to look out of without standing on a chair. The accom- modations seemed more suitable for a servant than for the wife of the son and heir. The furnishings were a far cry from those that had graced the rooms she'd seen on the lower floors; they consisted of a narrow bed with no hangings, a small dressing table topped by a spotted mirror, and a shabby commode holding a chipped washbowl. True, there was a coal fire in the fireplace, but it gave off more smoke than warmth. Worst of all, the room was located on the floor above her husband's bedroom. She hated it at once. She hated it even more when she returned to it after she'd gone down to Jack's room and been refused admittance. "Lieutenant Pilkington is sleeping," the butler had informed her in the hallway. "He gave orders that he was not to be disturbed." Poor Barbara climbed up to her room again, feeling miserable. Lonely, frightened and chilled to the bone, she wrapped herself in the bedclothes, threw herself down on the bed and wept herself to sleep.

Jack's father, Sir Matthew Pilkington, a large-bellied, bushy-haired man of huge appetites and easy temper, arrived home from his club to find his wife waiting for him in a state of agitation. "Jack's come home," she declared without preamble, "looking like death—all skin and bones—and accompanied by a doxy from the colonies to whom he's apparently *married!* The girl is completely unacceptable. She has not a shred of elegance or breeding. Matt, for heaven's sake, don't stand there gaping at me like a demented goldfish! Whatever are we to *do?"*

Sir Matthew, who had just won two hundred pounds at faro, was feeling self-satisfied and slightly but very pleasantly inebriated. Moreover, he was quite accustomed to what he liked to call 'female rodomontade,' so he refused to let his wife upset him or destroy the happy fog in which his brain was mired. He simply advised her to calm herself, and—promising to take care of everything in the morning—toddled off to bed.

Early the next morning, before anyone was stirring but the housemaids, Barbara climbed out of her bed, pulled a dressing gown over her nightshift and stole downstairs to her husband's room. To her delight, he was awake and looking well rested. She perched on the side of his bed—a massive structure with carved posts and fringed hangings—and prepared to pour her complaints into his ear. But before she could utter a word, he pulled her down beside him, quite like his old self, and kissed her with the same fervor he'd shown that first week on shipboard. With a contented sigh, Barbara slipped her arms about his neck and, forgetting her troubles, engaged with eager enthusiasm in the marital intimacy she'd missed so much.

Later, lying naked in his arms under the warm bedclothes, she spilled out her woes. She told him everything, from his mother's suggestion that she was with child to the distance of her bedroom from his own. But her woes didn't seem as woeful this morning as they had last night. Nor could she make her voice sound tearful when he kept her giggling by running his fingers over her ticklish places. "Stop it, Jack, you licentious devil!" she demanded at last, nevertheless nibbling at his ear. "Don't you care at all that your family despises me?"

He laughed and nuzzled her throat. "Silly chit," he murmured between caresses, "my family is not worth troubling yourself over. When we find our own place to live, you'll rarely be bothered with them. Besides, how can they possibly despise so gloriously luscious a—?" A knock at the door silenced him and made them both stiffen.

"Jack, my boy," came his father's voice from the hallway, "may I come in?"

"Oh, good heavens!" whispered the terror-stricken Barbara, "where shall I hide?"

"You needn't hide, my love. You're my wife. You have every right to be here." He handed her her dressing gown while calmly calling out, "Just one moment, Father."

Jack threw on his nightshirt, sat up in his bed and pulled the bedclothes neatly up to his waist, while Barbara hastily covered up her nakedness and ran across the room so as not to be found too near the scene of their debauch. "I shall die of embarrassment," she moaned, looking down at her flimsy dressing gown in dismay.

"Nonsense. Father will adore you," Jack promised, and he called for his father to come in.

Sir Matthew, his bulk wrapped in a frogged satin robe, entered eagerly. "My boy, how glad I—" he began, but then his eye fell on Barbara. She was standing barefoot in front of the fireplace and clutching the collar of her dressing gown tightly at her neck. It was clear that he'd interrupted a private moment, but before he could make an apology, he was struck dumb by the girl's loveliness. With her red hair enticingly disordered, her freckled cheeks flushed, her mouth reddened and swollen from recent embraces, and her thin gown only slightly masking her nubile body, she seemed to him utterly delectable. Where, he wondered, had his wife gotten the notion that this breathtaking creature was not worthy of his son? "Jack, you clever dog, I must congratulate you!" he chortled, his eyes fixed on Barbara. "However did you manage to convince this lovely girl to marry so sorry a specimen as you?" Smiling with enthusiasm, he crossed the room to the blushing bride and took her hand to his lips. "My dear," he said warmly, "we are delighted to welcome you into the family!"

Jack laughed aloud at this evidence of Barbara's misjudgment, but the laugh somehow caught in his chest and turned into a deep cough. He pulled out a handkerchief and held it to his mouth. While his father kissed his wife's hand, and Babs giggled in delight at having won at least one family member's approval, Jack noticed something that almost made him gasp. Keeping a smile fixed on his face, he surreptitiously tucked the handkerchief under his pillow. He didn't wish to spoil the felicity of the morning by dwelling on what he'd seen on the pristine whiteness of the square of linen—a spot of bright red blood.

Thirty-nine

Beatie dropped two dozen little candle ends into a basket and, with her usual dour frown, thrust it at Tom. He was standing just inside the kitchen door, bundled to the ears against the cold. "There ye are," she said.

Tom leaned down and kissed her wrinkled cheek. "Thanks, old dearie," he grinned.

Pretending not to be pleased, she rubbed away his kiss with the back of her hand. With her own daughter married and gone off to the frontier, she'd transferred her motherly affection to the handsome young bondsman and could deny him nothing. "Dinna ken what ye want with 'em," she muttered in her thick brogue. "There's scarce a half hour's burnin' left in any of 'em."

"It's better than darkness," Tom said.

"Aye. But ye needna let on to the missus that I let ye have 'em. She'd be bound to believe y're up to some mischief."

"No she wouldn't," Tom reassured her. "She'd guess I use them only for reading."

"A foolish waste o' time, readin' is," the bent old woman muttered, returning to her task of clearing away the breakfast remains. "These dark winter nights is for sleepin', if ye ask me. A bittock o' spare time for sleepin' is a real blessin'." Following that uncharacteristic rush of words, she shut her mouth and turned away, indicating that all discussion was at an end.

That's the great thing about winter, Tom thought as he wound a shabby muffler round the collar of his precious green coat and prepared to face the November wind outside, *a bittock o' spare time*. If it weren't for the cold, there'd not be a season he liked better. Winter was the one time of year he had real time to himself—time to sleep, time to read, time to steal off to meet with his friends without fear of being missed. Even the cold was something he'd learned to bear; what with the coat Patience had given him (tight though it was), and the clean wool blankets he'd found on his sheeted bed the night of the first frost, he didn't feel nearly as cold these days as he used to. And with these bits of candle that Beatie had saved for him, he could spend as much as three hours of the dark winter evenings reading. It was a pleasure so great it almost made up for the *un*pleasure of his days.

Repeating his thanks, Tom bade good-bye to the old Scotswoman, tucked the basket under his arm and went out the kitchen door. Passing the dining-room windows on his way to the stable, he was arrested by the sound of Hendley's loud voice. "They were supposed to be safe!" he was saying angrily. "A 'safe' Loyalist delegation!"

Tom couldn't resist looking in. The family was still at breakfast. Hendley was at the table's head, waving a newspaper at Benjy, on his right. Patience was seated with her back to the onlooker, who noted that a few stray locks of her hair had escaped from her cap and curled in enchanting disarray at the nape of her neck. The sight of the curled strands against the bit of bare skin clenched his innards. *I must be hungry for a leap,* he thought in self-disgust. *Perhaps I should tarry a bit with Freda after the tavern meeting tonight.*

To keep from thinking about kissing Patience's neck, Tom forced his eyes to Benjy's face. "Why did you think the delegation safe?" the boy was asking.

"Because," the father responded with the impatience of a schoolmaster to a thick-headed pupil, "the New York Assembly, which no more wanted to send a radical delegation to the Congress than I would, chose the right sort of people. Why, I'd have put money on the loyalty of men like Alsop, Duane and John

Jay! Good church, all of them, and strong advocates of the British constitution and the Crown. They were expected to keep the others temperate and loyal. Instead they've come home transformed!"

"What do you mean, Papa?" Patience asked. "How transformed?"

"Sam Adams worked his spell on them, that's how!" Hendley spat out in disgust. "They've come home *republicans! All* of them!"

Benjy, who was delighted at the outcome of the Congress, did not wish his father to read his true feelings in his face. He looked away and, in so doing, glimpsed Tom at the window. Tom winked at him. The bondsman would have liked to stay and hear more but, noting that Patience was turning in her seat to see what Benjy was looking at, ducked out of sight and walked off.

Hendley's word *republican* rang in Tom's ears. It was a word he'd often used but only recently had come to appreciate. The pastor of Fordham's Presbyterian Church had lent him a copy of John Locke's "Second Treatise," which persuasively argued the benefits of a voluntary compact among free individuals to form a commonwealth. A republic. A state in which supreme power would rest, not in a king, but in the body of its citizens. Tom was aware that the ownership of property would be the basis of that citizenship and that as a bondsman he would not qualify. But he would not be a bondsman forever. And even if he never qualified, he still believed a republican state would be far superior to one which kept a class of inherited nobility at the top and slaves at the bottom.

But Tom's ideal of republicanism took a hard blow that night at the tavern. His friends had gathered to discuss the final actions of the Congress, which had ceased deliberations at the end of October and whose acts were just now becoming public knowledge. The men seated round the table in the back room were delighted with the major decision of the Congress—the Declaration of Rights, which stated that the colonies would not give up the rights to tax and legislate for themselves. But Congress had come to another agreement, one more difficult to understand and even more difficult to implement: the agreement to form a Continent-wide association for the purpose of restricting trade with England. Nate read aloud from the *New York Gazette* the terms of the "Continental Association," an agreement to restrict both imports and exports, signed by all the delegates to the Congress.

To the men assembled at Samuel Peach's ordinary, the most pertinent part of that agreement was the statement urging "every county, city and town" to establish a committee to see to it that the decisions made by the "Association" were carried out locally.

"We've already got ourselves a committee," Jotham declared proudly. "The Sons of Liberty. Us!"

"Right," Daniel Styles agreed in his squeaky voice. "The Sons of Liberty are up to the task."

"It doesn't seem to me that the Congress intended for those committees to be self-appointed," Tom objected.

"You stay out of this, Tom Morrison," Jotham said belligerently. "A bondsman can't have no say in these matters."

"Drat you, Joth," Nate snapped in quick defense of his friend, "when have we ever stopped Tom from speaking on grounds that he's indentured?"

"Never before and not now," Samuel Peach said firmly. "As my mother used to say, 'Some speak *much,* and some speak *sense.*' Seems to me, Jotham, that you're the first kind and Tom's the second."

"Aye, I'm for ye, too, Tom, laddie," Charley McNab the Scotsman said, raising his mug.

Jotham glared at all of them. "Speakin' sense, is he?" he demanded. "What kind o' sense is he makin', eh? If we was to have an elected committee, most of the townsfolk who'd have the vote would be the very ones who'd like the Association to fail!"

The others, surprised by Jotham's sound logic, exchanged looks. "The gowk has ye there, Tom," Charley said with a laugh.

"So to gain your ends, you abandon the very principles you wish to uphold, is that it?" Tom asked.

"The ends justify the means, isn't that what they say?" Samuel Peach responded gently.

Daniel Styles stared into his mug of ale. "Samuel's maxims make sense for once," he declared, looking up after a long moment of deep thought. "Besides, to organize another committee when we already have one in place is a waste of time."

Most of the men nodded in agreement. Thus the committee was formed in spite of Tom's objection. "But what, exactly, are we supposed to do?" Nate asked, confused.

Jotham waved the newspaper under his nose. "You already read what has t' be done. Read it again."

Nate scanned the article to find the place. "Here it is. 'The Committees are conjoined to inspect Customhouse books, to publish the names of the Offenders in newspapers, to break off dealings with Violators, who from this day forth will be considered Enemies of American liberty.' "

"That's sure clear enough," Daniel said.

"Enemies of American Liberty," Samuel Peach echoed in a tone of foreboding. "I'd wager there's more'n a few around here."

"So how are we supposed to find them out?" Daniel wondered.

"Watch and listen," Jotham said. "That's all. We just watch and listen. If you see someone tradin' contraband or drinkin' tea, or overhear him cursin' the cause, you name him to the committee, and we make him pay the price."

"What do you mean, pay the price?" Nate asked. "What price? Fines?"

"An unauthorized committee extorting fines?" Tom exclaimed. "I wouldn't try it, if I were you."

Jotham shrugged. "There's other ways to make 'em pay. We can ban 'em from the tavern and the public places . . . you know the word I mean, Dan'l. Snub 'em, like."

"Ostracize 'em," Daniel supplied.

"Right. Then they'd have to come before the committee and recant."

"And if they refused," Daniel said, eyes brightening with the thought of these exciting prospects, "we could march 'em round a liberty pole, with a drummer markin' the beat and the whole town watchin'."

"And in the worst cases," Jotham added with a leer, "we can always give 'em a brush with a tar mop."

This turned Nate's dubious expression into one of horror. He dropped his head on the table and groaned aloud.

Tom merely shook his head in disgust. "Tell me, gentlemen, how you intend to go about this. Do you mean to spy on *everyone?*"

"On everyone suspicious," Jotham answered promptly.

"How admirable," Tom said with heavy sarcasm. "Spying on your neighbors. A noble enterprise, that is."

"It's noble enough if the cause is good," Daniel defended.

"It's said, Tom," Samuel Peach added, "that *he who spares the bad injures the good.*"

"But who's to decide who's bad?" Nate wanted to know.

"We already know the out-and-out Tories," Jotham said. "And we can find out the weathercocks by askin' 'em to join the Association."

"Compelling them, isn't that what you mean? They sign or get the tarbrush?" Tom rose from his seat and stomped to the door. "Even the *British* laws grant that a man is innocent until proven guilty. If I may borrow a leaf from Samuel's book, I, too, have a saying. Meant especially for you, Jotham. *He that hath the worst case maketh the most noise.*"

Jotham leaped up from his seat. "Damn you, Tom, you always fleer at me, whatever I say! My *case* is our *cause,* an't it? So are you sayin' that our *cause* an't good?"

"No, of course not. 'Tis a cause I'd die for. I'm saying that in the struggle for that cause—for liberty—we should be careful not to lose the very thing we're fighting for." And with one last glower, he left them to their deliberations.

In the taproom, Freda was waiting. "What a sour face you're wearin', my dear!" she said in greeting. "Did you have a bit of a row back there?"

"More than a bit," Tom sighed.

She slipped both her arms about him. "Give me half an hour, and I'll make you forget it all."

"That's exactly the half hour I came for," Tom assured her, his face relaxing into a smile. He put his arm about her waist and together they went to the stairs.

As they climbed, Freda undid two buttons of his shirt and commenced to plant tantalizing little kisses on his chest. Halfway up, Tom suddenly stopped. "Freda, no," he muttered awkwardly, holding her off. "I don't—! It's . . . er . . . late. Later than I . . . I'd best be going."

"Tom!" she cried, gaping. *"Now?"*

"Yes, now, this very moment," he said, backing down the stairs. "I'm . . . sorry." Without giving her a chance to recover from her astonishment, he turned and made a hasty exit from the tavern.

Lowering his head against the wind, he clumped up the hill toward home. He was filled with angry confusion, compounded by an overwhelming sense of self-disgust. Not only had he been revoltingly high-and-mighty with his friends, he'd ruined his night with Freda. Why on earth had he done it? He'd looked forward all day to a romp on Freda's featherbed. Not only had he wrecked his plan for the night, he'd probably lost the affection of the delectable tavern maid for good.

But in his bones he knew the cause: an unfathomable sense of loyalty to Patience. The feeling had come from only-God-knew-where. Even while fully responding to Freda's advances, he'd suddenly felt a profound need to escape from them. *Damnation,* he cursed, *I'm losing my mind!* There was no earthly reason why he should feel this inexplicable urge to be faithful to Patience. She hadn't let him near her in seven long months!

It was love, of course, that accounted for this insanity. Love! He was a bondsman to it as surely as he was to Hendley. Worse, in fact, for if it weren't for love, he would have fled his prison long ago. Yet if a man were strong-minded, he could make himself believe that love was as fragile a prison as any other. It was not impossible to escape. If he had a grain of gumption, he would rid himself of *both* sets of chains!

For the remainder of the way home, he filled his mind with plans of escape, carefully mapping out routes south, north and west. All the plans held possibilities of success. *What am I waiting for?* he asked himself.

But when he slipped between the sheets a few moments later and pulled the two woolen blankets up to his neck, he caught a whiff of peach blossoms. It was very faint, so faint that he might have been imagining it. But the mere possibility that one of those blankets had come from her own bed was enough to wrench his heart and undermine his resolve. Yes, he was going to escape, but not yet. Not quite yet.

Forty

Artemas "Black Hawk" Barlow was good at his job. Years of tracking escaping slaves and indenturers had taught him how runaways think. So tracing the movements of Sally and Aaron out of Spuyten Duyvil caused him little difficulty. He guessed from the first that the direction they took was north, for no Negro with a grain of sense would head south, and though going west to the frontier might offer possibilities for a black man of strength and stamina, it would be too dangerous for a woman and a boy. Barlow surmised correctly that the pair would head for Boston, where they could lose themselves among the hundreds of free blacks who lived there. They would undoubtedly keep to the woods for as long as they could. If they had sense, he reasoned, they'd keep hidden until they'd crossed into Connecticut.

It was this shrewd reasoning that brought him to the Old Anchor Inn outside of Stamford. When he learned that the innkeeper had given a day's employment to two Negroes who answered to the last detail the description Hendley had given him, he smiled to himself in triumph. He, Black Hawk Barlow, was hardly ever wrong.

But the innkeeper was a sullen sort, not eager to talk. All he would say was that he'd seen the runaways, that they'd been a pair of obstreperous troublemakers, and he was glad to see them go.

"Did you notice what direction they took?" Barlow pressed.

The innkeeper shrugged. "I took no notice. It's possible they made off with a damn Quaker who happened by."

That clue was helpful but not specific enough to make Barlow's task easy. He spent the next several weeks stopping at the homes of all the Quaker families he could discover on the road to Boston, but he found nothing. Sally and Aaron's trail seemed to disappear.

By the time he reached Boston, he was discouraged. And by the time he'd investigated a mere fraction of the Quaker households in the city—and had the door closed in his face more often than not—he'd just about decided to give up. He hated to admit defeat, but the search was taking too much time to be profitable. Nevertheless, his pride in his ability was badly shaken.

It was at that low point when the breakthrough occurred, but Barlow had to admit it came about more through luck than brains. He'd knocked at the door of a neat Quaker household and had been politely admitted. It was evening, and the head of the family, a man with a heavy red beard, had just come in from his place of business. While his wife busied herself setting the dining table in the next room, the man of the house ushered Barlow to a chair in the front parlor, but after hearing his request the man turned cold as ice. "We of the Society take no human being into slavery," he declaimed, as if Barlow hadn't heard it a hundred times before. "I have no information to give thee of the whereabouts of any persons of color."

"Are you certain, sir?" Barlow persisted. "A thin, tall woman and a fourteen-year-old boy? She might be working as a cook for one of the ladies of your congregation."

"I've heard of no one in our Society with a Negro cook," the man said, rising as if to end the interview. But Barlow was quick to notice that his wife, whose position in the dining room put her within hearing, had made a start and had looked up at the words 'Negro cook.'

Barlow rose, too. "The Negras I'm looking for are not in any danger of recapture," he said with unctuous insincerity. "Their owner only wants to be assured of their safety. He holds them in great affection."

"No doubt," the bearded man said with withering scorn. "All slave owners hold their slaves in great affection, don't they? But there is no more to be said, sir, I assure thee. Good even to thee."

Barlow left as he was bidden, but when the Quaker shut the door on him, the slave trader circled round the house to the dining-room windows. He often got more information eavesdropping *after* an interview than *during* one, and this time was no exception.

Luck was with him; one of the dining-room windows was slightly open. He knelt below and listened. The wife's voice reached him, clear and distinct. "Think thee 'tis a coincidence, Matthew?" she was asking. "Sister writ me she's taken her new Negro cook much to her heart."

"There must be many Negro cooks, my dear," the man responded. " 'Tis not likely to be this one."

"Perhaps not. But shall I write and warn her, just in case?"

"Thou art a ninny. Marblehead is miles from here. Will the fellow go searching through all of Massachusetts for one Negro cook? Set thy silly mind at ease."

Under the window, Barlow grinned. Success after all! His quarry was in *Marblehead!* Marblehead was a very small town. After Boston, finding his prey in Marblehead would be as easy as taking candy from a babe.

Forty-one

A little colored boy, playing in the December snow on the edge of the woods behind his mother's house, spotted a man's footprints. Instinctively, he hid behind a tree. Not more than a few minutes passed before he saw the man who'd made them. A white man. The child stayed hidden until the man went away. Then he ran home and told his mammy.

The free Negroes of Marblehead, Massachusetts, numbering fewer than a dozen families, lived clustered together in a row of wooden cabins on the western edge of the town. It was a small community in which all celebrations, privations, troubles and miseries were shared. Thus when the little boy reported that a white stranger had been observing their movements from the shelter of the trees behind their shacks, a tremor of fear spread quickly through the community. There was little doubt of the stranger's identity. He was—must be!—a slave hunter.

There was also little doubt of the objects of the stranger's surveillance: the most recent arrivals in their midst, Mary Baker and her son, Dee. Everyone knew that those were not their names, for they'd heard Mary call her son Aaron on one or two occasions when she'd been lulled by the warmth and friendliness of her new neighbors into relaxing her guard. No one had asked her about those slips. They all understood that there must have been a good reason for deception. Even *free* negroes had difficult lives; deception was often required just to survive.

The problem of the spying stranger was discussed among the

leaders of the little community, and Big John Berry, a cooper
and blacksmith who rented space for his forge in the livery stable
where young Dee was employed, was chosen to warn Mary Baker
that she was being watched. It was urgent, they decided. The
warning had to be made soon.

Big John set out for Mary's door early the next morning, when
it was still quite dark. It had snowed again during the night, and
he looked over his shoulder at the fresh prints his shoes made in
the thin veneer of white on the ground. If the stranger happened
to be watching, the footprints would surely reveal the destination
of this unusual morning visit. But it was very early; a spy would
be unlikely to be at his post before it was light enough to see.
And by the time half an hour had passed, so many others of their
small community would be on their way to work that the ground
would be a maze of new footprints.

Certain that Mary Baker would be up and dressed (for she
would shortly be starting out for the home of the Quaker Jonathan
Myers, where she was employed as cook and housekeeper), Big
John knocked at her door. "Miz Baker, cin I talk to you?" he
whispered hoarsely through the keyhole, his breath steaming up
in the icy air.

Sally, who even after five months of living as a free Negro
still started at every unexpected sound, opened the door only a
crack. "Somethin' wrong?" she asked, eyeing the man worriedly.

"Lemme in, Miz Baker. I got sompin' to tell ye."

As soon as she stepped aside, he clomped over the threshold,
shut the door behind him and looked around. The one-room
shack, like all the others in the row, had a dirt floor and one small
window, but Mary Baker had made it clean and pleasant. She'd
hung a neat pair of dowlas-linen curtains over the window, made
up the two pallets on the floor with sheets, and spread her table
with a clean cloth. Her boy, Dee, was sitting at the table sipping
a steaming cup of what smelled like camomile tea, but he put it
down and stood up slowly. "Mornin', Big John," he said, his eyes
wary.

"Mornin'." Big John nodded to the boy but fixed his eyes on the woman. "I ain't askin' ye any questions, Miz Baker," he said bluntly, "but if there's any reason someone might be wishin' to fin' ye, we reckon you oughta know someone's been nosin' round."

Sally swallowed. "Nosin' round?"

"In the woods back there. A couple o' days now."

"Damn!" Aaron swore.

"Hush, boy," Sally muttered, clenching her hands.

Big John noted her sudden stiffening. "We be yer friends, Miz Baker. No one's gonna say nothin' about when ye got here or where ye work or nothin' else."

"Thank ye kin'ly, Mr. Berry," Sally said absently, her mind already concentrating on evasive action.

"Is there somethin' we can do?" Big John offered. "There's a root cellar under Molly Vesey's kitchen—"

"No, thank ye, I don' believe we need to hide."

"A root cellar?" Aaron threw his mother a speculative look. "Maybe we should—?"

Sally shook her head firmly. "We already made a plan, boy. We gonna stick to it." She turned to Big John and led him to the door. "Thank ye again for the warnin', Mr. Berry. We gonna be fine. Don' ye worry none."

After the man departed, Aaron faced his mother. "Mus' ye be so mulish, Mama? Hidin' in the root cellar, we at leas' be together."

"We been over an' over this. What good's bein' together if we's caught? We sure be separated then. Don' waste time, boy. Get the clothes."

Aaron sighed in helpless resignation and pulled Barbara's old gown from its hiding place inside the pallet he slept on. While he once more dressed himself in girl's clothing and covered his head with a large-brimmed bonnet, Sally dug into her pallet for the little muslin sack in which she'd stored her worldly goods—a small cache of pennies and shillings that she'd saved from their wages. She dropped the sack into her pocket. Then she went to the window and peeped out from between the curtains to watch for movement in the woods. The sky was turning light when she thought she spotted something. "He be there," she said tightly. "Le's go."

She followed her son to the door, but before leaving she gave a pat to the bosom of her dress to make certain her precious writ of manumission, which she always carried with her, was still safely tucked inside. This done, she threw her shawl over her thin shoulders, went out and closed the door.

Arm in arm, they walked quickly down the road. "Keep yo' head down," she warned her son. "You gettin' mos' tall as me!"

Aaron glanced surreptitiously over his shoulder. "You sure he seen us? He be followin'?"

"Stupid! Don' look! He be followin' right enough."

By the time they reached the Myerses' house, day had fully dawned. They walked around the back to the kitchen door and went inside. "Goin' good so far," Sally muttered, shutting the door firmly.

In the kitchen Mistress Myers, a middle-aged woman with prematurely white hair that accented a pair of very dark, kindly eyes, looked up from the fire where she'd been stirring milk into a pot of porridge. At the sight of the boy in female garb, her eyes widened. "Mary!" she gasped. "Have they found thee?"

"I think so, ma'am," Sally said.

"Then we must go to Mr. Myers at once. Come with me, Dee. Mary, go upstairs and get Charity. We will need her."

The escape plan was known to the whole Myers family—Mr. Jonathan Myers, his wife, and his fourteen-year-old daughter Charity. In fact, Jonathan Myers had concocted the plan himself, when he'd first brought the two runaway slaves to Marblehead. After he'd saved the pair from the clutches of the Connecticut tavern keeper, he'd persuaded them to go with him to Marblehead, where he'd hired Sally as cook for his family and arranged for Aaron to work at the livery stable. In gratitude, Sally had revealed to him the truth of their situation, for it would not sit well on her conscience to reward him for his kindness by lying to him. The punishment for abetting runaways was severe; Sally did not wish to cause him such trouble.

The Quaker gentleman did not waver when he learned the truth. Although convinced that it was unlikely for the pair to be traced so far from their place of origin, he nevertheless understood the danger facing runaways. Thus he devised an emergency plan for their escape should escape become necessary.

Mr. Myers was found in the woodshed, stacking newly cut logs. As soon as he learned what had transpired, he took Aaron to his bedroom. There he helped the boy to strip off his female attire, which he then handed to his wife who was waiting outside the door. "Here, Dee," he said to Aaron, removing a a suit of clothes from a chest at the foot of his bed. "These belonged to my son Jacob, whom the good Lord took from us nine years ago. Put them on."

Aaron looked at the fine garments, so carefully folded and preserved, and hesitated. "I don' like to . . . 'tain't right, is it?"

"My Jacob, God rest his soul, would say it was putting his clothes to the very best use. Come, boy, put them on."

Meanwhile, Mrs. Myers hurried across the hall to her daughter's bedroom with Barbara's clothes thrown over her arm. Charity, a sweet-faced girl who, unfortunately for the day's purpose, had beautiful golden hair that fell almost to her waist, was already making herself ready for her part by hiding her hair inside a turban. Sally and Mrs. Myers dressed her exactly as Dee had been dressed, except for the shoes. But even in her mother's best shoes, with heels two-inches high, Charity was noticeably shorter than Aaron. "Oh, dear," her mother sighed, studying her daughter worriedly, "If only I could make thee taller. Wear the bonnet on the very top of thy head and carry thyself upright. 'Tis the best we can do."

A short while later, Jonathan Myers and Aaron joined the women in the kitchen. "Ready?" Mr. Myers asked.

"Jus' a minute, please," Sally said, drawing her son aside. She peered at him for a moment in his neat, well-made Quaker clothes. "Don' you look fine!" she whispered, smiling at him with lips that trembled. "Here, take these." She tried to thrust the sack and the writ into his hand.

"No, Mama," the boy said, backing away, "you may need 'em yo'self."

"Take 'em!" she ordered in the tone he'd learned to respect. "They be safer wit' you."

Reluctant but obedient, the boy took them and stuffed them into his breast pocket. "But what about you? How you gonna get on wit'out 'em?"

"It on'y be fo' one day. I'll fin' you in Salem, in the livery stable Mr. Myers tol' us of. Tomorrow night, lates'."

"Yes, Mama," he muttered tearfully.

She put out her hand and smoothed the lapel of his coat. "But Aaron, if I ain't there by nightfall, you mus' swear to me that you gonna set off west wit'out me."

His jaw set obstinately. "Damn it, Mama, don't ask me—"

"I ain't askin', I'm tellin'! Swear!"

"I *won't—!*"

"I's still yo' mama, boy! Don' you talk back to me! Swear!"

He threw his arms about her, openly weeping. "I swear, drat it all, Mama," he sobbed. "I s-swear."

She held him tight for a moment before wrenching herself from the embrace. Then she took his hand and drew him back to the others. "Ready now," she told Mr. Myers.

But Mr. Myers had one more act to perform. He motioned them all to kneel. Right there in the kitchen they bowed their heads. "Dear Lord," he said, "we give unto Thy hands the lives and fortunes of these thy servants Sally and Aaron, who now are called Mary and Dee Baker. They have known much travail and have suffered much, but they have never deviated from the paths of righteousness and honor. May Thou, in Thy infinite wisdom and kindness, keep them well and guide them to a safe harbor where, together, they may dwell in security, in peace of body and mind, and in blessed freedom. Amen."

The prayer said, Mrs. Myers brushed away her tears and helped Sally to rise. Placing a basket on her arm, she led the black woman to the door. Charity put the shabby bonnet over her turban and tied it under her chin. Pulling the poke forward so that her face was well hidden, the girl linked her arm in Sally's. They were ready.

With a last look at her son, Sally threw open the kitchen door, and she and Charity went out to perform their diversionary act.

Jonathan Myers ran to the window. "Is anyone following them?" his wife asked.

"I don't see— Wait! *Yes!* There he is, the blackguard! If I were not a man of peace, I'd—"

"Hush, Mr. Myers. Thou hast more urgent business. Dee is ready."

"Yes, thou speaks true. Come, boy, let's start thee on thy way."

Outside, Charity and Sally marched bravely up the road toward the center of town. Soon they could hear behind them the crunch of heavy footsteps on the snow. Sally began to tremble. Charity pressed her arm firmly. "It will be all right," the girl whispered. "Don't be afraid."

They marched on, not permitting themselves a backward look. When they reached the linendraper's, they went inside and loitered as long as they could, bending over bolts of cloth and studying the colors of the spools of thread until the clerk began to show impatience. He was only partially assuaged when they made the meager purchase of one spool of thread. They also made a protracted stop at the silversmith's, where they bought nothing. At the stationer's they spent almost an hour studying the samples before deciding on a packet of notepaper, which Sally purchased and dropped into her basket. By this time Sally estimated that almost two hours had passed since they'd started out, two hours during which Mr. Myers would have given Aaron a good start toward Salem in the buckboard and driven himself back home again.

Having exhausted all means of procrastination, Sally and Charity now picked up the pace of their stroll and walked quickly down the road that led south to Boston. They would now permit the stranger to believe they were making their escape. They'd given Aaron his chance.

Artemas Barlow was indeed following them. With his quarry right in front of him, he was ready to pounce. He was sure he'd found the right pair, for the woman was tall and gaunt, just as Hendley had described her, and she was accompanied by the boy. Barlow was too shrewd and experienced to be put off by a dress. Dressing up a boy in girl's clothing was too commonplace a trick to fool him! And if the woman thought her meanderings through the shops of Marblehead would put him off the track, she was about to learn the error of her ways. He hurried his step, came up behind the pair he'd been following all morning, and put a hand on Sally's shoulder. "Goin' somewheres, woman?" he asked.

Sally stopped and turned around. "Beg pardon?" she asked calmly.

"Don't give me that innocent stare," Barlow leered. "I know who you are, and I know yer boy, here, too." Without giving her a chance to reply, he reached out and pulled the bonnet and turban from the head of Sally's companion. A cascade of golden hair fell over his hand. Barlow gasped in surprise.

Charity swung around. "What art thou *doing?*" she exclaimed. "Whatever dost thou wish with my bonnet?"

Barlow's eyes bulged as he took in the girl's artless, white-skinned face. "Who the hell are you?" he asked, choking.

"I do not converse with strangers, especially those who blaspheme," the girl replied coldly. "Please be good enough to give me back my bonnet."

Speechlessly, his face reddening in frustration and chagrin, Barlow handed her the hat and the turban. Charity tossed the turban into Sally's basket and put the bonnet back on her head. "Let's turn back, Mary," she said as she tied the ribbons under her chin. "I am too disquieted to visit Aunt Lotty now."

With that, the two of them turned and walked back up the road arm in arm, leaving Barlow gazing after them with mouth agape.

When they arrived back home, Sally discovered that Mr. Myers, too, had safely returned. He'd driven Aaron by buckboard several miles north, to where the road forked west to Worcester and north to Salem. Mr. Myers tried to reassure Sally, who remained tense as a fiddle string despite the fact that the plan was proceeding smoothly. "Thy son looked so fine and proper as he walked away from me," Jonathan Myers said, "that anyone would know at once he was a sober, prosperous, hardworking freeman. He will be reunited with thee by tomorrow afternoon. I'm sure of it."

The plan to arrange for that reunion was relatively simple. On the chance that the slave hunter was still stalking her, Sally would return to her abode at twilight and wait there until midnight, by which time all the world—even slave traders—would be asleep. Then she was to steal out the back window and make her way along the edge of the woods to the north road, where Mr. Myers would meet her with his buckboard and take her as far north as time would permit, given the necessity of his being back home before the first light.

Sally went home to her shack at her usual time. If the slave hunter was following, she saw no sign of it. She locked her door, drew her curtains tightly closed and lit a candle. She had no clock, but Mr. Myers had told her to leave when three inches had burned down. He'd even drawn a mark in the wax. She shaded the candle on all sides so that no glimmer should show through the cracks in the walls or from beneath the window curtains. That done, she put on the black Quaker dress Mrs. Myers had given her and sat down to wait.

Three inches of candle burned very slowly, but eventually the flame reached the mark. She blew it out, opened the window slowly and silently, climbed up on the sill and slipped out to the ground below. She peered into the darkness, her heart beating so loudly she feared it would rouse the sleepers in the adjoining cabins, but she could see nothing in the starless night. Taking a deep, brave breath. she crept toward the woods, her light step barely making a sound on the hardened snow.

As she made her way along the edge of the woods, coming closer and closer to the road where she knew Mr. Myers would be waiting, her rapid heartbeats slowed down. By this time to-morrow, she told herself, she would be with Aaron again. She had only to take one step at a time . . . one step and another and another—"

"Sally!" a voice hissed behind her.

She spun around. "Who—?" Her eyes, showing white and wild, searched the darkness for a brief moment. Then she realized the mistake she'd made and uttered a deep, despairing groan.

"I *knew* it," Barlow chortled, pulling the cover from a lantern he carried as he closed the distance between them in two long steps.

Sally turned and began to run, a loud scream of agony escaping from her throat. A flock of juncos fluttered out of the nearby trees, cawing in irritation at being awakened, but no one else heard her. Barlow had chosen his capture site well; she was too far away from the huts behind her and the north road ahead. Fleet though she was for her age, Barlow caught up with her in a very few steps and flung her to the ground. Then, lowering his knee onto her back to hold her in place, he set the lantern on the ground, pulled her arms behind her and tied her wrists. "Get up!" he ordered.

But her spirits were so badly crushed she couldn't move.

He kicked her side. "Get up, I said!"

She struggled to her feet without even knowing that she did so. All she knew was that the heart within her breast had broken in two, and that the pain was so great she could barely breathe.

Her shoulders sagged and her head hung down as if her neck had lost its bone.

"Where is he?" Barlow said, thrusting his face close to hers. "The boy . . . where *is* he?"

The question revived something within her. Aaron was safe. That was what really mattered. She lifted her head and spat in the slave hunter's face. "Where you'll never get hold of him," she said.

He slammed her face with the back of his hand and then used it to wipe the spittle from his cheek. "I ast you a question," he snarled.

"An' I answered." She squared her shoulders and lifted her face boldly to him, her mouth twisted in a scornful yet triumphant smile. "He be in the groun'. Dead. No one get him now but God."

Forty-two

Barbara had escaped from her home in America to what she'd believed would be a life of easeful luxury in London among the *beau monde*. She'd imagined her wedded life as a constant frolic: grand dinners over which she would preside; elegant balls that she'd attend wearing brocaded gowns and jewels in the latest mode; trips to country estates where she'd be ceremoniously welcomed; routs and fetes and theater parties to occupy every evening of the week. It was to be a life of perpetual gaiety shared with the man she loved. The reality, however, soon demonstrated how childishly innocent her imaginings had been.

In the first place, her husband was not recovering his health with the speed she'd expected of someone with his youth and strength. His face was always pale, he had a small but persistent cough, and his appetite was so poor that in the two months since their landing on English soil he hadn't regained any of the weight he'd lost on the ship. While he managed to dress and come down for meals almost every day, and to walk out with her on brief sojourns, he still spent a great deal of time resting. And he'd not yet managed to kindle enough energy to venture out to find a house for them, though he promised every day that he would soon do so.

Meanwhile, Sir Matthew, showing a kindliness absent in the other family members, prevailed on Hetty to surrender her room to Barbara and move to another bedroom down the hall until the couple could find a place of their own. Hetty's old room was next to Jack's, which, Sir Matthew pointed out to his reluctant daughter, was the only proper place for Jack's wife. "A married couple," he insisted, "need proximity."

For Barbara, the room was a great deal more endurable than the garret room in which her mother-in-law had originally placed her. Being close to Jack made it easier to slip into his room and share his bed, although she had to admit that Jack's appetite for marital conjunction had become as weak as it was for food.

For this problem Barbara blamed herself as much as she did his weakened condition: she'd caused a rift between them. One morning, when she'd slipped into bed beside him while he still slept, she discovered that his nightshirt was soaked with sweat. Alarmed, she'd made a to-do, demanding that a doctor be called at once. Jack had become terribly angry, shouting that he would not be "babied," and he'd ordered her not to come to his bed again unless specifically invited. This quarrel, the worst they'd ever had, convinced her that he'd stopped loving her. She wept for hours afterward. It was only later, when rational thought returned, that she began to suspect something worse: that Jack was seriously ill and that the facts were being kept from her.

As if this were not bad enough, matters were made worse by having to live with two women who despised her. Although her father-in-law clearly held her in affection, Lady Olivia and her daughter Hetty refused to warm to her. When Sir Matthew insisted that they make every effort to provide the new bride with the proper clothing and accoutrements for London life, they obeyed him, but with obvious reluctance. So grudging were their attentions to her that Sir Matthew noticed. He tried to make up for their coldness by bringing Barbara expensive presents—a fur muff, a gold bracelet, a magnificent diamond and emerald brooch. The gifts were delightful, but they could not make up for the icy atmosphere of Barbara's daily life.

One day, Barbara overheard him berating his wife on the subject. She'd come down to breakfast earlier than usual, and when she reached the bottom of the stairs, she heard his voice. "What have you got against the child?" he was asking.

His wife responded in tones of sheer disgust. "What have I *not* got against her! How could our Jack have been taken in by a *provincial nobody* when he could have had a girl like Celia Holland or Lady Meg Clifton for the asking?"

Their voices were coming from the morning room where they were taking breakfast. Barbara crept closer to the doorway to listen. She knew that eavesdropping was dishonest and dangerous, but she could no more keep herself from listening than she could stop her breath.

"Because his provincial nobody, as you call her, has more charm in her little finger than Celia Holland has in her entire physiognomy!" Sir Matthew was retorting. "And as for the Clifton chit, what man wants a female with a chest as flat as a board?"

"Matt, really!" his wife snapped. "You become more vulgar every day."

"And you become more toplofty. It's quite beyond sense to find fault with the girl simply because she came from the colonies."

"It's not where she came from but what she is," Lady Olivia insisted.

"I don't understand your attitude. What do you find wrong with her?"

"Everything! Her slurred colonial accent, for one thing. And the free-and-easy manner she has with the servants, calling them by name as if they were long friends. And her way of walking, with those long strides like a boy's. A proper young woman should move with delicacy, with small steps that *glide*." Lady Olivia delivered herself of a deep sigh. "I suppose one shouldn't expect colonials to know what proper decorum is, much less to teach it to their daughters."

"Bosh!" her husband snorted. "I like the way the child walks. It has a swing to it."

"Of course you do. Another sign of your growing vulgarity."

"Everything you've said about little Babs so far is utterly trivial," Sir Matthew accused.

"Not to me. And, take my word, that's not all. There's the horrid way your 'little Babs' behaves when we dine with friends. She always manages to argue politics with anyone who—"

At that moment, Barbara heard approaching footsteps from the rear passageway. Jeffers was probably coming up from the kitchen with a tray. The eavesdropper immediately made a dash for the stairs and disappeared beyond the turning just in time.

But she didn't need to hear the rest. She knew exactly what flaws in her character bothered her ladyship. In Lady Olivia's eyes, Barbara Pilkington née Hendley was an upstart American: too brash, too unrefined, too unmannerly to know how to behave in polite society. And what bothered her ladyship most of all was Barbara's newly acquired penchant for speaking out loudly in defense of the colonies whenever any Englishman said a word against them. Barbara admitted to herself that it was quite true. Ever since that thrilling night when she met Benjamin Franklin, she'd felt impelled to do it, even though she knew it embarrassed Lady Olivia to hear her daughter-in-law intrude herself into what her ladyship referred to as "gentlemen's conversation." In Lady Olivia's mind such boldness made a woman conspicuous, and nothing was more unseemly than that.

If Barbara's behavior was unseemly, Dr. Franklin was the cause. She'd met him at a social gathering just before the new year, shortly after her first month in London. It was an experience that changed her irrevocably.

She would never forget that evening. The family had received an invitation to a large gathering at the home of Caroline Howe, sister to the famous Admiral Richard, Lord Howe and his younger brother, Major General William Howe. When Sir Matthew first asked Babs to join them, she'd refused. "I'd rather stay home with Jack," she'd said.

But Jack was feeling surprisingly well that evening and de-

cided to go to the affair, too. Barbara was overjoyed. She dressed
for the occasion with more excited anticipation than she'd yet
felt in London. She would have liked to wear one of those high,
ornate, heavily powdered wigs that were so much in fashion, but
she knew that Jack preferred her own wild hair to any wig. She
took a great deal of trouble dressing it, twisting it into a single
curl to fall over her shoulder in the style that Jack favored, giving
way to fashion only by powdering it. Then she donned a new
gown made from a rich lustring she'd chosen because it was in
Jack's favorite shade of green. As a final touch, she pinned the
diamond and emerald brooch that Sir Matthew had given her at
the center of her décolletage, just at the cleft of her breasts.

Jack's look of approval when she came down the stairs was
the perfect beginning for what was going to be a gala evening
with her husband—just the sort of evening she'd been yearning
for.

In the carriage on their way to Mistress Howe's, Barbara
looked across at her husband with dawning hope. In his full-
skirted evening coat, with its wide sleeves revealing the lacy
cuffs of his shirt, he looked a bit less thin. And his manner was
more animated than it had been in weeks. Perhaps he was finally
getting better!

Barbara couldn't take her eyes from him while he and his
father discussed what was on every Londoner's mind these
days—the tension between England and its American colonies.
News from America was growing worse every day, and the *possibility* of war was becoming *probable*. While most Britons were
in favor of punishing the colonies soundly for their upstart pre-
tensions, a few spoke out for moderation. Jack was one of the
latter. "One can't blame the Americans for finding the Port Acts
too severe a chastisement," he pointed out to his father.

Sir Matthew could not agree. "The laws of the mother country
must be obeyed on *principle*," he declared. "If the colonies refuse, they must be coerced, as any lawbreaker is coerced. How

can we keep the British Empire strong if we permit transgressions against our laws?"

"Americans don't react well to aggressive acts, even if they are made law," Jack said mildly. "It might be well for Parliament to consider how those laws might look to American eyes."

"Humph!" his father grunted in disapproval. "You sound like that damned Whig Edmund Burke."

The arguments about the colonies continued after they arrived at the gala. Jack, who was known to have spent more than a year in the colonies, was soon surrounded by men eager to debate the problem with him, the Howe brothers among them. Barbara would have liked to stay and listen, but Lady Olivia, giving the girl an order by means of a venomous glare, compelled Barbara to follow dutifully in her footsteps. With Hetty imprisoning her arm, Barbara was led round the room by her mother-in-law, who kept introducing her to friends as "my daughter-in-law from America" in a tone that was unmistakably disparaging. Barbara found herself being stared at through lorgnettes and quizzing glasses as if she were a specimen of an inferior species. They peered at her low décolletage with such disapproval that she began to wish she'd sewed in a strip of modesty lace. But that was not the only source of disapproval. "How quaint to wear your hair that way," one woman remarked. "Don't they have wigs in America?"

"Do they wear that particular shade of green for *evening* in colonies?" asked another in obvious disparagement.

But just as she was beginning to regret that she'd ever come, there was a stir near the entrance, as if a member of royalty were arriving. Barbara managed to slip away from her gaolers, and she edged into the crowd to see. But the new arrival was obviously not royalty. He was a cheerful-looking man, rotund and plainly dressed, with his own unpowdered hair hanging loosely down from a bald pate and a pair of square spectacles perched on his nose. "Who *is* that?" a woman near her asked aloud.

"That, madam," a man answered, "is Doctor Benjamin Franklin, the ambassador from North America."

"The North American Ambassador?" the lady exclaimed. "Dear me, look at him! How can an ambassador attend a *soirée* like this so shabbily dressed?"

"Hush, for heaven's sake," the man answered in a hissing whisper, "he's the man who bottles up thunder and lightning!"

Barbara choked back a laugh at this description of the American Ambassador's famous scientific experiments. But as she watched Dr. Franklin advance into the room, her amusement turned to astonishment at the warmth and respect with which he was being greeted, even by Lord Dartmouth, the highest-ranking Cabinet member present. If Americans were regarded, as she was regarded, as an inferior species, why was Dr. Franklin so highly revered? The question was particularly puzzling because she'd heard that he'd angered the British recently, when it was discovered that he'd disclosed to his contacts in America the contents of some secret correspondence.

When she was able to get Jack alone, Babs asked him why Dr. Franklin seemed so popular. "I thought he'd fallen into disgrace," she said.

"It's a matter of diplomacy," Jack explained. "It's rumored that Dartmouth is using Caroline Howe to press Franklin to assist him in an unofficial peace move. No one really wants war, you know, especially now, when there's trouble with the French. Look there, my dear! The Doctor is sitting down with Mistress Howe to play chess. She's a renowned player, and he's known to love the game."

If Caroline Howe was successful in her diplomatic mission, no one learned of it that evening. The game seemed to proceed pleasantly and was succeeded by another, and then another. Whatever serious diplomatic exchanges were made over the chess board were not overheard by anyone else. But much later in the evening, Babs noticed that Dr. Franklin was still playing chess, this time with a gentleman. Since she knew something about the game, having played with her brother years ago, she drew near to watch. Dr. Franklin seemed to be losing, for his king was in check. Instead of moving his king out of danger, however, the doctor, with a wicked gleam in his eye, moved another piece. "Sir," exclaimed the other gentleman in offense, "you can't do that and leave your king in check! It's against the rules."

Doctor Franklin nodded. "Yes, I see that my king's in check, but I shall not defend him. Were he a good king, he would deserve my protection, but he's a tyrant and has cost already more than he's worth. Take him, if you please. I can do without a king. I'll fight out the rest of the battle as a *republican.*"

A hoot of laughter issued from some of the watchers, mingled with a murmur of disapproval from others. Babs, unable to contain herself, cheered. "Good for you, Dr. Franklin," she cried aloud.

The doctor looked up. "Ah, that is an American voice, I think," he said, giving the pretty young woman a twinkling smile.

"Yes, sir," she smiled back, "from Westchester County in New York."

He got to his feet, took her hand and bowed over it. "You sound proud of it," he said. "That sort of pride pleases me."

She returned his bow, saying, "Yes, I am proud of it," and suddenly realized, with a jolt of pleasure, that it was true.

Her mother-in-law, who had passed by just in time to hear the exchange, promptly ushered her away, but not before Barbara heard Dr. Franklin remarking to his partner, "Now, there, sir, is a perfect example of the lovely sort of young woman we breed in the colonies."

The scolding Babs received for making herself conspicuous fell on deaf ears. Inside herself she was glowing. Benjamin Franklin, the most renowned American abroad, had smiled at her in approval of her loyalty to her native land. *He* had never felt shame at being an American, even while living for years in the midst of a host of disapprovers. With his example before her, she would from this moment refuse to let any Englishman—or woman—express any sentiment mocking America or Americans. *I, too,* she swore to herself, *will fight out rest of the battle as a republican.*

It was not to be an easy battle. Everywhere she went she met with supercilious disapproval. Her accent, her unruly hair, the informality of her manner, in fact, everything about her, was subject to criticism and scorn, as were the pronouncements from the first American Congress. But while she could not easily defend her own manners, she could and did defend Congress's position whenever the subject arose. It was only when Jack teasingly reminded her that she'd been a declared Tory when he first met her did she realize how much she'd changed.

The year was merely six weeks old when she experienced a greater change, one which altered everything in her life. She awoke one night to hear a loud coughing spasm from the room next to hers. The sound, loud enough to penetrate the thick wall that separated her from her husband, froze her blood. Jack was terribly ill; there could be no denying the fact any longer. Although he continued to make light of his persistent lassitude and to deny that the swelling in his neck or the ulcer she'd noticed on his tongue had any significance, she could no longer blind herself to the signs. She would not let another day go by without doing something about it.

She knocked at Sir Matthew's bedroom door the next morning before breakfast. His man, Ridley, opened it. "Sorry, Ma'am," the valet said, "but Sir Matthew has not finished dressing."

"But I must see him, Ridley. At once. Tell him it's—"

"Is that my little Babs?" Sir Matthew's voice boomed out. "Let her in, you nincompoop. I'm decent enough."

Barbara found her father-in-law in his dressing room. He was seated before a large mirror, clad in all but his neckcloth and coat, but his shoulders were covered with a protective cape. His valet had evidently been powdering his hair when she'd interrupted them. On the long table before which he sat were the dozens of articles necessary for a gentleman's toilet: shaving instruments, two wig stands, a box of black face-patches, a number of powder boxes, pomades, hair ribbands, combs, buttonhooks, laces and several sundries she couldn't identify. "Forgive me for intruding on you like this," she began, "but—"

"Nonsense, child," her father-in-law said from behind a cone-shaped mask with which he was protecting his face from the cloud of powder the valet was generating, "you can visit me whenever it suits you. You're quite one of the family."

"Thank you. That assurance makes it easier for me to say what I must. About Jack."

Sir Matthew lowered his face-protector and peered at the girl through the fog of powder. "Something serious, eh?" he asked, his cheerful smile fading. "Take yourself off, Ridley. I'll do the rest myself."

The valet bowed himself out. Sir Matthew, his forehead furrowed worriedly, rose and took his daughter-in-law's hand. "Come out where we can be cozy, child," he murmured, leading her out of the dressing room to the small sitting room next door. He seated her on a loveseat and lowered his bulk into the armchair facing it. "Now, tell me what's on your mind."

"It's Jack," Babs said, a little tremor in her otherwise-determined voice. "He won't permit me to call a doctor, but it must be done. I don't wish to alarm you, sir, but I believe he is terribly ill."

Sir Matthew dropped his eyes. "Apparently the time has come for some honesty."

"What do you mean?" She peered at him fearfully. "Is there something you've been keeping from me?"

He leaned forward and took her hand in his. "We agreed, Jack and I, to keep it from you as long as possible. A doctor *has* seen him and continues to see him regularly. We know what is wrong with him."

Barbara, her insides ashiver, braced herself for a blow. "Is it something very . . . bad?"

"Consumption," Matthew said bluntly.

The blow had come. Barbara shut her eyes with the pain. "Are you . . . certain?"

"Quite certain. The symptoms are plain. The cough. The loss of weight. You've seen them yourself."

"Yes," she admitted, "I've seen them. But surely they could be symptoms of other things?" As she spoke the words, however, she knew she was clutching desperately at straws.

"Not very likely," he said gently. "There are other signs, too. Night sweats . . . an ulcer on his tongue . . . and I'm afraid there's a family tradition of consumption. My wife's grandfather had a chronic cough. And her cousin Alfred died of it."

She withdrew her hand from his and, in a kind of daze, twisted her fingers together nervously, quite unaware of this sign of her inner agony. Then, after a long silence, the bewilderment in her eyes faded. She fixed those eyes on her father-in-law's face with a glittering look that spoke partly of fear, partly of anger but mostly of a fierce determination. "You've kept the truth from me long enough, sir," she said in a voice that matched the expression of her eyes, "so be truthful with me now. Will he die?"

Sir Matthew lowered his head. "I don't know. Some are cured of it."

Barbara clenched her fists. "Then we shall see to it that Jack becomes one of the cured." She got to her feet and strode purposefully toward the door. "I want to speak to the doctor, please, sir," she flung over her shoulder. "Today."

"Yes, if you wish, my dear," Sir Matthew agreed. He rose and followed her. "If there is anyone can make him well, it is you."

She paused and threw him a flashing, impenetrable look. "Does his mother know?"

"No. Nor Hetty. They are so . . . so highly strung. Jack and thought it best to wait—"

"*Tell* them," Barbara ordered and left the room.

That was when the changes came about. The whole household felt it. Lady Olivia, who had not let herself consider the possi

bility that her son had succumbed to the dread disease, collapsed
into distraught incompetence when the truth was made clear to
her. Hetty became so fearful of contagion that she never went to
her brother's room and rarely came out of her own. Sir Matthew,
kindly and sympathetic though he was, went to his club daily, as
he'd always done. Everything was left to Barbara. She ran the
sickroom—as well as the household—with one overriding goal:
to cure her husband of his ailment.

Every possible remedy the doctor could prescribe was tried.
Lemon tisanes were brewed daily. A mixture of raw turnips and
brown-sugar candy, said to have cured a patient of Dr. Hans
Sloane, was administered morning and night. Even an old-fashioned and repulsive concoction called Snayle Water (made from
roasted snails, earthworms, ale, herbs and several other unlikely
ingredients) was forced on the poor fellow until he put his foot
down, swearing that he'd had quite enough of the vile stuff.

Barbara spent most of her waking hours in the sickroom, reading to her husband from the newspapers, airing the room, helping
the maids to change his bed linens, adjusting his pillows or covering his forehead with cool compresses. Sometimes, when he
seemed well enough, she would help him take brief strolls down
the hallway. On good days, he might even dress and go downstairs. But the bad days became more and more frequent, and it
became hard for Barbara to keep her spirit hopeful.

February passed and half of March. Barbara had to admit that,
despite all her efforts, her patient seemed weaker. He was lethar-
gic, his eyes unfocused, his energy sapped. When she read to
him of the debates in Parliament over the American question, a
subject that in the past had piqued his interest more than any
other, he remained stuporous. She could not even stimulate him
to converse.

One evening at dinner—usually a dreadfully glum affair during which Hetty sniffed into a handkerchief and Lady Olivia
moved her food about her plate aimlessly, her eyes staring at
nothing—Sir Matthew came home from club and surprised them

with his presence. After exchanging greetings and asking about how his son had passed his day, he took a close look at his daughter-in-law. "You are looking very peaked, my dear," he declared, "and no wonder. You've been cooped up in the sickroom for weeks without a break. I insist that you go out tomorrow. Take yourself on a shopping expedition. Buy yourself some gloves. Or a new hat. Hetty can sit with Jack in your place."

"Papa!" Hetty gasped and burst into a flood of tears. "I *can't!* You know I can't. To s-see Jack so emaciated . . . it is more than I can b-bear!"

Sir Matthew bit back an angry retort and turned to his wife. "Then, Olivia, perhaps *you—*"

Barbara cut him off. "Thank you, sir, but her ladyship isn't strong enough to do what is necessary for Jack. Besides, I have no wish to shop. I don't need any gloves or hats."

"But you must have some relief, or you'll wear yourself out." He regarded her with knit brows. "There must be *something* you'd care to—Ah, I have it! The very thing! Edmund Burke is to speak to Parliament to propose conciliation with America. On the twenty-second, the day after tomorrow! I am not Whiggish myself, but I sympathize with your leanings in that direction. You'd enjoy hearing him, wouldn't you?"

Barbara brightened in spite of herself. "Edmund Burke? Oh, yes, I would indeed," she admitted, "but—"

"No buts, my dear. I'll see to it that a seat is reserved for you in the gallery. And *I'll* spend the day with Jack."

The morning of March twenty-second was dark and drizzly, but Barbara went all the way to the Parliament buildings on foot. It was good to be in the open, to feel alive and healthy, to take deep breaths of air that did not smell stale. She'd looked forward with unwonted eagerness to this visit to the House of Commons. She needed to set her mind on something other than sickness. When she was a girl, she'd irritated her father by her lack of interest in politics, but ever since she'd stepped on English soil and become aware of feelings of alienation—of not being a home in her mother country—she'd learned something important. She learned that matters of government could have a direct influence on one's own life—that politics was *personal*. She had a sudden yearning to go home to Spuyten Duyvil, to tell her father what she'd learned. *Heavens,* she thought, *wouldn't Papa be surprised!*

The gallery was crowded with gentlemen, many of whom looked curiously at the woman sitting among them. Barbara, blushing diffidently, lowered her eyes, but not before taking a quick glance down the long room where the members sat on benches lining the walls in ascending rows. However, she forgot her self-consciousness once the imposing orator was called to the floor and began to speak.

Edmund Burke took his stand facing the Chair, his hand resting lightly on the green-baize-covered table. He launched into his subject in a voice that was strong and authoritative but softened by a slight Irish burr. In the almost three hours of his oration, that voice never weakened. He spoke of America's amazing growth in population and in trade, and of the loss to England should this lucrative trade be damaged. He spoke of the errors made in the past to control the colonies by "the efficacy of arms." "The use of force," he pointed out strongly, "is but *temporary.* It may subdue for a moment, but it does not remove the necessity of subduing again; and a nation is not governed which is perpetually to be conquered."

Barbara was moved to tears when he spoke about Americans' rights. "In order to prove that the Americans have no right to their liberties," he said, "we are every day endeavoring to subvert the maxims which preserve the whole spirit of our own. To prove that the Americans ought not to be free, we are obliged to depreciate the value of freedom itself."

At one point she found herself hard-pressed to keep from standing up and cheering. It was when he said, "The Americans will have no interest contrary to the grandeur and glory of England, when they are not oppressed by the weight of it . . . and I confess I feel not the least alarm from the discontents which are to arise from putting people at their ease, nor do I apprehend the destruction of this empire from giving, by an act of free grace and indulgence, to two millions of my fellow-citizens, some share of those rights upon which I have always been taught to value myself."

On the way back to Pilkington House she repeated aloud as much of that statement as she could remember. She wanted to declaim it to Jack with as much accuracy as possible. But when Jeffers opened the door, one look at his ashen face drove everything else from her mind. "What is it?" she asked in terror.

"They are waiting for you in the drawing room, m'lady," was all the butler permitted himself to say.

She ran down the hall but stopped short in the drawing-room doorway. Sir Matthew was standing near the window, regarding her with eyes that showed both sympathy and pain. Lady Olivia was sunk deep in a large armchair, her head in her hands. And Hetty was curled up in a ball on the sofa, weeping loudly.

"Oh, God!" Barbara whispered, her hands clenched at her breast. "Is he . . . dead?"

Lady Olivia lifted her head and, with eyes red and swollen, glared at Barbara as if everything were her fault. "He asked for you," she accused, her voice trembling with grief. "He asked for you with his l-last b-breath. And you weren't even here!"

Forty-three

Sometimes, Patience thought as she walked down the path toward the south field, *spring can be too perfect.* The maples were shedding their little red flowerets and turning a soft April green, the forsythias were ablaze with yellow blooms, the river was a shimmer of sunlight, and the sky was so blue it hurt one's heart, all in spite of the tension and anger in the people who inhabited this God-graced land. *They don't deserve it,* she said to herself. *Those rebels, those idlers, those troublemakers . . . they don't deserve this Eden God has given them.*

It had been an active spring for the rebels. Sam Adams had barely evaded arrest in Boston, a man named Patrick Henry had made a speech to the Virginia assembly (heard by a cheering mob of hundreds who'd crowded outside the open windows to hear him) in which he brazenly declared that he wauld have liberty or death, and only last week her father had shown her a newspaper account of an earlier incident in New Hampshire in which a major of the militia had led a force of Patriots to attack a fort in Portsmouth Harbor. Wearing civilian clothes, they'd captured the commander of the fort and seized one hundred barrels of gunpowder. Her father had ranted for hours about it, swearing incoherently that he would have his revenge on the thieving miscreants soon enough. Though she didn't know what he meant, she knew enough to realize that such incidents could indicate that a war with England was almost upon them.

And tomorrow threatened to bring another troublesome incident, this time closer to home. That was why she'd come out seeking Tom. She shaded her eyes and looked across the field for him. She saw him almost at once, guiding a plow across the most distant border of the field. In order to catch his eye, she waved her shawl. As soon as he saw her beckoning, he tethered the plow horse and ran toward her, leaping over the furrows with a young man's grace. It was a pleasure and a pain to watch him.

"Morning, ma'am," he said, smiling tentatively as he drew near. "Something amiss?"

She wrapped her shawl tightly round her shoulders, suddenly shy and uncomfortable at having sought him out. "I wish to ask you about the meeting at White Plains tomorrow. Benjy says you know all about it."

"Not much more than he does." He pulled a ragged piece of osnaburg from the waistband of his breeches and mopped the sweat from his face and neck. "What is it you want to know?"

"Will there be rioting, as there was in New York last month? Papa insists on attending tomorrow, despite the doctor's warning that he not excite himself."

"I can't say for certain what will pass. But I'd not worry, ma'am. Westchester's not New York. There won't be so boisterous a crowd."

"But I do worry. You republicans are so determined to win that you'll find a way to send delegates to the next Congress whether the majority of the citizens want it or no."

Tom's eyebrows lifted in amused disapproval. "Did you come down here to pick a quarrel, ma'am, or to learn the facts?"

"You've a disrespectful tongue, Tom Morrison, and *that's* a fact. I suppose I shouldn't have come at all. I came but to learn if you think your Sons of Liberty and the rebel Whigs of Westchester County will resort to the same shameless nicknackery as the New York committee."

"If there was any 'nicknackery' in New York, ma'am," Tom retorted, but without real anger, "it was started by your damn Tories."

Patience frowned up at him. "Must you blaspheme in my presence? Using curses will not win an argument with me."

"Nothing I know of will win an argument with you," he teased, "though I've tried, God knows."

About to explode, she caught the gleam in his eye. "I didn't come here to encourage you to rally me," she said, lifting her chin and regarding him with proper queenly condescension. "And this is not a laughing matter."

"Sorry, ma'am. I do tend to forget myself when in your company. The mere sight of you brings a smile to my innards."

She dropped her eyes at that. "I knew I shouldn't have come," she murmured, coloring.

"I'm glad you did. Do not begrudge me this refreshing pause in my labors."

She bit her lip, warning herself not to permit herself to be charmed by him. "Let us stick to the subject, if you please," she said primly. "As far as the New York City fracas is concerned, I have it on good authority that the Committee packed the meeting with riffraff and rabble to swell their numbers and then pushed through their choice of delegates without polling the legal members, thus causing the riot."

"That's the Tory version of the event," he answered with a shrug. "We 'republicans' have another version. Believe what you will."

"Will it be the same tomorrow in White Plains? Will you and your rebel cohorts enforce your wishes on the others?"

"*My* rebel cohorts?" He'd made up his mind not to let her politics anger him, but he felt his anger rising in spite of himself. It was remarkable how she always managed to rile him without lessening his adoration of her. At this moment, however, he had all he could do to keep from shaking her. "In the first place, ma'am," he said with asperity, "I'll not even be there, since there's too much plowing still to be done. And in the second place, being a redemptioner, I have no right to vote and no influence on the 'rebel cohorts,' as you call them."

She did not miss the touch of anger in him and was sorry for it. "You needn't rise to a feather, Tom. I meant no offense. I only wish to know if there will be trouble."

"Yes, there may be a fracas, for aught I know. On one side, the Patriots purpose to elect a delegation to the second Congress. On the other, the Loyalists purpose to write a declaration opposing all illegal congresses. The atmosphere seems ripe for trouble. But should trouble come, it could be started as readily by the Tories as by the Patriots."

"Thank you, Tom, you've been a great help," she said dryly. "Sorry I took up your time."

"Nay, don't be sorry. You've been a joy to the eyes, standing there with the wind blowing your skirts and the sun making a halo of the lace on your cap. It only wants one thing more." Before she knew what he was about, he reached out and pulled off her cap. "There! It's something I've longed to see—your hair blowing in the wind."

"Tom!" she gasped, pulling her cap from his hand. "You *promised* me!"

"It's but your cap I removed, not your petticoat," he laughed, helping the wind to ruffle her hair.

She thrust his hand away, pulled the cap on again and hurriedly crammed her hair into it. "You doodle! What if someone were watching from the house?"

"Would it matter?" His eyes gleamed appreciatively as he helped her tuck in a last, recalcitrant lock of her hair. "Can I be horsewhipped for cap snatching? Or set on the ducking stool for hair-molesting?"

Shaking her head in reproof of his nonsense, she nevertheless couldn't keep the look of laughter from her eyes. "I shouldn't have come," she repeated guiltily, turning to go. "And don't say again that you're glad I did. For all you care, I could have simply sent my hair!"

He threw his head back and guffawed. "You know better," he

called after her. "The prime attraction of your hair is that it's attached to the rest of you."

She didn't deign to answer but stalked away, keeping her head high. And, certain that he'd watch her until she'd gone all the way up the path, she never once let herself look back. It would not be seemly to let him see that she was smiling.

Forty-four

Since Tom had failed to reassure her fears about the prospect of trouble at the Westchester meeting, Patience tried again to persuade her father not to attend. But Hendley would not be swerved. He left for White Plains the next morning after breakfast, after insulting Benjy by refusing to take him along. Before departing in the company of Clymer Young, he told Patience not to worry—that he felt quite well. "Like my old self," he assured her, "so don't expect me back before nightfall."

When Benjy disappeared shortly afterwards, Patience was not surprised. She knew where her brother had gone.

It was not yet nightfall, however, when Clymer Young's carriage reappeared at the door. At her first sight of it, Patience knew something dreadful had happened. She stiffened herself for a blow, but when her father was carried in on a litter by two of Mr. Young's servants, she realized that no amount of stiffening could have protected her from the shock of the actual sight of him. His mouth was horribly twisted and his eyes were open, one eye staring up and the other looking to the extreme right. He looked as if he'd seen the devil, and the sight had turned him to stone.

She fought back a scream. She had to control herself . . . to keep herself from surrendering to hysteria, as her mother always had in times of crisis. She had to hold on to her sanity. Her father needed her care, not her screams.

Later, after she and the servants had put him to bed and the doctor had come and gone, she went to her bedroom, sank down on the bed and surrendered to tears . . . tears of chagrin, tears to relieve the tension, tears of thanks to God that her father would live yet awhile. That's what the doctor had said, but he would not say for how long or in what condition. Only time would answer those questions.

When she'd again regained control of her emotions, Patience went downstairs to face Mr. Young and learn the details of what had happened. Mr. Young was pacing the drawing room floor. "It was dreadful," he said, his voice choked with fury. "A most disturbing affair. I thought I'd fall victim to stroke myself!"

Patience clenched her fists. "As bad as that?"

"Yes, indeed. We, the friends of law and order, were meeting at Hatfield's Tavern, but before we'd even begun—the men were still gathering—word came that the opposite party, those damned republicans (I beg your pardon, ma'am, for my loose language) had *already* met at Miles Oakley's Tavern. There, under the chairmanship of Lewis Morris, they'd underhandedly set about appointing delegates to the Congress! A Congress *we* had no intention of approving! They planned to come to us afterwards and present us with a *fait accompli!*"

"How dreadful!" Patience exclaimed. "No wonder Papa—"

"*Indeed* it's no wonder," Mr. Young agreed. "When we heard it, we were *all* highly incensed, I assure you. Your father and Isaac Wilkins and Frederick Philipse immediately led us out, heading for the courthouse where, we were informed, the opposition had by now surreptitiously reassembled. On the way, Isaac Wilkins begged your father to remain calm and to permit him to conduct a dignified protest. Hendley was in perfect agreement."

"And in sound health?"

"Yes, so it seemed to me. Angry, of course, but no more than the rest of us. When we arrived at the courthouse, we found that the opposition had amassed a number equal to ours—about two hundred or so in all. Isaac Wilkins, speaking for us, declared that the meeting was unlawful and that all congresses were unlawful.

Someone shouted for a poll, but Morris argued that our group
was filled with minors and tenants who had no eligibility to vote.
Your father shouted back that the Morris group had *more* illegals
than we. 'Everyone knows that two-thirds of the inhabitants of
Westchester are friends of the established government!' he cried.
Isaac Wilkins then added that we would not contest them by a
poll which would give tacit legitimacy to these disorderly pro-
ceedings. That was when your father cried out, 'God save great
George our King!' I turned to clap him on the back. That was
when I noticed his face had grown red and his eyes were bulging
out. During the ensuing outcry, he fell to the floor. By the time
Eb Simpson and I carried him out to my carriage, the confrontation in the courthouse had ended. The Morris group had won.
They'd elected their delegates in spite of us. We saw our group
marching back to Hatfields' bravely singing "God Save the
King," but they must have known in their hearts that we'd been
outmaneuvered."

Patience thanked him for his account and saw him to his carriage. "The fools," he muttered as he climbed up, "they know
not what mischief they do."

By the time Benjy returned, Patience had already noticed a
slight improvement in her father. His eyes were closed, his mouth
was less stiff, and he'd lapsed into a stertorous sleep. Since he
appeared to be in no immediate danger, Patience witheld the
news of their father's stroke from her brother until he'd eaten his
supper. In the kitchen, while wolfing down a cold chicken leg
and a piece of dry corn bread, the boy excitedly related his version
of the events at White Plains. "We were on the verge of riot," he
told his sister, his eyes shining, "but in the afterclap we managed
to vote for a second Congress and to name a delegation. And we
have a great man to head it. Lewis Morris is just the man to speak
for us."

Patience was quite at the end of her rope. To hear her brother
praising the very man responsible for her father's relapse was
too much for her. "Why was I cursed with such a mule for a

brother!" she cried, snatching up his trencher and throwing it into the fireplace, platter, bones, crumbs and all. Sparks sizzled up in all directions, and her brother recoiled in surprise, but Patience ranted on. "Do you ever think on what will come of all this? Do you wonder at all on where it may lead? Or does it *pleasure* you to envision your government destroyed, your land in anarchy, and yourself sinking a bayonet into another boy or having him sink one into you!" Then, her flare-up spent, she turned from him, sank down on the hearth and stared into the flames. "Mr. Young was right. You and your friends, in your ignorance, know not what mischief you do."

It was not kind to have at him so, she berated herself later, after she'd broken the news to him about his father and seen the guilt and misery in his eyes. She lay in bed for hours, relieved that this dreadful day had ended but still unable to sleep. Was the sleeplessness caused by the dire events of the day, she wondered, or the blasted rasp of a screech owl somewhere outside her window?

But the dreadful day had not yet ended. When at last she did drop off, she was immediately (or so it seemed) awakened by a repeated knocking at her door. "Who—?" she asked thickly.

"It's me, Benjy. I think there's someone outside. I heard carriage wheels . . . and a knocking . . . ."

Frightened, she reached for a shawl and, wrapping herself up in it, padded barefoot to her door and opened it. By the light of the candle he carried, she saw that Benjy was also barefoot and had nothing on but his nightshirt. She also became aware of a knocking at the door downstairs. "Yes, I hear it," she whispered. She clasped his hand and, together, they went down the stairs.

Near the door, Patience heard something else. "Benjy, did you—? I thought I heard a . . . a . . . baby!"

Benjy put his ear to the door but heard nothing. "Who's there?" he asked, making his voice as deep and angry as he could.

"Oh, thank God!" came a woman's tearful voice. "Open up! It's Hannah."

"Hannah?" Patience threw open the door at once, her heart pounding fearfully.

By the light of Benjy's candle she saw that her friend was in a state of extreme perturbation. Carelessly dressed, with her bonnet askew, and clutching her heavily bundled baby in both arms, Hannah was wild-eyed with terror. "Oh, *Patience,*" she cried, bursting into tears, "the most dreadful . . . ! You'd not *believe*—! The beasts kept *laughing* and *shouting* . . . and two of them held me back, so I couldn't help him at *all!* And with Stuart gone to New York, there was *no one!* Even the servants were too terrified to help!"

Patience was unable to make sense of the flood of words. But she did recognize the import of the hiccoughing sound that came from the baby. It was the sound small children make when their crying becomes exhausted. Poor little Caleb must have been sobbing all through their night ride. Patience gently removed him from Hannah's arms and handed him to Benjy. Then, murmuring meaningless words of comfort, she urged Hannah to come in.

But Hannah, still weeping, hung back, shaking her head and pointed to the carriage in the drive. "Papa," she managed between sobs. "Help Papa!"

Patience, bewildered and unnerved, felt for a moment that she was immersed in a nightmare. She had a presentiment of horror, but after the terrors she'd already endured this day, she could not believe that anything more could happen to her. This late-night occurrence, she told herself, couldn't be anything but a figment of her mind, a dream of horror that would surely dissipate by the light of dawn. She turned to where Hannah was pointing and pattered barefoot down the steps, shaking her head to see if she could break through this fog of nightmare and wake herself. But before she reached bottom, the Lovells' coachman leapt down from the box and threw open the carriage door.

A figure loomed up in the opening. Even in the dim light it was a sight so hideous that Patience screamed. The sound of the scream reverberated in her own ears in all its shrill intensity, shattering any hope that this was but a nightmare. She knew with sickening certainty that what she was looking at was real.

The figure being helped down from the carriage appeared at first to be a moving lump, oozing blackness that was dotted here and there with incongruous white feathers. Only when he stepped out and tottered toward her—and Patience could discern the face out of which stared a pair of terrified white eyes—did she understand what she beheld: Mr. Lovell, Hannah's father, had been tarred.

Forty-five

"If only Stuart had been home," Hannah wept. She and Patience were sitting on the bed in Barbara's room, little Caleb lying between them fast asleep. She'd taken off her bonnet but had refused to remove her traveling cloak.

Patience, who hadn't found time to dress but had managed to put on a kerseymere wrapper and a pair of slip-shoes, threw her friend a glance of tearful sympathy. "Think you Stuart could have prevented—?"

"Oh, yes. The committeemen know he is sympathetic to their cause. And I also believe that, if Papa had not been so miffy when they came and asked him to sign the Association agreement, it might all have passed over. But Papa'd drunk four glasses of Madeira at supper, and his color and his temper were both high. So when they threatened him with the tar mop, he became pot-valiant and shouted that they wouldn't dare." Hannah shut her eyes, shuddering at the memory. "That, of course, made their tempers flare up worse than before, and then the shouting began. There was a long, horrid scene, after which they dragged him out the door. I ran after them, screaming, but two of those vulgar creatures held my arms while they tipped the tar barrel over him, all the while laughing and shouting as if it were all a great game!"

"Good Lord!" Patience exclaimed, paling.

"Oh, Patience, I declare I've never felt such terror! It was hideous, like a nightmare. After they tarred him, they lifted him up on a rail and were about to carry him off to parade him round the village like a . . . a circus clown! But poor Papa fainted dead away, so they let the servants take him back inside."

"Savages," Patience muttered. "They are like savages."

"I was too frightened to remain in the house," Hannah went on, "so as soon as we revived Papa, we packed a few necessaries, I bundled Caleb up in a blanket—you can imagine how the child screamed when he caught sight of his grandfather!—and we fled. We're on our way to Stuart in New York, but we decided to stop here first to let Papa—"

A cry from across the hall made Patience wince. Hannah put her hands to her ears in a feeble and useless attempt to block out the sound. The cries were coming from across the hall in Benjy's room, where for more than an hour Benjy and the Lovells' coachman, assisted by Tom and Chester (who'd been roused from their beds and had come running with what medicinal supplies they could gather), were trying to remove the tar from Lovell's body. It was no easy task, for the tar was resistant to the whale oil and the brandy which the men were using as solvents. Some of the tar came off on the soaked cloths, but sometimes it took with it pieces of the poor man's skin. Since Lovell would not permit the women into the room, Patience and Hannah had to endure waiting helplessly in the bedroom across the hall listening to his screams of anguish.

It was almost dawn when Lovell was cleared of enough tar to enable his clothes to be removed. He would not lie down to rest, however, but insisted on being helped into clean clothes and taking an immediate departure. "The sooner we find Stuart," he explained to Patience, his eyes red with tears, "the sooner we can return to Lovell Hill. If we leave the house too long unoccupied, those miscreants will set to looting the place, which I don't for a moment doubt they intend to do. But with Stuart at home I don't think they'd dare. I'd hoped your father would supply us with a flintlock or two for protection—I think he has some arms hidden away. But of course, under the circumstances . . ."

His voice tapered off weakly. When he'd learned of his friend's illness, it had been another severe blow. Peter Hendley had been for him the very symbol of Loyalist strength. In this one day Lovell's pride had been leveled, his property endangered and his very person assaulted. Learning that Hendley was so badly in capacitated, he felt that the last support of his Loyalist leanings had been pulled from under him. His Whiggish son-in-law was now his only means of safety. He would not say it aloud, but the events of the past day had left him with a strong presentiment that the Loyalist cause was a lost one.

Patience had tears in her own eyes when she saw their carriage drive off in the predawn light. Mr. Lovell was a pathetic sight his neck still black, his eyebrows shaved off, and his skin, though oozing in places, too raw and sensitive to endure bandages. Hannah, too, looked distraught, her eyes red with weeping. Only little Caleb, who'd been well fed and had had several hours of sleep managed a smile as he waved goodbye with a fat little hand *What sort of world will he grow up in?* Patience wondered as she turned back to the house. *Dear God, may it be a better one than this!*

In the kitchen, she found Benjy and Tom perched on stools at the worktable. They'd started the fire and were now trying to ease their weariness by sipping possets of hot milk curdled with wine The very sight of them roused her ire. "I hope you're both satisfied," she fumed. "You and your 'cause'! The friends of your cause have brought tragedy to at least two households within a mere twenty-four hours!"

"I say, Patience," Benjy objected, "you can't denounce the cause of liberty just because a few of its supporters are damn brutes."

"There! More blaspheming! That cause is making a brute out of *you,* Benjamin Hendley!"

Tom had been studying her closely. The sight of her standing there in her slip-shoes, clutching her wrapper tightly over the white nightdress that peeped out below, made her look so sweetly vulnerable that he ached to hold her. Anger had reddened her cheeks, but weariness was evident underneath, in the shadows under her eyes, the pallor of her skin surrounding those flushed cheeks, and the tremor of her soft, soft mouth. But it was her nightcap, set haphazardly over the thick, tumbled hair he loved so much, that sent a wave of tenderness flooding over him. "Hush, woman, hush," he said softly, rising from his stool. "You're tired and sore beset, and no wonder. 'Tis a few hours of sleep you need."

She rounded on him angrily. "Don't tell me what I need! I need you to admit that your committees and your sons of liberty are inflicting useless pain and suffering on innocent people!"

"In the struggle for any cause, even a noble one, there must be a price to pay," Tom said gently. "The cost is always pain and suffering."

"Just so, Patience," her brother seconded. "Besides, you can't condemn the Patriots for one small incident—?"

"One incident! *One?*" She turned a furious glare first on one and then the other. Why were these two so unwilling to alter their views in spite of the evidence before their eyes? "Have you not heard tales *every day* of Patriot excesses?" she railed. "Committees spying on neighbors, going through private papers and reading mail, drumming people round liberty trees, abusing them in public for tiny offenses—like that farmer in New Britain shamed before the world for underselling eggs at a shilling a dozen—and publishing their names in the newspapers as 'persons inimical to the rights and liberties of America.' Inimical, indeed! I heard only yesterday of a gentleman who was forced to sit on a cake of ice 'to cool his loyalty'! And is poor Mr. Lovell the only man to suffer tarring? 'Tis a practice that grows more popular every day! In one case I read of in Papa's newspaper, the poor fellow was dragged through a brook afterward, tar, feathers and all, and *he* was the Reverend of the New Cambridge Church!" Overwhelmed by her own oratory, she covered her face with trembling fingers and began to weep. "And . . . and what about your poor father lying upstairs half paralyzed? Are not your patriots responsible for *that?"*

Benjy opened his mouth to protest, but Tom put up a restraining hand. Circling the table that stood between them, he took the shaken woman in his arms. "Don't cry, Patience," he murmured, nestling her head on his shoulder and rubbing his cheek against her crooked cap. "It was a hellish day for you, I know. But from this day on, I swear that no one, Patriot or Tory, will molest anyone in this house. Not while I have breath."

His words were a balm to her soul. A knot of fear that had been tightening her chest since her father was brought home—the painful existence of which she had not acknowledged to herself—melted away. How did Tom guess how fearful she was when she hadn't known it herself? This was not the first time that his presence, his words, his arms had brought her comfort in a crisis. To find such comfort in him was a sin, but, God forgive her, she was thankful for it.

For a moment she rested against him, letting herself breathe in the strength of him. Then she remembered that Benjy was watching. *Heavens,* she thought, with a stab of shame, *what must he think?*

She pushed herself from Tom's hold and looked around. Benjy was coming toward them, his expression revealing nothing but innocent affection. "Tom's right, Patience," he said, putting an arm about her shoulder. "You have nothing to fear, not while we're here."

Forty-six

It seemed as if spring were making a mockery of humankind,
for the days grew more glorious as the affairs of men worsened.
On April twenty-third, an afternoon when the sky glistened with
purity and the warming earth smelled sweeter than baking pears,
a post rider from Boston named Israel Bissel, racing on horseback to New York and Philadelphia, paused at the foot of the
King's Bridge and shouted out the news that a battle had been
fought four days earlier at Lexington and Concord—an actual
battle between regiments of armed men. Blood had flowed. Men
had died.

Although the full import of the news would not be understood
for many weeks, there was a strong sense in both the messenger
and those who heard him that the event had portentous significance. The news sent the men who were lounging in front of the
tavern hurrying into the back room. It sent the members of the
militia running home to ready their flintlocks. And it sent Benjy
dashing up the hill to bring the word to Tom and to Patience.

Tom brooded on the matter for a long time. It was war, that
he was sure of . . . a war in which he might have a real stake.
But he didn't know if he could play a part in it. He was indentured,
to Hendley legally and to Patience morally. He knew the legal
bond would not hold him, but the other was stronger: he'd sworn
to give her his protection. But he'd sworn to himself to fight for
America's liberty, and his own. If it came down to a choice, which
had a higher claim?

Benjy had no such problem. His promise to protect his sister had been made in the warmth of the moment and quickly forgotten. As soon as the call should come for recruitment into a Patriot army, he would go. There was no question about it.

The news raised all sorts of questions in Patience's mind. What did it mean, she wondered? Was it the first battle of a war or just another in the long series of minor conflicts between the colonies and the mother country? Would it require her brother and her indentured man to increase their despicable militia duties? Should she put her foot down about it? Would it do any good if she did? And what about her father? He was now alert and speaking (although his speech was slurred) and beginning the long dreary effort required to regain use of his muscles. Should she tell him what had passed? If she did, he might become overly excited. But if she didn't, might he not soon learn about it anyway in the newspaper? Wouldn't it be better if she broke it to him first?

The next few days brought little change, except that the town militia increased the time they spent drilling. One day, Patience discovered that Benjy and Tom were gone all afternoon. She was furious! Chester and the drunken Jeb could not possibly do all the work required in this busy season. True, she'd hired Beatie's husband Charlie McNab to work for them and had installed the couple in Sally's old room, but McNab was too busy helping with her father to be spared for work in the fields. There was nothing for it but that Patience should give Tom Morrison a piece of her mind!

When she saw from the kitchen window that he'd returned, she flew out through the kitchen garden and accosted him on the path to the stable. "How dare you disappear all day," she stormed, "with the planting not half done and Chester busy with the livestock and Jeb good for nothing! Have you no conscience at all?"

"I've too good a conscience," Tom answered calmly. "My work with the militia makes demands on my conscience, too.

"Blast the militia! Dash it, Tom, is the militia more important to you than the needs of this house? I thought I . . . we . . . meant more to you than—"

"You know well enough what you mean to me. I wish you meant less, so that I could do my duty for my cause without this conscience that you say I don't have tearing me apart."

She was too upset to hear the pain of his inner conflict. "How can you believe you have a *duty* to a cause that is not only illegal but im—?"

But she was not to finish her tirade, for at that moment Beatie came trotting up behind her, breathless and wide-eyed. "There's a man for to see ye, missus," she said, pointing to the house. "A gentleman. Come in a fine carriage. Wearin' fine clothes, too. He's waitin' in the drawin' room."

Patience threw Tom a last, withering look and turned back to the house, Beatie pattering at her heels. Tom, not only curious but struck with a premonition of disaster, followed after them. In the corridor between the kitchen and the main house, Patience pulled off her apron and handed it to Beatie. If she noticed Tom behind them, she made no sign.

She paused in the drawing room doorway. A tall, bewigged gentleman in a brocaded coat and a necklet of exquisite Mechlin lace turned from his contemplation of the painting over the fireplace and smiled. "Ah, there you are, my dear! A little thinner than I remember but still lovely. And not aged nearly as much as I."

Though she didn't yet fully recognize him, something about him chilled her through. "Excuse me, sir, but I don't—" she began.

"I know it's been many years," he said, advancing toward her, "but not so long that you can have forgotten your husband."

"Oh, my God!" she gasped. *"Orgill?"*

"Yes, of course, my dear. I've come back."

Shock made everything freeze—the blood in her veins, the breath in her throat, Lord Orgill in midstep with his arms stretched out to her, everything. Then the world began to spin about her, whirling and whirling in ever-increasing speed. *I suppose I'm going to faint,* she thought. The prospect brought a sensation of relief. Fainting would be a way to escape, at least for the moment. But before she let herself slip into unconsciousness she took a step backward into the corridor, to keep from letting him take her hand as he seemed determined to do. *No,* she thought, *no, don't touch me!*

With the world still whirling crazily, she tottered backward another step. It was then she saw Tom. Suddenly there was nothing in her line of vision but his face. He looked fierce, but also stricken, white-lipped, like a enraged man in a bout of fisticuffs who'd received an unexpected blow to his stomach and did not yet know he'd been hurt. Unaware of anything or anyone else, she put out a hand to him. "Tom," she begged hoarsely, "don't—"

But by now he knew how hurt he was. He did the only thing he could: he turned and ran back down the corridor out of her sight.

She yearned to run after him, but she knew she could not. Orgill was her husband. To run after Tom was a sin. To refrain from sinning required strength, strength to keep from fainting, strength to renounce her adulterous love feelings, strength to face a husband she had no wish to see. She had to find that strength. She was her father's daughter. She knew how to survive.

Somehow she got through the rest of the day. Somehow Lord Orgill accepted her dazed behavior as a normal reaction to his shocking return. Somehow she played the role of polite hostess, sat opposite her husband on the sofa and explained to him the condition of the family. Somehow she took in his explanation of his return to America: that his life in England had become stale, that he'd realized he needed the excitement of life in America, and that therefore he'd taken a diplomatic assignment to assist the New York governor to control the colony—a mission, he told her proudly, "that may very well lead to an important appointment later on." Somehow she arranged for dinner and sat at the table with him and her astounded brother and watched them make polite conversation. Somehow she served him his sweets and poured his wine.

Then it was time for bed. Time also, she warned herself, to dispel the fog in her brain. With every muscle tense, she led her visitor up the stairs. "I've put you in Barbara's old room," she said, rigidly distant.

"Come now, my dear," he said in his booming voice, cheerfully indifferent to the past, "you are my wife. Shouldn't we begin at once to make up for the lost years?"

Patience lifted her chin. "My Lord, you may be my husband by law and even in the sight of God, but in my eyes you lost that position years ago. I've not had sufficient time to consider what duties I still owe to someone who is my husband in no way but the name, but *conjugal duties I do not owe.* Until I decide what to do about our situation, you may consider yourself no more than a guest in this house." And leaving her husband gaping after her, she marched off to her bedroom and shut and locked the door.

Tom came to the kitchen the next morning just after sunup. Beatie was building the fire and Patience was pouring cream into the butter churn, her back to the door. "Mornin', Tom," Beatie said, cocking her head at him, birdlike in her curiosity.

He nodded to her but said nothing. Patience, who'd stiffened at the sound of his name, had not the courage to look at him. He came up behind her and waited. After a long, strained silence, she turned around. He looked bone-weary, but he was dressed as he would for town, with his green coat brushed and worn over a Sunday shirt, and his boots polished. Patience gulped, trying to push down the heart that had jumped into her throat. "Are you going somewhere?"

"Yes. I've come to say good-bye."

She knew what he meant. Her nervously bobbing heart sank into her chest like a stone. "You promised, did you not," she asked desperately, "that you would be here to protect me? And less than three weeks past. While you had breath, you said."

"So I did. But now you have your husband for protection."

She dropped her eyes. "I . . . we . . . need you," she said, her voice almost a whisper.

"You'll manage."

"They'll catch you." It was more desperation. "When Papa learns of it, he'll send the sheriff after you, and they'll catch you. Then where will you be?"

"They won't catch me, not this time. And if they do, I've nothing to lose. They extended my indenture and took away all my freedom dues the last time."

"Tom!" Her eyes widened in disbelief for a moment, and then, accepting the truth, she winced in agony. "I didn't know. You should have told me." She turned away from him, pressing a hand against her mouth to keep from crying out. It was a long moment before she could speak. "I'm so sorry. I never thought . . ." Her trembling knees gave way, and she sank down on the stool. "Dear God! All these months! Why did you stay?"

"You know why."

She looked up at him, her eyes pleading. "Then why go now? Just because Lord Orgill is here doesn't change—"

"Oh, doesn't it?" He flicked a look at Beatie, who immediately turned to the fire. Then he grasped Patience's shoulders and pulled her to her feet. "I can't bear it, don't you see that? I couldn't close my eyes last night without seeing . . . Dash it, woman, I can't stay here, knowing he's in the house with you!"

"No, Tom, please don't think— You musn't believe—!" She clutched at the opening of his coat in despairing urgency. "I didn't! I *wouldn't* . . . not ever!"

He thrust her from him. "Don't say it. I don't want to hear about it. All I know is that he's your husband, and he's here. It drives me crazy. It's something I can't endure, so don't ask it of me."

He took one long look at her and went to the door. "If you

should ever really need me," he said, not looking back, "ask Benjy. He'll know to go to Nate Cluett. I'll keep Nate informed of my whereabouts."

"Benjy won't be here either, not for long," Patience said numbly. "He'll run off, too.

"Then you'll have a house cleared of rebels," he threw back. "Isn't that what you wanted? A completely Loyalist household!" And he slammed out the door.

Patience stared at the door, drained of feeling. He was gone. She knew it was the worst thing that had ever happened to her, but something—a numbness—was protecting her from the pain of loss. She felt nothing, nothing at all . . .

Then the door flew open again, and Tom came striding back to her, his mouth set and his eyes glittering. Her heart leaped up to her throat. *He's changed his mind,* she thought joyfully as he took her face between his two hands. *He's going to stay after all!*

He studied her face for a long breath and then kissed her, a gentle, lingering kiss that neither of them wanted to end. When she felt him end it and start away, she clutched tightly at his arms. "Tom, my dearest," she whispered forlornly, *"please—!"*

But he shook his head. With the same abrupt determination of his reentry, he freed himself from her, strode back to the door, and was gone.

Beatie made a clucking noise with her tongue. Patience looked over at her and knew, from the look of sympathy in the Scotswoman's birdlike eyes, that Tom would not be back. Not again.

She sat down and began to churn. And then the pain came.

Book Four
Liberty Flaming

Winter to Fall 1776

Dearest Hannah,

How Sorry we are to learn that your father has left America for England. It is a sad reflection on these times of Distress and Upheaval when such good men are driven from their Birthplace. We shall all miss him. It must have been hard for you to say Goodbye to him, and to have had to make the choice of Marital over Filial Duty. I hope you do not doubt the Wisdom and Rightness of that choice; neither Duty nor Sense could have demanded otherwise.

Your letter reveals that, in choosing to stay with Stuart and raise your son in America, you, like Stuart, have chosen to support the cause of Rebellion over Loyalty. Do not believe, Sweet Hannah, that I am Critical of your political choice. We women tend to be influenced in our political opinions by the Men we love. It is not a thought that makes me Proud of our Sex, but I fear it is True. You are fortunate that your husband is a man of Sense and of Honor. To be influenced by such a Man does you no discredit.

In my case, however, I find it difficult to be influenced by the Men in my life. I haven't sufficient Confidence in their views. Papa is too vehemently Emotional to think wisely, I fear. And Benjy too full of youthful Naivete. So, although Stuart may still find me Toryish, I often find myself wavering in my views. When men like Stuart speak of Liberty, they make the Cause sound noble, yet when the Sons of Liberty abuse those who oppose them with Beatings and Lootings and Washings with the Tar Mop, one must wonder what sort of Liberty they are fighting for. I often think of your little

Caleb and wonder what the America will be like that he will grow up in. If the Rebels win, will it be Stuart's America—Kind and Fair and Generous to all citizens? Or will it be an America cut off from old Traditions and Restraints and made free for Anarchy and Chaos?

Papa (whose mind is as Active as ever, though his left side is still paralyzed) remains Obsessed with political concerns. Every bit of news from the Congress in Philadelphia drives him to Distraction. You can't imagine how Vituperative he became when Congress decided to adopt the Army that was camping out near Boston and appointed Mr. Washington of Virginia its General. The name of Washington, which until six months ago was Unknown to me, has now become all too Familiar; it is Reviled daily in this house!

Then, when Congress authorized our neighbor, Captain Richard Montgomery, to plan Fortifications around the King's Bridge to secure the approaches to the City, Papa became quite Wild with fury. He wrote Captain Montgomery so abusive a letter that I feared the Captain would demand Satisfaction, but the captain (now a General—so Quickly do things change these days!) has gone off to fight with the Americans in the Canadian campaign, so the letter was returned unopened, to my immense Relief.

Isn't it dreadful how these Hostilities have taken over our lives? There seems to be nothing else on our minds but the latest Skirmish or the most recent Act of the Congress. However, there are other things to claim our attention—among them my desire to see you all. Please pay us the Honor of a Visit soon. This house is dreadfully quiet these days, with Barbara (whom I miss dreadfully) gone and even my Lord Orgill (whom—if I may admit honestly to my best Friend—I don't miss at all) away on an extended Stay with Governor Tryon. When the Governor still lived in his New York house, his lordship Orgill divided his time more or less equally between the Governor's abode and ours. Since October, however, when Governor Tryon decided that New York was Unsafe and took up residence aboard the Duchess of Gordon *in the harbor, my Husband spends most of his time on shipboard visiting with the Governor, who, he claims, needs the Bolstering Presence of his Friends.*

Please do come soon. To have more than three at my table would be my Greatest joy.

With fondest affection, I remain your loving Friend,

Patience.

Letter from Patience Hendley
to her friend Hannah LeGrange
Spuyten Duyvil, New York,
9 January, 1776

Forty-seven

Tom had known cold, but never like this. He was lying face down on the frozen ground of Quebec's Lower Town, in the midst of the worst blizzard he'd ever experienced. The wind screamed over him in deafening hysteria, and torrents of snowflakes attacked him in intermittent barrages of icy fury. His hands felt frozen, but he couldn't even feel his feet. He wondered if his legs would be able to carry him away from this scene of destruction when he finally could generate the strength to get up and run.

But right now he couldn't get up, for his head ached so badly he couldn't lift it. It seemed comforting to lie motionless and let the snow cover him. He hoped he was well-covered, so that he wouldn't be noticed by any redcoat looking down at this scene from the barricades on the cliffs above or the blockhouse just ahead. He would rather freeze to death out here than to be taken prisoner. He hadn't joined the army to sit out the war in a British gaol.

To keep his spirits up and his blood warm, he muttered curses under his breath. He cursed the British General Guy Carleton for having eighteen hundred trained men (so it was rumored) against the Americans' eight hundred. He cursed Congress for deciding that the conquest of Canada would be useful to the American cause. He cursed the decision of General Benedict Arnold and General Richard Montgomery to storm the citadeled city from below. He cursed the blinding blizzard, the landscape that gave Quebec protective cliffs on three sides, the woefully inadequate tunic that passed for a uniform in the American army, and the trick of fate that had brought him to this place at this time. *Yes, indeed,* he thought, *there's no end to the list of things I can curse.*

Tom now knew the meaning of the words *military disaster.* The attack—after six months of preparation, after weeks of tortuous marching through forests and across rivers, after days and nights of cold and hunger and endless waiting—had lasted only two hours. Two hours . . . during every moment of which he knew it would fail.

The two American generals had agreed that an attack on the Canadian city would have a better chance of success at night under the cover of snow, but a blizzard was probably not what they'd had in mind. General Montgomery's plan, as far as Tom's scant information went, was to lead the New York divisions through Quebec's Lower Town from the south, while General Arnold led his brigades down from the north. They would skirt the southeastern edge of the city through the narrow Lower Town, meet at a street called Sault au Matelot, from which point they would storm the Upper Town and win the city. Tom had misgivings about the plan from the first moment he'd heard of it, but, in his admiration for Richard Montgomery (whose home was near the King's Bridge and whose farmhands had often told Tom of his estimable character), had let himself be persuaded that it had a hope of success. He'd even volunteered to be part of the advance battalion under Captain Jacob Cheesman.

The order to march had come on the last day of the year, at two o'clock in the morning. The weather was unbelievably severe, freezing the men through. The generals should have called off the attack when it became clear that what had begun as a mild snowfall was becoming a blizzard, but since the enlistments of many of the men—whole companies, in fact—ran out on this very day, the generals must have believed they could not wait. Tom, feeling in his bones that the enterprise was doomed, nev-

ertheless marched forward bravely with the advance company,
carrying an axe in one hand and a musket slung over his shoulder.

The march north was a nightmare. The snow blinded them,
icy hailstones cut at their cheeks, the wind whirled the snow into
huge drifts, and the passage between the cliffs and the river was
so narrow and so dangerously clogged with huge blocks of ice
from the frozen river's edge that movement was slowed to a crawl.
The pass permitted, at most, a group of five abreast, but it was
sometimes so narrow that only one man at a time could squeeze
through. Tom was nevertheless inspired by the determination and
courage of General Montgomery and his aides, Captain McPherson and a nineteen-year-old volunteer named Aaron Burr, who
took places at the very front of the line.

The British General Carleton had barricaded the approach to
Sault au Matelot with two log barricades. Tom and the other
advance men had hacked and sawed their way through the first
barricade without opposing gunfire, although they could hear
shooting in the distance. The general, fearing that they might be
late for the rendezvous with Arnold's force, shouted the men
on, at one point pulling a saw from the hand of the man
next to Tom—a sturdy frontiersman named Gideon Jones who'd
marched beside Tom all the way up from Albany—and sawing
through a post himself.

As soon as a passage through the barricade was hacked out,
General Montgomery and his aides stepped through the narrow
opening, with Captain Cheesman and his advance company just
behind. Ahead of them they could see an ominous-looking brick
building showing a dull light in its upper story. It had once been
a brewery, but Tom could see that ports had been cut into the
wall for cannon. The small building had obviously been converted to a blockhouse, though it now appeared to be deserted.

Suspicious, Captain Cheesman signaled his men to pause, but
General Montgomery was eager to push on. "Men of New York,"
he shouted, "you will not fear to follow where your general leads!
Push on! Quebec is ours!"

They all surged forward. When about fifty men had squeezed through the opening in the barricade, General Montgomery, feeling that to be a sufficient number to take the blockhouse, ran forward, his aides and Cheesman following. At that instant, there was a flash of light, and a tremendous roar broke over them from the blockhouse, spewing grapeshot through the air. Tom saw, to his horror, a spray of blood burst from General Montgomery's head. The general fell over on his back, his dead eyes staring. His aide, McPherson, and Captain Cheesman fell at the same moment. The other aide, young Aaron Burr, tottered about in blind confusion, unhurt but unhinged by shock.

Before Tom could become aware of anything else but the taste of bile in his mouth, a burst of rifle fire issued from somewhere, whether from the blockhouse or above he could not tell. Gideon Jones stumbled forward and fell on his face. Screams and shouts filled the air, and a number of men around Tom began to push and shove in their hurry to back away. Then an avalanche of fireballs came whirling down from the palisades above, lighting the hellish scene with an orange glow and revealing a number of terrified men pressing themselves against the palisade and perhaps ten other bodies sprawled in the snow.

Something struck Tom just above his left ear, and he too stumbled and fell. Dazed, he lay unmoving, waiting for the whirling world to right itself. Over the scream of the wind, he could hear from the other side of the barricade Captain Mott, whose company was just behind Cheesman's, shout orders urging his men to renew the advance, but in the hubbub and shouting that followed, it was clear that, with Montgomery dead, they were too disorganized to do so. The noise soon receded, and Tom, dazed as he was, knew that the rest of the brigade had retreated.

When the pain in his head eased, Tom lifted himself on his elbows and looked about him. The snow reflected enough light to reveal details that made him feel sick. The narrow passage was strewn with bodies. They formed a ragged line of mounds in the snow. Here and there a lifeless arm or a hatless head, brushed clean by the wind, stood out in grim, starkly colored contrast to the whiteness surrounding it. One man's face, the eyes open and the skin blue, was turned toward him as if, even in death, he was pleading for a warm drink.

Swirling over the bodies of the dead, whipping about through the air like leaves, were bits of debris, the remains of this fruitless skirmish: a bloody kerchief; a broken ramrod; a wad of batting that someone had pinned to his coat a few hours earlier to protect his shoulder from the kick of his musket when he fired; a British fur cap to which an American had pinned a note. (Tom knew what the note said, for many of the men wore those fur caps, acquired from supplies captured from the British at Montreal. They'd pinned pieces of white paper to them to distinguish themselves from the enemy. Those papers always read *LIBERTY OR DEATH*.) But what sickened Tom most of all was the sight of three bodies at the head of the line of dead. General Montgomery's body, first in the line, was almost completely buried in the snow. Close behind, angled on either side of the general, were the bodies of his aide, McPherson, and of Captain Cheesman. The positions in which they fell formed an arrowhead pointing to the blockhouse that had undone them.

To the east, the sky was beginning to show the faintest sign of light. If Tom was to save himself, he had to move before daybreak. When he convinced himself that no redcoats were lurking about, he poked at the shoulder of the man lying alongside him. "Are you all right, Giddy?" he shouted over the wind.

"I can't nohow tell," came Giddy's gruff voice.

Tom exhaled a steamy breath of relief. Gideon Jones, though older by a decade than Tom, was lean and tough. He'd come through the long march up from Albany without a sign of strain. But now he seemed unable to do more than turn over on his side and watch Tom struggle to his feet. Tom shook his head to clear the dizziness from his brain. "Get up, old man," he said, offering a hand to the fellow lying at his feet. "We've got to get out of here before daybreak. The redcoats'll be swarming all over this place by then."

Giddy Jones was well accustomed to hardships and cruel weather, but this time he found himself unable to stand on his feet. "Go on without me, boy," he muttered with a groan, his long face tight with pain.

"What is it? Are you shot?"

"It's my ankle. I must've twisted it when I dodged that cannon fire."

Tom, cursing, helped the fellow up. "Can you walk on it?"

Gideon tried, but the pain was too great. "Go on, Tom. Leave me. I'll give myself up."

"No, we'll make it." Tom shifted his pack, pulled Gideon's arm across his shoulder, and half carried, half dragged him back in the direction from which they'd come. "As soon as we find some shelter, we'll take a look and see how bad it is."

"Ye're none too good yerself," the older man muttered. "There's blood on yer temple."

"It's nothing," Tom assured him. "Just a graze."

Slowly they inched their way back toward Cape Diamond, just south of the city, the place from which they'd started out a few hours before. It was full daylight now. They heard no gunshots, nor could they discern any signs of continuing military action. Silent and discouraged, they climbed the steep, mile-long pass to the plains above. Here, too, they could detect no military movement. Evidently the attack was over on all fronts.

Neither man spoke. Tom, with the image of the dead general imprinted on his memory, was too disheartened to speak. And Gideon, using Tom's shoulder and his musket as crutches, concentrated on hopping forward through the snow, his teeth clenched to keep from crying out with pain. The snow still beat at their faces, and the wind screeched so loudly in their ears that they didn't hear the sound of hoofbeats closing in behind them. When the horse was almost upon them, Tom wheeled around, his heart pounding. *It's a redcoat,* he thought in terror, *a redcoat with murder in his eyes and his bayonet at the ready.* But one good look reassured him. The man on horseback was too shabbily dressed to be British. He wore the buff and blue American uniform, but it had seen better days. If the red sash tied round his middle could be believed, the rider was an American officer. "It's all right," Tom said to his companion in relief. "He's one of ours."

The officer pulled up on the reins and stopped alongside them. "Were you with Montgomery?" he shouted over the wind.

"Yes, sir," Tom answered, not bothering to salute. "Fifth Company, First New York."

"Have you heard what's become of him?"

"General Montgomery? Shot in the head. And our captain, Jacob Cheesman, killed also. It's all over, here in the south sector."

The officer nodded. "In the north, too. General Arnold's been wounded. What a damned day! I figure fifty or sixty casualties and more than half our force taken. What's left of Arnold's contingent are regrouping about a mile west, so if you're looking to join us, you're heading in the wrong direction."

"Thank you, sir, but I think the survivors of the Yorker regiments will be heading south."

"Back home, I have no doubt," the officer said with a touch of disdain.

"Some will, I suppose," Tom admitted.

The officer sneered. "Damn deserters!"

Gideon Jones lifted his head at that. "This is December thirty-first, ain't it? Mos' of our enlistments run out today. Mine does."

"So I suppose you'll be heading home."

Gideon Jones wiped the snow from his face and fixed the officer with a look of pure scorn. "You can bet on it," he spat out. "First chance I git."

"How can we be expected to fight," the officer exploded, "when you damn riffraff bolt whenever things go badly? If the two thousand who deserted us on the march up had stuck it out the outcome today might have been altogether different!"

"Well, we two 'riffraff' are still here, aren't we?" Tom retorted coldly. "We stuck it out through this damned ill-timed battle."

"True," the officer granted, "but the struggle isn't over."

"It is here."

"And how about you?" the officer asked Tom nastily. "Are you also going home 'first chance you git'?"

"If I had a home to go to, I might."

"Does that means you're staying in?"

Tom shrugged. "Might as well. I've no love for the British."

"Good fellow!" the officer said by way of apology. "Then why don't you come along with me to General Arnold's camp?"

"No, thanks. No point in hanging about Quebec. Besides, with our company without a captain, I suspect that those of us who managed to get away will probably head back to Albany and rejoin General Schuyler."

The officer nodded. "Suit yourself," he said, preparing to ride off.

"Sir," Tom asked, "we left some dead back there. What will happen to the bodies?"

"Sir Guy Carleton will permit a detachment of prisoners to take care of them, I expect. After this damn blizzard dies down. Well, good luck to you."

Tom and Gideon stood watching as the officer rode off to the west. But after riding only a short distance, the officer suddenly pulled his horse to, turned around and came galloping back. "Will you do something for me?" he asked Tom, taking a folded sheet of paper from inside the breast of his coat. "When you get back to New York, will you get this to my wife? The direction is on the back."

Tom frowned at the paper the officer thrust at him. "But, sir, it will take me weeks to get there, if I make it back at all. Haven't you a more reliable way to—?"

The officer looked him over through narrowed eyes. "You'll make it," he said with an assurance that Tom found unaccountable. With a salute, the officer turned his horse once more. Before

Tom could find his tongue, the horse had disappeared into the cloud of snow.

In the woods that fringed the Plains of Abraham, just west of Quebec, Tom and Gideon found four other survivors of the morning's battle. One had taken a musket ball in his upper arm, and another was bleeding from a gash in his neck. All of them were shivering, ragged and dazed. This small group, after only a brief discussion, banded together and followed Tom, who seemed to be the only one among them who had a plan. "We should follow the river south," he suggested. "Either we'll catch up with one of the Yorker regiments, or we'll make our way back to Albany on our own."

By nightfall they were well below the city, but they'd not yet seen a sign of the retreating regiments. Frozen and weary, they found passable shelter among the crags that lined the rivershore. There they constructed a lean-to and settled down for the night.

While one man made soup over a smoking fire by dropping his last piece of dried salt pork into a pot of snow, another bandaged the wounded man's arm. Tom reassured the fellow whose neck was gashed that he'd suffered only a superficial wound that was already scabbing over, and then he turned his attention to Gideon Jones. He cut off the top of Giddy's boot and strapped the swollen ankle with a strip of osnaburg that he'd torn from the bottom of his shirt. With the wounds thus tended, and the blizzard dying down, the men's condition became more bearable. They slopped up the snow-soup hungrily and prepared for sleep.

Gideon sat near the fire with his ankle propped up on a log as Tom undid both their packs. "That there officer, today," the frontiersman said thoughtfully, his eyes on his neat bandage, "he took your measure pretty good."

Tom looked up curiously from the bedrolls he was spreading on the ground. "What do you mean?"

"He trusted you. Respected you enough to give you his letter.

Smart fellow, that. But it's got me to wonderin' about you. Why ain't you an officer, Tom?"

Tom gave a short laugh. "Don't be daft. I'm riffraff, just as he said I was."

"No you ain't, an' he knowed it. I been wonderin' about you since we started out together. You talk good, you read good, you think things out good. And men listen to you. So why ain't you an officer?"

Tom, stretching himself out on his bedroll, threw Gideon a grin. "No one ever asked me."

"I bet they did. I bet you didn't take the offer 'cause you're afraid of somethin'."

Tom's grin died. "What makes you think that?"

Giddy hopped over to his bedroll and, gingerly protecting his ankle, stretched out on it. "It would explain a lot. Officers get noticed. But if you're hidin' from someone or somethin', you don't want to be noticed."

Tom pulled his bedding tightly round him and rolled over on his side. "You've a colorful imagination, Giddy," he murmured sleepily. "If I weren't so deuced bone-weary, I'd ask you to use that imagination to make up a bedtime story. But it'd be best for all of us if you'd just shut up and go to sleep."

Gideon Jones, knowing enough about Tom not to press, shut up.

Soon the whine of the wind was augmented by the sound of the heavy breathing of sleeping men. But Tom couldn't sleep. Gideon's questions had stirred up the anxiety that always dogged him: that someday, somewhere, someone would discover that he was an escaped redemptioner. This anxiety would probably have plagued him in any case, but it was made worse by the memory of an event that had occurred in New York not long after he'd arrived there. He could not forget that scene . . . that line of chained men . . . that memory with the power to clench his innards . . .

It happened last July, before he enlisted. He'd arrived in New

York in June, having taken several weeks making his way south
after leaving Hendley's estate. He hadn't hurried, this time, because he knew that Patience would not send the sheriff after him.
He may not have been happy, for leaving Patience had torn him
in two, but at least he felt free.

He found New York to be a very strange place. The city was
in turmoil, for two opposing factions governed it side by side.
Governor Tryon's Assembly, the entity sanctioned by the Crown,
was the official governing body, but a Provincial Congress,
elected by the people and answerable to the Continental Congress
in Philadelphia, made the laws and ran the city. Governor Tryon,
knowing he could not disband the Provincials without force of
arms, wisely let them be. He knew that the British gunboats,
positioned in the New York harbor, could destroy the city at will.
That threat alone was all the power he needed. Thus the city
existed part Tory and part rebel.

The strangeness of the situation was typified by an incident
that occurred on June 28th. The newly chosen general of the
Continental Army, George Washington, arrived in the city on the
very same day that Governor Tryon, just returning from a year-
long trip to Britain, was landing at the New York harbor. Both
men were greeted by official delegations and large crowds, the
general first, and then, four hours later, the governor. When Tom
learned that many of the same people had joined both crowds
and cheered just as enthusiastically for the rebel general as for
the king's own governor, he found it more laughable than
astonishing. In New York, he was beginning to discover, the in-
credible was commonplace.

Within a month, both factions were actively recruiting for their
armies. It amused Tom to see a redcoat recruiter soliciting men
on one side of the street while a Continental Army man recruited
on the other. Recruitment on both sides was active, for unem-
ployment was high and men were desperate. The British recruiter,
however, put on the better show. Resplendent in his red regimen-
tals, he periodically took a stance before a placard he'd hung on

a post behind him. "Hear ye, all intrepid, able-bodied *heroes,* " he'd shout, quoting the words on the placard, "who are willing to serve *His Majesty King George the Third,* in defense of your country, laws and constitution against the arbitrary *usurpations* of a tyrannical *Congress.* You will now have not only an opportunity of manifesting your *spirit* by assisting in *reducing to obedience* your *too-long-deluded countrymen,* but also of acquiring the *polite accomplishments of a soldier,* by serving only *two years,* during the present *rebellion* in America."

"We'll accept *six-month* enlistments," the Continental recruiter would shout in response. "You can acquire *polite accomplishments of a soldier* without wasting two years of your life!"

Someone on the street always asked at this point, "How much is the pay?"

The redcoat was always ready with his reply. "All recruits will earn a bounty of five dollars, as well as arms, clothing and accoutrements."

Then the Continental Army recruiter would shout back, "We also pay five dollars and supply arms, clothing and accoutrements."

"Continental dollars," the redcoat would sneer. "But *we* will promise *fifty acres of land* at the end of the war."

"That's if you win," the Continental would rejoin.

Tom stopped to listen to the badinage every time he walked past. He wondered how many men were tempted by that promise of land to enlist with the British. He himself would have endured many hardships for fifty acres of land, but joining the British army was not one of them. He intended to join the American army, even though the pay was merely continental scrip. But first he wanted to earn enough money to buy himself a good pair of boots. Everyone knew that the Continentals did not offer much in the way of accoutrements (most of the recruits weren't even issued proper uniforms), so Tom, knowing that good boots were essential, wanted to have a pair on his feet before enlisting.

Earning money for boots was not easy. The times were uncertain, and work was scarce. Tom eked out a bare subsistence by taking odd jobs in taverns and stables. But he'd almost saved enough money when, one day in July, he saw a group of men being marched through the streets in leg chains, with a guard at the front of the column and one at the rear. The prisoners were mostly youths—the oldest of them looked to be about nineteen—and they wore American army uniforms.

Tom fell in step with the rear guard. "Who are these fellows?" he asked.

"Runaway indenturers and apprentices," the guard replied. "On their way to jail."

Tom felt the blood drain from his face. *Indenturers!* He almost stumbled from the paralyzing spasm of alarm that shot through him.

The guard threw him a curious glance. "Ain't you heard? We found 'em in the two regiments Brigadier General Wooster brought down from Connecticut. The ones billeted over on Bowery Road, that we sent for to scare the inimicals."

"Yes, I've seen the Connecticut men," Tom said. Everyone in the city had seen the army of fifteen hundred men who'd come at the request of the New York Provincial Congress to help in routing out the non-Associators (now being called 'inimicals' because they were 'inimical' to the cause of the Association) who were so numerous in Queens County. "But this is New York. Are you saying these are *New York* runaways? What were they doing in an army from Connecticut? And so many of them!"

"Connecticut's the closest colony a New York redemptioner can escape to," the guard explained. "That's the first place these boys think to run to. See, the Connecticut regiments are no different from any other—they always need men. So they don't ask too many questions when a fellow signs up. That's how it is those regiments have so many of these lawbreakers on their rolls."

"But how did you manage to catch them?" Tom asked, trying to keep his voice casual.

"Easy. A couple of 'em was reco'nized at a tavern they went to when they was off duty. After that—"

"After that," one of the prisoners cut in bitterly, "the rest of us was identified quicker'n you could say skedaddle." He shook his head in sad disbelief. "I never figured a Connecticut regiment would be called to serve in New York. The minute we crossed the border, I felt in my bones we'd be reco'nized."

"Yeah, well, you were," the guard snapped, "so move along and don't be jawin'."

Tom walked alongside the prisoner silently for a moment. "What will become of you now?" he asked at last.

"God knows," the fellow said glumly. "A term in jail, a whipping, and two more years on my indenture, I suppose."

"Two more years at least," the guard smirked. "But no more gabbin', you hear? Move along, you wretches! Smartly now!"

Tom watched the line of men shuffle off down the road, their shoulders hunched in despair. His own shoulders sagged with the thought that he might one day be one of those 'wretches.' He could almost feel the shackles on his legs.

For days afterward, every time he thought of those poor young men, he felt sick. It kept him vacillating on the subject of his enlistment. Although joining the American Army had been his desire from the first, he now feared that he, like those captured runaways, might be discovered in its ranks. He walked about the streets in a fog of indecision.

But his belief in the cause of freedom was stronger than his fear. After a while the fear faded, though the memory of those shackled men did not. He finally decided that, since Hendley was ill and not likely to recover for months, and since Patience would not ever give him away, a six-month enlistment under another name would be safe enough.

Thus, in due course, and calling himself Tom Morgan, he became a soldier in the Fifth Company of the First New York Regiment. And that was how he now found himself shivering in his bedroll under an inadequate lean-to on the shore of the St.

Lawrence river just below Quebec. Yet even here, so far from where he'd started, he was not free from his ever-present fear of discovery. Someone was becoming suspicious. Gideon Jones was asking questions.

Not that Giddy, if he guessed the truth, would ever give him away, Tom realized as he burrowed deeper into his bedroll. Giddy Jones could be trusted to keep a secret. He was as loyal as . . . well, as Patience.

Patience. The very thought of her was a balm to his soul. Tom shut his eyes and tried to conjure up her face, a ritual he indulged in every night before he fell asleep. Some nights her image was so clear he could almost believe he smelled her hair. On those nights he would bury his head in his arms and pretend he was resting on her breast. When the vision was real enough, when the scent of peach-blossoms actually seemed to tingle his nostrils, he would experience a moment, in that instant just before falling asleep, that was pure bliss. Of course, he warned himself as he clutched the bedroll tightly around him, that moment happened only on rare occasions. Very rare occasions. But maybe tonight . . .

Forty-eight

It was snowing again, the third snowfall in as many weeks, and with February still to come it was not likely to be the last. Patience, setting the table for dinner, glanced up at the heavy flakes drifting past the dining-room windows and sighed. Though not yet four in the afternoon, it was as dark as night out there. Spring seemed very far away.

Beatie looked in at the door. "Carriage comin' up the drive."

"A carriage? In this snow?" Patience set down the plates and started toward the front room.

"Charlie went afore ye," Beatie informed her. "He'll see to't."

Both women turned curious eyes toward the doorway. In only a moment, Patience saw a caped figure striding in through the shadows of the front room. It was Orgill, back from New York. Patience took an instinctive step backward.

His lordship, shouting a hearty hello, threw his cape at Charlie McNab. "Am I in time for dinner?" he asked in his booming voice as he pushed Beatie aside and crossed over the threshold of the dining room. He smiled broadly at the sight of Patience. Without a pause in his step, he grasped her around her waist, lifted her off her feet and swung her about. "There you are, lovely wife! Have you missed me?"

Patience winced. "Put me down, please, my lord."

"Come, woman, give your lord a smile," he insisted, "or I shall be forced to conclude it's as cold indoors as out." He lowered

her onto his chest, holding her tightly against him with one arm
while moving his free hand smoothly over her buttocks.

She pushed herself as far from his chest as she could. "I sug
gest you use the fireplace for warmth," she said firmly. "It wil
serve you more effectively than—"

"Orgill? Is that you?" came her father's voice from the hallway

Orgill set her down and turned to watch as Hendley swung
himself into the room on his crutches. "Yes, Hendley, old fellow
I'm back," he said, slapping his father-in-law's shoulder cheer
fully, "and with news that will fill you with more good spirit
than a firkin of aqua vitae."

As Patience resumed setting the table, she saw from the corner
of her eye how her father's face brightened. Lord Orgill's com
panionship had become almost the only thing (other than the
weekly visits of Clymer Young) that gladdened her father these
days. In truth, the past six months had given Peter Hendley littl
reason for gladness. His recovery had been slower than the las
time, and less complete. His mouth was more twisted than ever
causing a real facial distortion; his lower left side was still para
lyzed, necessitating the use of crutches to get around; and ther
were days when his hands shook so badly he could not write
Charlie McNab helped him dress and undress, and his bed ha
been taken down to his office so that he would not have to b
carried up the stairs. In short, he'd aged many years in a few
months.

Her father's spirits had not recovered either, for the conditio
of the province was not at all to his liking. The Loyalist positio
had considerably weakened since the day he'd gone to the elec
tion meeting and fallen ill. Six months ago, the rebel sympathiz
ers in Westchester County had numbered (by his own calculation
less than a quarter of the population. Now, he feared, the propor
tion had reversed itself. The number of citizens who openly de
clared themselves Loyalists could be counted on one hand! Tha
this shocking decrease was more the result of coercion and cow

ardice than political conviction was cold comfort to Peter Hendley.

If he found comfort, it was in complaining. Patience had to listen every day to her father's ranting against what he called "creeping corruption." Corruption, he felt, was inherent in the very concept of American self-government. A typical symptom of that corruption was the increasing aggression of the Sons of Liberty toward those whom they called Non-Associators. An atmosphere of fear was growing all through the colonies, fear of what the lawless committees might do to those who refused to take the oath of Association. The fears were not without foundation; more and more reports of abuse were circulating—cases of destroyed property, tarring and feathering, harrassment of whole families, even arrests and imprisonments. Therefore, most of the erstwhile Loyalists signed the oath when they were pressed; it took a man of very strong convictions and almost foolhardy bravery to stand up against the rising tide of intimidation.

Worst of all, from her father's point of view, was the news from Philadelphia. When the Congress (which seemed to grow more powerful with each passing day) decided to support an American army and appoint a commander in chief, Peter Hendley fumed at their effrontery! But behind his ire lay a dismaying conviction that all-out war was inevitable. In all quarters, hopes for a last-minute conciliation with England were rapidly receding, and an increasing number of the members of the Congress were actually discussing—some reluctantly and others eagerly—the possibility of complete independence, a subject that hadn't even been considered six months before. This was deeply disturbing to her father. And as the pace of events quickened, he grew more and more unhappy.

That was why Patience swallowed her irritation at Lord Orgill's arrival. If his lordship's presence brought some cheer to her father's spirit, she would grit her teeth and endure it. Nevertheless, it was a bitter pill to swallow. How ironic that her father had become so attached to Orgill in these last few months! Patience could understand, of course, that Papa needed the companionship of someone whose sympathies so closely matched his own. But it was sad to reflect that the one man whose company she detested was the one man whose company her father most enjoyed.

But there wasn't time to indulge in reflection when dinner was waiting to be served. Patience sent Charley to fetch Benjy, and the four sat down at the table. Orgill did not need much encouragement either to eat or to talk. "I'll save the best news for last," he said as he hungrily devoured Beatie's savory barley soup. "First, I have a tale that is certain to amuse you. It has to do with the fortification that the New York Provincial Congress authorized to be built on the Hudson."

"Do you mean Fort Constitution?" Benjy asked interestedly.

"That's the one. Not many miles north of here, I understand. Lord Tryon's informant, who is himself a member of the Provincial Congress and regularly reports to his lordship about the goings-on at their meetings, could hardly contain his laughter as he told us about it. It seems that those idiots who've taken over the running of New York went ahead and funded the work without really studying the plans. Then, after the money was spent, they discovered that they never should have built there in the first place. The site was utterly wrong. It's at the widest part of the river, where an attack on passing ships is *least* likely to be effective."

"Ha!" Hendley chortled. "Just what I might have expected."

"Right!" his lordship guffawed. "Any fool knows the site should be at a narrows. And, even sillier, they located the fort in a valley, at the bottom of a natural bowl, surrounded on three sides by high ground!"

"What?" cried Hendley. "A fort open to artillery fire from *above?* Who was the idiot who chose such a ludicrous site?"

"That, my dear father-in-law, is the most amusing part. The Provincial Congress hired for the project a man whose credenials and experience were evidently not investigated. It seems they hired him on the basis of the beauty of his drawings!"

"His *drawings?*" Hendley shook his head incredulously.

"Can you believe it? After the stupidity of his planning came to light, they finally checked his credentials. Only then did they learn that the best job he ever held was in the Floridas, as His Majesty's *Botanist!*"

Hendley and Orgill laughed until their eyes teared. Benjy maintained a stoic silence. Patience, noticing that Benjy's ears were turning red in repressed chagrin, reached under the table and pressed his knee comfortingly.

Hendley wiped his cheeks. "Can you tell me, Orgill," he asked, grinning his twisted grin, "how such idiots expect to wage a war with Britain?"

"It will be the most ludicrous war in history," Orgill prophesied.

"Not if the Americans win it," Benjy muttered.

The other men either did not hear Benjy's remark or considered it unworthy of notice. "There's another item you may find amusing," his lordship went on. "My Lord Tryon has tricked the city yet again. He convinced three of the city's four gunsmiths into departing for England to make weapons for the Crown."

"Indeed?" Hendley rubbed his hands together gleefully. "How did he do that?"

"Bribery. He paid their passage and then some. That leaves all of New York City with only one gunsmith. Their militia, as well as the regiment they've recruited on the orders of the Continental Congress, will be hard-pressed to find muskets."

Benjy stuck out his chin. "There's more than four gunsmiths in the city," he stated emphatically. "I know that for a fact. Your Lord Tryon doesn't know how to count."

"Is that so?" Orgill raised one brow and threw Benjy a look of supercilious disdain. "Then you may be sure they aren't skilled enough to be counted." He turned back to Hendley and smiled broadly. "But the news I've been withholding—the best news of all—is this: Guy Carleton has trounced the rebels in Quebec!"

"Oho!" Hendley chortled, his eyes widening in excitement. "I knew he would! I just knew it! It was stupid of the rebels to even *try* to fight for Canada."

This was too much for Benjy. "It wasn't so stupid when General Montgomery marched right over Montreal, was it? You weren't laughing then."

Hendley's twisted grin died. "That was a fluke," he snapped. "And I can't say I like your tone, boy."

"Well, I don't like your gloating," Benjy retorted truculently. "If poor Richard Montgomery hadn't been killed the first day of battle—"

"Richard Montgomery? Was that the Captain Montgomery who used to live near here?" Patience asked, appalled. "How terrible! He was so promising . . . so young . . ."

"Yes," Benjy muttered, lowering his head so that no one would see the tears in his eyes. "It was a damned shame."

"So you heard about the defeat at Quebec before tonight, did you?" his father asked, leaning toward him. "You *knew?*"

Benjy threw him a nervous glance. "I heard . . ."

"How did you hear?"

The boy shrugged. "I hear things . . . in town . . ."

"Your militia friends, eh?" Hendley's hands began to shake. "I thought I'd made it clear that you were not to associate with that rabble."

"They're *not*—"

His father cut him off with an angry gesture. "Did I or did I not give you an order?"

Benjy's jaw clenched so tightly that a muscle in his cheek throbbed. "Yes, sir, you did."

"And you *disobeyed* me? Knowing my state of health, you still—?"

The boy met his father's eyes and tried to explain. "Papa, I—"

"Answer me! If you can't respect my wishes when you're out-

side the house, you can at least show me some respect at my own table!"

"It has naught to do with respect," Benjy mumbled miserably.

"Papa," Patience put in, "can we drop the subject, at least for now? We're eating dinner—"

Hendley ignored her. "I want to know! Did you deliberately disobey me?"

Benjy turned red-faced in humiliation. "Yes, I disobeyed you," he burst out, jumping to his feet. "What else could I do? You refuse to respect *me!* So I have no choice. In this one matter, the one thing most important to me, I disobeyed you. And I'll continue to disobey you."

Hendley heaved himself up by pressing down on the arms of his chair. "You'll continue *nothing!*" he said through tight lips, his eyes burning with rage. "I am still your father. While I live, you will do as I tell you to do. And right now, you will get out! You will leave this table, and you will go to your room until I give you leave to come down! *Go,* do you hear? *Out of my sight!*"

"Very well, I'll get out of your sight!" Benjy pushed back his chair, his knees trembling. "And out of this *house,* too!" He wheeled about, stumbled out the door and slammed it behind him.

Peter Hendley lowered himself slowly to his seat. With a conscious effort to restore his calm, he took a deep breath and resumed eating. But Patience could not eat. Her emotions were in turmoil. White-lipped, she got up from her place and looked from her father to her husband, waiting for one of them to offer to stop the boy . . . to keep him from dashing out into the snow. But neither one met her eye. With a sputter of disgust, she stormed out of the room and shut the door. "Benjy, wait!" she cried, running after him.

The large vestibule was dark and chilly; only a small candle burned on the chest near the front door. Benjy stood just in front of it, shrugging into his greatcoat. "Don't try to stop me, Patience," he said quietly. "I can't bear it here with him. Not any longer. He despises me."

"No, he doesn't, dearest. It's just this horrid war . . ."

"It's not this war. There's another war between Papa and me. There has been from the first. I can't be what he wants. Our differences will kill him if I stay. I don't want to fight him any more."

His words surprised her. They sounded so adult. And he seemed suddenly so tall. The caped greatcoat that she'd made for him a couple of years ago, that used to hang down almost to his ankles, now only reached to the top of his boots. When had she begun to look *up* to him when they stood together like this? When had Benjy become a man?

He took her hands in his and tried to smile. "Don't look at me that way, Patience. I can take care of myself. I'll be all right."

Her shoulders sagged in surrender. "What will you do?"

"I'll join up. Colonel Holmes is recruiting for the Fourth New York, to fill in the gaps left by the men whose enlistments ended in December. I'll sign with him."

"But Benjy, you're too young. Surely they won't take you!"

"I'm seventeen. There's men younger than me been in since summer."

She started to cry. "Benjy, please don't go! Is Papa's temper . . . or even American independence . . . important enough to . . . to die for?"

"Maybe they both are." He took her in a rough embrace. "Don't cry, Patience. I won't die."

She held him tightly. "But it's snowing!" she pleaded foolishly. "Can't you stay home one more night?"

A muffled sound from the dining room reached them. Their father and his crony were laughing in there. *Laughing!* The raucous sound revolted the two listeners. Benjy's arms dropped from her. "I've got to go, Patience. Now! I won't spend another night under this roof." He snatched his tricorn from the coatrack, put it on and threw open the front door. A blast of cold air filled the hallway. But before stepping out, he took one last look at her. "Don't worry, my dear," he said in a tone that was almost fatherly. "I won't sleep in the snow. I'll stay the night with one of the boys in town."

"Wait," she begged. Hurriedly, with hands that shook, she opened the lid of the chest near the door and pulled out a knitted muffler. "Promise me, Benjy," she urged as she wound it twice round his neck, "that you won't do anything foolish."

He kissed her cheek. "I won't. I promise."

She stood at the open door and watched as he walked quickly down the drive, his head erect under the cocked hat and the cape of his coat flapping in the wind. Icy flakes blew against her cheek and accumulated on her cap and shoulders, but she didn't notice. The shadow that was her brother's form became fainter and fainter. Soon the dark swallowed him up, as it had swallowed Sally and Babs and . . . and everyone else she loved.

With the heel of her hand, she wiped the wetness from her cheeks and went back inside. She was not sorrowing, she realized with a shock. She could not sorrow for Benjy. He'd freed himself. She was *glad* for him. This clench of pain in her chest was something else, a feeling she couldn't for the moment name.

As she turned back to return to the dining room, her eye fell on the band of light that glimmered out from beneath the dining-room door, behind which the two men left in her life sat laughing over their victories. Suddenly she knew the name of that feeling about Benjy's departure. It was called envy.

Forty-nine

Although he would never admit it, Peter Hendley was far from indifferent to his son's disappearance. Benjy was not everything Hendley wanted in a son, but the boy was blood of his blood, the carrier of his name, his passport to posterity. Benjy's absence from the household caused Hendley real pain. He was a father, after all. Fathers are rarely immune to feelings of love for the sons they sire.

Therefore Hendley sent Charlie McNab into Fordham with instructions to question every one of Benjy's friends. And if McNab learned something of Benjy's whereabouts, he was to find the boy and drag him home, bound and gagged if need be. But McNab came home empty-handed.

The atmosphere in the house became too gloomy for Lord Orgill, whose life in London—and even in the limited society of Lord Tryon's New York—had accustomed him to nightly carousing. Thus, after a stay of only three days, he announced his intention of returning to the *Duchess of Gordon,* the ship on which Lord Tryon was taking refuge. Before he left, his father-in-law entreated him (with what Patience felt was unusual earnestness and humility) to search the New York inns and taverns for any sign of Benjy. Orgill acquiesced promptly, so promptly that Patience was convinced his lordship had not the least intention of troubling himself to honor his word.

Waiting for news of Benjy made Peter Hendley even more impatient and crotchety than usual. Patience could have ended her father's suspense by telling him that the boy had joined the American army, but, fearing that the news would bring on another apoplectic stroke, she held her tongue.

A week went by. The weather cleared, though the air remained icy. On a particularly frosty morning, when even the sun's glimmer on the wind-whipped river looked cold, Beatie beckoned Patience to come out of the dining room where she and her father were breakfasting. "There's a soldier come to the back door, ma'am," the little Scotswoman whispered, "but no' a redcoat. He winna say a word to anyone but ye."

"Shh!" Patience hissed, throwing a glance at her father. But she needn't have worried, for he still sat sat hunched over his porridge bowl, abstractedly stirring the thick lumps with his spoon. He'd probably not even noticed that she'd left the table. Patience closed the door quietly. "Do you think it's a message from Benjy?" she asked Beatie over her shoulder as she hurried down the passageway.

"He dinna say," Beatie answered, trotting eagerly behind.

The man warming himself before the kitchen fire was a lanky fellow with a long, narrow face and straggly hair hanging unkempt from beneath a weatherbeaten tricorn. "Did you wish to see me?" she asked him.

"If you be Patience Hendley," he said, turning to face her and removing his hat politely. But the shrewd eyes that took her in from top to bottom were more appraising than polite.

"Yes, I'm she."

He smiled at her broadly, showing a row of large, uneven teeth. "I figured you'd look like this," he said, nodding as if in approval. "My name's Jones. Gideon Jones."

"How do you do?" Patience offered her hand, observing him closely as he bowed over it. He was dressed like a frontiersman, in a heavy, fringed shirt that hung over his breeches like a coat. The only sign that the fellow was a soldier was the military strap slung diagonally across his chest, from which a leather pouch was suspended. "I'm told you have a message for me," she prodded.

"Not a message. I'm only to give you this." He took a small, flat package from his pouch and handed it to her.

Patience, completely confused, stared down at it. It was wrapped in rough brown paper and tied with fraying string. "What is it?"

"Can't say, ma'am. I'm only to deliver it into yer hands. Your hands and no one else's."

"But who sent it?"

"Can't say that neither. He said you'd know." He put his hat back on and made another bow. "I'll best be off, with your permission, ma'am. I shouldn't leave my horse standin' in the cold. An' I've a long way to go. Good day to you."

"Surely you'll take a bit of refreshment first. Some breakfast, perhaps? Or at least a hoecake and a drink of hot cider?"

"Thank ye kindly, ma'am, but yer woman already gave me a posset to drink. I'll take the hoecake in my pouch fer the journey, though, if yer willin' "

"Yes, of course. Wrap one up in a napkin, Beatie, and put in some comfits, too." Patience smiled at the fellow, trying to encourage him to loosen his tongue. "You appear to be a soldier, Mr. Jones. Can it be that you're serving in the Fourth New York, with my brother?"

"No, ma'am. Never met anyone from the Fourth New York. An' I ain't serving in the army no more."

"But the Continental Army hasn't even been in existence for more than a few months. Don't tell me you're disillusioned with your cause so soon."

"Oh, I b'lieve in the cause right enough, but I got a fam'ly to feed an' land to till. I gave six months, an' I might sign up again later on, but right now I'm on my way home"

"I see. And where would home be?"

"A long ways from here, in the Mohawk Valley."

"Heavens, that *is* a long way."

"An' a good bit longer for havin' stopped here, I can tell you," the man said with a kind of pride. "I'd say comin' here added an extra week to my travels."

"Did it indeed? Then it was certainly very good of you to go so far out of your way, just to deliver this."

Mr. Jones shrugged cheerfully. " 'Twarn't much. He done more'n that for me."

"He?" Her expression sharpened. "The man who sent this?"

"Yes, ma'am. Him."

Patience could see, from the glint in Mr. Jones's eyes, that he would not be tricked or cajoled into revealing anything more. "Well, Mr. Jones," she said in defeat, "since you've come so far out of your way, I hope you'll let me offer you more than a hoecake. Beatie, take Mr. Jones to the smokehouse and give him some salt pork and cheese and anything else that might last him on his travels."

Mr. Jones thanked her profusely, favored her with another of his approving, toothy grins, and followed Beatie out the door.

Patience sat down on the hearth and studied her mysterious parcel closely on both sides, but the wrapping gave her no hint of its contents or the sender. So, with almost breathless eagerness, she tore off the wrapping.

The contents proved disappointing—nothing but a slim pamphlet whose flimsy cover was worn soft by much handling. It was called *Common Sense,* written by someone who merely called himself "an Englishman." Patience immediately recalled hearing Lord Orgill speak of it to her father. "A nasty piece of sedition," he'd called it, and he'd gone on to say that it was circulating through the colonies with the most amazing rapidity. "I can't understand its popularity," he'd fumed, "since it's just another revolutionary diatribe. The writer, Tom Paine, didn't sign his name to the document, but now that it's caused such a sensation, he's perfectly willing to admit his authorship. In the city every fool who can read is clamoring to get his hands on it."

Why, Patience wondered, would Benjy (and it had to be Benjy, even though Mr. Jones had denied knowing him) go to such lengths to send her so blatantly partisan a publication? Did he really believe that a journalistic diatribe would convert her?

She opened the pamphlet and discovered that something had been written on the fly-leaf. The writing was as boyish and unartful as Benjy's, but it was not Benjy's. Her heartbeat quickened as her eyes flew over the words: "To thank you for teaching me and changing my life forever, I send this to teach you, and perhaps to change your life forever."

There was no signature, but none was needed. A note from Tom, after all these months! In a burst of emotion, she clutched the pamphlet to her breast. *Tom,* she thought delightedly, *you still think of me!*

But after rereading the words the little flare of delight died down. There was nothing in those words, really, to warm a woman's heart. Words of gratitude were pallid and sickly when one was looking for signs of love. With a sigh, she slipped the pamphlet into her apron pocket and started back to the dining room, consoling herself with the thought that at least Tom hadn't forgotten her. After discovering a piece of writing that he wanted to share with her, he'd taken a great deal of trouble to send it . . . cajoling another man to go miles out of his way to deliver it into her hand and no other. It was—

She stopped short. That man—Gideon Jones—must have been well acquainted with Tom to have done him such a favor. Then he probably knew what had become of Tom!

With a gasp she turned around, flew back to the kitchen and out the kitchen door. "Mr. Jones!" she cried, running toward the smokehouse. "Mr. Jones! Where—?"

Beatie, who'd been standing in the drive watching the visitor ride off, turned in surprise. "He's gone," she said, shrugging her Gaelic shrug. "See, there's his horse, just disappearin' down the road."

"Oh, *blast!*" Furious with herself for having missed the opportunity to learn something—anything!—about her Tom, Pa tience kicked the side of the smokehouse with such force that she bruised her toes. She had to limp back to the house.

She read the pamphlet that night, burning down two candles to their ends. When she finished, she lay awake mulling it over. Mr. Paine had written some very daring things. He had no respect for monarchy and made no bones about saying so. He claimed that the British constitution, far from being one of the glories of civilization, was founded on what he called "two ancient tyrannies"—monarchy and aristocracy. Mr. Paine's scorn for monarchy was quite shocking: "the most prosperous invention the Devil ever set on foot for the promotion of idolatry," was how he described it, adding that the kings of history had brought nothing but misery. And the hereditary succession of monarchs, he pointed out wickedly, "often gave mankind an Ass for a Lion." Patience, when she read those words, became quite out of patience with his rudeness.

But on she read. "To know whether it be the interest of this continent to be Independent," he wrote, "we need only to ask this simple question: Is it in the interest of a man to be a boy all his life?"

The question was a good one, Patience had to admit. It made her think of Benjy. In order to make himself a man, Benjy had had to rebel against a parent who kept too tight a control over him. Was England's king just such a parent over America? And was it necessary for *everyone* to rebel in order to become fully adult—even women? Even herself?

The questions were troublesome. She pushed them out of her mind and went on with her reading. Mr. Paine claimed that "simple facts, plain arguments and common sense" proved conclusively that the American condition would only deteriorate if a reconciliation with the mother country were achieved. "Reconciliation is a fallacious dream," he warned. There was no going back. And to go forward in thrall to Britain would mean enslavement for the colonies. He showed in forceful detail how the British government's colonial aspirations were in direct opposition to American rights and liberty. The Americans, he said without mincing words, had no choice but to free themselves of monarchy by declaring independence.

He went even further. Not only was American independence common sense, he declared, it was, in reality, something more, something of immense importance in the history of the world. "The cause of America is in a great measure the cause of all mankind," he wrote. "We have it in our power to begin the world over again. A situation, similar to the present, hath not happened since the days of Noah until now."

Patience lay in the dark and thought about that statement for a long while. Begin the world over again? What presumption! Sitting up in bed, she lit a third candle and read those words again. They seemed even more arrogant than the first time she'd read them. If her father ever read this tract, he would have another attack of apoplexy for certain! "Tom Morrison," she muttered as she closed the book and slid back under the covers, "do you really believe it in your power to make the world over again?" She herself couldn't imagine putting her faith into so monumental a task. Besides, she didn't want to. Wasn't the world fine enough the way it was?

With a shake of her head to indicate that as far as she was concerned the subject was closed, she blew out her candle and went to sleep.

Fifty

In the days and weeks that followed, however, Patience could not keep Mr. Paine's audacious words out of her mind. There was an excitement to the words in that pamphlet, a fervor that she could see would be inspiring to readers who were in sympathy with the cause—readers like Tom. It might even ignite the passions of the Americans who'd been wavering. She herself was often tempted to reread it. Some of the phrases repeated themselves in her memory verbatim. She saw quite well why Tom had sent it to her.

While Mr. Paine's impassioned argument was preoccupying Patience's mind, something very different was preoccupying her father's. Several weeks had passed with no word of Benjy from any source. During that time, Hendley's emotions toward his son had undergone a curious development; from a guilty awareness of his own fault in the quarrel and a wish to conciliate, his feelings quickly progressed to an irritable resentment and from there accelerated into passionate fury. Such fury needed to be vented. It was not enough to declare that he never wanted to see his rebel son again, or that Benjy was no real son at all. Somewhere, sometime soon, there would have to be an explosion.

It came on a March morning when all of nature seemed in a foul mood. The wind whipped around the corners of the house with an angry whine, and the rain beat against the windows like drumming fingers. Hendley stared out the window of his office-bedroom, watching the weather tear disastrously at the new little buds on his orchard trees and thinking about the fact that his son and heir would never care for those trees as he did. The thought was more than he could bear. *"Patience,"* he shouted loudly, "come in here *at once!* I want Benjamin Hendley's name *expunged forever* from the family Bible, and I want you to help me write a *new will."*

Patience came running from the kitchen, wiping her hands on her apron. "What are you saying?" she asked in alarm.

"I'm too much atremble to hold a pen today," he said, motioning her to a chair beside his desk. "Write down what I say to you. I'm going to dictate a new will."

She stiffened. "Why must you have a new will?"

"I won't leave my properties to a rebel ne'er-do-well. Take paper and write as I direct you—"

"Papa, this is foolish. An impulsive response to the silence from Benjy. But, it's only a mood. It will pass."

"It will *not* pass! Do as I tell you! Pick up the pen."

"Please, Papa, you needn't do it today. Think about it for a fortnight. Then, if you still wish—"

"Damnation, woman, does *nobody* in this house respect my orders any more? Pick up the pen, I say!"

Patience, seeing his color rise, did as he ordered. To prevent the occurrence of another stroke she felt it necessary to avoid altercations whenever possible. No matter how much she disliked doing it, she wrote down what he dictated. But when he came to the place where he named his beneficiary, her pen faltered. "Me? You're leaving everything to *me?"*

"Well, of course. Who else but you?"

"But the property would not come to me but to my husband, wouldn't it?"

"He would have the rights to its use, but you would own it," he mumbled, not meeting her eyes.

Patience had no choice but to pursue the matter, even if it meant raising her father's dander. This was too important. "What does that mean, 'rights to its use'?" she asked.

"It means that the husband can retain any rents or profits obtained from the properties."

"Could I sell any of it, if I wished?"

"No. He would have to sign—"

"Or any other agreements relating to it?"

"No. A married woman is not an independent entity. She cannot make contracts."

Patience rose from her chair. "Then, Papa, think what you are *doing!* Lord Orgill could sell or buy or manage the income of the land any way he wanted," she declared indignantly. "And since he is unlikely ever to be guided by *my* wishes, I would have *less* influence on what becomes of this property than I would if you left it to *Benjy!*"

"Well, whose fault is that?" Hendley retorted sharply. "Is it my fault you and Lord Orgill are at odds? You have it in your power to exert influence on the man. If you were any kind of proper wife to him, you could make his lordship putty in your hands."

Patience's head came up sharply. "What do you mean, proper wife?"

"You know very well what I mean! Do you think me blind? I may be weakened in my legs, but my eyes are sharp enough. I'm well aware that you've been denying your husband his conjugal rights."

Patience stared at him in horror. "That is sharp-eyed indeed! Am I to believe that my father spies on me in my bedroom?"

"Of course I don't spy on you. The suggestion is insulting. Everyone in this household knows you lock your door to him. Orgill complained to me of it himself."

"Oh, he did, did he? How very admirable of him. Am I to take it that you are on *his* side in this?"

"Yes, I am. The man is your husband. Take him to your bed, Patience, and you'll be able to get whatever you like from him."

She winced at the thought. "Good heavens, Papa," she exclaimed, appalled, "are you making yourself his *procurer?"*

"I'll ignore that indelicate remark. It does you no credit. I shall simply point out to you, my girl, that a man's conjugal rights are a God-given part of the marriage contract, and that it's a wife's duty to—"

"It is *not* my duty," she cried, rising angrily. "As far as I'm concerned, Lord Orgill broke our marriage contract when he deserted me for seven years."

"Nevertheless, he is your husband by law and in the eyes of God."

"The law perhaps, but the eyes of God must surely see the circumstances with more clarity than the law does."

"I will not bandy words with you on this matter. I've given you good advice. Take it or not, as you wish."

"I will *not* take it. Nor will I write another word of this monstrously unfair document. If you'll take *my* advice, Papa, you'll leave your original will exactly as it was."

"I will not leave it as it was! But you needn't write any more of it if it offends you to do so. Clymer Young is coming this afternoon with some papers. He'll write the will for me and sign as witness. I shall manage without your help or advice."

"Yes," Patience muttered, clenching her teeth in baffled frustration and turning to go. "When have you ever paid heed to advice from me?"

Peter Hendley was stung by those words. Patience was the one person in all the world to whom he felt close. He believed that his affection for her was obvious. How could she believe that her words meant nothing to him? There was only one time in all these years when their relationship unraveled. Hadn't she forgotten it yet? "If you're referring to the matter of Sally and Aaron," he muttered sullenly, "it only proves how poor your advice is. If you'd listened to me, Sally would still be here and Aaron would be—" Here, suddenly aware that he'd said more than he should, he caught himself up and clamped his lips shut.

Patience stopped in her tracks. "Aaron would be what?" she asked, wheeling around.

"Nothing. Never mind."

She came slowly up to the desk, an icy feeling gripping her heart. "You've *heard* something of them! What *is* it?"

Hendley shifted uncomfortably in his chair. "This argument has wearied me. Go and leave me in peace."

"Tell me!" She leaned across the desk and grasped his shoulders. "Finish your sentence. Aaron would be—"

"Alive!" He thrust her hands from him but could not meet her eyes. "He'd be alive."

She felt the floor lurch beneath her feet. "Aaron . . . *dead?* It can't be!" Holding the desk for support, she peered at him in utter disbelief. "I don't *believe* you! How can you *know?"*

He lowered his head. "My agent had it from Sally herself," he said in a subdued voice.

"He *found* her? That dreadful man found her? Oh, my God!" She pressed her hands against her trembling mouth until she could regain control of herself. "Then where *is* she?" she asked hoarsely when she was able to speak. "Why hasn't he brought her home?"

"Brought her *home?* Are you mad?" He glared at her, unable to understand why she had so little appreciation of his position in this matter. Couldn't she see that this entire business had become a point of pride with him? "The woman ran off! I won't have a runaway slave in my house. She's been sold."

Patience could hardly believe her ears. Aaron *dead* . . . Sally *sold* . . . it couldn't be! Her mind would not accept it. It was a mistake, she told herself, and in a moment her father would surely say she'd misunderstood him. But he said nothing, and when she looked at him, her heart beseeching him to deny those words, she saw something in his face—a look that was both guilty and hideously self-justifying—that told her with hopeless certainty he'd spoken the truth. It was an ugly, heartbreaking truth, but she had to face it. And as for her father, he knew his guilt, though he'd never admit, even to himself, what his soul was telling him: that he'd committed a grievous, grievous sin!

She couldn't bear to look at her father's face another moment. With every muscle quivering, with her breath caught somewhere in her chest, with her heart torn between revulsion and the crushing pain of loss, she backed slowly from the room. Once in the hallway, she looked about her in confusion. What was she to do? She had to do something, for there was a tumult inside her that needed to burst out, in sobs or screams. But somehow she could neither cry nor cry out. All she could do was run.

So she ran . . . down the hallway . . . across the vestibule . . . out the door. The rain beat down on her, drenching her hair and soaking her dress, but it made no impression on her mind. Her brain, teeming from a jumble of dreadful feelings, took no notice of the messages being sent by eyes and ears and skin. On she ran, stumbling dazedly down the steps . . . across the drive . . . over the sodden lawn. She did not realize where she was or what she was doing until she crashed into the large oak. The pain of the blow was nothing; she barely noticed it. But it stopped her headlong flight.

Dizzily, she clung to the trunk until her head ceased its reeling. Then she slowly slid down to her knees. It was, she noted in surprise, the position of prayer. But what was she to pray for? Aaron was dead, Sally captured, everyone she loved gone.

What had happened to her life? Everyone who'd lived in this house, everyone she loved, had left her . . . Babs and Benjy, Tom, Sally . . . and Aaron. Poor dead Aaron. They'd all been driven off in pain and despair by Peter Hendley, the Monarch of his Property.

Yes, her own father had driven them off, leaving her with no one but himself . . . and Orgill.

Was this her reward for being a dutiful daughter, for accepting her father's precepts and patterning her life by his standards? Suddenly the words that she'd been mulling over all week sounded loudly in her ears: *Nothing but misery has come from Monarchy.* All at once Mr. Paine's words rang very, very true.

How blind she'd been, how blind! It had taken the tragedy of

Sally and Aaron to make her see. "Dear Lord," she found herself saying, hands clasped at her breast, "forgive me for my ignorance, for my blindness, for my lack of courage. Forgive me for listening to the wrong voice."

Her father had been her guide, the monarch who ruled her life. But he'd not managed to rule anyone else. Everyone else she loved had discovered that there was a time for rebellion . . . for independence. They had struggled against their bonds, not meekly accepted them. They knew that tyranny had to be fought. Wasn't it about time she discovered it too?

Slowly she pulled herself to her feet, walked out from under the shelter of the tree and lifted her face to the cleansing rain. *Dear Lord,* she prayed, *thank you for making me hear new voices. And thank you, Aaron, and Sally and Benjy and Babs and Mr. Paine and you, Tom Morrison . . . all of you . . . for changing me forever.*

Then, brushing away a dripping lock of hair from her forehead, she turned and strode purposefully back to the house. Perhaps it was not too late for *her* revolution. Like the rest of the rebels in the land of her birth, she, too, was going to try to begin the world over again.

Fifty-one

Jotham Dillard and Daniel Styles, lowering their heads against a March-like April wind and holding onto their hats, made their way up the drive to the Hendley house. "Now, let me do the talkin', Joth," Daniel warned. "You always get miffy an' rile folks up."

Jotham would have argued the point, but they were already at the door. Beatie answered their knock. "We come t' see Mr. Hendley," Jotham said quickly, throwing Daniel a defiant glance.

"Bringin' trouble, no doot," Beatie said under her breath, shaking her head in disapproval. She let them in and pointed toward the front room. "Wait there," she ordered.

A few minutes later Patience came into the room. The two men, who were seated nervously on the edge of the settee, jumped to their feet. "G'mornin', ma'am," Daniel said.

"We come t' see yer pa, not you," Jotham said, his nervousness before this proud woman making him more pugnacious than he meant to be.

Daniel gave his friend a warning poke with his elbow. "I apologize for Jotham, ma'am. What he means is, may we speak to Mr. Hendley? We have important business to discuss with him."

"I know what Mr. Dillard means," Patience said dryly. "I am not unfamiliar with the graciousness of his manners." Inside herself, she was wryly amused at the timing of this visit. Just as she was learning to view the rebellion in a sympathetic new light, these two 'representatives of the cause' appeared. They were a daunting reminder of what she might expect in the character of her new confederates. That she and such men as Jotham Dillard could be on the same side in *anything* was a subject for mirth. However, she smothered this inclination to drollery and focused her attention on the problem at hand. "I'm sure you know, gentlemen, that Mr. Hendley is not well. If I might convey your message to him—"

"If he's well enough to see his Loyalist friends," Jotham burst out angrily, "then why ain't he—?"

"Shut up, Jotham," Daniel snapped under his breath. "What Jotham means, ma'am, is that we know Mr. Hendley had a visit from his friend Mr. Clymer Young yesterday, so . . ." Meeting Patience's cold eye, his voice failed him.

"And how do you know that, Mr. Styles?" Patience asked. "Have you been spying on us?"

"It's the job of our Committee to know what goes on in this town," Jotham declared.

"Is it, indeed? And is it also your job to question my word?"

"What Jotham means, ma'am," Daniel said, glaring at his friend, "is—"

"Mr. Styles," Patience interrupted, "you needn't keep telling me what he means. I understand him perfectly well. But I think you should try to understand *me*. My father's condition requires that he be shielded from undue excitement. Therefore, be good enough to tell me the purport of your visit, and I shall willingly convey it to him at a time and in a manner I deem appropriate."

"We have t' see him hisself," Jotham said in exasperation. "In person. We have somethin' for him to sign."

"Then the matter is simple to resolve. Just give me the document, and I'll see that he gets it."

Jotham threw up his hands. "I never *could* get a nod from this woman! Dan'l, you said you'd do the talkin', so do it."

"Y'see, ma'am," Daniel said earnestly, "we need to tell him what will . . . er . . . transpire should he decide *not* to sign it. There's things he ought to kn—"

"I know enough!" came an angry voice. They all looked around to see Peter Hendley standing in the doorway glaring at them. "And you know damned well I won't sign your damned Association agreement no matter what you have to say!"

"Papa," Patience said, putting a hand on his arm to help him to a chair, "you needn't blaspheme—"

"Blaspheming is all these idiots understand." He thrust her hand away and hobbled into the room, supporting himself on his crutches. "One might think you feather merchants would know better than to waste your time and mine trying to coax me to sign your blasted oath."

"We was hopin' you'd feel different by now," Daniel suggested, "seein' how the situation has changed."

"And just how has it changed?"

"Almost everyone in the county's signed by now."

"Only because they've succumbed to coercion. You may take my word, their feelings toward the king haven't changed."

"Even if that was true six months ago, Mr. Hendley," Daniel argued, "their feelin's are different now."

Hendley sniffed scornfully. "People don't change as quickly as all that. Six months ago, no more than two out of ten were real revolutionaries. Another two held firm to their loyalties. And the other six, cowards that they are, would bend to the strongest wind. Well, the wind's changed, that's all."

"An' no wonder," Jotham muttered. "It's a pretty strong wind."

Daniel nodded in agreement. "In all of New York City, I hear, there's hardly a Tory to be found."

"Maybe not. But there are plenty of them in Queens County, and plenty here in Westchester, just waiting for the right time to show themselves."

"That may be, Mr. Hendley, but there's army men, like Colonel Isaac Sears, who's trackin' 'em down. Every New York county's drawn up lists of those inimicals. We just come to warn you that you're on our list."

Hendley drew himself up, glowering. "Are you threatening

me, you jack-pudding? So I'm on a list! What do you intend to do about it, eh? Bring around the tar barrel? Try it, and you'll face the barrel-end of my musket."

"We ain't threatenin' the tar mop," Daniel said placatingly. "We on the Fordham committee don't hold with tarring, but—"

"No," Jotham cut in sourly, "Nate Cluett talked 'em all out of it."

Daniel gave his friend another jab with his elbow. "As I was sayin', we don't hold with tarrin' but that ain't sayin' you ain't in danger. Do you want to be taken into custody by the army an' brought before the Provincial Congress fer questioning?"

"Let them take me! I'll give them as good as I get. And just you wait! The wind will change again. When General Howe gets here, the shoe will be on the other foot. You know who'll be on a list then!"

"I wouldn't bet my neck on it, if I was you," Jotham said belligerently.

Hendley swung around on his crutches to Jotham with such a fierce glare that the heavyset fellow took a step back. "Don't you come to my house and tell me what to bet my neck on!" he snarled. "Just take yourself out of here!"

"Papa," Patience put in gently, noting that her father's color was becoming dangerously high, "no need to lose your temper."

"No need at all," Daniel agreed.

"Humph!" In an attempt to calm himself, Hendley refrained from saying more.

Daniel tried once more to accomplish his aim. "You mustn't pay mind to Joth," he said, holding out a sheet of paper on which the pledge was printed. "He didn't mean nothin'. Just take this an' look it over. Think about it, is all we ask right now."

The sight of the printed pledge was Hendley's last straw. He struck at the paper so hard it flew out of Daniel's outstretched hand. "Out, do you hear!" the crippled man shouted, raising one crutch and brandishing it at the visitors. "Take your blasted oath and go! Out of my house!"

To get out of the way of the swinging crutch, Daniel and Jotham backed out of the room. With Hendley hobbling in pursuit, they turned and made quickly for the front door. Once safely outside, however, Daniel looked back. "This ain't over yet, Peter Hendley, not by a long shot," he yelled.

This was more Jotham's style. "You ain't seen the last of us!" he chimed in loudly.

"Go and be damned!" Hendley shouted from his stance in the doorway.

Patience came up behind him and touched his arm. "Papa, come back in—" she began. But at that moment the sound of horses' hooves drew all their eyes to the bottom of the drive, where an elegant black chaise drawn by four horses was just turning in. Daniel and Jotham peered at it as it trundled past them, but, unable to see inside, they went on their way.

The carriage drew to a stop in front of the door. The coachman jumped down from the box and ran quickly around to open the door, but the passenger, not waiting to be handed down, had already thrown it open. Out stepped a woman dressed in exquisite black silks and a veiled bonnet trimmed with plumes. She lifted her skirts just enough to reveal a pair of small feet shod in silver-buckled slippers and ran with eager grace toward the stairs. At the sight of the two figures in the doorway, however, her step faltered, and one gloved hand flew to her bosom. Then, with hands that shook, she threw back her veil and favored the two onlookers with a tremulous smile.

Patience and her father stared at the visitor blankly for a moment. Then Patience gasped. "Babs!" she cried, flying down the steps. "It's *Babs!*"

Barbara, tears flowing down her cheeks, opened her arms to her sister's embrace. "Oh, Patience," she wept on her sister's shoulder, "I've missed you so!"

They clutched each other tightly for a long while. Then Patience stepped aside to permit her sister to make her second greeting. Barbara slowly mounted the stairs. "Hello, Papa," she said softly, trying to accustom her eyes to the grizzled, crippled, aged man who was her father.

Peter Hendley submitted to her embrace but said nothing.

"Are you still angry at me?" Babs asked, wiping her cheeks with a gloved finger. "Well, whether you are or not, I am so very glad to see you."

"Let's not stand here in the doorway where the coachman can hear our private conversation," he said gruffly. "You'd better come in."

The two sisters, hands clasped, followed their father to the front room. "Where's Benjy?" Barbara asked eagerly. "He must be quite the man by this time."

"He's run off," her father said, "like his sister. Perhaps a tendency to running away is an inherited trait."

Babs threw Patience a questioning glance, but this was a subject Patience did not wish to dwell on. "Babs, my dearest, what a lovely woman you've become!" she said, partly to change the subject and partly to express her glowing admiration. "You're so very beautiful and stylish! I'm quite overcome."

As Barbara removed her bonnet, Patience stared at her sister in amazement, taking in her severe coiffure (Barbara's wild hair was almost unrecognizable pulled back that way in a tight bun), her face in which the girlishness had vanished, replaced by a lean, womanly strength, and her new, confident carriage. Even Barbara's clothes seemed to have acquired a new dignity. They were subdued, yet stylish. Though the unremitting black of her gown was somber, the darkness was relieved by the lace ruffles that fell from the cuffs of her wide sleeves, by the beautifully intricate embroidery of her stomacher, and by an exquisite diamond and emerald brooch that pinned together the halves of her fluted collar. Awestruck, Patience drew her sister down beside her on the settee. "But do tell me, you magnificent creature, is wearing black in the afternoon the fashion in London these days?"

"No." Babs lowered her eyes. "I'm in mourning, you see. Jack died a couple of months ago." She looked over at her impassive father and smiled sadly. "Your daughter is a widow, Papa, before you even learned to know her as a wife."

"Oh, my dear!" Patience enveloped her sister in another embrace. "I'm so sorry."

Hendley showed no emotion. "So you're now a widow. I suppose that means you want to come back here to live," he said with a tiny touch of satisfaction.

"No, Papa. I knew you wouldn't want me back after . . . after all I've done. I've taken a house in New York."

"Oh, Babs," Patience groaned, *"no!"*

"It's all right, my love," Babs said, pressing her sister's hand. "Sir Matthew, Jack's father, saw to it that I was awarded a quite adequate competence. I've rented a sumptuous town house. I shall manage very well."

"Then I'll leave you to gossip about competences and town houses," Hendley said coldly, pulling himself to his feet. "I shall retire to my room."

Barbara jumped to her feet in disappointment. "But, Papa, I've hardly seen you. I can only remain here for an hour or so if I'm to get back to the city before dark. Can't you stay?"

"I've already had too much excitement for one day." Without another word or a nod of his head, he hobbled out of the room.

Barbara stared after him. "He's greatly aged," she murmured sadly, "but in many ways he hasn't changed at all."

"But you have," Patience said, shaking her head in wonder. "I hardly know you. Sit down, Babs, and tell me what has changed my willful, spoiled, wild little sister into this resolute, self-possessed woman before me."

The hour was spent catching up. They spoke about Benjy, about their father's illness, about the return of Lord Orgill, and, tearfully, about Sally and Aaron. But most of all, they talked about Barbara's marriage and its tragic ending. The account left Patience with a real admiration for her sister's maturity in dealing with her fate. "I suppose," she sighed as Barbara rose to leave, "that you'll be going back to London soon."

"Back to London? Never!" Barbara picked up her discarded bonnet and set it firmly atop her neatly bound hair. "I hate it there. I tell you, Patience, one never feels so American as when one stands on foreign soil. You won't approve of me when I admit to you that I've become an intractable Whig, but that's the truth of it. I want nothing less than complete independence for the colonies. A rebel to the core. So there!" She threw her sister a mischievous glance from under the brim of her ostentatiously plumed hat. "Have I completely lost your esteem by this admission?"

Patience took her sister's arm. "That look was my first reminder of the Babs I used to know," she laughed as they strolled to the door. "No, you haven't lost my esteem, my dear. I believe I'm becoming a rebel myself."

Barbara stopped short. "No! Not Mistress Patience Hendley, the Tory spinster of Spuyten Duyvil!" she exclaimed. "Whatever happened to change your mind?"

"Oh, many, many things. But the final straw, I think, was what's happened to Aaron and Sally."

"Yes, I can see how that would change you."

"It's made me question everything Papa stands for. You have no idea how I itch to act on this urge I feel toward rebellion. My mind teems with schemes."

"What sorts of schemes?"

"Mostly schemes to rescue Sally." Her eyes darkened with the agony she could not shake. "I can't really concentrate on anything else until I find her." They went down the front steps to the carriage, where the waiting coachman jumped to attention.

"How can you possibly find her?" Babs asked. Though she recognized her sister's pain, she did not think it sensible to dwell on a situation that had no solution.

"I think I can discover where she is, for I know the name of the agent who sold her," Patience explained, "but I don't know how to find the money to buy her."

Barbara's face brightened. "But you have *me* now, you idiot."

"You? How—?"

"I told you I have a competence."

"Yes, but we're speaking of . . . oh, perhaps as much as two hundred pounds!"

"Leave it to me," Barbara said with a smile. "Come to me in the city, as soon as you can get away." She threw her arms about her sister and gurgled happily. "Oh, Patience, how lovely it will be to scheme together!" And she jumped up into her carriage and waved goodbye.

Meanwhile, hiding behind the curtain of his window, Peter Hendley saw his daughter climb into the carriage. Another leave-taking. Another offspring disappearing into the distance. The words Babs had said to him an hour ago—*I knew you wouldn't want me back*—still rang in his ears. He couldn't imagine how she could believe that. How was it, he asked himself bitterly, that one's own children always thought the worst of their parents? As he watched the chaise trundle off down the drive, he forced himself to clench and unclench his left fist, an action that always brought sharp pain. But neither the pain nor the tight grip of the fist could keep his shoulders from shaking with the sobs he would never, never permit to escape from his chest.

Fifty-two

Tom was on digging detail when the fight broke out. Since digging footings for fortifications for New York City was strenuous but not grueling work, and since the weather was comfortably cool for April, the men had been in good spirits, so the fight—a loud and bitter brawl—suprised him.

New York City had become a rebel stronghold. Because Tom's regiment was quartered in the city, with nothing to do until General Howe made his move, every man in the regiment—and in the other regiments as well—was assigned to assist with the construction of fortifications. But the soldiers were not the only men involved in the task; from the middle of March onward, by order of General Washington, all able-bodied civilian men of New York City, from the rich and wellborn to their slaves and redemptioners, were required to spend every third day assisting in digging trenches and fortifications at strategic places throughout Manhattan Island to protect the City of New York from attack. It was known that General Howe had left Boston with all his army and that New York was his destination. New Yorkers were, for once, united in their conviction that the city be defended at all costs.

That was why fisticuffs and arguments were not commonplace among the workers on the ramparts. Some of the wealthy citizens (those whose hearts were not with the cause of freedom) could pay unemployed laborers to substitute for them on the work detail, but many others—even those who had not wielded a pickax or shovel in their lives—took their places on the work-teams and performed their labors in fine spirit, proving to be a source of inspiration and good fellowship. Despite differences in class and station, the men, understanding that they labored equally toward a common goal, were ordinarily quite congenial.

This customary congeniality was the reason Tom was surprised at the fierce fistfight that broke out between two of the diggers in his section. And he was even more surprised by the number of men who crowded round the fighters, shouting and taunting and urging them on. For a few minutes he merely stood with the watchers and observed the fighters trade blows. One of the combatants was a soldier in his own company, a short but cocky young buckskin named Nick Brewster. The other was a thin, middle-aged, half-bald civilian wearing clothes that were much too fine for this sort of work. Tom surmised that he was one of those who could have bought a substitute if he'd wanted to. Tom had the impression that he was a sincere, good-hearted fellow, but he was not nearly as handy with his fists as Brewster. Right now the civilian was getting the worst of the battle—his right eye was swelling and his nose was dripping blood.

Tom became more and more uncomfortable as the observers continued to goad the fighters, working them into a frenzy. He hoped an officer would come along and stop the brawl. As a matter of fact, an officer did come along, but he paused on the other side of the road, keeping his distance and merely observing the scene. Neither the combatants nor the onlookers noticed him.

Nick Brewster, sensing his pugilistic superiority, landed a punch on the older man's jaw that sent him tottering to his knees. The civilian, humiliated to desperation, snatched up his shovel and raised it with the obvious intention of swinging it at Brewster's head. At this point Tom deemed it time to intervene. "Hold off there!" he yelled, breaking through the crowd and grasping the civilian's raised arm in a tight grip.

"Damn you, mind your own affairs," the civilian cursed at Tom as he struggled to free his arm. "I'm going to split his head open, the foul-mouthed jack-pudding!

"Try it!" Nick Brewster retorted belligerently. "You bloody macaroni! We can do without you whifflin' about pretendin' to work."

"Stow it, Brewster!" Tom snapped. "This fellow's been working as hard as anyone."

"Damn right!" the civilian muttered, relieved that the soldier holding him back was nevertheless taking his side. "That deuced little pimp's been riding me like that ever since we started this morning. I've had a bellyful of him."

"You ain't heard the half," Nick Brewster sneered, hopping about like a boxer and taking unfair advantage of his opponent's constraint by repeatedly swiping at his chin.

"Someone hold that fool down!" Tom ordered. "Let's stop this nonsense and see if we can make peace here."

Two soldiers, recognizing a tone of command when they heard it, came forward and caught hold of Nick Brewster's arms. With a quick twist, they pinned his arms behind his back and held him fast. The civilian, as soon as he saw his opponent imprisoned, lowered his shovel. Tom released his hold on the man and patted his shoulder comfortingly. "If you have a handkerchief, friend, now's the time to use it. You don't want that fine neckband of yours to be bloodied."

The fellow nodded. "Thanks," he said, obediently mopping at his nose.

"Look," Tom suggested to him, "there's no law saying you have to work side by side with this fellow. Why don't you take your shovel and join the men down there on the other side? And you, Brewster, can stay here beside me. If you must rattle your tongue spitting out insults, spit them at me."

The watchers laughed and began to disperse. Brewster, assuring his captors that he was now calm, was released. And the civilian, throwing a last, fulminating look at his tormentor, walked away to the lower rampart. Everyone returned to work.

The officer who'd been watching at a distance now crossed

the road and approached Tom. "I say, fellow," he said, tapping Tom on the shoulder, "are you in Ritzema's regiment?"

Tom turned round. "Yes, sir, D comp—" But his voice failed him, for the officer was frighteningly familiar. It was Henryk Bogaerde. In the two years since Tom had last seen him, Bogaerde had changed greatly—adolescent plumpness had become muscular manliness—but not so greatly that Tom didn't recognize him at once. And if he could recognize Bogaerde, Bogaerde could recognize him. This encounter would surely mean recapture. Tom could almost feel the shackles being locked around his ankles.

Henryk Bogaerde did recognize him. "Good Lord," he chortled in sincere delight, "it's Hendley's Tom. Tom Morrison, isn't it?"

"Damnation!" Tom cursed. "Of all the blasted luck."

Henryk's eyebrows rose. "You don't sound glad to see me," he said, half amused and half puzzled. "You do recognize me, don't you?"

"Oh, yes, Captain I remember you quite well."

"But from your tone, one would think I'd done you ill. I haven't trod on your toes in the past, have I?"

"No, of course not. There's nothing personal in my want of warmth at seeing you again. In fact, if you were to promise to wait a few days before telling Hendley you saw me, I'd be very happy to give you the warmest greeting you've ever received."

Bogaerde eyed him in utter confusion. "Good God, fellow, why would I tell Hendley *anything* about you?"

"You must know I'm an escaped indenturer. Your sort usually believes the proper punishment for runaway redemptioners is prison."

"My sort? I'm an American army officer, not a blasted bounty broker. Besides, even if I wanted you caught, I couldn't do anything about it. You can't be taken while you're in the army. Didn't you know that?"

Tom's brows knit. "I don't like to contradict an officer, Captain Bogaerde, but you're quite wrong. I myself saw a line of shackled indenturers being marched off to jail, every one of whom had been plucked from Colonel Wooster's Connecticut regiment."

"Did you indeed? And when was that? A year ago, I'd wager."

"Yes, I suppose it was," Tom admitted, a feeling of hope surging up in his chest for no discernable reason. "Why—?"

"Because the law's been changed. Any indenturer enlisted in the Continental Army is immune from arrest."

Tom could only gape. Could it be true, he wondered? Had his worst, most constant fear been groundless? "That can't be so," he argued stubbornly, afraid to let himself believe what Bogaerde was saying.

"Of course it's true. I don't know how you can have remained ignorant of it. The army's become the safest place for an indentured man to run. Why, just the other day Captain Roosevelt of the First New York Militia swore in a redemptioner just *minutes* before his pursuer—a bounty man named Leary—caught up with him. There they were, runaway and bounty broker, as close to one another as you and I, and Leary couldn't *touch* him! So what have you to say to that?"

Tom felt as if a weight had been lifted from his chest. He grasped Captain Bogaerde's hand and shook it with hearty enthusiasm. "I'd say that I'm *very* glad to see you, Henryk Bogaerde."

Henryk laughed. "You ought to be. I came over here because I saw how you handled that fight just now. I wanted to compliment you . . . and to make you an offer." He squinted at Tom curiously. "How is it you're not an officer, Tom? You used to drill the Fordham militia, if memory serves. That alone might have qualified you—"

"You should guess the answer to that. I was afraid to be recognized. I thought that being in the ranks was my best hiding place."

"Well, now you know it's not necessary. My company happens to be short a lieutenant. What would you say to my recommending a field promotion for you?"

Tom's head was swimming. "I . . . hardly know what to say," he muttered. This was too much good luck to grasp at once. It made him wary. Good luck, in his experience, was always followed by bad.

Captain Bogaerde smiled serenely. "Lieutenant Thomas Morrison. How does that sound to you?"

Tom had to smile back. "Like music. It sounds like music."

Fifty-three

Barbara left her house on Cortland Street, opened her frilled parasol and walked briskly along the cobbled street. She crossed Broadway and turned down Maiden Lane to the east. Her mood was as bright as the April sunshine, full of warmth and the promise of spring's renewal. Her step was light, and she twirled her parasol gaily until it occurred to her that it was unseemly for a widow to dance down the street like a girl. She slowed her step, berating herself for feeling so cheerful—after all, it had been only five months since Jack's death.

But one can't force one's spirit to grieve forever, she rationalized in her mind. *One's spirits are often beyond the control of the will.* Since her return from England, her wounded soul had been steadily healing. All the weights that had oppressed her in England had been lifted from her shoulders. Here in America, living by herself in her own home, she was for the first time in her life her own mistress. She had no father to disapprove of her, no mother-in-law to despise her. She'd never before been able to come and go as she pleased, with no one to judge her, no one to require her attention or demand her company. *Jack, forgive me,* she murmured to herself. *I truly loved you and will always miss you, but I cannot deny that it is wonderful to be so free.*

With her conscience thus assuaged, she put her feelings of guilt aside and looked about her with interest. The city was much changed since that icy day when she'd come to visit the New York Bogaerdes. The streets were still as busy, attractive and prosperous as they'd been then, but now she could see signs that the inhabitants had become fearful of the possibility of devastation in this time of war. Many of the larger houses were boarded up; the owners had shut their city dwellings and run off to their country houses on Long Island or in Westchester. And there were now several British battleships in the harbor—like the *Asia*, with its sixty-four guns—posing a constant threat. The *Asia* had already fired on the city twice, as a warning during times of civil disorder. If the British ever decided on an all-out attack, the *Asia* alone could blow the city to smithereens.

Danger to New York could come from the American side, too. There had been rumors of a plan by the Continentals to burn the city to the ground if the American army had to surrender it to the British. New York was very vulnerable to disaster, and everyone who lived there was aware of it.

But the New Yorkers who remained in their homes (and there were many more of them than of runaways) were becoming accustomed to the threat; they went about their business with the same vitality as if this were a time of peace. The streets teemed with humanity—blue-coated soldiers, ladies with children, laborers, black men, and even a few wealthy citizens decked out in finery.

As Barbara moved east, the character of the street changed, becoming more commercial than residential. She'd never walked so far east before, and she was surprised by the bustle of commerce. This was where many of the city's shops were located. The vivid assortment of shops within this small area included a bakery, a haberdashery, a milliner's, a stationer's, a livery stable, a saddlery and at least four taverns. Carts and carriages fought their way through streets crowded with humanity. And down at the bottom of the street, at the East River, she could see a group of men digging fortifications. There was nothing unusual about that. Fortifications were being dug up and down the island of Manhattan. On General Washington's orders, the city was putting up defenses along both the east and the west side. Barbara found it all terribly exciting. New York was preparing itself for a battle, and the fact that she might actually become a witness to it was both frightening and exhilarating.

But she had not come out today merely for sightseeing. She was looking for the shop of a Mr. Vernon, silversmith and jeweler. She'd been told he might be persuaded to buy her diamond and emerald brooch. Barbara was not certain of its value, but if the man offered her two hundred English pounds (or its equivalent in New York dollars at the rate of three dollars per pound), she would sell it . . . for Patience's sake, and Sally's.

She was busily looking at all the wooden signs in order to locate the silversmith's shop when a passing soldier stopped short and stared at her. "Babs?" he asked in astonishment.

She lowered her parasol and looked at the speaker blankly. The soldier was of average height and unspectacular appearance except that he carried himself with the proud bearing of an officer. He was neat and trim in his buff and blue coat with its gleaming buttons and crossed straps, but his tricorn shadowed his face. It was not until he removed it that she recognized him. "*Henryk!*" she gasped. "Is it *you?*"

"Captain Henry Bogaerde now," he grinned, making her a smartly-military bow, "though I'm still Henryk at home. Damme if this isn't my week to come face-to-face with old friends! Just a few days ago I met—but that's neither here nor there. What's more interesting is what you are doing *here,* Babs! I was told you were in England!"

"I was. But I'm home now, and glad of it. Henryk Bogaerde, look at you! So trim and military . . . and in *rebel* uniform! How did this happen? Your father must be livid."

"No, not at all. My father has always been a Separatist, and so have I. In the old days, I tried to give you hints of it, but you never paid me any heed."

"Well, no one could doubt your position now." She smiled up at him with approving warmth. "Really, Henryk—or should I say Captain Henry?—you are most marvelously changed. You've quite taken my breath away!"

"While you, Babs, are as lovely as always." His words were those of an insincere, if practiced, rake, but his eyes roamed over her with a touch of the old admiration. All at once, however, he became aware of her black gown, and his face fell. "But are you in mourning?" he asked in quick sympathy. "Don't tell me your *father—?*"

She shook her head. "My husband."

"Pilkington? Good God!" He gaped at her, knowing neither what to say or what to feel. "I *am* sorry," he managed after an awkward moment.

"Thank you," she said.

Henryk bit his underlip, unable to think of anything else to say. Barbara couldn't help noticing that a slight flush suffused his cheeks. What was he thinking that caused his embarrassment, she wondered? Was he realizing that she was now a free woman, again available for his attentions? That thought now having occurred to *her,* she felt her color rising, too. Not that she was at all interested in being courted. Love and courtship and wedlock had brought her enough pain to last a lifetime. She was not in the least eager to endure that pain again.

To end the uncomfortable silence, Barbara smiled and held out her hand. "Well, I see that the silversmith I've been searching out is just down the street, so I must be off. It was good to see you, Henryk. I would ask you to remember me to your family, but I suppose they would not take kindly to greetings from me. I'm glad that you, at least, do not still hold me in contempt."

Henryk immediately recovered from his abstraction. "I never did," he said with convincing sincerity. He kissed her hand and made a quick bow. "Good-bye, Babs. It was good to see you, too."

They walked a few steps in opposite directions. Then Henryk stopped and turned. "Babs?"

She looked back over her shoulder. "Yes?"

"May I call on you one day soon?"

"Yes, of course," she replied promptly, and with a wave she continued on her way. But with each step she felt a stronger and stronger twinge of guilt. Perhaps she'd agreed to his request too quickly. What had he meant by calling on her? Was he merely making a polite request for a casual visit, or did he mean something more? Could he be asking permission to *woo* her? That's what a man calling on a woman usually meant. *But he couldn't be,* she assured herself, for he'd plainly seen that she was still in widow's weeds.

Besides, she told herself after another moment's reflection, *he doesn't know my address. He can't call on me even if he wanted to.* She sighed in relief as she entered the establishment of John Vernon, silversmith, and turned her mind to her business. Her dealings with Mr. Vernon were a good deal more pressing than the intentions of Captain Henry Bogaerde, whatever those intentions might be.

Fifty-four

Six weeks later, Patience and Barbara sat disconsolately side by side on the driver's seat of the Hendley landaulet as the Paulus Hook ferry carried them, horses and all, across the Hudson from New Jersey. It was midafternoon. Although a May-bright sun sprinkled the ripples of the Hudson with glints of gold and a refreshing breeze blew across the water from the west, the two women were too depressed to take pleasure in their surroundings.

On the New York side, the ferry slip was situated at the top of Cortland Street, the very street on which Barbara lived. Patience had only to drive off the pier and over the cobbles for a few dozen yards before pulling the horses to a stop before Barbara's door. Once there, she passed a weary hand over her brow. Barbara took notice of the pathetic gesture and placed a light, comforting hand on Patience's shoulder. "Stay with me tonight," she begged. "I can't bear to think of you driving back to Spuyten Duyvil all alone, especially today, when you're so blue-deviled."

"I'll be just as blue-deviled tomorrow," Patience sighed. "I must get back. I've already been away for four days. As it is, I'll be hard-pressed to explain this long absence to Papa."

"Don't explain it!" Barbara said angrily. "It's all his fault in the first place."

"There's no gain in blaming him. Papa is what he is." She took her sister's hand affectionately. "But you, Babs! How can you have changed so much and Papa not at all? You've made me so proud! Such a wonderful support you've been to me. I couldn't have taken a step without you. I hope you know how grateful I am."

"I know. But what good has it all been? After all we've done, after more than a month of scheming and trying, to have it end like this . . ."

Patience shut her eyes in pain. It was all true. After all their effort, the search for Sally had come to naught. It had taken half of April and all of May to accomplish nothing. Yet the prospects had seemed so promising at first, especially when Babs had sold her brooch for such a good price and they'd managed to find Black Hawk Barlow (although that had not been easy—if Henryk Bogaerde hadn't come to Spuyten Duyvil looking for Babs, and if he hadn't volunteered to help them in their search, they might never have found him). A simple bribe had loosened Barlow's tongue; he told them that Sally had been sold to a Lemuel Peters in Trenton, New Jersey. All they had to do then, they thought, was to drive to Trenton and buy her back.

With that goal before her, Patience told Papa she was going to spend a few days with Barbara in New York. Firmly ignoring his obvious disapproval of her "jaunting about unescorted" and leaving him alone, she ordered Chester to ready the landaulet. "Beatie is as capable of seeing to your needs as I am," she told her father, the excitement of rebellion bubbling in her veins. "You'll hardly notice I'm gone."

In New York she took Babs up, and the two drove all the way to Trenton in a state of elation, laughing and joking and feeling closer than they'd ever felt before. But when they arrived at the Peters homestead, they were told that Sally had been "traded" again. Neither their pleas, their tears, nor their offers of bribes had persuaded Mr. Peters or anyone else on the property to give them additional information.

The return from Trenton had been a sad, silent journey. It was only now, when they were about to part, that they felt compelled to speak. "Here, Babs, take back your money," Patience said, thrusting her reticule into her sister's hand. "Perhaps the silver-smith will sell the brooch back to you."

But Barbara shook her head and dropped the reticule back into Patience's lap. "No, keep it. Please. Something may yet come to pass to lead you . . ." But she knew that there was little hope of that. "I don't want the brooch anyway," she finished lamely.

Patience looked down at the little drawstring bag with a small, wan smile. "You *have* changed, Babs. 'Tis astounding! Do you remember Henryk's ruby ring? You could hardly bear to give it up. And it wasn't half as lovely as your brooch."

"I was such a fool in those days! As if such fripperies as rings and brooches mean anything, or make a difference in one's life."

"Your brooch might have made a difference to Sally," Patience said, her throat tight with heartbreak.

They sat in silence for a moment more. Then, knowing that the time for parting could no longer be postponed, Barbara threw her arms about her sister and held her close. "Perhaps she's in a good place, where they'll be kind to her," she whispered, snatching at a last hope.

"I shall pray so," Patience said, but her voice was too shaken with despair to project conviction.

Fifty-five

The long journey home from New York City to Spuyten Duyvil did nothing to ease Patience's despair. It was well past nightfall when she turned the carriage into the drive. Weary to the bone, and as low in her spirits as she'd ever been in her life, she was ill-prepared to face another blow. But the blows of life come when they will, and she came face to face with another one as soon as she caught a glimpse of the house. "Oh, God in heaven, no!" she cried aloud at the scene before her.

The front lawn was alive with movement, made frighteningly sinister by the flare of torches. There seemed to be six or seven bobbing about. The sight filled her with terror, for she knew who carried them. The Fordham Committee of Safety had come for her father!

She whipped up the horses and wheeled up the drive at dangerous speed, not slowing down as the carriage neared the door. The torchbearers, who'd been preparing to block her way, had to jump aside. At the door, she pulled the horses to an abrupt halt and, without permitting herself a moment's hesitation, leaped from the carriage and ran quickly up the steps.

"Hold off," said a voice' in the darkness. "It's only Mistress Patience."

The front door was cautiously opened, and Beatie's head appeared. " 'Tis ye, missy, thank the Lord!" the little Scotswoman cried, stepping aside to make way for Patience. "Come in quick!"

Beatie shut the door as soon as Patience slipped inside. "Some of 'em's in the parlor," she whispered, "arguin' whether or no to break into yer da's room. An' Mr. Hendley, he's locked hisself in wi' a *musket!* Says he'll shoot the first one who tries t' get in his door!"

"Oh, Lord!" Patience put a hand to her breast to still the pounding in her heart. "Is there a tar barrel out there?"

"I dinna think so. Charley promised me he wouldna permit it."

Patience could only hope that Charley's word was good. With her knees shaking, she took a turn about the vestibule, trying to think. "Tell Charley to take a stand in the back hallway with a good, stout broomhandle and not to let anyone pass through to Papa's room," she said, taking off her bonnet, her eyes fixed on the parlor door. "I'll try to talk to the committee."

"But ma'am," Beatie said, biting her lip, "Charley's *wi'* the committee."

Patience winced. "Yes, of course. I wasn't thinking. Chester, then. Do you think you can slip out and get Chester?"

Beatie nodded and ran down the hall toward the kitchen. Patience threw her bonnet and reticule on the chest near the door, squared her shoulders and went into the parlor.

Five men stood together near the windows, conferring. Patience anticipated seeing Daniel Styles and Jotham Dillard, of course, and Beatie had warned her that Charley McNab would be with them, but she was surprised to see Samuel Peach, the innkeeper, and Nathaniel Cluett, whom she knew to be Tom's good friend. What were they doing with the three hotheads? And who were the rowdies marching about outside with torches?

She cleared her throat to let them know she was there. They turned to her at once. "Good evening, gentlemen," she said with all the calm she could muster. "Just what is going on here?"

Daniel Styles pulled off his hat. "We warned ye, Mistress Patience, months ago—"

Nathaniel Cluett came forward, hat in hand. "I tried to stop this, ma'am," he explained quietly, "but they're spoiling for a confrontation. Can't you convince your father to be reasonable? The oath only requires him to declare he'll do nothing to impede our cause. Is that too much to ask of him?"

"It's as good an offer as he'll ever get," Daniel put in.

Samuel Peach nodded in vigorous agreement. *"He who won't when he may, when he will shall have nay,"* he quoted in tones of dire foreboding.

Jotham Dillard groaned in disgust. "There goes Sam'l with his blasted proverbs."

"You all know perfectly well that my father will not sign an oath, " Patience said. "It is more than a matter of political conviction. His pride is at stake."

"We'll see how proud he is when we set fire to his office," Jotham said menacingly.

"Fire?" Patience paled, her terror increasing so greatly she could hardly maintain her facade of calm assurance. "You can't really intend to burn—!"

"Stop it, Joth!" Nate snapped. "We agreed to use reason, not threats and violence."

"Yes, let's try to reason," Patience said desperately. "Of what value is my father's signature on an oath? Words on a piece of paper. They wouldn't signify a change of heart. We all know that many—indeed, *most*—of those you've convinced to sign an oath would not honor their sworn words if circumstances should change. They'd deny the oath in the flick of an eye if the British took over the province."

"That *ain't so!*" Jotham shouted angrily.

"Your words, ma'am, are an affront to the honor of all the signers," Daniel declared.

"A man's word is his bond, as they say," Samuel added.

Patience turned to the innkeeper. "I can offer a saying, too, Mr. Peach. *Vows made in storms are forgotten in calms."*

"She got the best o' ye there, Sam'l," Charley McNab laughed.

"I told you it wouldn't be no use to reason with 'em," Jotham said sullenly. Then, in a burst of spirit, he waved his fist in the air in a gesture intended both as a threat to Patience and a provocation to goad the others to action. "We came here to get Hendley's oath or to *teach him a lesson,* so *let's do it!* If he won't sign—"

"Wouldn't you rather have a man state his feelings honestly than sign an oath dishonestly?" Patience asked, trying to delay them from following Jotham out the door.

Jotham had no patience left. "Honestly or not," he sneered, lowering his face so close to hers that she had to jump back, "if he won't sign, he pays the *price!*"

"What price?" came a voice from the doorway. "Tell me, Joth, are you going to hang the fellow all by yourself?"

Everyone turned. A gentleman in a crisp and gleaming uniform of an officer of the Continental Army was leaning on the doorjamb grinning at them.

"Tom!" Nate gasped. "Good God, it's Tom!"

The gentleman took off his jaunty cocked hat and bowed. "Lieutenant Thomas Morrison at your service."

Patience's breath caught in her throat, for he was indeed a sight to take one's breath away. Resplendent in his smart blue coat with its buff revers shining with rows of brass buttons, he was stalwart and elegant from the top of his head (his wild hair tied back with a neat black bow) to his sleek tan breeches that showed off a pair of shapely, muscled legs. He looked for all the world like a hero she'd conjured up out of the air . . . out of girlish dreams, out of loneliness, out of dire, desperate need. *He can't be real,* she thought. *He can't be.*

But he was evidently real enough to the others. "Tom Morrison, as I live and' breathe!" Daniel was exclaiming. "You've gone and joined up!"

"More'n just joined up!" Jotham chortled, so proud of his old friend that he'd forgotten his anger. "Damn me if he's not an *officer!*"

In a hubbub of excitement, the five men surrounded Tom, pumping his hand and clapping him on the shoulder and shouting their welcome. But over their shoulders, his eyes sought out Patience. The look he gave her was so warm and intimate and told her so clearly how he'd hungered for the sight of her that it was all she needed to melt away the dread and tension that a mere moment ago had threatened to overwhelm her. Everything in the world changed. In her stormy night, the clouds parted, and suddenly the stars were shining.

Tom took one look at her face, and the stars shone for him, too. He made a small, polite bow in her direction. "Can you fellows excuse me for one minute?" he asked the men surrounding him. "I must have a word with Mistress Hendley, if she'd be good enough to step outside. I'll be right back."

The men exchanged curious glances before moving aside to let Patience pass. Tom held the door for her. She did not look at him as she crossed over the threshold. Only after he'd closed the door and they stood alone together in the entryway did their eyes meet again.

They smiled at each other in awkward silence until Patience, in an impulsive act that came from a part of her being that had never before asserted itself, flung herself into his arms and kissed him fervently. He was so surprised he tottered back a step, but the surprise was not so great that he let her go. In fact it took hardly a breath before his arms enclosed her in an equally fervent embrace. They clung together—arms, lips, bodies pressing tightly to one another—until they both had to stop to breathe.

At that moment, shyness overcame her, and she tried to release herself from his hold, but Tom wouldn't let her go. " 'Tis a warmer greeting than I expected," he said softly. "Have I done anything to deserve it?"

She blushed. "I was hasty. It was . . . gratitude. I shouldn't refine on it too much if I were you."

"Shouldn't I?"

"Your friends are to blame," she babbled, trying to extricate herself from his arms. "They frightened me, you see . . . and I

was so grateful to see you back . . . and at the very moment you
were so urgently needed."

He tightened his hold on her and forced her to look up at him.
"Is that how you'd reward any stranger who'd interceded? You'd
fly into the arms of *anyone* who happened along?"

Too embarrassed to meet his gaze, she hid her face in the curve
of his shoulder. "Anyone in such a beautiful blue coat," she murmured against his chest.

He chuckled. "Is it not magnificent? A gift from Henryk
Bogaerde. I admit, ma'am, that I make an impressive appearance,
but I refuse to accept this coat as the cause of your bestowing
on me so . . . so *indecent* a kiss."

She gave a gurgling laugh. "It *was* indecent. But you see, I've
never before seen you in a coat that fits you. I was quite overcome."

He rubbed his cheek against her hair. "I will not believe," he
murmured, continuing the silly badinage just to be able to keep
holding her a little longer, "that my Patience would toss aside
her high principles of behavior merely for a coat."

"Your Patience?"

"I always think of you as mine. Despite the fact that you have
a husband. By the way, where is his lordship, your noble husband,
in this time of urgent need? Hiding in the attic?"

Her eyes fell. "On the governor's ship, with the other king's
men."

"And a good riddance. From what you admitted to me when
I left, I assume you concur in that sentiment. Is it presumptuous
of me?"

"No," she admitted bluntly, "no more than it was presumptuous of me to kiss you as I did."

"Oh, but that was very presumptuous!" He lifted her up in his
arms, swung her around in sheer joyousness and kissed her again.
"You've become shockingly daring, ma'am," he mocked as he
set her back on her feet.

"I blame your Mr. Paine," Patience laughed. "He has made a wild radical of me."

Tom's brows rose in surprise. "You received my parcel! Then Gideon found his way here after all?"

"Yes. I do thank you, Tom. Getting that book from you was a lovely surprise."

He was gazing at her with delight, but at her last word, his expression changed. "Speaking of surprises," he said, abruptly dropping his hold on her and eyeing her with a strange, unreadable expression, "there is a very great one waiting for you in the kitchen."

"A surprise? For *me?*"

"Yes. Do go at once."

"Now? But the committee—"

"Go along. I'll take care of the committee."

"Are you sure? Shouldn't I stay with you?"

He took hold of her shoulders, turned her around and pushed her in the direction of the kitchen. "I've held off too long already. Run!" he ordered.

She threw him one questioning look and then did as he bid her. As she hurried down the passageway, she wondered what on earth the surprise could be. Another parcel with another pamphlet? That seemed unlikely. But whatever it was, why had he left it in the kitchen? Why couldn't he have handed it to her himself?

The kitchen was dimly lit, the fire having been banked for the night. The only light came from a candle on the worktable. But it was light enough for Patience to see Beatie, who stood right inside the kitchen doorway looking wide-eyed and bemused. "Did Tom leave a parcel here for m—?" Patience asked. But she never finished, for her eye was caught by a movement near the fire. A woman had been sitting on the hearth . . . a woman who, at the sound of Patience's voice, was rising slowly to her feet.

Patience felt the ground lurch beneath her. "Oh, my God!" she cried, stumbling forward, her arms outspread. *"Sally!"*

Fifty-six

Sally, at Patience's insistence, was stretched out on the bed in Barbara's old room. Patience sat beside her, smoothing back her hair. "Oh, Sally, it's all white," she said sadly.

"Boun' to turn white soon or late," Sally said. "I don't min' it."

"I do. And I mind that you're so thin. Are you certain you won't have another bowl of pudding. I'll cover it with bonny-clabber just the way you like it."

"I be a'ready like to bust." Sally sighed contentedly and rubbed her stomach. "I couldn' take in one mo' mo'sel. An' don' be waitin' on me no more. 'Tain't fit."

"It's more than fit. And 'tis but for one night, since you insist that we must part again tomorrow." She looked down at the beloved black face and sighed. "Where will you go?"

"West. To fin' Aaron."

"Aaron?" Patience stared at her. She hadn't been able to bring up the subject of Aaron in the two short hours of their reunion. It had been the one shadow over her happiness. The mere sound of his name on Sally's lips was enough to set her trembling. "But Papa told me . . . I thought . . ." Her voice failed her. She could not say the words.

Sally sat up, her eyes searching Patience's face. "What is it, missy? What's achin' you?"

"Oh, God, Sally, I can barely stand to speak of it. Papa said he heard from the dreaful man who caught you that . . . that . . ."

Sally's eyes widened with understanding. "That Aaron be dead? Is that what's gnawin' you?" She took the trembling girl in her arms. "No, no! I didn' figure the tale be comin' back to you like that. Aaron ain't dead. I tole a lie to that slave-hunter man so he'd quit lookin' fo' him."

Patience blinked at Sally for a moment and then burst into tears of relief. "Oh, thank God!"

The two women clung together, Patience's sobs bringing tears to Sally's eyes, too. Finally Sally took herself in hand. "Stop it, missy!" she said, wiping her own eyes. "We be soakin' this pretty nightdress you give me."

Patience found it hard to take in so much good news. "Tell me," she asked, wiping her cheeks, "are you *sure* about Aaron?"

"Not Aaron. Dee. Dee Baker. I ain't heard nothin' of him these past months, but my boy has his wits, an' he has the writ to keep him safe. If he was dead I'd feel it . . . right in here."

"So you're going to search for him. But how? Where?"

"I ain't sure how, but I knows where. When we was together in Marblehead, we used to hear 'bout free Negras goin' west to the frontier, an' him and me, we'd talk 'bout one day goin' there, too. We'd make plans to follow the Mohawk trail. So that's where I'll fin' him." Her black eyes took on a shine that Patience had never seen in them before. "I tell you, Miss Patience, somewheres along the Mohawk river there be a buildin' with a sign— Dee Baker, Stable an' Forge."

"Oh, Sally, I pray it may be so!" Patience wiped her cheeks with the back of her hand and sighed. "I can hardly take it all in. Aaron *alive* . . . you *free* . . . with a writ of manumission that's not forged! And full of hopeful plans . . . it's more than I would let myself dream! And . . . *wait!* I just remembered—" She jumped to her feet and clasped Sally's hands in hers excitedly. "I even have six hundred and fifty New York dollars to help you in your search! You can hire a horse and wagon, and pay for lodgings with it. Here." And she removed the reticule from the pocket where she'd tucked it only a few hours earlier and pushed it into Sally's hand.

Sally stared at the plump little bag. "Oh, Lordy!" she breathed. "You *can't*—"

"Of course I can. It was *meant* for you. It's the money we intended to use to buy you from Mr. Peters. Come to think of it, Sally, how did Tom manage it? I know he must have learned from Hendryk Bogaerde where you were, but where did he find enough money to buy your freedom?"

Sally pressed her lips together. "I ain't s'posed t' say."

"Oh, dear." Patience brows knit in a worried frown. "That means he did something dreadful. Stole it or something."

"He didn' steal it, but it be somethin' dreadful enough." With her eyes fixed on the reticule, she took a deep breath. "May the Lord forgi' me for breakin' my word, but I has to. Tom, he trade two years of indenture fo' me."

Patience did not understand. "Traded an indenture?"

"He sign a paper. He gonna work fo' Mr. Peters after his army service end. I s'pose Mr. Peters figure two years of Tom's labor on his land is worth more'n what years I has lef' to work in his kitchen." She threw Patience a sudden grin. "See how these white hairs done some good? They make folks b'lieve I ain't got long to last."

Patience finally understood. Tom had enslaved himself anew just to do this wonderful thing for Sally . . . and for her. She sank down upon the bed, overwhelmed.

"Don' tell him I tole you all this, please," Sally begged.

"I won't."

Sally held out the reticule. "You take this, Miss Patience, an' buy his freedom back with it."

"No, you keep it. I'll buy his freedom somehow." She smiled wryly. "Perhaps Babs has some more jewelry to sell."

Later, after settling Sally comfortably in bed and promising to wake her before dawn (to assure that Peter Hendley would not catch a glimpse of her), Patience returned to the parlor. Neither

Tom nor the committee members were anywhere about. Nor was there a single torch flickering across the lawn. She strode quickly down the passage to her father's room and tapped on the door. "It's I, Papa. I'm back."

"I know it," Hendley said shortly. "I saw Chester taking away the carriage. Come in if you wish."

She found him sitting at the window, a blanket covering his legs and the musket lying across his knees. "Why aren't you abed, Papa?"

"I was making certain those miscreants are all gone. Idiots! They can't be coaxed to come up here to do a day's work, but they're here quick enough when they smell a chance to make trouble. Running up here full of shouts and threats and then slinking off with their tails between their legs! There's no understanding them. I wonder what drove them off. Did you say something to fright them, Patience?"

"I only told them that your honest refusal to sign the oath is preferable to a dishonest signature. Perhaps they saw the reasonableness of that."

"If they did, it's the first time they acknowledged *anything* reasonable."

"In any case, they've gone now, so you can give up this vigil and go to bed."

"Yes, I may as well. 'Tis late enough. Send McNab in to give me a hand, will you?"

"Yes, of course." She opened the door. "Good night, Papa."

"Good night," he said gruffly. Before she could close it behind her, however, he called her name.

She turned back. "Yes, Papa?"

"I'm glad you're back," he muttered, lowering his head so that she couldn't see his eyes. "I missed you."

She blinked at him, startled. He'd not said an affectionate word to her in months . . . nor she to him. But now, seeing him sitting there with his head bowed, aging and lonely, with the blanket covering his almost-useless legs, her heart went out to him. With

Sally safe upstairs, and Aaron alive, it was hard to keep hating him for what he'd done. She crossed the room, bent over him and planted a kiss on his temple. "I missed you, too, Papa," she said.

She walked back along the passageway and through the house without seeing another soul. She tried not to keep wondering where Tom had gone; she hated to think that he might have left without saying goodbye to her. She supposed he'd gone to spend the night at the inn with one of his wenches. She couldn't blame him if he had. A man had his needs, after all.

But she couldn't bear thinking of it. Instead, she tried to concentrate on finding Charley for her father. The kitchen was a likely place, but it, too, was deserted. Just as she was about to climb up to Beatie's room, Charley and Beatie both came in the kitchen door. "There you are," Patience greeted them. "I was looking for you, Charley. Papa needs you."

"We were seein' to Tom," Charley said, crossing quickly to the passage. "I'll go to Mr. Hendley now, but I'm nae lookin' forward to the dressdown he's like to gi' me."

"Dressdown?" Patience asked. "Why should he scold you? He doesn't know you're one of the committee."

"Fer certain sure he does." Charley did not pause, for he knew his master's impatience, but his voice floated back to them from the passageway. "No fool, your da."

Patience turned to Beatie. "What did he mean about seeing to Tom?"

"We made up the wee bed in Tom's old quarters. Tom said he wanted to sleep there. Fer old times, he said." Beatie's unreadable bird-like eyes flickered up to her mistress's face. "We dinna think ye'd mind."

"I don't mind," Patience said, trying to keep her eyes unreadable also. "Not at all."

Fifty-seven

Later that night, Patience sat at her dressing table brushing her hair. She was still dressed in the wrinkled traveling gown she'd worn on her trip to New Jersey. It was a stiff, dark blue eyesore of Kentin linen with a prim white tucker buttoned from waist to neck. It had no embellishments like bodice embroidery or jeweled buttons, nor had she put on a hip hoop that a more stylish woman would have worn to emphasize a small waist. Patience would have liked to change into something more becoming—her lilac silk, perhaps, with its neckline that showed her womanliness—but it was too late now. Tom would certainly notice so blatant a change. But one change she *would* make, no matter how blatant: she would go to him without the cap he so disliked. With her hair hanging loose, her attire might appear less repressively prim. Tonight, of all nights, she didn't wish to look prim.

When she was convinced that everyone was asleep, Patience stole out of the house and made for the stable. She carried a lantern shrouded with a piece of dark cloth so that only the smallest beam of light was permitted to escape to light her way. Although her step was eager, her mind was full of misgivings. *He will be asleep,* she warned herself. *He will be unclothed. He will look at me askance and think me unladylike, or even lewd. I should not be doing this. I should go back.*

Nevertheless, her feet carried her down the path and up the dark stairway to his door. A faint light shone from beneath it; he was not asleep. Before she could bring herself to rap on his door however, her courage failed her. She turned to flee back to her room, but as her foot touched the top stair she remembered Sally telling her that he had to leave before dawn to get back to his regiment on time. If she was to thank him properly for what he'd done, there was only tonight. She went back to his door and lifted her hand to knock.

Before her knuckles touched wood, however, the door flew open. Patience froze, startled, for it was not Tom but a woman standing in the doorway. The woman's face was turned away; she was looking back over her shoulder into the room. "If you must be such a *damned fool*—" she was saying.

Patience, completely taken aback, gasped.

The woman looked around. "And who might *you* be?" she demanded, placing her hands on her hips in a pose of aggressive hostility.

Patience felt the blood drain from her face. Though the light was dim, she recognized the woman—the young barmaid from the tavern, a woman called Freda. She couldn't help noticing that the creature's mop of curly hair, which had been pinned up high, was half tumbled down, and that the bodice of her dress was half unlaced. She could also see Tom, in his shirtsleeves, standing in the room beyond. He looked utterly dumbfounded.

"I might've knowed," the woman, Freda, was saying nastily. "It's Mistress Priss-face herself."

A hot flush surged up into Patience's cheeks. "I beg your p-pardon!" she stammered.

"Patience!" Tom took a hasty step toward the door.

But Patience, not only hideously embarrassed but hurt beyond words, could not bring herself to face him. "I . . . I only—that is, I didn't mean to—" she babbled as she gathered up her skirts, turned and fled. The lantern, still dangling from her fingers, swung wildly about, shedding its shroud and throwing crazy shafts of light from the rafters above to the ground below.

"Patience, *wait!"*

Though his voice was a desperate plea, she didn't answer. Her pulse was pounding in her ears. The sound was deafening, but over it she could hear his footsteps clambering down the stairs after her.

She ran out of the stable and down the path with such desperate speed that she was halfway to the kitchen garden before he caught up with her. "Please," he pleaded, catching hold of her arm, "it wasn't what it seemed. Let me explain."

"You've no need . . . to explain anything . . . to me," she said, her breast heaving from her exertion and the upheaval of her emotions. "I'm dreadfully . . . sorry I intruded."

"But you didn't intrude. I wasn't expecting her. It was *you* I—"

"Please! Don't say it!" She wrenched her arm from his hold. "Explanations will only humiliate me further."

"But I *must* say it. I never invited her. Someone else must have told her I was here."

"I don't want to hear this. You have every right to invite your . . . your friends."

He grasped her by the shoulders and pulled her around to face him. "But why would I invite *anyone* when I was expecting a visit from *you?*" he demanded.

She stiffened in his hold. "You were *expecting* me? How could you be? I wasn't sure myself if I should go to you."

He managed a smile. "In truth, it was more of a hope than an expectation."

She remained obstinately cold. "I believe it was neither one nor the other. You obviously had other things on your mind."

His smile died. "Damn it, woman, do you think I *lie?*" he demanded furiously. "I've never lied to you!"

Tears sprang unbidden from her eyes, but she blinked them away. She had to admit to herself that she'd come to his door with the intention of rewarding him in the same way that Freda had. The sight of Freda, tousled and uncouth, had dealt her a double blow: not only had it aroused a monstrous jealousy in her heart, it had degraded her own actions in her eyes. But Tom would never learn of her debased intentions, not if she could help it!

She looked up at him with her head pridefully high. "Please don't say anything more on this subject. It demeans us both. I assure you that I make no harsh judgment of your conduct. You are your own man now."

"No harsh judgments? Your every *word* is a harsh judgment!" he retorted. "And your thoughts even harsher."

Her knees trembled at the possibility that he could read her thoughts, but she kept her expression stern. "You cannot know my thoughts, much less judge them."

"Can't I? When your every word reveals that you believe I'd taken Freda to my bed?"

"My thoughts do not dwell on that at all! I have no interest in your doings with your Freda. My thoughts are occupied with . . . with the difficulty you've placed on me to do what I came to do—to express properly my gratitude for what you did for me today."

The change of subject bewildered him. "What are you talking about?"

"Sally, of course. Seeing her again . . . and seeing her *free* . . . 'twas like a miracle. I must thank you."

"You *must?*" He glowered down at her. " 'Tis a reluctant thanks."

"Not at all. If I sound reluctant, it's because you are holding me against my will."

He lifted his hands from her. "There. I free you, too."

She stepped away from him stiffly. "This awkward situation makes it difficult to express my gratitude. Yet I *am* deeply grateful. You performed *two* miraculous feats for me tonight. You dispersed the committee and their torchbearers, and you brought me Sally. That's why I blundered in on you. I came to . . . to thank you."

"No need to thank me," he muttered churlishly, unable to shake his anger. "Dispersing the committee was easy. I merely told them that you, the true head of the household, have recently and enthusiastically converted to our cause. I think that news made an impression. You've nothing more to fear from them. And as for Sally, I didn't free her for your sake. When I heard from Lieutenant Bogaerde that Sally'd been sold, I was determined to win her her freedom somehow. I did it partly to keep your father from a gloating triumph, but mostly because I knew how much Sally must have been suffering. She'd already tasted freedom, you see, and servitude is much more galling after one has had a taste of being free."

"Yes," she sighed sadly, painfully aware of the sacrifice he'd made of his own freedom, "it must be."

He dropped his eyes from her face. "I may as well be fully honest. I admit that I did seek her for your sake, too. I wanted to see the gladness in your eyes. And now, because of a stupid mischance, there is none."

"Nevertheless, 'twas the most wonderful gift I've ever been given. I shall be grateful to you for it all my life."

He grasped her shoulders in a cruel grip. "Blast it, Patience, I don't want your damned gratitude!"

"Well, Lieutenant Morrison, you have it whether you want it or not."

"Lieutenant Morrison? Is that what this foolish mixup has made of me—a distant acquaintance? Did I dream it or did you not, a mere four hours ago, throw yourself into my arms and kiss me?"

"Yes, I did . . . to my shame."

"There was nothing shameful in kissing me," he snapped. "What should shame you is *this*—this distrust of me."

Her head came up, her face tight with more hurt than anger. "Do you ask me to distrust my own *eyes?*" She thrust his hands from her and turned her back on him. "Dash it, I told you more than once I don't wish to speak of it!"

"But I do! I cannot meekly accept the change from the warmth of your earlier greeting to this empty offering you call gratitude."

"My gratitude is *not* empty!" she cried, wheeling around. "It is truly sincere. And as for my earlier greeting, that kiss was an error . . . no, it was a heinous *sin*. Perhaps what I saw tonight—what you call a foolish mixup—is the good Lord's way of reminding me of my transgressions."

Tom winced in pain. He was ever at a loss when she reminded him that their relationship was an offence against God. He had never suffered from religious guilt. He believed that the love he felt for her was purity itself. Whenever she reminded him that it was sinful by church law, he did not know how to respond.

He stepped back, defeated. The happiness that had glowed between them so short a time ago was now extinguished. Distrust had poisoned every feeling, even her gratitude. "Twas not the good Lord who brought Freda to my door," he muttered helplessly as she turned from him, "but Satan."

He watched her walk away, the gloom of night swallowing her up until all he could see was the light of her lantern. He too had had dreams that this night would bring her into his arms. As her light receded into the distance, his high hopes receded with it. He remained standing motionless in the path until he heard the kitchen door close and saw the light disappear from the kitchen window. Then he turned away and, kicking disconsolately at the small stones in his way, walked slowly back to the stable through the uncaring darkness.

Fifty-eight

On a hot evening early in July, Tom came into the barracks near the Common where his regiment was housed and fell upon his cot. He was dripping with sweat and weary to the bone after a long session of training new enlistees. The need to train new troops was constant; men were dropping out and new men enlisting every day. If all the regiments were as unstable as this one, Tom didn't know how General Washington could possibly fight his war. And now that the British Admiral Richard Howe's ships (one hundred and thirty of them, carrying his brother's army of more than twenty-five thousand men aboard) had finally been sighted approaching New York harbor, matters were becoming critical.

But even when matters were critical, a man needed his rest, so Tom stretched out his booted legs and shut his eyes. He was just drifting off to sleep when he heard someone call his name. He opened his eyes to find Henryk Bogaerde standing over him. "You've been invited to visit a lady," Henryk said, grinning down at him. "Get up, you lazy croaker, and come with me."

Tom's pulse began to race. "A *lady?* Not—?" But he stopped his tongue in time.

Henryk cocked his head and peered at Tom with curiosity. "What lady were you about to name? Speak up, fellow! Have you lost your heart to some female and not told me of it?"

Tom swung his legs over the side of the cot and sat up. "Not I. I'm no fribble dallying with women like some I know."

Henryk, in the act of pulling Tom to his feet, pushed him back down again. "Calling a fellow officer a fribble is grounds for a court martial."

"Are you going to tell me the lady's name," Tom demanded, foolishly hoping that Patience had miraculously proferred this strange invitation, "or do you have some reason to keep me in suspense?"

"No reason at all. It's Babs."

Tom's heart sank. "Have you been to see Mistress Barbara *again?*" he taunted to cover his disappointment. "That's the second time this week you've taken French leave. Do you never have work to do?"

"Why do you think I helped you win a commission?" Henryk retorted, throwing Tom his coat. "It makes things easier for me."

"I can't call on her in all my dirt," Tom objected, getting up.

"You are to come just as you are."

Tom shrugged and threw on his coat. "What on earth does your Babs want with me?"

"I wish she *were* my Babs," Henryk sighed with rueful sincerity. "She's been holding me at arm's length since I was a boy. As for what she wants with you, you'll have to wait and see. Have patience."

"Patience I'll never have," Tom muttered under his breath as he followed Henryk out the door.

They quickly covered the three city streets between the Common and Barbara's house. Their hostess was waiting for them in her small, modestly furnished drawing room. Tom bowed over her hand. "I hope there's nothing amiss at home," he said after the proper greetings were exchanged.

"No, no," Barbara assured him. "I visited Spuyten Duyvil only yesterday, and I found the household quite as usual. They are muddling through the summer as best they can without farm help. Do sit down, Tom. I have something for you"

She sat down beside him on the sofa and handed him an envelope, while Henryk perched on the arm of a wing chair opposite them and observed them with bright-eyed interest.

Tom looked suspiciously from one to the other and then opened the envelope. Inside were two documents, both torn in half. He caught his breath, because he recognized them at once. One, yellowed with age and crumbling at the edges, was the letter of indenture that he'd signed with Hendley, its expiration date extended three times and crossed out twice. The other was the new indenture he'd signed with Lemuel Peters of Trenton. "Good God!" he exclaimed, looking up at Barbara. "How on earth did these papers come to you? And why are they torn?"

"They're torn because they are no longer in effect. We would have burned them, but she . . . we . . . thought you should have the exquisite satisfaction of igniting them yourself and seeing them turn into ash."

The papers in his hand began to tremble. Tom could not keep them steady. Here, in this unexpected place, at this unexpected time, he found himself holding his freedom in his hand. "I don't understand," he mumbled in utter confusion. "How did you—?"

Barbara looked down at her hands folded in her lap. "We're not supposed to say."

"But you must tell me," Tom pleaded.

"Of course we must," Henryk agreed. "See here, Babs, you can't expect the man to believe he is truly free if he doesn't know how those papers were obtained."

"But we promised!" Babs exclaimed.

" 'Twas a foolish promise. Your sister is too modest."

Tom's head came up abruptly. "Is it Patience you speak of? What has *she* to do with—?"

"She has everything to do with it." Henryk leaned toward Tom eagerly. "She organized this entire campaign. First she stole—"

"Henryk!" Barbara cut in. "I don't think you should be revealing what we promised to keep hidden."

"Nonsense, Babs. It seems to me that your sister was *proud* of what she did; so why shouldn't Tom be told?"

Barbara, surrendering to temptation, joined Henryk in the delicious sin of spilling secrets one has sworn never to reveal. "Patience actually stole the indenture from Papa's drawer!" she said with a giggle.

"She justified that shocking act," Henryk laughed, "by explaining to us that stealing for a good cause was acceptable behavior for a rebel, which, she tells me, she has recently become."

"It was not really a crime," Barbara hastened to add in defense of her sister, "for everyone knows that the indenture agreement should have been surrendered to you long ago."

Tom could only stare at them speechlessly. That Patience had done this thing for him, especially after what had happened when he'd last seen her, was bewildering enough. But that was only the *beginning* of his confusion. "But . . . the new one I signed with Mr. Peters," he asked when at last he found his voice. "How on earth did you get that? How did you even *learn* about it?"

"Sally divulged your secret to Patience," Barbara said. "Now, don't be angry with Sally, Tom. She could not bear to keep silent. How could she carry your tremendous sacrifice on her conscience? And once Patience heard of it, she could not let the matter rest. As she explained to us, you would have had your freedom two years ago, if Papa hadn't cheated you of it. How could she—or any of us—permit you to fight for *our* freedom with the cloud of two more years of servitude hanging over your head?"

Tom was still bemused. "But . . . Mr. Peters would not have sold this paper for less than two hundred pounds!"

"We persuaded him to accept five hundred and eighty New York dollars," Henryk said with satisfaction. "And let me tell you, old man, raising that sum required a community effort. Fortunately there were several people quite eager to contribute to the Thomas Morrison Freedom Campaign."

"Sally, for one," Barbara said. "And I, of course. And Patience, who not only contributed a bracelet she had from Mama but also her precious Italian cameo."

"She also spoke to your friend Nathanial Cluett," Henryk went on proudly, "who took up a collection at the tavern. All your friends contributed handsomely."

"And, though Henryk will not wish me to divulge this," Barbara said, throwing Henryk a glowing look, "he made the most valuable contribution—an antique ruby ring."

Tom stared at them for a moment before covering his eyes with a shaking hand. He sat that way for several minutes. "I don't know what to say," he muttered when he was at last able to speak.

"You don't have to say anything," Barbara said, patting his shoulder affectionately. "But don't you want to burn these things?"

"We've made elaborate preparations for the ceremony," Henryk joked, producing a bowl and a candle from the hearth.

Barbara jumped up and, with appropriate solemnity, took a flint from the mantel and handed it to Tom. "I wish Patience could be here to see this," she said, "but for some mysterious reason she didn't want you to know she had a hand in this."

" 'Tis no mystery to me," Tom said, his eyes fixed on the torn papers in his hand.

Henryk and Babs exchanged looks but did not ask him to explain. After a moment, Henryk urged him to his feet. "Well, go on and *do* it!"

In a kind of daze, Tom lit the candle. Then, as he held the documents to the flame, the meaning of the occasion burst upon him in all its significance. Barbara's earlier words came back to him: *she . . . we . . . thought you should have the exquisite satisfaction of igniting them yourself and seeing them turn into ash.* His dear, beloved Patience! Who but she would have said those words? His heart overflowed with gratitude to all who had helped in this enterprise—Henryk and Babs and Nate and Sally and all the rest. But it was Patience who burst it apart. How strange it was that whenever he was most angry with her, she found a way to disarm him.

With a hand that was far from steady, he set the papers aflame, dropped them into the bowl and watched them burn. The satisfaction was more than exquisite. The same flame that curled and blackened the torn pages and reduced them to a little mound of ash licked away at the place in his soul that had been sickened by years of servitude . . . and burned it clean.

Fifty-nine

A week later, on the evening of July 9th, Tom's entire regiment assembled on the Common, which had been commandeered from the city for General Washington's army and was now being used as the parade grounds. Several other regiments had also gathered, making two brigades, and filling the square to its limit. They were forming to sound retreat, which was scheduled for six o'clock, half-an-hour earlier than the usual retreat, so every man in this assemblage knew that this was no ordinary affair.

Somehow, word was spreading among civilians, too, that this gathering portended something extraordinary. All around the Common, numbers of civilians, attracted by the stir, began to gather and fill the adjoining streets. Before the chimes of nearby church bells tolled six, there was no standing room left.

Promptly at six, General Washington and his aides rode into the square. Roll was called, and Tom and the other company officers shouted to their regimental commanders that all were present or accounted for. The men stood at attention while several routine announcements were made, and then the formation was ordered to stand at ease. One of General Washington's aides came forward and announced that he was about to read a declaration from the Continental Congress. This was greeted by a murmur of excitement from the crowd of civilians, but the soldiers remained silent. The aide began to read in the loudest voice he could raise:

> When in the course of human events, it becomes
> necessary for people to dissolve the political
> bands which have connected them with another . . .

An awed hush fell over the assembled crowd as they listened intently to every word. But long before the reader came to the words, "we mutually pledge to each other our Lives, our Fortunes and our sacred Honor," Tom knew what had happened: the Congress had made the final break with England. Independence had been officially declared at last. What would happen next depended on him, on the other men now standing there, on the grim-jawed general sitting erect on his horse in front of them, and on God above.

Sixty

By August, Benjy had been a bona fide soldier for seven months but had had not a day of excitement or elation. Though he'd been made a corporal (not an insignificant achievement for a seventeen-year-old), he'd experienced nothing in all that time but drilling and digging. What was worse, he hadn't gone anywhere. He'd spent the entire time digging redoubts along the Hudson—working his way north from Haerlem Heights to what they'd recently named Fort Washington, near the northern tip of Manhattan Island—in an area that was at most four miles from his home. "No one warned me," he often complained to his next in command, Sergeant Blake, "that war can be so great a bore."

But that feeling underwent an abrupt change at midday of August twenty-ninth. The company captain came walking along the line where the men, despite a heavy rain, were laboriously piling up stones to form an escarpment. Benjy at first assumed that the captain had come out to give encouragement to the men by getting wet along with them, but he soon realized that the captain had a more specific purpose, a purpose that had something to do with Benjy himself. As the boy watched, the captain paused to exchange words with Sergeant Blake, who nodded and pointed right at him. This act gave Benjy a twinge of apprehension, for he had no idea what the sergeant could possibly be saying about him.

The captain came directly over to him. "Hendley?"

Benjy saluted nervously. "Yes, sir."

"Sergeant Blake tells me that you've some experience sailing the Hudson. Is that true?"

"Yes, sir. My home is at Spuyten Duyvil, just north of the bridge. We have a farm there. In summer and fall, it was my task to sail our dory down to the city with the produce we harvested. Every week, in season."

"Your own dory?" the captain asked, his brows rising interestedly.

"My father's."

"I say! Do you suppose you could go home and borrow it?"

"Borrow it?" Benjy asked in surprise. "Papa's *dory?"*

"Yes, corporal, that's what I asked."

Benjy hesitated. Not only did the request bewilder him, but he didn't know how to respond. He knew that his father was not likely to grant him permission to spend a night under his roof, much less to borrow his boat.

The captain frowned. "This is not a casual request, corporal. General Heath had an urgent message from General Washington, requesting that he round up as many boats as possible to rendezvous in the East River at nightfall. They need everything that can navigate the river." He pulled a paper from the shelter of his coat and read from it. "Any flat-bottomed boat or craft using either oars or sails that is fit for transporting troops, Colonel Hutchinson writes."

"For transporting troops?"

"Yes, those are his words." The captain dabbed away the drops of rain that had flecked his letter and put it away. "Don't ask why. We weren't told. It's not necessary that we always understand our duty, only that we do it."

"Yes, sir," Benjy muttered, lowering his head awkwardly.

"Your father's boat fits the requirements, does it not?"

"Yes, sir . . . but . . ." His voice failed him.

The captain observed him thoughtfully for a moment, then shrugged and spoke more kindly. "I suspect the need for boats has something to do with the battle on Long Island. There must be trouble there. 'Tis known that fully half our numbers were sent to face the enemy at Brooklyn Heights. Perhaps they need to ferry in additional troops from New Jersey. Whatever the purpose, the message said the need is urgent. If you could borrow your father's boat and sail it down, Hendley, I believe it would be a great help to General Washington."

Benjy lifted his head, his jaw set with determination. "Yes, sir," he said, his heart beginning to pound. "I'll do it. When, sir?"

"Right away. You've got to get it to the East River by dark."

"Then, with your permission, sir, I'll take off at once."

The captain nodded. "Good lad! Go along. I'll tell the sergeant not to expect you at roll call."

Benjy, splashing off through the puddles at a run, caught a glimpse of Sergeant Blake looking after him enviously. He almost laughed aloud in glee. He was leaving the shovels and the mud behind. The sergeant and the rest of his company would have to deal with those blasted earthworks without him. He was going into action. Not actually *in* a battle, perhaps, but close to it.

While he hurried over the three miles to the King's Bridge, he made his plans. He could not borrow the boat, he knew that. He couldn't even ask. His father would have an attack of apoplexy at the mere sight of him in rebel uniform! He would have to stay completely clear of the house, that much was certain. He would take the boat in the only way possible—by stealth.

Stealing it, he realized, might not be easy. He had to pray that no one would be lurking about near the landing. If Chester and the other hands were all busy elsewhere—which was very likely—all he'd have to do would be to untie it and sail off.

One of the guards at the bridge was a fellow he'd known all his life, so he was permitted to pass without difficulty. As he climbed the Spuyten Duyvil hill, his spirits climbed too. The rain was keeping everyone indoors. He would probably get to the boat with no trouble at all!

He passed the gate and, sideslipping his way along the line of trees that edged the drive, made his way past the house. As he rounded it, he wondered what Patience might be doing at that moment. He had the strongest urge to stop in at the kitchen to see her, to have her make a fuss, and cry over him, and make him a mug of hot chocolate as she used to when he was a boy, and while he was drinking it down, he could hint to her about this brave mission he was embarking on. But he knew better than to do it. *Dearest Patience!* he said to her in his mind. *What a grand adventure I shall be able to tell you of when next we meet!*

He moved on past the house, keeping low and ducking behind every available bush and shrub. Cautiously he descended the hill to the river, but when he came in sight of the pier he got his first shock. The boat was not there!

Then he remembered Orgill. *"Damn the fellow!"* he cursed aloud. "His blasted lordship must have taken the dory downriver on one of his visits to the *Duchess of Gordon!*"

His spirits fizzled like glowing ashes doused with a barrel of rainwater. What was he to do now? He supposed he'd have to go back to his company with his tail between his legs and admit to the captain that he'd failed. The captain would undoubtedly excuse him very politely—after all, this had been a voluntary mission. But he'd never win the man's respect again.

No, he was *damned* if he'd go crawling back a failure! There were other boats. If he couldn't steal his father's, he'd steal someone else's!

His mind raced about, desperately trying to remember who else might have a boat. Betts, of course, just a mile up the river road—he had a skiff and two small sloops! Surely one of them would be moored at the pier on a rainy day like this.

He raced up the road, no longer feeling concerned about being seen. Somehow his mission had taken on enormous importance in his mind. He didn't yet understand just what his mission was but General Washington needed him! That fact was enough! Moreover, his self-respect hinged on the outcome. How could he consider himself a soldier—or a man—if he couldn't accomplish this one simple task?

When he drew near the Betts's pier, he saw with a sinking heart that only one of the three boats was tied to it. If it was the little skiff, it would hardly be worth—

But as he drew closer he saw that it was the largest of Betts's three, a thirty-footer, five feet longer than his father's. Benjy knew it well. It was in the old Dutch style, broad of beam and a bit heavy in planking, which made it slow, but its single mast was well forward to give it good cargo space. Benjy couldn't have come upon a better vessel. He shut his eyes and offered up a prayer of thanks to God for it.

He ran down the pier, leapt into the boat and began at once to untie the ropes. As he undid the last one, a figure loomed up at the far end of the pier. "Who's that there?" came an angry voice.

Benjy, desperate, pushed off at once. The boat slowly began to move downstream.

Heavy footsteps pounded along the planks of the pier. Benjy glanced over his shoulder and recognized Dick Crocker, one of Betts's redemptioners. "It's me, Dick. Benjy Hendley," he said with a cheerful wave.

"Benjy?" The heavy old fellow gaped in astonishment. "What in blazes do ye think ye're doin'?"

"Are you an American, Dick, or a damn Loyalist?"

Dick Crocker scratched his bare head at the unexpectedness of the question. "I been indentured eight years," he admitted. "What do ye *think* I am?"

"Then, if you care about our cause, you won't say anything 'bout this."

"You steal in' boats for the *Americans?*" the old man asked in disbelief.

"For General Washington himself. Besides, I'm only borrowing it. So go on back to what you were doing and don't say a word to a soul that the boat is missing."

The old fellow, confused, shook his wet head, shedding raindrops from his long gray hair like a dog, and considered the problem. The boat was already too far away from the pier for him to retrieve it, that much was plain. It was also plain that if he reported the theft to his master, he'd only be tonguelashed (or even whiplashed) for incompetence. "What's to be gained by talkin'?" he shouted to Benjy who'd already steered into the current and was rapidly increasing his distance from the pier. "I ain't never seen you."

Benjy laughed in sheer joy and sat down at the tiller. The current was so strong and the wind so violent that he didn't need to hoist the sails. He merely let the current take him south. Already soaked to the skin, he took no notice of the rivulets pouring from the brim of his hat. As he steered past Haerlem Heights, he looked up at the redoubt, the walls of which he could see from his position on the river below. He wondered if the captain and Sergeant Blake were watching the passing boats. He knew they wouldn't be able to make him out, even if they were watching, but he gave them a triumphant wave just in case.

He drifted past a number of British warships anchored in the river, but their nearness did not trouble him. The river was always heavily trafficked with small boats; the lookouts were not likely to bother about another little cargo boat.

It was not quite dark when he reached the southern tip of Manhattan Island. As he turned his boat abeam to maneuver around the island into the East River, he was surprised to see a veritable armada of small boats, most of them even smaller than his—whaleboats, dories, scows, even rowboats and an Indian canoe or two—all milling about near the Manhattan shore. He steered among them, wondering what he was expected to do next.

A large sloop pulled alongside him, and a fellow with an insignia on his hat that Benjy didn't recognize leaned down from its deck. "You, there," he called to Benjy over the wind, "identify yourself!"

Benjy, having expected a grateful welcome, was irritated at the arrogant manner of the questioner. "Corporal Hendley of the ourth New York," he snapped, "sent at the request of General Heath. And who the hell are you?"

"You're cursing at Lieutenant Halleck of Glover's Marbleheaders," came an amused response.

Benjy, embarrassed, got up and saluted hastily. "Sorry, sir."

"Forget it. We all feel like cursing in this damned blow."

Benjy, sprayed at that moment by spume blown up by a sudden ust of wind, silently agreed. "Can you tell me what I'm suposed to do?" he asked, wiping his face with his sleeve.

"Nothing right now. We can only use oars while this conounded nor'easter keeps blowing. Our regiment's been assigned o handle the boats, so when the wind dies down and we can aise sail, I'll assign someone to man your boat, unless you can o it yourself."

"I think I can handle it," Benjy assured him. He'd heard of the Marbleheaders, John Glover's regiment from Marblehead, Masachussets. All excellent seamen, they'd given up their nautical ursuits to fight for independence. It would be an honor to man he boats with them. "What is it we have to do?" he inquired gain.

"We've got to get across the river to Brooklyn and bring back ome men and supplies. It's a kind of troop transfer, that's what we're told."

Benjy nodded. Getting across the river would not be difficult or him. But the orders were puzzling. "Transfering troops at his time of night?" he couldn't resist asking.

The Marbleheader shrugged. "Those are the orders. But it's ot to be done silently. We don't want to draw the attention of he British. They're camped up there just below Brooklyn Heights. See their campfires—up there to the left?"

Benjy nodded. "Yes, sir, I see 'em. Just barely." Though the ires were not easily seen through the rain, they nevertheless ooked uncomfortably close.

"Soon as you can hoist sail," the officer instructed, "cross to

the Brooklyn side, just right of the Fulton ferry slip. Don't show
any light. There'll be a Marbleheader to guide you in."

The lieutenant withdrew his head, and his boat began to move
off. "Beg pardon, sir," Benjy called after him, "but I saw at least
two British frigates sitting in the Hudson right beyond the bend,
and I'd wager there's more up the East River side. What if they
should come round—?"

"Don't think about it, boy," came the answer as the boat moved
off. "Don't even *think* about it."

Benjy couldn't help thinking about it, however, during the next
three hours, for the nor'easter persisted in its violence, forcing
him to hug the New York shore in useless inaction. It was obvious
that, if the British frigates sailed around the tip of the island, they
could put an end to this enterprise with but a few rounds of their
cannon. Could it be that they didn't notice this huge number of
small craft right under their noses? Were they blind? But perhaps
the Marbleheader was right—he shouldn't think about it.

Meanwhile he could see small, oared craft bringing in their
loads from the other side—all sorts of supplies, foodstuffs and
even light cannon . . . and a stream of soaked, weary, silent men.
After he'd watched dozens of the small craft unload their burdens
(and Benjy had spotted a number of wounded among them), he
deduced what was really going on. It was a *retreat!* The Americans must have been beaten at Brooklyn Heights, and General
Washington was trying to save what was left of his army. Benjy's
captain had said earlier that more than half of the entire American
army was there at Brooklyn Heights. From the look of the
wounded it was clear that they'd taken a terrible drubbing. Benjy,
utterly dejected by this realization, wondered how many there
were left to save.

After what seemed hours of waiting, he saw that the wind was
dying down. The men who were manning the other sailing craft
must have noticed it, too, for there was a flurry of movement as
dozens of sails were raised. The rain stopped, and the river became smooth as glass. A southwest breeze blew up—just the

ight wind for the American purpose. And—another good sign—
one of the British frigates had made an appearance. Benjy felt
his spirits lift as he set off for the opposite shore.

The span between New York and Brooklyn was about a mile
in length. The favorable breeze made it possible for him to cross
in less than an hour. Near the other shore, a Marbleheader in a
kiff motioned him into line with other boats.

He could see through the gloom of the night a long line of
men making their way down the narrow steps from the fortified
heights above. The line seemed endless. As each boat took on
its load, another group of men moved down to the shore to await
the next. The smoothness of the enterprise was amazing. The
men held hands to assist each other to make their way in the
darkness. But what most amazed Benjy was the silence. Not a
word, not a whisper was exchanged. The men had even muffled
their shoes, tying them round with strips of cloth ripped from
their shirts.

When Benjy's turn came, two Marbleheaders waded out and
pulled his sloop close to shore. Twenty men trudged into the
water and heaved each other into the boat. Then the Marbleheaders, deciding that there was still room, signaled for another five.
When those were aboard, they shoved Benjy off.

It was slower going back. On the New York side, the unloading
was accomplished with equal dispatch and equal silence. But the
silence here was more the result of weariness and dejection than
of necessity. The dejection, Benjy supposed, was to be expected.
A defeat of this magnitude was bound to take its toll on a soldier,
despite his having managed to escape alive.

As Benjy waited for the men to disembark, he fell into conversation with the skipper of the sloop behind him. Clement
McFadden (who said everyone called him Ruddy) was a red-
bearded fellow from a Connecticut militia company which, like
Glover's regiment, was made up mostly of former seamen. They'd
been sent over from New Jersey to assist the Marbleheaders.

Ruddy McFadden had been given the details of the battle by

one of the wounded men he'd ferried over earlier, and he was eager to share his information. "The Brooklyn battle was a disaster," he told Benjy bluntly. "The British had fifteen thousand or more, all trained to use their bayonets without hesitating. They outsmarted us by marching round our rear. Whole companies were taken by surprise. Even the Pennsylvania riflemen were massacred right there in the trees. They might've been sharpshooters in their woods back home, but their wonderful rifles weren't so wonderful here. In the time it took them to reload after their first firing, the bloody redcoats were able to fire three rounds. And then there were the Hessian bastards, bayoneting everyone they could see, even those who surrendered! We must've lost a goodly number, dead and captured. And when the main battle was over, what was left of our army found themselves cornered up on the heights, completely surrounded."

"Damn," was all Benjy could say. "Damn!"

Benjy made two more trips before the sky began to show light. And still the line of men continued to move down the slope from the heights. By that time, Benjy had noticed a tall, imperious officer on horseback riding up and down the shore, overseeing the movement of the men and boats. "Is that *him?*" he whispered to an infantryman standing near him.

The man nodded. "Washington hisself. I wish he'd get aboard. Likely get hisself killed, out there in the open."

Benjy stared at the general in awe. The man had been on his horse all night. And probably on duty for hours or days before that, arranging for this retreat. Undoubtedly exhausted and soaked to the skin, he sat his horse as straight and firm as if he were fresh from his bed. Benjy could understand why the infantryman beside him was so troubled, for the sky was brightening rapidly. If someone from the British camp spotted the action, the general's very life could be in danger.

But Nature was once again kind. A heavy fog settled over the water, so thick that Benjy, on his next crossing, could not see the boat ahead of him. When he got close to the Brooklyn shore however, he did see that the once-endless line of men was dwindling. "Last load," a Marbleheader informed him as he shoved him off.

Benjy gaped at him aghast, for he could see through the mist that General Washington still had not embarked.

Out in the river a few minutes later, with his boat completely enveloped in fog, Benjy heard gunshots. The redcoats had discovered the retreat! Were they shooting at Washington?

He quickly trimmed his sails to slow his advance. The boat behind him hove into view, with Ruddy McFadden at the tiller. Benjy signaled him to pull alongside. "They're *shooting* back there," he yelled as soon as Ruddy was close enough to hear. "Have you seen General Washington?"

"He was still ashore when I pulled off," Ruddy answered worriedly.

"Were there any boats behind you?"

"Only a skiff." The bearded man frowned. "It'd be just like the general to be the last man off."

Both men let their boats drift into the wind as they watched for the skiff to catch up with them. In a few minutes the skiff materialized out of the fog. Ruddy and Benjy exchanged smiles of relief as they saw General Washington, obviously hale, standing near the mast in deep conversation with another officer.

Without exchanging a word but following similar instincts, Benjy and Ruddy McFadden maneuvered their crafts so that they flanked the skiff, Ruddy at its portside and Benjy off its starboard. Although their escort had not been requested, they gave the skiff convoy across the river. General Washington appeared to be too engrossed to notice the escort, but when he disembarked, he smiled and tipped his hat to them both. Benjy was overwhelmed. He felt as if he'd been awarded a medal.

"If any man can lead us to victory, 'tis he," he muttered to himself as he watched Washington being surrounded by his aides and moving off.

Later, after his human cargo had all disembarked, he went

ashore to shake Ruddy McFadden's hand in farewell. "Did you hear?" Ruddy asked excitedly. "We ferried over *nine thousand men* this night! I had it from a man who had it from John Glover himself. We may have had a defeat at Brooklyn Heights, but Washington's cunning ploy has snatched the victory right out from under General Howe's nose." He clapped Benjy on the shoulder. "And it was us, with our little boats, that did it!"

Benjy, remembering the weary wretchedness on the faces of his passengers, could not feel quite so sanguine. But Washington had tipped his hat to him—General George Washington himself! That, at least, was something he could someday boast of to his grandchildren.

Sixty-one

Peter Hendley told anyone who would listen that the summer of 1776 was the worst of his life. Everything infuriated him. Everywhere he looked he saw something that raised his ire. There were the redoubts built all around Spuyten Duyvil by the Americans, at least three of them so close to his property that he could see them from his office window every time he looked out. There were the cannon, brought by the American General Knox to fortify the King's Bridge. Worst of all was the insolent epistle from Philadelphia that the illegal Congress called its Declaration of Independence. "The damn fools have lost their minds!" he shouted at Patience when he read the text in the Westchester *Gazette*. "They'll pay for their arrogance, mark my words! Every last one of 'em will hang!"

Added to his fury was a pervasive and dispiriting sense of his own helplessness. From every window he could see his neglected fields. His physical weakness seemed not only an insurmountable obstacle but another symptom of the corruption of his world, for there was nothing he could do, even on his own property, to stop the deterioration. There were very few men available for hire. All the help he had to work his vast acreage were Chester, Jeb and two day laborers that Charley McNab had managed to cajole into accepting employment. And they could barely handle the care of the livestock.

Then, in late July, Hendley received a blow that brought his dejection to its lowest point. His friend Clymer Young, who always visited him weekly and spent several hours conferring with him in his office, one day failed to appear. " 'Tis strange," Hendley remarked to Patience. "He usually sends me word if he cannot come." The following Sunday, in church, Patience learned that poor Mr. Young had been struck with putrid fever, a disease that some doctors called typhus. It was an often-fatal illness, notorious for attacking its victims with abrupt violence. It had killed Clymer Young in three days.

She broke the news to her father as gently as she could, but it struck him hard. When the shock wore off, Hendley began to speak of papers that had been in Young's possession that he had to reclaim. Weak and dejected as he was, he planned to make the trip to the Young household. But before he could do so, Mr. Young's son, a boy of thirteen, appeared at their door carrying a parcel. He'd driven a two-wheeled chaise all by himself from White Plains. "My father told me on his deathbed to deliver this to Mr. Hendley," he told Patience, "so it must be important."

"How brave of you to come all alone," Patience said, putting out a hand for the parcel.

The boy shook his head. "Papa instructed me most particularly that this was to be delivered into Mr. Hendley's hands and none other."

She smiled at the boy's self-assurance and obediently led him to the office. When her father saw the parcel, his face lit up with relief. It was the first time in months the man did not look utterly miserable.

Patience then took the boy to the kitchen to give him some refreshment before he drove home. After expressing her sincere condolences, she tried to question him about the parcel. "Did you wrap it up yourself?" she asked, feeling like a spy.

"Yes, ma'am," the boy said proudly. "Papa told me to pack up everything in the last two compartments on the left side of his desk, and so I did."

"Two whole compartments?" Patience placed a large portion

of rasberry syllabub in front of him. "That must have been a great pile."

"Not so great," he said, stuffing his mouth hungrily. "There was only a ledger, a bundle of receipts and a document with Papa's seal. Papa was a protonotary, you know." He smiled up at her. "That's a clerk of the court."

"My! A protonotary! But 'tis no wonder. Your father was held in great respect. You must be very proud of him."

The boy's information was enough to set her mind racing. The ledger and receipts, she suspected, had to do with the purchase of arms. She knew her father had never given up his plan to help supply the British, but he hadn't enough money to do very much about it. Even with the contributions Clymer Young must have made, they couldn't have accumulated enough to matter. What interested her more was the document with the seal. What was it, she wondered, that could be important enough to worry her father and to cause Mr. Young to mention it on his deathbed? *Good God,* she thought with a shock, *is it a will? Did Papa change his will, as he once threatened to do?*

This possibility was very disturbing. If Benjy were disinherited, the entire property would, in the end, fall into Lord Orvill's possession. And to Patience's mind, no one in the world was less deserving. His lordship had come to see Papa no more than twice in the last six months, even though the trip up river from the *Duchess of Gordon* was an easy journey and, with the British naval vessels in full control of the Hudson, as safe for a member of Lord Tryon's circle as a trip by land would have been dangerous. Orgill's devotion to her father was as self-serving and erratic as his devotion to his wife. For him to be rewarded with the fruits of her father's lifelong labors was nothing short of a travesty of justice.

By the end of August, however, Patience had even more serious concerns, for the war was suddenly being fought in earnest, and right nearby—in Brooklyn. She first got news of the impending battle in a message from Barbara, who'd heard the details from

Henryk Bogaerde. General Howe had at last begun to move, threatening New York City from a position on Gravesend Bay on Long Island. General Washington, Barbara informed her, was going to defend the city by removing most of his army from New York and taking a defensive position on Brooklyn Heights. Barbara believed that both Henryk and Tom were with this American force.

The battle, Patience later learned, was fought on August twenty-sixth. By the next day, the British had the Americans surrounded. When word of the disaster reached Westchester, Patience was frantic. She was terrified at the possibility that Tom and Henryk had participated in the battle, and, as far as she knew, Benjy, too, had been involved. Any or all of them could have been killed, injured or captured. This was a fear she'd not known in her life before, a constant dread that gnawed away at her insides. She remembered reading the words of Herodotus: "In peace sons bury their fathers; in war, fathers bury their sons." These words now had a terrifying ring.

Her father, knowing nothing of his son's whereabouts, had no such concern. The British had a victory, and he rejoiced in it. But a few days later, news came that set him wild. General Howe, notorious for choosing inaction over action, had not immediately followed up on his advantage. He waited two days before ordering his army to close in and finish off the Americans. By that time that accursed General Washington had managed, in a single night, to transport what was left of his army—almost ten thousand men and boatloads of supplies—back across the river to the city.

Hendley was beside himself. "William Howe had the *whole rebel army* in his grasp, *and* their *commander in chief!* He had the fleet to assist him! He had three times the number of men! He could have ended this damn insurgence *then and there!* Whatever *possessed* the fellow to lose what he'd won? Is he *mad?*"

Patience, who'd spent the morning on her knees in her bedroom, praying that three particular men were among those who'd gotten away, responded calmly that perhaps General Howe had not wished to incur huge losses of men.

"Losses must be *expected* if one is to gain a great victory, as this would have been!" he shouted at her.

She didn't bother to express her feelings about the value of human life, for it would only have enraged him further. She merely cautioned him mildly not to let himself become choleric. "Remember what the doctor said," she warned.

But her warning did no good. A few days later, after repeating his tirade endlessly not only to Patience but to Charley McNab and to Chester (who'd merely come for instructions on what to do about a horse who'd gone lame), he spewed forth his grievances upon Beatie while she was serving breakfast. She was alone in the dining room with him, for Patience had gone to kitchen for the buttermilk spoonbread her father particularly liked, that she'd made especially to cheer him. Poor Beatie, always so frightened when the master raised his voice that she lapsed into a kind of stupor, did not understand a word he said. She believed that he was scolding her for something she'd done wrong. "I'm . . . I'm . . . sorry," she mumbled, close to tears.

"It could all have been *over,* don't you understand?" he bawled at her, his face reddening alarmingly. "This whole stupid rebellion could have been *over!*" He lifted himself by the arms of his chair, opened his mouth to explain to her what she obviously didn't understand, and suddenly stiffened. His eyes bulged, he went into a momentary paroxysm of shaking and then fell face down on the floor, unconscious.

"Blessed *God,*" the little Scotswoman cried, bending over him and wringing her hands, "what hae I done? What turrible thing hae I *done?*"

Sixty-two

Although Hendley regained consciousness, the doctor offered Patience no hope of a recovery. "It won't be long," he predicted frankly. " 'Tis best you prepare for it."

Patience did not know how to prepare for death. She only knew that she needed her brother and sister at her side. She didn't know how to reach Benjy, but she sent Charley McNab to the city with a message for Barbara. The whole of Manhattan Island was chaotic with military activity, for the British were moving up the east side, pursuing the Americans who were moving up the west, but Charley assured her that he would get through safely.

Hendley seemed to guess that the end was near. For two days he tried to tell Patience something that seemed important to him, but he couldn't speak. On the third day, however, he managed to say two words from the right corner of his twisted mouth: "Get Orgill." It was an urgent plea.

Whatever her inner reluctance, Patience could not ignore her father's dying request. She asked Chester to borrow Betts's skiff, take it down river to the *Duchess of Gordon* and leave a message with someone on board. If Orgill had an ounce of human feeling, he would come back in the dory he'd taken away weeks before.

Meanwhile, Charley returned, with Barbara at her side. The sisters embraced wordlessly and, hands clasped tightly, went together to their bedside vigil.

Lord Orgill returned that very evening, imminent death being a strong motivator. Patience took him to her father at once, but it was plain that Peter Hendley was breathing his last. His eyes were open, but they seemed already to be looking at another world. He showed no recognition of the faces that bent over him. Patience, Barbara, Beatie, Charley and the doctor all stood around his bed, but he seemed unaware of any of them.

Orgill leaned close and put a hand on his cheek. "Peter? 'Tis I, Orgill. You sent for me."

Hendley blinked, and a light of recognition glimmered in his eyes. The right corner of his mouth twitched, emitting a faint sound. Orgil bent down and put his ear against the dying man's lips. Hendley made a valiant last effort to tell him something, but only one small sound came from his mouth before he gasped and died.

"Did you hear it?" Barbara asked, feeling a desperate need to know her father's last word.

Lord Orgill's brow knit in a puzzled frown. "Magazine. I think he said 'magazine.' What do you suppose he meant?"

But the doctor was covering the dead man's still-twisted face with a sheet. This was not the time to hazard guesses on the meaning of inappropriate words. It was a time to mourn.

Late that night, after Barbara had gone to sleep in her old bedroom and Lord Orgill in Benjy's, Patience crept out of her room and, carefully shielding her candle, tiptoed downstairs to her father's office. There was a document she was determined to examine before anyone else could see it.

She closed the office door and crossed the room, keeping her eyes averted from the sheeted form on the bed. She placed the candle on the desk and began to rifle through its seven drawers. She found, in the topmost drawer on the left, the ledger that Clymer Young's boy had brought. She leafed through it quickly, noting in passing an inventory total of thirty-six barrels of powder. The number astonished her. Thirty-six barrels! That amounted to a veritable arsenal! How much armament had her father actually acquired?

But this was not the time to think about that. She was looking

for the will. And there it was, right under the ledger—a folded
sheet of heavy parchment. She sat down at the desk, pulled the
candle closer and read it through. As she feared, it was the document willing all the Hendley properties to her, signed by her
father and witnessed by Clymer Young.

She sat for a moment in deep thought. Then, with a determined
shake of her head, she took the paper to the fireplace, laid it on
the empty grate and set it afire with her candle-flame. *No one
will ever know it existed,* she told herself as she watched it burn,
and the property will go to Benjy just as it ought.

Before leaving, she paused at the bed, pulled back the sheet
and looked down at her father's face. Her heart seemed to swell
up painfully in her chest. " 'Tis for the best, Papa," she whispered
in a shaken voice, "If you truly meant for the property to be
mine, then I'm in my rights to do what I did. Besides, if you
weren't crazed by anger, you'd never have taken away Benjy's
birthright. You always underestimated Benjy. Oh, Papa, if now
you be with God, looking down on me, please give your blessing
to what I've done."

She took a last look at him. In the glow of candlelight it seemed
to her that his expression was almost benign. She found herself
suddenly shaking with sobs. They poured out of her from some
inner well of affection deeper than she'd suspected. *Poor Papa,*
she thought, ineffectively wiping at her cheeks, *if only you could
have shown us a benign face in life!* Then she covered him
quickly, to insure that this final impression would remained fixed
in her memory.

She stayed beside him for a long while until she regained her
equilibrium. But before going out the door, she remembered that
she had one more chore to do in this room. She returned to the
desk, pulled out the ledger and tucked it under her arm. She knew
what the word *magazine* meant, even if no one else did. The
mystery was answered in this book, but Lord Orgill would not
get his hands on it. He'd learn the secret—and the meaning of
magazine—only over her dead body.

Sixty-three

The funeral was held at midmorning of a cloudy, breezy September day. The pastor, friends of the family like Hannah and Stuart LeGrange, and several of the Fordham villagers—Nate, Jotham, Samuel Peach and all the other committeemen among them—joined the procession from the house to the gravesite. It was a long walk, past the orchard, through a fallow field and over a rise to the far edge of the north field where Peter Hendley had built his mausoleum.

As the coffin was lowered into the ground, Patience found herself staring at the monument Clymer Young had built for her father. It was a structure she'd never approved of, and she'd therefore not looked at it closely before. But she now saw that there was nothing about it to dislike—it was merely a simple obelisk set on a large, high, rectangular stone base. In front of the base, on a burnished bronze plate, the name HENDLEY was engraved in large letters. The only other decorations were similar bronze plates on each side of the base from which a pair of laurel wreaths, sculptured in bronze, were hung on rings. The design was modest, but the size was not. Patience, still very much a Puritan in her soul, could not help feeling that it was too pretentious for the grave of a man who, to all but his family, was obscure.

The pastor took his place at the head of the grave and opened his prayer book. "Be thou my judge, O God, and plead my cause—" he began. But he was interrupted by the clatter of horses' hooves on the stony ground. Three horsemen came riding over the rise toward them. The riders pulled to a halt a short distance from the gathering, tethered their horses to a tree and strode quickly toward the mourners. Patience recognized two of them before they dismounted—Tom and Henryk. But the third, when she got a look at his face, caused her to gasp.

Barbara saw him too. "Benjy!" she cried aloud.

Benjy, his lips pressed together to keep them from trembling, broke into a run and took both his sisters in his arms. They clutched each other tightly but could not speak. The pastor gave them a little time and then cleared his throat. They broke apart and stood shoulder to shoulder facing him. Henryk took a place beside Barbara, but Tom hesitated. Although he wished he had the right to stand beside Patience and support her in her grief, he didn't know if she wanted him near her. But then he saw that Lord Orgill was present. His lordship had taken a proprietary place just behind his wife. Tom had to inhale deeply to adjust to this circumstance. Then, his jaw set, he turned and went to stand with the servants. Patience watched him move away, but when he took his place and looked across at her, she dropped her eyes. That one small, evasive flicker was enough to tell him he was not forgiven.

The pastor spoke at length about the brevity of earthly existence and the rewards of the life hereafter. Although it was unseemly to display one's grief at a public ceremony, Patience was aware that Barbara's eyes were streaming and that Benjy's shoulders were shaking with the sobs he was trying his best to suppress. She also tried to suppress any outward show of her own grief, until her eye fell upon a fallen tree just a little distance beyond the clearing. It was a pathetic sight, its trunk still partially attached to the stump and its leafless branches turned upward, like a prostrate man with many arms, all beseeching. The tree had no connection with her father, none at all, for her father had never in his life beseeched anybody for anything, but somehow the sight of those yearning limbs pierced her

hest like an arrow. She raised her shaking hands to her eyes
o keep back what she feared would be a sudden rush of tears,
ut she discovered that her cheeks were already wet. She'd been
rying all along.

She hardly heard the words the minister spoke, nor was she
ware of it when he ceased. It was only when Orgill put a hand
n her elbow to help her walk back to the house that she
ealized the ceremony was over. Too overcome with emotion
o concern herself with Orgill, she let him lead her a few steps
p the rise, but some instinct made her look back over her
houlder to take another look at her father's grave. Benjy still
tood there with head lowered. She broke from her husband's
old and went back to her brother. "Benjy," she whispered
oftly, slipping an arm about his shoulders, "walk home with
ne."

Benjy lifted his head and looked at her, his face tortured with
rief. "He never tried to know me," he said in a choked voice.
"He never even looked at me."

"Yes, he did, in his way," Patience comforted. "His land, his
abor, his dreams . . . they were for you. Look around you, Benjy.
Ill the way down to the river. And over there, past the orchards,
ast the house, over the rise to the Spuyten Duyvil channel. Look
t it, so beautiful, so . . . rich. It's all yours—everything he
vorked so hard to accumulate. That's how he showed his love—in
is legacy to you."

But as she spoke those comforting lies, a kind of comfort
verwhelmed her, too. If the words were not quite true for
Benjy, they were, in a sense, true for her. Her father had left
is hard-won property as a legacy for *her,* not Orgill. Perhaps
hat was why he'd done it. It was an unwise act, perhaps even
 cruel one, but it put into legal terms what he'd said to her so
ong ago—that she was the one, of all his offspring, who loved
his land as he did. In the long run it would have turned out
o be a bad decision; she was not at all sorry she'd burned the
vill. But perhaps Papa had done it for a reason she'd not

thought of before: to tell his eldest daughter in the only wa
he could—for he could never have said the words aloud—ho
very much he'd loved her.

Sixty-four

By late afternoon the ceremonies were over, the condolences
expressed and most of the guests departed. Those who remained—the three soldiers, Hannah and Stuart LeGrange, and
Lord Orgill—were invited back to the house for a repast with
the family. Tom, however, did not join them. "I'll take my dinner
in the kitchen with the McNabs and the other servants," he muttered to Henryk, "and I'll meet you at dusk for the return to the
regiment."

Henryk opened his mouth to object, but there was a look in
Tom's eyes that made him hold his tongue.

It was a motley group of men gathered round the table: Benjy
and Henryk in the uniforms of the Continental Army, and Stuart,
a well-known and active American sympathizer, sitting down to
take a meal with a member of the British aristocracy, Lord Orgill.
But it was tacitly understood that they were meeting under a kind
of truce. Military matters would not be discussed.

This was a source of deep frustration to the Americans, all of
whom would have liked to exchange news. Since his return from
England, his lordship had not been welcomed into this house by
anyone but Peter Hendley. Now that Hendley was gone, it should
have been obvious to him that his presence was not desired. But
if Orgill felt unwelcome, there was nothing in his demeanor to
show it. He behaved quite as if this were his own manor house,
and he was its boisterously affable host. He took Peter Hendley's
seat at the head of the table without so much as a by-your-leave

to Patience and proceeded to ladle out the soup. "Our Beatie' barley soup," he boomed cheerily, "is the best of its kind thi side of Scotland."

His lordship's possessive manner made Patience and Hanna exchange looks of chagrin. The others also found his heartiness if not his proprietary air, obnoxious. But no one was in the moo to confront him, and they maintained a glum silence.

At the end of the meal, they all repaired to the parlor. Everyon was now more relaxed. Barbara and Benjy, who had not see each other since her elopement, sat down on the sofa and spok together in low tones. It was an emotional reunion. With thei father gone, Barbara a widow and Benjy a soldier, they were n longer what they'd been when they'd last seen each other. Wit a mixture of happiness and sadness, each one marveled at th maturity of the other.

Later, Barbara asked Henryk how they'd managed to locat Benjy. "We assumed Benjy'd be with one of the Westcheste regiments," Henryk explained, "so it was not too difficult to fin him." Then he glanced toward the fireplace, where Lord Orgil was leaning on the mantel, smoking a pipe and watching then "But don't ask me anything more," he added in an undervoice "I don't think we should discuss matters concerning our troop while Lord Orgill is with us. General Howe has been gettin quite enough information from his spies."

"Henryk!" Barbara said, eyes widening. "Surely you don think—!"

"What I think, Babs, is that I must be going. Benjy has offici leave, but Tom and I have not."

"Heavens, Henryk, where on earth *is* Tom?" Babs asked, be latedly realizing she'd not seen him for hours.

Henryk shrugged. "Something is amiss between Tom and you sister, but if you want to know more, you'll have to ask her."

Henryk took his leave of the other guests and went out fror where he spotted Tom leading their two horses around the corne of the house. He waved a greeting and started toward him whe the front door opened, and Patience came out. "Henryk, wait," she said quietly, looking over her shoulder to make certain no one was nearby. "I have something to ask—" And then she saw Tom. "Oh!" she exclaimed in surprise, her cheeks reddening. "I thought you'd . . . gone."

"I took my dinner in my usual place," Tom said with his jaw clenched. "In the kitchen with the servants."

"Dash it, Tom, that's not fair," she burst out. "You know you are always welcome at my table."

"Thank you, ma'am, but perhaps this is not the time for us to be discussing my welcome in this house. You came out to talk to the captain, did you not? Please go ahead and do so." He reached for his horse's curb-strap. "I'll meet you down at the gate," he said to Henryk and started down the drive.

"No, Tom, don't go," Patience begged, looking directly into his eyes for the first time that day. "I need advice from both of you."

Henryk had been observing their exchange with interest. "What sort of advice?" he asked, glancing from one to the other.

Patience took a deep breath before plunging in. "If someone— a civilian, say—should find a supply of powder and arms . . . a rather large supply . . . what should she, this civilian I mean, do about it?"

"That's a strange question," Henryk said.

Tom frowned at her. "What are you getting at, Patience? Are you in some sort of fix?"

"Should this civilian keep it hidden?" she persisted. "Should she—he!—notify someone? Or load it on wagons and take it somewhere?"

"Load it on *wagons?*" Tom asked, appalled. "How large a supply are we speaking of?"

Patience bit her lip. "I'm not sure."

"Damnation," Tom cursed, "is this a result of one of your father's blasted schemes? He was up to something, wasn't he?"

"Cease your blaspheming, Tom Morrison!" she scolded. "The

man is not cold in his grave! Besides, all this is purely hypothetical."

Tom glared at her. "And where is this hypothetical cache?"

Her eyes fell. "I don't know yet."

Tom's horse, agitated by the delay, reared up and whinnied
Tom kept his eyes fixed on Patience as he steadied the animal
"See here, ma'am, all my instincts tell me that you're in some
sort of serious trouble. Whether you welcome my attentions or
not, I'm *not* going off and leaving you until I find out just how
serious it is."

"Oh, yes, you are," Henryk said firmly. Though the charged
air between his lieutenant and the lady fascinated him, he knew
they had no time for dalliance. "Even our *horses* are on French
leave. We must get back before dark or the serious trouble will
be ours."

Patience's eyebrows rose. "You *stole* the horses?"

"Only borrowed them," Henryk assured her.

"But Henryk is right," Tom admitted with a sigh. "We must
get back before we, or the horses, are missed."

"Look here, Patience," Henryk said, climbing up on his mare
"We're stationed only a short distance below the bridge. At Haer
lem Heights. If you find this hypothetical cache of arms, send
us word there. I'm sure our regimental commander will be de
lighted to relieve you of it."

"But don't do anything dangerous," Tom added, mounting hi
horse reluctantly. "If you injure yourself, or in any way fall int
difficulty, I'll come back and wring your neck!"

They spurred their mounts and rode off in a shower of gravel
Patience watched as they disappeared down the road. Then, feel
ing inexpressibly bereft, she turned back to face her other guest

Sixty-five

Patience felt even more bereft the next day, when the others all departed, Benjy to return to his regiment, Barbara to close up her house in New York to prepare to move back home with Patience, and Lord Orgill to sail back to Lord Tryon's ship. After she waved her last good-bye, Patience walked back to a house that was lonelier than it had ever been.

She had difficulty falling asleep that night. The house seemed so quiet. Beatie and Charley were the only other occupants, and their room over the kitchen was too far away on the other side of the house to give her a feeling of security. As the hours passed, she became uneasy and frightened. She seemed to hear ghostly noises . . . the sound of footsteps, the creak of stairs. She even imagined that her door was opening . . . quietly . . . stealthily . . .

But it *was* opening. She sat up in bed, her pulse racing, her hands clutching at the coverlet. "Who—"

The light of a lantern illuminated the opening and silhouetted the outline of a man. "Who should it be, my dear, but your adoring spouse?" came Orgill's hearty voice.

"Why are you back?" she demanded, raising the volume of her voice above the hammering of her heart. "And how dare you come into my room without knocking?"

The room was now fully lit by his lantern. He closed the door and set the lantern down on her bedside table. "I have no need to knock," he said. "Matters are quite different now, you see. It is I who'll make the rules."

He looked horridly forbidding standing above her, with th lantern behind him throwing his enormous shadow across th ceiling. Her throat tightened in alarm. "What rules? Wh-wh do you mean?"

He chuckled at the little stammer that gave away her fear. "I' the man of the house now, am I not? Your father told me of h new will. All his property is yours, and what is yours is mine.

"That's not true! He changed his mind about the will. He nev rewrote it."

"We'll see about that. But in any case, *you* are mine. I did n demand my husbandly privileges while you were under the pr tection of your father, being too good-natured to wish to mak scenes. But now that he's gone, you are under *my* protection He sat down on the side of her bed and reached for her. "Com my sweet, don't be adamant. Permit yourself to enjoy a secon honeymoon."

She backed away from him until the bedpost stopped he "How can you demand husbandly privileges?" she gasped ou "You cannot pretend to care for me, after deserting me as yo did."

"I care for you as much as for any woman. No woman hol my eye for long."

"Then cast your eye elsewhere. I am not available for yo momentary satisfaction."

"Ah, but you are, my dear, if I say you are. I am accustome to taking my satisfaction when and where it pleases me." Wit that, he lifted her in his arms, coverlet and all, so precipitousl that she was tangled in it and couldn't struggle. Without a mo ment's hesitation, before she do anything to prevent him, h pulled her upon him and pressed his mouth on hers. Sh wrenched her mouth free, almost retching in disgust. Unheedin of her obvious repugnance, he raised her higher on his chest. H laughed in triumph as, holding her with one arm, he slipped hand under her nightdress, slid it up the rear of her leg and thig until it reached her buttocks. He began to fondle her, snickerin with vengeful pleasure. "I'd forgotten what a soft little filly you are," he said, his fingers roaming where they willed.

Pinioned as she was, she could only kick her legs. But in desperation, she managed to free one arm and beat on his face with her fist. Neither the kicking nor her fist made least impression on him. His touch on her bare skin sickened her. Her insides clenched as if in defense against an onslaught, the same way her body used to react to his earlier lovemaking. *I'll die,* she swore, *before I let him enter me again.*

Her eyes searched for a weapon, but the only thing within reach was his lantern. She reached out for it slowly, but once her fingers curled around the handle she moved decisively. Before he guessed what she was about, she swung it at his head. The glass of the lantern cracked, and as he let out a pained cry, the broken lantern fell to the floor. The candle-flame guttered out, leaving the room in darkness.

His lordship flailed his arms about, roaring in angry pain. Patience, free from his hold, threw off the coverlet, slipped to the ground and ran in her bare feet out the door to the back stairs. She heard him curse as he blundered about in the darkness. She was halfway down the stairs before she saw a light from above. Dash it all, she thought, he's found the tinder on the mantel and managed to light a candle all too quickly!

She could hear his footsteps coming after her. Her only advantage was knowing her way in the dark. Impelled by sheer terror, she sped down the passageway to her father's office. *Let it be there!* she prayed silently as she shut the door. *Dear God, let Papa's musket be leaning against the window where I last saw it!*

But it wasn't there. She could hear his footsteps coming closer. "Charley! Beatie!" she cried as loudly as she could, but she had no real hope that they would hear. She felt her way along the wall to the fireplace, hoping that someone had put the musket where it properly belonged—on hooks over the mantel. Her fingers found it just as he threw open the door. She blinked at the sudden flood of light but managed to take aim. "Stop where yo are!" she ordered, steadying the gun against her shoulder. "Tak another step and I'll shoot."

He laughed his booming laugh and continued to advanc "Ninny!" He said it almost fondly, wiping away a smudge o blood from his forehead. His smile was as broad as always, b his eyes glittered with a threatening coldness that terrified he "I'd wager you've never held a musket in your life."

"You'd lose." She cocked the gun with more expertise tha she really had, for terror had sharpened her responses. "On more step and you'll see what a marksman I am."

He stopped but continued to smile. "And I'd wager it isn even loaded."

"You may be right. I hadn't time to check. Do you wish t chance it? Back away now. Straight back . . . out of this room.

He kept his eyes on her as he followed her orders. The candl in his hand highlighted the creases in his cheeks and made h persistent leer look positively Satanic.

Patience followed him into the passageway, keeping her gu steady, though her knees trembled so badly that she wondere how she managed to keep erect. "Now, turn around and take you leave. At once."

He made as if to turn, but instead made a lunge for the muske She knew she ought to pull the trigger but she could not—she never shot anything in her life, not even a rabbit. Desperatel she swung the muzzle upward. It caught him on the chin. He le it go, cursing, and tottered backward.

But it was a minor injury. He quickly recovered and cam toward her again. "I was certain you wouldn't shoot," he chortle "You may as well give over."

"Don't push me too far," Patience retorted, lifting the muske to her shoulder again. "You may be sor—"

But at that moment Charley came dashing down the passag from the other side of the house, with Beatie scurrying behin him, holding a candle. "What's goin' on here?" he demande grasping Lord Orgill's arm and pulling him around. Then he saw who it was. "Oh! Yer *lordship!*" he gasped.

"Is he troublin' ye, missus?" Beatie asked. She glared at Orgill and took a brave stance beside Patience, ready to fight to the death.

"His lordship was just leaving," Patience said, keeping aim with her gun. Breathless, and with every muscle aquiver, she was surprised that she could hold it so steadily. "I only wanted Charley to see him out to whatever conveyance he used to bring him here."

Charley nodded and gestured toward the door. "This way, yer lordship, if ye please."

Orgill hesitated, looking from the adamant Patience to the determined servants. Then, with a shrug, he turned and strode to the door. "Very well, I'll go," he said over his shoulder. "As I told you, I'm too good-natured to make scenes."

At the doorway he looked back at his wife. "I'll be back," he said, his eyes still lit with that threatening gleam but his smile quite gone. "And next time I'll not forget to be armed."

Sixty-six

Even after several days, Patience continued to suffer the after-effects of that frightening night. Lord Orgill stalked her in her dreams, in many forms. Then one night, as she dreamed about going rabbit hunting with Benjy (the rabbit having light hair like his lordship, and a persistent, evil smile), a startling idea filtered into her sleeping brain. In her dream she was tracking the rabbit with a musket too heavy to lift, when the animal hopped across the north field and leaped up on her father's monument. At that moment, her eyes popped open, and she sat up in bed, wide awake. "Of course!" she cried aloud. "It's in the mausoleum. The arsenal is somewhere in the mausoleum."

It was still dark, but she couldn't bear to wait for morning. She dressed, took a lantern and flint, and slipped out of the house. Since she knew her way in the dark, she did not light the lantern until, breathless from her long dash over the fields, she came up to the monument. The light from the lantern did not show her anything unexpected. The structure was exactly as she remembered it; there was nothing about it that looked remotely like a storage place. The base was large—much too large for the obelisk it supported—but not large enough to hold the thirty-odd barrels of powder and all the other items she'd found listed in the ledger.

But she could not believe she was wrong about the arsenal's location. The more she thought about it, the more logical it seemed. She'd always believed it strange that her father had wanted a mausoleum. He was not the sort to care about an imposing grave-marker. And Clymer Young's construction work had been strange, too. It had taken weeks, much more time than this simple structure seemed to warrant.

She circled the monument several times before realizing that the bronze panels on the sides were almost as large as doors. She fingered the edges of one of them, but the panel did not come loose. Then, on an impulse, she lifted the sculptured wreath and turned it round. There was the sound of a lock unlatching, and the panel swung aside, revealing a gaping opening.

Within the opening, all was darkness. Patience shuddered with apprehension. It took all her courage to lift the lantern and peer inside. There was a narrow wooden stairway leading down. Heart beating, she bent her head (for the opening was wide but not as high as a door) and crept in.

Seven steep steps took her down to an underground room, larger than the parlor at home but with a ceiling so low that she couldn't stand erect. Piled along the walls and filling most of the space were more barrels, boxes and crates than she'd expected to see. Here was Papa's magazine!

With a feeling of triumph, she climbed back up the stairs and closed the bronze panel. The latch caught with a satisfying click. Then she blew out the candle in the lantern and went home. The next step would have to wait till morning.

Morning brought a surprise. From the kitchen window she could see a line of men coming across the King's Bridge—a long, endless line slowly moving north. Wagons were moving among the lines, and several men were pulling heavy artillery behind them. From their ragged uniforms—with only an occasional blue coat among them—she knew they were men of the Continental Army. Was General Washington deserting New York? It was unexpected, for there had been word of a small American victory in the battle for Haerlem Heights.

She threw a shawl over her shoulders and ran out. If the men were leaving Haerlem Heights, she might never find Tom or

Henryk. But perhaps someone in that line could tell her where they might now be. It was a foolish hope, she supposed, but she had to try.

At the bottom of the hill she came upon Nate Cluett heading toward the moving line with a pack on his back. "Good morning, Mr. Cluett," she greeted. "Do you know the meaning of this parade?"

"Yes, ma'am, I do. General Washington is removing his army from Manhattan Island and taking them north. 'Tis rumored they are going to White Plains."

"I see. And are you going with them?"

"Yes, ma'am," he told her proudly. "I'm going to join up at last. I'm looking for Tom's company. I've been told that Ritzema's regiment is not very far ahead."

"Then I'm most fortunate to have met you. Will you carry a message to him or to Captain Bogaerde?"

"I'd be honored to, ma'am."

"Tell either one of them—but no one else, please—that the cache has been found and that they'll need at least two wagons."

He peered at her, baffled. "Cache? Two wagons?"

"Yes. They'll understand."

Tom and Hendryk evidently did understand, for later that afternoon they rode up to her door, each driving an open wagon drawn by two horses. They wasted no time on formalities, for they had to be loaded and on their way back to the regiment before dark. Tom was still awkwardly distant in his greetings, so Patience climbed up on the seat beside Henryk, and the two wagons trundled up the path past the stables and over the fields to the rise that marked the north field. At the monument, Patience unlocked the panel, hiding her excitement behind a veneer of calm dispassion. "Go down and see it for yourselves," she said, stepping aside and waving them in.

The two men climbed down into the underground hideaway. She heard them gasp at what they saw. "Patience, you *angel!*

Henryk shouted up at her in enthusiasm. "You should get a medal for this!"

Henryk supplied Patience with a pencil and paper with which to record each item as it was carried up. The carrying was heavy work, for the stairs were steep. By the time the wagons were loaded it was twilight. "I can't believe it!" Henryk said, tired but overjoyed. *"Twenty* barrels of gunpowder!"

"Twenty?" Patience echoed, puzzled. "I thought the ledger gave a figure of more than thirty."

Tom looked over the list Patience had kept. "Twenty-two," he corrected. "Quite enough to make our commander very, very happy. And eight crates of musket balls, six boxes of flints, eighteen muskets and fifteen gun cartridges." He wanted to lift Patience in his arms and swing her around in delight, but he only took off his hat and made a low bow. "We can only say, ma'am, that General Washington thanks you, Colonel Ritzema thanks you, Captain Bogaerde thanks you, and I . . . well, I would thank you too, if I thought my thanks would be acceptable to you."

Patience flushed. "If you defeat the British and come safely back, that will be thanks enough for me."

He met her eyes, a look of longing in his own. "Don't believe for a moment," he said quietly, "that I don't know what going against your father's wishes has meant to you." As he climbed up on his wagon, he couldn't help smiling down at her. "What a daring little rebel you've become! I know I predicted that you'd become a revolutionary, but you've surpassed my most extravagant expectations."

She watched the wagons roll back down the hill and out of her sight, an ache in her heart. If anything happened to Tom in this war, she thought, and she never set eyes on him again, she would have to live with the pain of not having made things right between them.

She walked back slowly, wondering what might have been if she'd never met Orgill, if she'd been unmarried when she taught

Tom to read, if she'd never seen the barmaid in his bedroom. If . . . if . . .

But when she arrived home and entered the kitchen, Beatie gave her news that drove everything else from her mind. *"He was here again,"* the Scotswoman said, "an' he said he'll be back in an hour."

"Who?" Patience asked. But she knew the answer. The instinctive clench of her stomach told her.

"His persnickity lordship, that's who. He was in yer da's office an' in yer bedroom, searchin' fer somethin'. I couldna stop him."

He was looking for the will, Patience thought, momentarily relieved. The will was something he'd never find. But he might have found the ledger. Would he have made sense of it? Would he then understand the meaning of magazine?

She flew up the stairs to her room. The ledger, which she'd hidden in the back of her escritoire, was open on the writing surface. He'd found it . . . and he'd read it.

But it doesn't matter if he did, she told herself. *The supplies are already gone. Orgill is too late.*

She glanced at the open page. It was the last page of writing, the one with the totals: *Gunpowder, 36 brls . . . Musket balls, 11 crts . . .*

She blinked curiously at the figures. They were not right. The numbers were higher than the totals of the supplies that Tom and Henryk had taken. What could account for the discrepancy?

It was then that a dreadful thought smote her: what if Clymer Young had dug out *two* rooms under the monument? She hadn't thought to try the wreath on the other side!

Alarmed, she snatched up her lantern and raced back across the fields. It was now becoming dark. She cautiously approached the second panel and turned the wreath. Just as she feared, the second bronze plate was another door that opened on another stairway. She lit her lantern, climbed down and found, to her dismay, another room, twin to the first. It was not quite as crowded with supplies as the first had been, but it was bad enough: she could count *fourteen barrels of powder* alone!

By this time Orgill would no doubt be back at the house, waiting for her. He would surely ask about the ledger, and he might even persist in a search for the storage place until he discovered for himself what she'd discovered. She could not let that happen. This supply must not be allowed to fall into British hands.

Her mind raced about, trying to determine a course of action. It would take too long to notify Tom and Henryk; a full day or more might go by before they could be located and return with their wagons. There was only one thing to do: destroy everything in this room!

It can be done, she assured herself. Gunpowder would surely burn easily. And the heat generated by the flames would undoubtedly destroy everything else in this room. Setting this room aflame was what she had to do.

Her mind made up, she pried the lid from one of the barrels of gunpowder, removed the candle from her lantern and planted it in the powder, leaving only a half-inch of candle visible. When the flame burned down to the level of the powder, she reckoned, it would set the barrel burning and eventually ignite the other barrels. It was a terrible waste, but better to burn it all than to let the British get hold of it.

Her task completed, she climbed up the stairs, took one last look to insure that the candle-flame was still burning, and carefully latched the panel. Then, forcing herself to breathe calmly, she made her way back across the fields.

She had just reached the path to the kitchen, just beyond the stable, when someone reached out from the darkness and enfolded her in a tight grip. "Where is it?" Lord Orgill hissed in her ear as he pulled her arms behind her.

She shuddered in fright. She'd tried to prepare herself to face him, but he'd taken her by surprise again. She glanced over her shoulder at him. His expression was different from anything she'd ever seen on his face. Gone was the smile and the veneer of robust good-nature that he showed to society. Instead, his mouth was narrowed into a thin line, the lines of cheek and jaw were rigid, and there was a look of icy determination in his eyes that said without words that he would trample anyone underfoot who stood in his way. "Let me *go,* my lord!" she said bravely, trying to wrench herself from his hold. "I told you there is no will."

"Don't play with me, my girl. You know I'm not speaking of the will. Where's the magazine?"

"I don't know what you're talking about."

"Thirty-six barrels of gunpowder can't be easily hidden," he said, twisting her arms more tightly behind her. "Let's try the barn."

He pushed her before him, keeping her hands locked behind her in a crushing grip, and stomped through the barn and then the stables. The other outbuildings were obviously too small. As his frustration grew, so did his cruelty. *"Tell* me!" he snarled, ripping off her cap and pulling her head back by her hair. "Where else—?"

"Is this the good-natured Lord Orgill you've so often described to me?" she asked, too proud to give him the satisfaction of gasping from the pain.

But he paid no heed, his mind busily considering the possibilities. "Wait!" He stared down at her face, a light dawning at the back of his eyes. "There must be some sort of *vault . . ."*

"You're twisting my neck! Let me go!"

"A vault, of course! An underground vault. It must be . . . the *gravesite."* Instead of his usual booming laugh, he emitted a single, loud snort of triumph. Then he turned her to him and forced her to look up at him. "It is the gravesite, isn't it?"

She stared at him icily. "I have nothing to say to you."

"Yes, I've guessed it now. I have no need for you." He pushed her away from him so roughly that she fell to the ground, and he set off across the field.

Patience looked after him, brow wrinkled. *The magazine must be a veritable inferno by this time,* she thought. Shouldn't she warn him? She pulled herself to her feet and ran, stumbling with every other step. "My lord, wait!" she cried.

He did not stop. Determined to do what she felt was honorable, she lifted her skirts and sped after him. "Please wait," she said as she caught up with him and grasped his arm. "I think I ought to tell you—"

He shook off her hold. "Do you take me for a fool? Don't think you can cozen me into changing my course."

She stepped in front of him. "Please, my lord, you must listen! I set a fire—"

"Out of my way, woman!" And he struck her a blow back-handed across her face.

She reeled from the shocking pain of it and fell to the ground, dazed. When her head cleared and she looked up, she could see no sign of him. *Let him go!* she told herself furiously. *He's an evil barbarian! He deserves to injure himself!*

But her conscience would not permit her to ignore the possibility of danger to him. She tottered to her feet and set off as quickly as she could toward the gravesite. As she came over the rise at the edge of the north field, she could just barely see him through the darkness.

He was approaching the monument, but something made them both stop. Patience thought she heard a peculiar rumble . . . an ominous underground growl. Then she saw Orgill totter, as if the earth below him had shifted and he'd lost his footing. The rumbling become louder, like thunder, and with a blood-curdling crack, the bronze panel on the monument blew open. A huge flame burst out of the opening like a suddenly erupting volcano. Before Patience's horrified gaze, the whole monument exploded into bits. The bronze panel flew through the air, struck Lord Orgill's head and hurtled off into the distance. His lordship dropped down like a stone.

Despite the glowing debris falling all about her, Patience tried to run to him, but flames were shooting into the air, giving off

waves of unbearable heat. She had to pause and shelter her eyes
with her hand. In the light of the fire Patience saw something
that made her knees give way. She shut her eyes, retching, as she
sank to the ground. Half of Lord Orgill's crushed and bloody
head was gone.

Sixty-seven

A group of Virginia Riflemen, stopping for the night along the road to White Plains, were bedding down in tents and lean-tos along the edge of the Bronx River when one of them spotted a glow in the sky. "Somethin's burnin' back where we jus' came from," he said aloud.

Three of the others got up and stood alongside him to see. "Yup," said one of them. "That's a purty big fire."

Henryk and Tom, looking for their own regiment, were driving their wagons by at just that moment. Tom turned on the seat to see what the men were looking at. The sight froze his blood. As far as he could judge, the fire appeared to be as close to the Hendley property as makes no matter. He pulled the wagon to and leaped down. Henryk was behind him and therefore obliged to stop as well. "What's the trouble?" he asked.

"Look!" Tom pointed to the sky.

Henryk's jaw dropped at the sight. "You don't think—?"

"I don't know, but I'm going to find out." He began to untether one of the horses from his wagon.

"What are you doing?" Henryk demanded in alarm. "You can't go back now! What about the wagon?"

Tom glanced over at the Virginia riflemen who were watching. "Will one of you drive this wagon to our regiment? It won't take long. They can't be far off."

Henryk was about to order his lieutenant to get back on the wagon and move on, but he thought better of it. He'd already determined that Tom's emotions were strongly bound up with Patience, perhaps so strongly bound that he'd refuse to take orders. Besides, there was Babs to think about. "There's two New York dollars in it for the man who'll do it," he offered to the Virginians, to show Tom his support.

One of the Virginians promptly scrambled up on the seat, while Tom leaped up on the untethered horse. "Thanks, Henryk," he said as he galloped past. "I'll make it up to you. If anyone asks for me, assure him I'll be back by morning."

It was an unpleasant ride back; Tom's thighs were rubbed raw from riding without a saddle, and his thoughts gave him even more pain. *Something's happened to Patience,* one part of his mind forewarned, while another part argued that even if the fire *was* on the Hendley property, it didn't necessarily follow that Patience would be caught in the blaze.

The closer he came to the fire, the more it became clear that it was on the Hendley land. But when he actually came up to the site of the flames and saw the blackened debris that had been Peter Hendley's monument, he couldn't make sense of it. How could a monument burn?

He slipped from the horse and broke through the little crowd of onlookers—folks from Fordham Village and neighboring farms, who'd gathered to watch the conflagration. The fire, he saw, was coming from the underground magazine, but it was now dying. He felt a surge of relief, for apparently the blaze had not caused damage to anything but the monument. But the feeling of relief was short-lived. To his horror, he spied Chester kneeling on the ground not more than ten feet from where he stood, wrapping a shroud around a charred body. "Oh, my Lord!" he gasped, his blood freezing in his veins. He dropped down on his knees beside the wrapped body. "Who *is* it?" The eyes that searched Chester's face were wild with terror.

"Tom?" Chester's face lit up with welcome. "What're you doin' here?"

Tom clutched at Chester's shirt. "For God's sake, *who?*"

Chester looked down at Tom's white knuckles. "It's Lord Orgill. Dash it, Tom, I didn' think you was so fond of him."

Tom sat back on his heels, letting out a long breath. Lord Orgill, dead! The significance of that fact burst in his skull like an exploding shell, but he couldn't let himself dwell on the ramifications at this time. There was a more important question to be answered before he could let himself think about it. "Was anyone else hurt?" he asked tightly.

Chester shrugged. "Dunno. It'll be a while 'fore we can go down t' look in that hole. Lord Orgill was the o'ny one I foun' so far. Appears like he was hit on his skull wi' that heavy plate layin' over there, an' he died afore the flames got 'im."

Tom stared at what was left of the mausoleum. The hole in the ground that still burned was not the place from which he'd taken the supplies earlier that day. He rubbed his brow in confusion. "Have you seen Mistress Patience since the fire?" he asked Chester.

Chester shook his head.

Tom got up and ran back to his horse. He galloped the animal at breakneck speed over the fields to the house. As he approached the driveway, he saw a carriage draw up to the door. It was Barbara. Unaware of any untoward circumstances, she climbed down and started for the front steps. "Ma' am?" Tom addressed her, pulling up at the bottom of the steps. "Have you seen Patience?"

"Tom, good evening," she greeted him cheerfully. "I've only this moment arrived from the city. Isn't she inside? And shouldn't you be with your regiment?" She took a closer look at the horseman. Tom was white-faced and tense. "Is something wrong?" she asked. Then a thought struck her, and she herself turned pale. "Good heavens, is it . . . *Henryk?*"

"No, no, Henryk is fine. But I must find your sister."

Barbara, now fully alarmed, led him in. Without pausing to question him, she helped him make an exhaustive search of the house, but it availed them nothing. And Beatie could offer no help. "Where can she have gone at this hour?" Barbara muttered nonplussed.

All at once, the answer burst upon Tom as clearly as if Patience's spirit had whispered it into his ear—the overlook at Spuyten Duyvil, her special place. A glow of hope lit his eyes "Why don't you sit down and have some tea?" he suggested to Barbara. "I still have one place to look." And without waiting for her to respond, he went quickly from the house.

He ran on foot to the bottom of the knoll overlooking the Spuyten Duyvil creek and looked hurriedly about. A three-quarter moon tipped the ripples of the river with glints of pearl and shed a silvered whiteness over the east face of the hill, bathing the land with a mystical, unworldly magic. The only touch of reality came from across the creek, where little glimmers of light from the campfires of the American troops at Fort Washington reminded him of the fighting that was still ahead of him. But he could not think of war . . . not now. He climbed up the rise, his pulse racing. He was almost at the top when he saw her. He breathed a heartfelt thanks to God for keeping her safe and took a quick step forward. But he immediately stopped and stared in astonishment. She was dancing! As if in a trance, she was slowly turning round and round, arms outstretched and waving about with unearthly grace. He could not move, watching her, for she seemed to him at that moment to be a moon goddess set on the earth to enchant him, and he had no wish to break the spell.

But she must have sensed his presence, for she stopped, lowered her arms and turned. Peering into the shadows, she asked breathlessly, "Is someone there?"

He stepped out into the moonlight. "Were you *dancing?*" His voice was awestruck.

"Tom!" Her eyes lit with utter gladness. "You came back!" She ran toward him. "I prayed you would, so that I could tell you . . . so that I could make things right between us."

He gathered her in his arms. "The look on your face just now has done it better than words." He lifted her chin and gazed down at her. Now that he was close, he could see that she was no moon goddess. Her hair hung in bedraggled disarray down her back, and her clothes were muddy and covered with a dusting of ash . . . and he'd never seen anyone so beautiful. "I thought you were a figment of the moonlight, dancing that way," he said softly.

"I couldn't help myself." Her eyes shone with a light he hadn't seen in them before. "It was this feeling of *freedom*. Oh, Tom, I never knew before what a truly glorious feeling it is!"

He pulled her closer. "So I tried to tell you."

"Yes, you did. How could I understand . . . ?" But suddenly the glow in her eyes clouded over and she looked up at him in alarm. "Why are you back? Has something gone wrong?"

He shook his head. "I saw the flames. I had to learn if you were safe."

"You came back . . . just for that?"

"Is that not reason enough? Damnation, woman, I love you! I couldn't have borne it if something had happened to you."

She stared into his face. The truth of his feelings was plain in his eyes. "Oh, *Tom!*" The cry came from deep in her throat, a sound both agonized and full of gladness. She flung her arms about his neck and hid her face in his shoulder. "I have no right to feel so joyful," she whispered. "I *killed* him."

He was finding it difficult to concentrate on her words when the sheer joy of holding her was setting his innards atremble. "Do you mean Orgill? What nonsense is this?"

She poured out the story in a rush of words. "So you see," she finished, tearfully, "though I never dreamed the magazine would explode, I did set the fire. It must be considered my fault."

He took her face between his hands and made her look up at him. "We are at war," he said firmly. "Today you were a soldier, and Lord Orgill was the enemy. He was a casualty of war. You did what anyone calling herself an American had to do. You should be proud."

"Oh, God, Tom, how can I be proud? He was my husband, and . . . and in some part of me I . . . I *wished* him dead."

He brushed her tears away. "If wishes were deadly, my love, we'd *all* hang. You cannot have wished him dead with more passion than I."

He lifted her up, carried her to a nearby tree and set her down with her back against the trunk. "This is how you were sitting when I first saw you," he said, drinking her in with his eyes. Just then the moon ducked behind a cloud. He looked up at the sky in annoyance. "Why, Lady Moon, must you hide yourself away at the very moment I want you?"

Patience, feeling her tension and guilt subside, glanced up at the sky with a sigh of relief. "Perhaps the Lady Moon is a rebel who will not jump to a man's commands."

"Just the sort of female I most admire," he grinned, taking off his coat and placing it over her shoulder. By the time this was done, the moon had coyly peeped out again. He sat down beside the woman he'd dreamed of for so long and studied her face. It was smudged with soot except for two clean tracks down her cheeks where her tears had dripped. "How can you be so dirty and look so lovely?" he murmured, running a finger thoughtfully along her cheek. There was so much he wanted to tell her, and yet he remained silent. In this one day, everything between them had changed. Whole new prospects had opened up. He yearned to speak of them, but perhaps this was not yet the time. On the other hand, he would not soon have another chance; the army was on the march, and there was no telling how long it might be before he could manage to come back. *Come on, chicken heart,* he urged himself. *Now or never.*

He plunged in boldly. "Do you realize, ma'am, that you're a widow now?"

"Oh, yes," she sighed. "I realize it quite well."

"And do you realize that you may now consider marrying again?"

She flicked him a surprised glance, and then looked down at her hands. "And whom might I consider marrying?"

"I have a candidate to suggest. That is if you can lower yourself to accept the hand of a redemptioner with no money, no property, no looks, no refinement, and no prospects."

She shook her head. "Don't speak so lightly of so serious a matter," she said softly.

"I'm deadly serious, I promise you."

"You can't be serious when you say such things of yourself. 'Tis a blatant exhibition of false modesty! In the first place, you are no longer a redemptioner. As for your prospects for money and property, those are quite promising, for when Benjy takes over his inheritance, he will surely pay you all the freedom dues that my father withheld, with which you can purchase enough property to hold your head up with the best. And as for refinement, you never lacked that. Even when you came here as a boy there was something about you . . . the way you spoke . . . the way you carried yourself . . ." She paused, seeking the right word.

"Don't stop, ma'am, don't stop," he grinned. "I could sit here and listen to you say such things all night. You've so flatteringly dispensed with all my qualms. Let's recount. You've covered, firstly, the matter of my finances. Secondly, my prospects. And thirdly, my refinement. Ah, but wait! You haven't yet covered my looks, ma'am. It seems you cannot make an asset of my looks."

This last sally finally brought a smile to her lips. "I refuse to be maneuvered into saying I admire your looks, you coxcomb. The tavern wenches who surrender so easily to your blandishments must be considered ample proof of the acceptability of your appearance."

His own smile died. "On the subject of my tavern wenches," he said, taking her hand in his, "I hope you will believe me when I say that I've not had anything to do with them since the night so long ago when you were foolish enough to say you loved me. No other woman could tempt me after that. I have only one wish now—that what you said that night might still be true."

She lifted his hand to her cheek. "Oh, my dear! You must see that it is."

"Truly?" His heart bounced up in his chest, and he pulled her close. "Then you *will* wed me?" he murmured, his lips against her forehead.

She lay for a moment in his arms, but then withdrew from his embrace. "You must think more carefully on marriage, Tom. The world has vastly changed already, and will change even more when this war is over. 'Tis you would do the lowering if you were to wed me. You're a gentleman with prospects, while I'm an aging, quarrelsome, dirty, spinsterish, impoverished widow."

He'd felt a twinge of alarm at her first words, but by the time she finished he only laughed. "Dirty I grant," he teased, "but spinsterish? And impoverished?"

"Indeed. I have not a penny nor a bit of property for dower, so what man of sense would have me? I shall have to live a spinsterish existence with my widowed sister until Benjy returns from the wars. And then, when he marries and has children, I shall either remain in his house on the charity of his wife, or I shall be sent out in the cold to make my way as best I can."

Tom snorted. "In the first place, ma'am, you shouldn't count on spending time with your widowed sister. The frantic manner in which she asked me, a little while ago, if anything was wrong with Henryk Bogaerde convinced me that she cares for him almost as much as he for her. They'll make a match of it before long. And as far as your being tossed out in the cold," he added, taking her back into his arms, "I shall save you from so bleak a fate. I am willing, in charity, to wed you and keep you warm."

She slipped her arms about him in contented surrender. "So you are *willing* to wed me, are you?"

"Yes, ma'am."

"To keep me warm?"

"Oh, *yes,* ma'am. Very warm."

"In *charity?* "

"Yes, ma'am. I'm a very charitable sort."

She lifted her head and frowned at him in mock disdain. "But what if I don't need charity? What if I can manage without a husband?"

"Tell me, ma'am," he murmured absently as he reached up and toyed with her hair, "just how you propose to do that."

"I shall search along the Mohawk River till I find Sally. Then she and I will open an inn and serve wholesome meals to the men of the frontier."

"Not on your life," he said, using her hair to draw her face close to his and kissing her roughly. "You will marry me, Patience Hendley, and you'll serve those wholesome meals to me and our children! Though I'm willing to become a man of the frontier and make our home somewhere on the Mohawk, if that is what you wish."

She slipped her arms around him and nestled against his chest. "That, my love, is what I wish above all else."

They held each other closely, not speaking, his cheek resting on her hair, her hand in his. The channel waters gurgled away below them, and the silver oval of the moon darted in and out among the clouds. For this brief moment everything was perfect. There would be time later for the pains and joys, the defeats and triumphs, the mishaps small and great that are part of the unexpectedness of life. There would be time later to fight a war and build a country. For now there was only hope, and love, and the self-respect that comes from knowing they were strong enough to struggle and to sacrifice for a great cause. For this tiny breath of time it was paradise enough to sit together, happy and at peace, under the rebel moon.

To the reader:

I grew up in the Bronx, quite near Spuyten Duyvil. From our living-room window I could see the Hudson and, to my left, the majestic span of the George Washington bridge. In my childish innocence, I didn't realize that from this cramped lower-middle-class apartment I had a millionaire's view.

Nor did I realize, when I used to catch my bus on Kingsbridge Road, that there had once actually been a King's Bridge at the bottom of that road and that George Washington, John Adams and many other heroes of history had stood on the very ground that was my neighborhood. Once I made that discovery, however, everything about the neighborhood changed for me. I couldn't keep myself from imagining what it had looked like before the twentieth century—with its cement sidewalks, proliferating apartment buildings and elevated subway tracks—erased all signs of the past.

But now, when I go back to Kingsbridge Road, I see it in three different ways: as it is now, as it was in my childhood, and as it was for Patience. If I shut my eyes, the George Washington Bridge, the crush of houses, the streets with their rows of autos all disappear, and it's as if I can *remember* the wooden bridge, the Spuyten Duyvil creek, and the dirt road that wound through the trees leading up to the top of the hill where Patience's house stood. It's become as real to me as my memories of my own childhood. That's what writing this book did for me. It turned history into memory.

Paula Jonas

PINNACLE BOOKS HAS SOMETHING FOR EVERYONE —

MAGICIANS, EXPLORERS, WITCHES AND CATS

THE HANDYMAN   (377-3, $3.95/$4.95)
He is a magician who likes hands. He likes their comfortable
shape and weight and size. He likes the portability of the hands
once they are severed from the rest of the ponderous body. Detec-
tive Lanark must discover who The Handyman is before more
handless bodies appear.

PASSAGE TO EDEN   (538-5, $4.95/$5.95)
Set in a world of prehistoric beauty, here is the epic story of a
courageous seafarer whose wanderings lead him to the ends of
the old world — and to the discovery of a new world in the rugged,
untamed wilderness of northwestern America.

BLACK BODY   (505-9, $5.95/$6.95)
An extraordinary chronicle, this is the diary of a witch, a journal
of the secrets of her race kept in return for not being burned for
her "sin." It is the story of Alba, that rarest of creatures, a white
witch: beautiful and able to walk in the human world undetected.

THE WHITE PUMA   (532-6, $4.95/NCR)
The white puma has recognized the men who deprived him of his
family. Now, like other predators before him, he has become a
man-hater. This story is a fitting tribute to this magnificent animal that stands for all living creatures that have become, through
man's carelessness, close to disappearing forever from the face of
the earth.